SEARCHING FOR ELSIE

Eagle Point Search & Rescue, Book 2

SUSAN STOKER

Edited by Kelli Collins

Cover Design by AURA Design Group

Manufactured in the United States

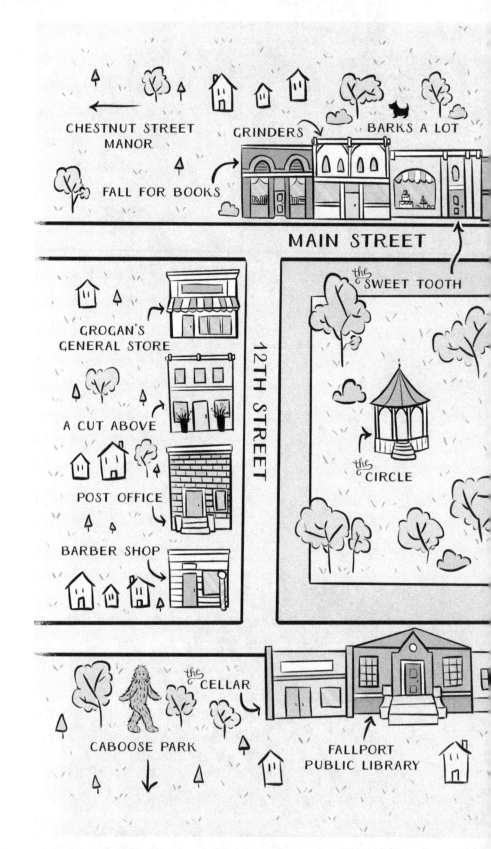

AUTHOR NOTE

The map on the previous page is a rough rendition of Fallport's main square. It doesn't include the parking lots behind the buildings and the businesses on the bottom of the page are actually facing the square.

It's difficult to accurately depict every single thing about the town that's in my head in a 2D image.

But the map should give you general idea of the areas that appear in all of the Eagle Point Search & Rescue books!

Enjoy!

SEARCHING FOR ELSIE

CHAPTER ONE

Zeke checked his watch for what seemed like the twentieth time.

Elsie was late.

She was *never* late.

He'd gotten to know her pretty well over the last year and a half, and her reliability was the first thing he'd noticed. At first she was just another employee...but she was so much more than that now.

As time went by, Zeke's attraction to the sweet brunette grew, and slowly, he'd begun to see through the easygoing façade she presented to the world to the woman underneath. No matter how much she tried to hide it and pretend otherwise, she was stressed, exhausted. It made him want to do whatever he could to help.

He also wanted On the Rocks to be a safe space for her. A place where she could let down her guard and know she had people to rely on.

He wanted to think he was succeeding, at least a little bit. She smiled more frequently, was a touch more outgoing, and she seemed genuinely happy while at work.

And little by little, she was finally beginning to loosen up around *him* as well.

Zeke had only kissed her once. That evening, he'd lost his shit when one of the customers had grabbed her ass, and he'd pulled her into his office and told her he was done tiptoeing around his attraction. Instead of getting upset or telling him he was overstepping his bounds, that she didn't want any kind of relationship, she'd melted in his arms. The kiss they'd shared had been short but hot, and Zeke definitely wanted more.

He was trying to take things slow. Give her time and space to come to terms with the fact that she had a protector. Him.

It was one of the hardest things he'd ever done. All he wanted was to take her home and spoil her and Tony, her nine-year-old son. Wanted to show them both that whatever had made them so skittish and uncertain was behind them. But even after he'd declared his interest, Elsie had remained guarded.

So he'd backed off, while making it clear his interest hadn't waned. He frequently found reasons to touch her. A hand on her back. A brush against her arm. Standing just a little bit closer when she was talking to him. Nothing threatening or overt. Just intentionally clear. And it was working. Slowly but surely, since that first kiss, she was relaxing her guard.

Most people wouldn't agree. Would observe how she acted around him and argue she was just as wary now as when she'd first arrived...but they'd be wrong.

Her reactions toward him were even more subtle than his own, but Zeke could read them loud and clear. She smiled shyly at him often. Her sweet blushes when he complimented her came more frequently. And just the other day, *she'd* touched *him*.

It had been one of the first times she'd deliberately initiated contact, and Zeke wouldn't ever forget it. He'd been slammed behind the bar, as both his bartenders called in sick so he was the only one making drinks. He'd been on his feet since arriving right before lunch. In addition, he and his friends on the Eagle Point Search and Rescue team had been out most of the night before, looking for a mentally handicapped teenager who'd slipped out of the house without anyone's notice and disappeared into the wilderness behind his home. Luckily, they'd found him, cold and scared but without any major injuries.

Zeke had been exhausted and two seconds from blowing up at a customer when Elsie had come behind the bar, loudly announced to the whole place that he was taking a twenty-minute break and their customers needed to just chill, before taking his hand and leading him down the hall to his office.

It had been *extremely* uncharacteristic. Elsie didn't like to be the center of attention. She preferred to fade into the background. But for Zeke, she'd faced down the rowdy patrons and forced him to take a break. It had been a surprise to see her standing up to him, as well. Pointing at the couch and ordering him to sit and relax for a few minutes.

He had. But not without pulling her down next to him. She'd hesitantly settled against him, and they'd both just sat in the semiquiet of his office and decompressed.

Afterward, she'd gone back to being shy and reticent, but Zeke wouldn't forget how

she'd had his back—not to mention how good she'd felt at his side, literally.

Some people might get frustrated with how slowly their relationship was progressing, but not Zeke. His time in the Green Berets had taught him to be patient. That the most worthwhile outcomes came from persistence.

And besides...after his ex, he'd avoided relationships himself for years.

He suspected Elsie rarely had anyone watching her own back. It was obvious she hadn't had an easy life before coming to Fallport, Virginia. Hell, she *still* didn't have an easy life. But she didn't complain. Never bitched about how hard she worked to keep a roof over her and her son's heads. She just did what needed to be done and kept moving forward.

The bell above the door finally rang, and Zeke looked up in

relief, expecting to see Elsie rushing into the bar, apologizing for being late and promising it would never happen again. But instead of Elsie, Reina Caudle waved at him as she entered.

Zeke's brows furrowed. "What are you doing here? You aren't scheduled until later."

"Wow, good to see you too," Reina said with a smile. "And I know that. But Elsie called and asked if I could do her shift. She's sick."

"Sick?" Zeke asked, his brow lifting skeptically.

"That's what I thought," Reina agreed. "The woman's never sick. Remember a few months ago when everyone in town seemed to catch that flu? But not Elsie. She did so many extra shifts for all of us, it was mind-boggling."

Zeke *did* remember. Elsie had worked two weeks straight without a day off, most of the time pulling ten-hour shifts. She'd been a godsend to the other servers, and everyone, including Zeke, was grateful she'd been willing to pick up the slack.

"What's wrong with her?" he asked.

Reina shrugged. "I don't know. She just said that she felt like crap but she should be in tomorrow as usual."

Zeke's frown deepened. One thing he knew about Elsie was that she never admitted a weakness. Ever. When asked how she was doing, she always said "great." When asked if she was tired, she insisted she wasn't. When the bar patrons got overly rowdy, she never admitted to being annoyed or frustrated. She had a calm personality and always stayed positive, no matter what was going on in her life or around her.

So for her to flat-out admit she felt like crap was unusual enough to worry him.

Hank Blackburn was behind the bar, getting ready for the lunch crowd. They didn't have near the amount of people coming in for lunch as Sandra Hain did over at Sunny Side Up, the diner in town, but they were busy enough to warrant opening at eleven-thirty every day.

Now that Reina had arrived—joining Valerie, another server—Zeke was confident he could leave the trio to handle things for a while.

Without thinking twice, he headed for the door.

"Boss?" Reina asked, watching him go with a questioning expression on her face.

"I should be back later," he told her, speaking loudly enough that Hank and Valerie could hear as well. "If anything happens that I need to know about, just call."

Valerie grinned. "Tell her we all hope she feels better soon!"

Zeke wasn't surprised the others knew where he was going. He hadn't made his interest in Elsie a secret. By now, everyone—including the regular patrons—knew better than to say anything inappropriate or to touch her.

Zeke waved as he headed out of the door. The bar was at the end of the row of businesses on one side of Fallport's main square, and Zeke quickly walked around the building to the parking lot in the back.

He knew some people would think he was crazy. That there was no need to personally go check on Elsie. If she was sick, she'd probably feel better in the next day or two and would soon be back at work. But his intuition had never let him down in the past. When it came to his job, he had a one hundred percent accuracy rate. He seemed to always know when shit was about to hit the fan.

Unfortunately, the Army didn't run on intuition. There were layers and layers of bureaucracy, and after being forced into one too many situations Zeke knew were going to go bad before his team was even sent in, he was done. He'd been honored to serve his country, but he couldn't blindly lead his team into deadly situations simply because someone who outranked him gave an order.

So he'd quit, once again following his intuition. And luckily, Ethan "Chaos" Watson, a Navy SEAL he'd gotten to know over the years, had heard he was out and brought up the possibility of Zeke joining the Search and Rescue team here in Fallport. It was one of the best decisions he'd ever made.

The only time his intuition had failed him involved his ex-wife. It wasn't something Zeke liked to think about. The bitch had betrayed him in the worst way a spouse could. Every time he was off fighting for his country, putting his life on the line, she was back home, sleeping with other men. Lots of them. She'd had affair after affair, and he'd had no idea. At least...not for a long while. Even then, it wasn't until he'd gotten home from a deployment earlier than expected that he'd been faced with the irrefutable truth.

He'd caught her in their bed with an eighteen-year-old private. She'd seduced the kid...and had the gall to blame *Zeke* for her adultery.

He hadn't been serious with a woman since. Nothing beyond a single date...but somehow, Elsie had slipped under his radar.

She was *nothing* like the bitch he'd married. No subterfuge. No deviousness. Every emotion showed on her face. She did her best to hide her thoughts from others, but Zeke had learned to read her like a book. He could tell when she was putting on a happy face for the patrons at the bar. Could tell when she was content, worried, or just plain tired.

But she never complained. Not once.

Which brought Zeke back around to the here and now. Not only was calling in sick unlike her, Elsie needed every cent she earned. Admitting she didn't feel good was akin to holding up a huge flashing sign that something was wrong.

She was currently living in the Mangree Motel and RV Park at the edge of town. It was somewhat dated and rundown, but had a small sparkling pool and was kept clean. Everyone at On the Rocks knew Elsie was trying to save up enough money for an apartment. But it wasn't cheap to raise a nine-year-old, and she hadn't quite made it to the point where she could afford the move, facing one setback after another.

The most recent was a flat tire on I-480, the thirty-mile stretch of lonely road that connected Fallport to Interstate 81, the main thoroughfare stretching from the southwestern-most point of Virginia to the northern border. Afterward, Zeke asked Brock, his friend and SAR teammate, to do a complete inspection of her car. He'd wanted to pay for the four new tires she'd needed, as well as the other work Brock had done, knowing it would take a huge cut of her apartment fund, but Elsie refused.

So Zeke lied his ass off and cut the price in half.

He hated to do it, but Elsie had more pride than most, and he refused to do anything to damage that.

It didn't take long for Zeke to reach the motel. He pulled into the mostly empty lot and parked outside of room twelve. It was next to the office, which he thoroughly approved of. He didn't want Elsie and Tony to be on the end of the row of rooms; that was less safe. He climbed out of his truck and headed to her room.

Frowning when Elsie didn't answer the door after he knocked, Zeke tried to look into the window but the curtains were pulled shut. The hair on the back of his neck standing up, he entered the office. He smiled at Edna Brown, the older lady who worked the front desk every day. She and her husband owned the motel and had lived in Fallport for decades.

"Hi, Edna," he said as he approached the small desk.

"Zeke! It's good to see you. What brings you out here? Everything all right?"

"I'm not sure. I'm here to check on Elsie. She called in sick today. Asked Reina to take her shift. I knocked, but she's not answering. I was wondering if you might let me in so I can check up on her?"

Edna frowned. "Yeah, the poor thing didn't look good this morning. I found her passed out on top of the sheets she was folding earlier."

Zeke was confused. "The sheets she was folding?"

"Yep," Edna said with a nod. "In the mornings, after Tony goes to school and before she heads into town for her shift at the bar, she's been working for me. If there are rooms that haven't been cleaned by my regular housekeeper for any reason, she gets them ready to rent. She's also been finishing up the laundry as well. It takes a while to get all the sheets and towels washed and dried, so she finishes up whatever the housekeeper couldn't get done the day before. She's been extremely helpful."

Zeke sighed in frustration. He'd had no idea Elsie had been working a second job before her shifts at the bar. He shouldn't have been surprised. The woman was one of the hardest workers he'd ever met, and she'd do whatever it took to make sure her son had everything he needed and wanted.

"Anyway," Edna continued, "this morning I went to check on her because I hadn't seen her in a while, and she was slumped over the laundry table where we fold the sheets. The poor dear was burning up. I helped her back to her room and got her settled in."

Zeke's worry didn't lessen at hearing Edna's story. "She's not answering the door. I'm sure it's because she's just exhausted, but I'd feel better if I checked on her."

Edna's eyes narrowed as she stared at him, and Zeke did his best not to fidget. Some people might take one look at the Mangree Motel and RV Park and make a lot of assumptions. But Edna and her husband ran a tight ship. They didn't tolerate drugs, didn't rent their rooms by the hour, and definitely didn't approve of anything illegal taking place in or around their property. It was one of the reasons Zeke hadn't already attempted to move Elsie and Tony out. The Mangree was a safe place, even if it wasn't exactly ideal or practical to live in a motel.

"I'm not sure I should be letting a man into her room," Edna hedged. "I can check on her and let you know how she is."

Leaning forward, Zeke met Edna's gaze. "I'd never do anything to disrespect her, or you. I'm worried about her, Edna. She hasn't asked anyone to take her shift the entire time she's worked at On the Rocks. I care about her, and I need to make sure she's okay. I'd never forgive myself if something happened to her and I didn't do anything about it."

Edna eyed him for a long moment. "Haven't seen you around much," she said skeptically.

"I'm takin' things slow because she needs that. I think she's been hurt in the past, and I'm taking care not to rush her into a relationship," Zeke said.

Edna took a deep breath and turned, reaching for a key ring hanging on a hook behind the desk. Zeke wasn't thrilled that the master key to all the rooms was so accessible, but he'd have a word with Edna about that later. At the moment, all he wanted to do was put his eyes on Elsie and make sure she was all right.

The elderly woman moved slowly around the counter and toward the door. Zeke wanted to snatch the key out of her hand and rush out of the office, but he knew better. He was getting what he wanted, so he'd be patient for just a bit longer.

They stepped over to room twelve, and Zeke held his breath as Edna knocked on the door.

"Elsie? It's Edna. Are you all right?"

There was no answer.

Edna frowned. "I'm going to open the door to make sure you're okay. Zeke is here with me. Are you decent?"

Still no answer.

Edna put the key in the lock and turned it. She quietly opened the door and stood back, giving Zeke room. He nodded at her, thankful she was letting him take the lead. She waited in the doorway as Zeke entered.

The room was dark, all the lights off and the curtains pulled shut. It might as well have been the middle of the night. Zeke saw a lump on one of the full-size beds and made his way toward it immediately.

The space was typical of any other motel room. Two beds, a nightstand between them, a small circular table near the window, a dresser holding a TV. There was a sink against the far wall, with clothes hanging on a rack next to it. Everything was clean and orderly. Zeke caught a glimpse of a few toys on the table and shoes lined up against the wall under the clothes rack.

A coffee maker sat on a narrow shelf between the sink and the rack, and Elsie had set up a kind of pantry using milk crates beneath. Even though the room was clean, it was depressing to know that she and her son lived here full time.

Frustrated that he hadn't considered the realities of her living conditions sooner, Zeke sat on the edge of the bed next to Elsie.

"Else?" he said quietly, reaching a hand out to pull back the covers.

For just a moment, Zeke's absolute worst fear swamped him when he saw her. She was so pale, and she didn't even flinch when he touched her. Zeke had seen plenty of dead bodies while in the Army, and even during searches in the forest around Fallport. But *nothing* could have prepared him to see Elsie so deathly still.

He touched her cheek and almost collapsed in relief when he felt her warm skin. But the relief turned to worry when he realized *how* warm. She was burning up.

"She okay?" Edna asked worriedly from the doorway.

Zeke forced himself to look at the older woman. She was wringing her hands as she stared at him.

"She will be," he said with determination.

Zeke heard a car pull up outside and saw Edna look over her shoulder before she turned back to him. "I need to get back to the office. You'll tell me if there's anything I can do?"

"Of course." Making a split-second decision that felt more right than anything he'd done in a long time, he said, "I'm taking her home with me."

Edna's reaction went a long way toward reinforcing how worried she was for Elsie. She nodded and said, "That's probably for the best." Then she narrowed her eyes at Zeke and said, "But no hanky-panky, young man. She's a good girl."

In any other situation, Zeke would've laughed. No one said "hanky-panky" anymore, and Elsie was a grown-ass woman. But instead, he merely nodded and said, "Of course not. I just want her to get better."

Edna stared at him for another moment before abruptly turning. She tugged the door closed behind her as she went to greet whoever it was who'd pulled into the parking lot.

Zeke leaned over and clicked on the light next to the bed. Now that the door was shut, the room was pitch black.

Elsie moaned a little at the glare of the light, but didn't completely rouse.

"Else?" Zeke asked, leaning toward her and palming her cheek. "I'm gonna take care of you."

To his surprise, her eyes opened and she stared up at him.

"Hi," he said softly.

Her eyes seemed cloudy and her brows furrowed in confusion.

"It's me. Zeke. You're going to be okay."

"I'm sick," she whispered.

"I know. That's why I'm here."

"I'm never sick," she said almost petulantly.

"I know that too. I was worried when Reina came in and said you asked her to take your shift."

"I'll be better tomorrow," Elsie said.

"We'll see."

"I'm cold..."

Zeke frowned. He knew it was the fever talking, since she was burning up. It increased his urgency. "Okay, Else. Rest. You'll feel better soon." He hoped.

Elsie nodded and closed her eyes again, tilting her head into the palm that was still resting on her cheek.

Determination rose within Zeke. He hated seeing her like this. Between two jobs and caring for her son, she was burning the candle at both ends, and her body was paying the price. But he'd get her back on her feet, whether she wanted his help or not. Leaning down, he kissed her forehead gently. She sighed at the touch of his lips to her skin, and he took that as a good sign.

Forcing himself to leave her side, Zeke looked around the room and saw a duffel bag on the shelf above the hanging clothes. He grabbed it. He needed to pack some things for Elsie. He wasn't sure how long she and her son would be staying with him, but it would at least be until she was back on her feet, and she'd need some things. He'd get Tony to pack more stuff when he came back to pick him up after school.

Zeke didn't think twice about packing her clothes and toiletries. She took care of everyone else, it was about time someone returned the favor. Once the bag was filled to overflowing, Zeke left the room long enough to bring it out to his truck and open the door. Then he returned to the room. He leaned over Elsie once more.

He pulled back the covers, ignoring the moan that left Elsie's lips at the loss of warmth. He gathered her into his arms and strode toward the door.

She roused enough to put an arm around his neck and mumbled, "What's happening?"

"Nothing. Go back to sleep," Zeke told her.

She nodded against his chest and burrowed into him.

Zeke's heart swelled in his chest. Her unconscious trust, when she was at her most vulnerable, meant the world to him. He wasn't going to let this woman down. No way in hell.

He settled her on the passenger seat and clicked the seat belt around her. She was slumped over in what looked to be a very uncomfortable position. Luckily, it wasn't a long drive to his small house. He'd found the place when he'd first moved to town. At the time, it was practically falling apart, but with Ethan and Rocky's help, he'd been able to fix it up so it was somewhat respectable. There was still more work he wanted to do, but he was enjoying taking his time with the more cosmetic renovations.

Zeke stood there a moment, studying the sleeping woman in his truck. Elsie was petite, at least half a foot shorter than his six-foot-two. She had thick, curly brown hair and, when awake, expressive brown eyes. She rarely wore makeup, but she didn't need it. She was slightly older than his thirty years. She was also too thin in Zeke's eyes, and he had a feeling that was because she made sure Tony ate before she did, and probably went without too often herself, just to save a buck.

He'd been hungry before, was all too familiar with that gnawing feeling of an empty belly, and hated that the woman in front of him had probably gone through that and more. As far as he knew, Elsie didn't have any close family to rely on.

Zeke wanted to be the one to slay all her dragons and reassure her that she'd never go without again. The thought of her or Tony suffering tore him apart inside.

When Elsie made a small groaning noise, Zeke shook himself. He needed to get going, not stand here staring at the vulnerable woman all day.

He couldn't resist leaning down and kissing her forehead once more, hating how hot her skin was against his lips. He closed the truck door before going back to shut the door to the motel room. Edna stepped outside, and he met her gaze before he climbed into the driver's side of his truck. She gave him a nod. It was as much of an endorsement as he was going to get from the woman, and he'd take it.

His mind worked with the things he needed to do. Call the clinic and see if he could get Doctor Snow to make a house call. Get Elsie's fever down. Figure out what he had to eat in the house, both for a sick patient and a nine-year-old boy. He was sure one of his teammates would volunteer to go to the store for him, if necessary. He also needed to pick up Tony after school. Maybe Lilly would come over and stay with Elsie while he got Tony...

Shit, he also needed to call Hank and let him know he wouldn't be back at the bar today. Maybe not tomorrow either, depending on how Elsie felt. Lance or Reuben, his other two bartenders, wouldn't have a problem picking up the slack. They did it all the time when he was called out for a search. They'd be thrilled for the extra hours.

Unable to resist, Zeke reached for Elsie's hand. He gripped it in his and whispered, "Don't worry, Else. I've got this."

He didn't know if he actually did, was feeling a little over-whelmed, but he wanted to reassure her. Elsie didn't respond verbally, but her fingers briefly tightened around his own.

Feeling panicky but unsure why—she had the flu or something; she wasn't dying—Zeke drove carefully toward his house. He'd wanted to invite Elsie over for weeks now, but this wasn't how he'd imagined it would go. He'd promised himself a month ago, when that jerk had touched her ass in the bar, that her life would change for the better. But he'd been too slow in actually backing up that promise, and a proud, reticent Elsie hadn't made it any easier. Now she was sick, probably because she'd worked herself into exhaustion.

No more. He'd fallen down on the job, but Zeke was going to right that wrong. Starting now.

More plans swirled in his head, and Zeke pressed his lips together. He knew Elsie would fight him every step of the way, but he could be persuasive when necessary.

It was time Elsie Ireland figured out that she didn't have to do everything on her own anymore. She had him. His search and rescue team. Lilly. And the citizens of Fallport.

First, he had to get her well, then he'd ensure she didn't work herself to exhaustion ever again. It was time to stop tiptoeing around and make sure Elsie knew just how much she meant to him.

The thought that she might not feel the same never crossed Zeke's mind. He'd seen the glances she'd shot his way when she thought he wasn't aware. There was no way a woman who wasn't interested revealed such...longing. She just needed the confidence to trust in her feelings. In *him*. It wouldn't be easy, but nothing worth doing ever was.

CHAPTER TWO

Elsie couldn't help but groan when she felt herself being moved. Every muscle in her body hurt. And she was so damn cold. She couldn't seem to get warm. She was also trying to remember something, but at the moment, she simply felt too awful to think.

"Open your mouth, Else," a deep, sexy voice said.

For just a moment, Elsie thought she was dreaming, but when someone put their arm around her shoulders and forced her to sit up, she realized she wasn't. Opening her eyes, Elsie saw a black-haired man's face close to her own. She blinked, and a well-trimmed beard came into focus, and she knew immediately who it was.

"Zeke?"

"Yeah, it's me, sweetheart. Can you open your mouth and take some pills for me? It's just to try to reduce your fever. I've called Doc Snow and he'll be here soon, but in the meantime, I'm worried about how high your fever is."

Elsie frowned. Fever? Doctor? She looked into Zeke's hazel eyes and shook her head. "No doctor," she said in a voice she didn't recognize.

"Yes," he said firmly.

"Can't afford it," she told him, too sick to be embarrassed.

"I've got it," he told her.

She shook her head again. It made the room spin, but she didn't regret it. "No, Zeke."

"Yes, Elsie," he returned firmly. "You're sick. *Really* sick. You passed out folding sheets at the motel. And we'll talk later about the fact that you took on a second job in the first place. You could've talked to me if you needed more money, sweetheart. We could've worked something out. Anyway...you've worked yourself into exhaustion. If you don't see the doctor, you'll be sick longer, and therefore out of work longer. I know you don't want that."

Elsie frowned. He was right, she definitely didn't want that. Couldn't afford to be out of work.

"Not only that, but you don't want to pass on whatever this is to Tony, do you?"

Elsie closed her eyes and relaxed into Zeke's hold. "No," she whispered.

"Right, so take these pills, then I'll let you relax until the doctor gets here. Later, I'll go pick up Tony and bring him back here."

Elsie opened her mouth and waited for Zeke to put whatever he wanted her to take on her tongue. She supposed she should muster up the energy to open her eyes and at least make an attempt to take care of herself. But she was so tired. And cold. And lonely.

Where that last one came from, she didn't know. But it was true. She'd spent the last few years going full speed. After leaving the DC area with very little to her name, she did whatever it took to keep her and Tony from being homeless. She was proud of how far she'd come, and while some people might not consider living in a motel and being a waitress very impressive, she knew better.

She'd barely finished high school and hadn't even considered college. After graduating, she'd gotten a waitressing job and took to it immediately. She enjoyed meeting people and was able to make decent tips. She shared an apartment with three other women, and her life was moving along just fine.

Then she'd met Doug Germain. He swept her off her feet and they'd gotten married within six months. She moved into his large house and quit her job when he'd asked. From the outside, she'd spent the next few years living a seemingly carefree life as Doug's wife.

In reality, being married to the man hadn't been easy. He was extremely hard to please. She couldn't do anything right in his eyes. Her hair wasn't styled right, she didn't dress like he preferred, she couldn't cook up to his standards, the house was always a mess...

Slowly but surely, he'd beaten her down. He didn't use his fists; his words were enough to smash whatever self-esteem she'd managed to build. While dating, they'd had a good sex life, but once married, even that had waned.

She'd been ready to call it quits—she wasn't going to stay in a marriage where she was treated like crap—but then Doug changed. He began to pay more attention to her. Compliment her. Take her out for dinner more often. Giving her flowers. He became more like the man she'd married.

She'd had no idea why he'd changed for the better, but she was relieved and thrilled at the time. He talked about starting a family. Elsie was over-the-moon happy with the idea, and they began to try immediately. Doug was still working long hours and late nights, but he was doing his best to be home as much as he could.

When she'd found out she was pregnant just a few months later, Elsie couldn't wait to tell Doug that their dream was coming true.

But within mere weeks of her sharing the news of his impending fatherhood, Doug had inexplicably changed yet again.

He'd become cold and distant. He stopped touching her, began working even longer hours than before. His changing personality had given her whiplash, and for the longest time Elsie thought it was something *she'd* done wrong.

It wasn't long before she discovered why he'd become attentive so suddenly—and so briefly. He was in line for an upper-management position at work, and his boss had told him the CEO was a proponent of families. In order for Doug to secure his promotion, he'd decided Elsie needed to have a baby to increase his chances.

Elsie was devastated. She, and her child, were nothing but pawns. The truth hurt. A lot. And making the decision to leave her husband became a hundred times more difficult after she got pregnant. Her parents had both fallen ill and died several months earlier, leaving her no place else to go. She needed Doug's health insurance to make sure her baby boy was as healthy as he could be.

And despite wanting to leave...she had a feeling Doug would've done anything to make sure that didn't happen. Not because he cared about her or their baby, but because he would do whatever it took to secure that promotion.

Doug never did touch her again after finding out she was pregnant, not that Elsie cared. Once she'd realized his entire change of heart had been a ruse, she didn't *want* him to touch her.

The day she'd had Tony, she was home alone. Doug had left on a business trip with his secretary—Elsie was well aware he was fucking the woman, but she didn't care—and she'd gone into labor. She drove herself to the hospital, pulling over every couple of minutes because of her contractions, and ended up giving birth without anyone by her side.

The second the nurses put Tony in her arms, Elsie fell in love. She might not have wanted to bring a child into the hell that was her marriage, but she vowed right then and there to do whatever it took to protect him.

And she'd done that and more over the years. Surprisingly, Doug seemed proud to have a son at first, but that pride quickly turned to irritation. Literally everything about having a baby in the house annoyed him. He never changed a diaper, bitched about Tony crying in the night, and soon began to spend more and more time away from the house. Though, his nasty comments never stopped. During the few minutes he saw her each day, he never wasted an opportunity to tell Elsie she was a horrible mother, along with a thousand other digs.

Nothing he said mattered. All that mattered to Elsie was her son. But she *did* try to leave Doug when Tony was two. She was sick of the insults, the constant degradation. She was especially worried about how her awful relationship with her husband was affecting their son.

Doug refused to let her go. He'd gotten the promotion he wanted so badly, but he still needed her to show face at work events, sometimes with Tony, to continue the charade. His insults turned to threats, swearing that if she tried to break up their "happy family," she'd regret it. The meaner he got, the more Elsie was afraid of Doug.

She also felt stuck. She had no money of her own, no place to go. No special skills or college education. Getting a job that would earn her enough money for childcare and all the other things she'd need to raise Tony safely seemed impossible...at that time. But that didn't mean she wasn't constantly trying to figure out how to get herself and her son out of their situation. She bided her time, watching, waiting...documenting.

That day finally came when Tony was four and a half. Doug told their son that he was as stupid as his mother—and Elsie was done. She could take her husband yelling at her. Telling her she was no good and would never amount to anything. But the second he turned on Tony, all bets were off.

Doug was pretty much living with his secretary at that point. He'd actually bought her a house and was shacking up with her almost every night. His promotion came with a huge raise, and he spent most of it on his mistress.

Elsie searched online and found a legal website, paying to print off a no-frills divorce agreement. She was well aware that she could fight like hell and get a good chunk of Doug's money, but she didn't want it. She simply wanted to be free of him.

The night she'd told him she wanted a divorce, Doug laughed at her—then realized she was serious when she presented the divorce papers. She'd already signed them. She hadn't asked for alimony.

Hadn't brought up his infidelity. Had even granted him visitation rights with Tony.

When he refused to sign, Elsie got *pissed*. For the first time in her marriage, she'd stood up for herself.

She told him if he didn't sign the papers, she'd take him to court. Would ask for half of his investments, his savings, the house. She would reveal his years of verbal abuse. But most importantly, she would drag his precious "family man" reputation through the proverbial mud—sharing the letters his unbelievably *stupid* secretary had sent him over the years, along with the naked pictures of the woman Elsie had found on Doug's phone and forwarded to herself...just in case.

She'd been scared to death of the rage on his face at her threats, but in the end, he'd agreed to sign the divorce papers—as long as she was out of his house and his life by the next day.

It wasn't nearly enough time to pack all of her and Tony's things, but Elsie didn't even hesitate. She left the next day. With two hundred bucks, her car, and the little she could fit inside it. Tony was confused and didn't understand what was happening, but at the time, it was for the best. The last thing Elsie wanted was for him to grow up to be anything like his father.

They didn't need Doug Germain. All they needed was each other and a fresh start.

It took her longer than she'd have liked to find one.

Immediately upon leaving Doug, one of the women she'd shared an apartment with before her marriage had agreed to let her and Tony stay with her. She was a flight attendant at the time, and away from home more often than not. She was a godsend...but even with Elsie temping, and despite the reduced rent her friend requested, Elsie couldn't afford staying in the city for longer than a year.

Next, she found work south of Washington, DC, and moved her and Tony again, but the job ultimately didn't work out.

She always tried to stay in one place as long as she could, so Tony could make friends and get consistent schooling, but money was the constant struggle. She continued to scrape by, and it wasn't easy, but Tony was worth every blister, every late night she lost sleep, trying to figure out how to pay rent and buy enough food to tide them over.

Eventually, after three and a half long years, Elsie and Tony moved to Fallport, where the cost of living and the crime rate were low, the schools were great, and the locals were friendly.

Her life *still* wasn't easy. She was thirty-three years old and sometimes felt as if she was at least fifty. But all Elsie had to do was look into Tony's innocent eyes, and she knew if she had to do it all again, she'd make the exact same decisions.

"Else?"

She jerked, suddenly ripped back to the present, and realized where she was. She'd swallowed the pills Zeke had given her and was lying in his arm, clutching his wrist as he held a cup of water to her lips. Revisiting the past wasn't her favorite thing to do, and she hated that she'd done so in front of Zeke.

The man confused her. A month ago, he'd kind of gone a little nuts when one of the patrons at the bar had touched her ass. Zeke had dragged her to his office, informed her that no one was allowed to touch her but *him*, then proceeded to kiss the hell out of her. Since then, he'd been overly attentive, very touchy-feely...but he hadn't kissed her again.

Meanwhile, she replayed that kiss *constantly*. She'd never felt chemistry with someone like she did with him.

Attraction aside, he never talked down to her. Always complimented her, looked out for her and Tony. She felt closer to him than she ever did toward Doug, despite barely knowing Zeke. He worked hard, was respectful to everyone, and *always*, every single day, praised and thanked his employees. He had more consideration for those who worked for him than her own husband ever had for her.

"You're worrying me, Elsie. Talk to me," Zeke said.

Shit. She'd done it again. Gone into her head. "I'm here," she said somewhat lamely.

"How do you feel?"

"Like I was run over, then forced to march ten miles, then dropped off in the middle of the North Pole wearing nothing but shorts and a T-shirt."

Zeke chuckled, and the sound went through Elsie like a warm blanket.

"That good, huh?" he said. "I'm sorry, sweetheart. But Doc'll be here soon and he'll get you fixed up in no time. All you have to do until then is rest. Okay?"

"'Kay."

Zeke slowly lowered her backward, and when her head hit a pillow, Elsie turned her face and inhaled deeply. "Mmmmm."

"What?"

"Smells like you," she mumbled.

"It should, since it's my bed."

Elsie might've been alarmed by that statement, but his words weren't fully registering. She closed her eyes...

It seemed as if it was seconds later when Zeke was shaking her awake again.

"Elsie?"

"What?" she asked a little harshly. "I thought you wanted me to sleep," she complained. "I would if you'd leave me alone."

To her surprise, instead of getting mad—Doug would've torn her a new asshole if she dared speak to him like that—Zeke simply chuckled.

"You've been sleeping for an hour and a half. Doc's here."

Elsie opened her eyes and stared up at Zeke in confusion. "Really?"

"Yeah, he's really here."

"No, I've been asleep that long?"

"Uh-huh. But you don't feel quite so hot anymore, thank goodness. I think the Tylenol did some good. Can you sit up?"

"Of course." But that was easier said than done. Elsie pushed herself up and leaned against the headboard of the large bed.

Looking around, she realized she wasn't in her room at the motel. "Um, where am I?"

"My house."

"How'd I get here?" she asked.

Zeke frowned. "You don't remember?"

"No."

"I got concerned when Reina came in and said you'd asked her to take your shift. I went to check on you, and Edna told me she'd found you passed out on top of the sheets you were folding. She got you to your room. You were still completely out of it when I got there to check on you, and I brought you here so I could keep an eye on you. Now Doc Snow is here to make you feel better."

"Oh. Um...Thanks."

Zeke smiled and reached a hand out to smooth a lock of hair off her forehead. "You're welcome. Now are you going to give the doctor a hard time, or are you going to be a good girl?"

Elsie wanted to laugh. She wasn't eight. She was thirty-three years old. But since Zeke hadn't sounded condescending, and it was obvious he was teasing her—something she didn't have a lot of experience with—she merely stared up at him.

"Hey, Elsie. It's good to see you...not under these circumstances though," the doctor said as he entered. Robert Snow was in his mid-forties, blond, blue-eyed, and sporting a slight paunch. He wasn't married, but had a longtime partner, Craig, who lived with him and served as his admin assistant at the clinic. "Now, what ails ya?"

Elsie smiled at that. She'd always liked the doctor, even if she'd never sought him out for herself in the past. She simply couldn't afford his services. "I'm sick," she informed him.

It was his turn to chuckle. "Right." He turned to Zeke. "Out," he said sternly.

Zeke crossed his arms over his chest. "I'm staying."

"No, you aren't," the doctor said. "You're hovering. And there is such a thing as doctor-client confidentiality. I need to ask questions about her medical history, and you standing there frowning and being all worrywartish isn't helping."

Elsie wanted to laugh at the doctor's words, but all of a sudden she felt exhausted again. She closed her eyes and swayed against the headboard.

"Out," Doctor Snow ordered in a firmer voice.

"I'll be right outside the door if you need me," Zeke said.

Elsie opened her eyes and met his gaze. Surprisingly, his words reassured her. "Thanks," she whispered.

He held her gaze for a moment, then turned and left the room.

"Whew! I've never seen him so intense before. That's quite a sight," Robert said with a wink. "Now, why don't you tell me when you started feeling poorly while I take your temperature."

Ten minutes later, Elsie was once again lying under Zeke's covers and the doctor was talking to Zeke quietly by the door. He believed she had the flu, and because she'd worked her body until she was exhausted, it was hitting her harder than it would otherwise. He'd told her to drink as much liquid as she could, take Tylenol to keep the fever down, and to rest. If she didn't feel better in a few days, she was to call him back and he'd re-check her.

Elsie didn't have a few days to be sick. She'd just started feeling as if she was climbing out of the hole she'd been in for so long, and she was so close to being able to rent a real place for her and Tony. Taking a few days off would be a hit she couldn't afford. Hopefully she'd feel better tomorrow and could go back to work.

She felt the bed depress next to her hip and opened her eyes. She was hugging one of the extra pillows on Zeke's bed to her chest, too sick to be embarrassed about it. His sheets smelled so damn good. It had been forever since she'd been with a man, and having Zeke's scent, in particular, surrounding her was a huge comfort.

Zeke once again pushed her hair back from her cheek, and this time left his hand on her head as he spoke. "How you doin'?"

"I'm great. Ready to run the Fallport half marathon. Just give me another minute and I'll get up and be ready to go."

He chuckled, and Elsie smiled at him in return.

"I don't doubt you'd do just that if you had to," he said. "You're one of the toughest women I've ever met."

There he went with the compliments again. Elsie stored that one away for the future when she was feeling down and needed a pick-me-up.

"You feel like eating?" he asked.

Elsie shook her head.

"All right. I'll pick up some Pedialyte when I'm out so we can keep you hydrated. Anything else you like when you're sick? Chicken soup?"

"Velveeta Shells and Cheese," Elsie mumbled. "And bread. That sweet bread."

"Hawaiian bread?" Zeke asked.

"Yeah. And cheese sticks."

He grinned. "Got it. When's the last time you were sick, sweetheart?"

Elsie wrinkled her forehead, trying to remember. "I think it was when Tony was around two. I was throwing up practically every thirty minutes while trying to keep him from destroying the house."

"You were married, right?"

"Uh-huh."

"Where was your husband? He should've been there to watch Tony."

Without thought, the words spewed out of Elsie. She'd been so very careful not to talk about her ex. Didn't want to badmouth him around Tony. Or even think about him. But when her guard was down, and she felt so awful, she couldn't keep the bitter words back. "Probably fucking his secretary. He thought I was useless and weak. There was no way he would've lifted a finger to help me with Tony. He saw that as my job...whether I was sick or not."

"What an asshole."

Elsie blinked up at Zeke. Then nodded. "He was."

"For the record, raising a child isn't a *job*, it's a privilege. And I'm sorry you didn't have anyone to take care of you. That sucks. But I'm here now, and the only thing you have to worry about is getting better."

His concern for her was almost overwhelming in her current emotional state. "I'll be okay in a while. I'll get out of here soon."

Zeke didn't reply to that. "Tony gets home from school around four, right?"

Elsie frowned. "Yeah, why?"

Instead of directly answering, he said, "I've got just enough time to get to the store and pick up some things for you before meeting his bus."

"Oh, shit!" Elsie tried to sit up. "What time is it?"

"No," Zeke said, putting his hand on her shoulder and pushing her back down. "I've got this."

Elsie frowned. "Got what?"

"You. And Tony. I'll meet the bus at the motel and bring him back here."

"Oh, but—"

"No buts," he said firmly. "You stay here and sleep. Do. Not. Get. Out. Of. This. Bed."

Elsie shook her head. "You're really bossy."

"Yup. When it comes to your health and wellness, you bet I am. Sleep, Else. That's what your body needs right now."

She knew she should protest more. She should get out of bed and pick up her son. But she was so damn tired. She relaxed against the mattress and her eyes closed.

She felt Zeke's lips on her forehead, and she was certain he'd done that before. While he was carrying her? She wasn't sure. But the feel of his lips against her skin wasn't something she could ever forget. It was...comforting. Intimate.

"I'll be back soon," he said softly.

Her eyes popped open, and Elsie reached for him, grabbing hold of his arm before he could stand up. "Wait."

"Yeah? What's wrong?"

"The code word. You have to tell it to Tony before he'll go with you."

"Code word?" he asked.

"Yes. We change it up every month. It's silly, I know, but I've taught him never to go with anyone, even if he knows them, if they can't say our code word."

"It's not silly," Zeke praised. "It's smart as hell. What is it?"

Elsie frowned and panicked for a second, not able to remember what she'd decided on that month. Then it came to her. "Austere."

Zeke was silent for a moment, then he said, "Wow. Okay."

"I know it's weird, but I went online and found a list of the vocab words on the SAT test. I want it to be a word that won't normally come up in conversation, that someone won't accidentally guess, but I also want him to learn something at the same time he's being safe."

"It's not weird," Zeke insisted. "It's...awesome. You're an amazing mom."

Again, his praise made her feel really good. Every time he said something nice, especially about her being a good mom, it seemed to patch up a hole Doug had created with his caustic words.

Zeke stood up and headed for the door.

"Zeke?"

He turned. "Yeah, Else?"

"I...Thanks. I appreciate you picking Tony up. We'll be out of your hair before dinner."

Zeke walked back to the bed and sat again, leaning over her. "No, you won't."

"You can't want us to stay here. I love my son, but he's...exuberant. He asks a ton of questions, and he'll probably have even more once he realizes you're there to pick him up."

"And you think I'm gonna get annoyed by questions?" Zeke asked.

Elsie winced. "Well, um..." She hedged, not wanting to offend her boss. He'd been extremely nice to her today, and she didn't want to say or do anything that might insult him.

To her surprise, Zeke smirked. "Right, it's probably good we have this conversation sooner rather than later. This might not be the right time, since you're sick, but I'll remind you in the future that we had this talk, if you don't remember. I *like* kids, Else. They're honest, and inquisitive, and yes, even a challenge. I have no problem with Tony asking me questions. I'm happy to teach him whatever I can."

Then he smirked. "Although, I'm thinking he'll probably be more interested in getting to know Ethan and Rocky better, and even Brock more than me. They can teach him fun things, like taking a toilet apart, how not to electrocute yourself while hooking up a ceiling fan, how to change the oil in your car. Not sure knowing how to make mixed drinks is something you want me to teach him...or something he wants to know at this point in his life."

Elsie reached for his hand. "He's starved for a man's attention. I can give him lots of things in his life, but I can't be his dad. He's at the age where he's understanding that he's different from a lot of his peers, and I hate that. I was thrilled when Lilly taught him how to change our tire, but it opened a can of worms I can't seem to shut again. He wants to know all sorts of 'manly' things that I have no clue about. I'm not saying I want you to teach him how to make a Tom Collins, but just being around you, a guy who's more mascu-line than anyone I've ever met, will thrill him to no end."

Zeke smiled down at her. "Thank you. Now, no more talk about leaving tonight. You're sick, I'm looking forward to getting to know your son better, and I love not being alone in my house."

Well, damn. How could she insist on leaving after that? She couldn't. She simply nodded. "Drive safe," she whispered, not knowing what else to say.

"Of course. I'll have precious cargo with me. Sleep, Else. I mean it. Relax. There's nothing you have to worry about for the next twelve hours, at the minimum."

Elsie nodded. He was right. She'd already asked Reina to take her shift. She didn't have to worry about anything until the morning, when she needed to get Tony ready for school and get back to the motel to work, before starting her shift at On the Rocks.

Once again, Zeke leaned down...but this time, instead of kissing her forehead, he touched his lips to hers.

Flustered, Elsie blushed and blurted, "Germs. Don't want to get you sick."

"It'd be worth it," Zeke told her, brushing his thumb over her cheek before he stood. Elsie didn't stop him again when he reached the door and closed it gently behind him.

She closed her eyes and sighed. She wasn't sure what had just happened, but she was too tired to think about it anymore.

It felt amazingly good not to have to worry about anything at the moment. She should feel guilty about that, since her life revolved around her son, but knowing Zeke would take good care of him, she let herself relax. She was asleep in seconds, content in the knowledge that for now, however briefly, she had absolutely no obligations. It was heavenly.

CHAPTER THREE

Zeke hated to leave Elsie alone, but the sooner he left and picked up some food she might eat, then picked up Tony, the sooner he could get back to her.

He went to old man Grogan's general store in town instead of heading out to the better-stocked big-box store, because he wanted to make sure he was waiting for Tony's bus when it arrived at the Mangree Motel. The store didn't have everything Elsie wanted, but he got the cheese, the Pedialyte, and the Velveeta Shells & Cheese. Grogan didn't carry the sweet bread, but Zeke grabbed some regular rolls.

He also picked up hamburger meat, hot dogs, some fresh fruit, and a box of doughnuts. The latter wasn't the healthiest thing he could get for Tony's breakfast, but he could eat some fruit and that should balance things out. It wasn't as if one morning of junk would hurt the kid. He hoped.

He was leaning against his pickup truck when the school bus rumbled up the road and stopped outside the motel parking lot. Tony was the only kid who got off, and he immediately saw Zeke.

He smiled and ran toward him. "Hi, Zeke!"

"Hey, bub. How was school?"

The boy shrugged. "Fine." Then, as if he realized that Zeke being there to greet him wasn't normal, lines formed in his little forehead. "What's wrong? Where's Mom?"

"She's at my place. I'm here to pick you up," Zeke said.

"Why?" Tony asked, the suspicion easy to hear in his question.

"She's sick, bub. She called in sick to work, and I was worried about her. I came over here and she had a fever. So I took her to my house where I could look after her."

His words didn't make the boy feel better, if his step backward was any indication. "Mom's never sick," he declared.

"I know," Zeke said, doing his best to stay relaxed. The last thing he wanted was to freak Tony out. "Which is why I came to check on her. She's gonna be okay. She just needs some rest. She's been working really hard lately, and I think it all just got to be too much."

Tony nodded at that, but the worried look didn't fade from his face.

"I stopped at the store before I came to pick you up and got stuff to make hamburgers for dinner. You like hamburgers, right? If not, I also got some hot dogs, just in case."

Tony swallowed hard. Then he asked tentatively, "Do you have the code word?"

Zeke mentally smacked his forehead. Shit, he should've said that right away. Tony knew him, but it was still better to be safe than sorry. He crouched down on the balls of his feet so he was eye-to-eye with the boy. "Yeah, bub. It's austere. You know what that means?"

Upon hearing the word, Tony visibly relaxed. "Yeah. There are actually a couple meanings. The most used one is plain. But it can also mean stern."

Zeke was impressed. "Yup. I'm sorry I didn't reassure you with the code word right away."

Tony shrugged, then asked, "Is my mom really gonna be all right?"

"Of course. Doc Snow came by and thinks she has the flu. She just needs lots of rest and fluids, and she'll be right as rain again in a few days."

Tony's eyes got big. "She saw the doctor?"

Zeke chuckled. "Yeah. Didn't want to, but I didn't give her a choice."

"She doesn't like doctors. Says they're too expensive. She makes me go every year for a checkup, and calls him when I get sick, but *she* never goes."

"Yeah, that's what she told me."

Tony frowned and glanced at the door to their room. "She's gonna eat ramen for a long time."

"What do you mean?" Zeke asked.

Tony met his gaze, saying bluntly, "When she has to spend money on something she didn't expect to, she doesn't eat much for a while. She claims she's not hungry, but I know she is." The boy shrugged and turned his gaze to the ground.

Zeke was getting an even clearer picture of how hard Elsie's life had been, and he didn't like the image. He'd been such an idiot. Admiring her work ethic, worrying about how skinny she was, yet not doing anything to help in his bid not to overstep. "Look at me, Tony." Zeke waited until he had the boy's attention. "Your mom not eating ends right now," he said, quietly but firmly. "I'm gonna take care of her. And you. Not that she hasn't done an awesome job of taking care of you all by herself, but everyone needs help now and then."

"Even you?" Tony asked.

"Especially me."

"What do you need help with?" the boy asked with an inquisitive tilt of his head.

"Not working so much. Stopping to enjoy life. Taking a breath and looking around me more often. I need help not being lonely."

Tony eyed him with an expression that belied the fact he was only nine years old. This kid was much wiser than most his age. A fact Zeke was proud of and hated at the same time. "Mom gets lonely too. She pretends she doesn't, but she does."

Zeke nodded. "Right. So starting today, food's no longer an issue for you guys. Neither is seeing a doctor when either of you need one. Okay?"

Tony nodded.

"Great. Now, since you're spending the night at my house, how about we get some clothes for you to wear to school tomorrow, and anything else you might want from your room, and get going so we can check on your mom?"

"I'm spending the night?" Tony asked with wide eyes.

"Yup. That okay?"

"Yes! It's awesome!" he exclaimed. Then he dropped his back-pack and raced toward the office.

Zeke chuckled. He picked up the bag and followed. He'd just reached the lobby door when Tony burst outside. "Mom doesn't like for me to carry a key with me at school, so when I get home, I have to go to the office and get one," he explained as he passed Zeke and headed for room twelve. "Edna always has it waiting for me." He looked back at Zeke as he pushed the key into the lock. "I know it's also because Mom wants to make sure I get home all right, and she has a deal with Edna to let her know if I don't get home on time. But that's cool. I get it." He pushed open the door to the motel room and hurried inside.

Zeke didn't like the thought of Tony being on his own between the time he got home from school and when Elsie's shift was over. Tony was a pretty mature kid, and it was obvious Edna kept her eye on him...but still.

Tony rushed around the motel room, opening a drawer, pulling out clothes and throwing them on the bed. He then went to the bathroom and got his toiletries. He also grabbed a small fire truck that was sitting on the table, as well as two books and a couple of Matchbox cars.

Then he hesitated, biting his lip and looking up at Zeke.

"What's up, bub?"

"Nothing. I'm done. I don't see our bag, though. Did you already bring it to your house?"

Zeke looked around and realized there was nothing to put Tony's things in. He and his mom probably shared the duffel bag he'd packed earlier. He made a mental note to pick up another suitcase or bag the next time he was at the store. "I did. Not a big deal. We can use your backpack," Zeke said, unzipping the bag he was still holding.

"No! Wait!" Tony exclaimed.

But it was too late.

Zeke looked into the bag...and did his best to keep his dismay to himself. He looked up at Tony. "Want to explain this?" he asked, nodding toward the open bag in his hands.

Tony looked down at the floor. "Not really."

Feeling unsure, not certain how to handle the situation, Zeke sat on the end of the bed closest to the door. "When I was growing up, my parents didn't have much money. And what money they did have, they spent on drugs," he told the boy quietly. "Most of the time it felt as if they forgot I was even there. There was never enough food in the house. Weekends were the worst. At least when I went to school, I could get the free lunches they offered to people who needed it."

Tony was looking at him now, so Zeke went on.

"I'm not proud of what I did, but sometimes I stole food from the store so I wouldn't go hungry. Or when my parents remembered to buy food, I hid some of it in my room, so I'd have it for later," he said. Zeke hadn't talked about his childhood with *anyone*, but this kid needed to hear that he wasn't alone, more than Zeke needed to keep his embarrassment about his upbringing quiet.

"I didn't steal it," Tony said quietly. "At lunch, I do some of the other kids' homework in exchange for some of what they brought to eat. I bring it back and add it to our stash while Mom's still at work," he said, gesturing to the milk crates that served as their pantry. "I don't like it when Mom doesn't eat. She hasn't noticed the extra stuff, and as long as it looks like there's food there, she'll take something for herself. When it gets too low, she insists she's not hungry and makes me eat what we have."

Zeke had to swallow hard twice before he was able to talk. Fuck. Once more, he wanted to kick his own ass. He'd not even guessed how little Elsie and Tony had. He should have. Especially after what he'd gone through growing up.

He put the backpack on the mattress and gestured for Tony to come closer.

The boy shuffled toward him, and when he was close enough, Zeke put a hand on his shoulder. "You're a good kid," he said firmly. "The fact that you worry about your mom and want to take care of her is awesome. But you won't need to do other kids' work for food anymore. Hear me?"

Tony didn't nod or say anything. He just stared at Zeke with a blank expression.

"If she lets me, I'm gonna take care of your mom," he said earnestly. "I knew she was working hard, I just didn't fully understand the reality of your situation. From here on out, she's gonna eat lunch at the bar, *and* she'll bring home dinner for the both of you. Every day, bub. Neither of you will have to go hungry again."

The relief in the little boy's hazel eyes was painful to see. "Okay."

"Okay. Now, go ahead and take this food and put it over there," Zeke said. "Then take out your school stuff and put your overnight things in the backpack. You have a lot of homework for tonight?"

Tony shook his head. "Just a few worksheets. They're easy."

"And how many of those have you already done for other classmates today?" Zeke asked.

Tony's lips twitched. "Three."

Zeke chuckled. It probably wasn't appropriate, he shouldn't be laughing at the fact that the poor kid had to do the same work for himself that he'd already done for three other kids, but he couldn't help it.

"You aren't mad?" Tony asked.

"At you? No."

The little boy tilted his head and studied Zeke. "Who are you mad at then?"

"Myself."

"Why?"

"Because I don't like the thought of either of you being hungry. I experienced it often enough when I was little to know it sucks—sorry...it's not fun. I should've noticed. Should've paid more attention. Here's the thing...I like your mom, Tony."

"I'm glad," he said.

"No. I *like* her," Zeke emphasized gently.

Tony's eyes got big. "Oh! Like...you want to go out with her?"

"Yes. Is that okay with you?"

His head bobbed up and down enthusiastically. "Yes! Does that mean you'll be her boyfriend?"

Zeke smiled. "Yeah. If she'll let me."

"She will," Tony said with a huge smile. "And can we maybe do stuff?"

"Stuff?" Zeke asked.

Tony shrugged. "Yeah. All my friends do stuff with their dads."

Zeke knew he wasn't this boy's dad. But hearing him use that term when talking about him made his throat tighten up. "Like what?" he managed to ask. He had no frame of reference for what kinds of things a dad might do with his son because of his own upbringing, but he could probably figure something out. But he wanted to be sure to do something with Tony that the boy would enjoy.

Tony looked down at his feet once more and shrugged. Zeke

was beginning to realize he did that any time he was unsure or embarrassed.

"I'm not a car expert like Brock. Although I can change a tire like Lilly showed you," Zeke told him. "And while I can do simple things around the house, I'm also not as good at construction stuff as Rocky and Ethan are. But you know what I love to do?"

Tony looked up. "What?"

"Hike. And camp. Make dinner on a fire and roast marshmallows afterward. And I love to fish. You ever been fishing?"

Tony shook his head.

"You want to?"

"I don't know how."

"I'll teach you."

And just like that, Tony's eyes lit up again. "Cool," he breathed.

"But not today. We need to get back to my house to check in on your mom. And make dinner. You ever made hamburgers?"

"No. Mom's always made all our food."

"It's probably about time you started to learn how to do that for yourself, don't you think?"

The little boy nodded once more. "Yeah. That way if Mom gets sick again, I can take care of her."

Zeke had the strong urge to assure Tony that if his mom got sick in the future, he'd be there to take care of them *both*—forever. But he figured he'd pushed his luck far enough for one day. Elsie hadn't exactly complained when he'd staked his claim a few weeks ago, but telling her kid that they were going to get married and live happily ever after was going a bit far.

"Right. So...let's get you packed up and get going, yeah?" Zeke prompted.

Tony spun and ran over to the corner to unload his backpack.

Elsie had to know that the food in the corner of the room wasn't magically appearing out of nowhere, but she obviously hadn't said anything to her son about it. Probably wanting him to feel as if he was contributing. But he was pretty sure she didn't know he was doing other kids' schoolwork in return for the food. She probably just figured it was items given to kids on the free lunch program.

It was obvious to Zeke that Tony was an exceptionally smart kid, one who spoke like an adult and was more astute than people probably realized. He wondered if there were special classes he could take or programs that would help stimulate him academically. He also understood a little more about the code words Elsie chose for him. A college-entry-level word no longer seemed odd. Tony soaked in information like a sponge took in water.

He was finished packing his stuff in minutes and stood in front of Zeke with a smile. "Okay, I'm ready. Let's go!"

Smiling, Zeke headed for the door. "You need to return that key to Edna?" he asked, nodding at the key on the dresser.

Tony shook his head. "Nah. She'll come and get it when we aren't here."

"All right. Let's get a move on then." Making sure the door was closed and locked behind him, Zeke shook his head at the abundant energy Tony seemed to have as he practically bounced to the truck. He got buckled in and Zeke carefully backed out of his parking spot.

When they were on their way to his house Tony asked, "Did you mean it?"

"I don't say anything I don't mean," Zeke said calmly. "But what specifically are you talking about?"

"You'll take me camping?"

"Of course. It's one of my favorite things to do. And once you're up for it, I'll even take you to Eagle Point Lookout. It's a ten-mile hike one way though," he warned. "So it'll be long and tiring."

"Cool!" Tony exclaimed. "I've heard about it, but none of my friends have ever been there."

"It *is* cool," Zeke said. "It's an old fire watchtower. You know what that is?"

"Uh-huh. It's where people used to live and watch over the forest for signs of a fire."

"Exactly. Of course, it's pretty rundown and no one actually lives out there anymore. There are more high-tech ways of discovering fires these days. But the view from up there is unbeatable. You think your mom would want to come with us?"

Tony laughed. "No way. She doesn't like bugs. Or hiking. Or the outdoors."

"Okay, then it'll just be us guys then," Zeke said.

"Yeah," Tony sighed. "Us guys."

It was obvious Else was right—the kid was starved for male attention. Not that she hadn't done a great job of raising him. But sometimes a boy just wanted to be a boy. Get dirty. Play in the forest. Find bugs. Zeke might not be able to teach him some of the things his friends could, but he could definitely take him camping. One of his favorite things to do was get out in nature as often as possible.

"Zeke?" Tony asked, interrupting his internal musings.

"Yeah, bub?"

"This is the best day *ever*."

"I'm having a good day too, bub," Zeke told him. He hadn't lied to Elsie. He liked kids. They were generally so open and enthusiastic about everything. He couldn't wait to get to know Tony better.

CHAPTER FOUR

Elsie felt awful. But even though she was sicker than she'd been in a very long time, she somehow also felt content. After the doctor had left and Zeke had gone to pick up Tony, she'd dozed, but hadn't fallen into a deep sleep. She couldn't. Not until she knew her son was safe.

When they'd arrived, Tony had immediately come to check on her and excitedly said that Zeke was going to let him help make dinner. Zeke had asked if she wanted to come out and lie on the sofa in the living room, and she'd eagerly agreed.

Now here she was. Alternating between being hot and cold, trying not to throw up at the smells coming from the kitchen...but loving every second of watching and listening to her son interact with Zeke.

"Just like this. Squish the meat together so the burger doesn't fall apart when it's cooking," Zeke told Tony. The look on her son's face as he concentrated on making the hamburger patty exactly as Zeke instructed wasn't something Elsie was going to forget anytime soon. Not having a real kitchen was tough. She wanted to teach

Tony how to cook, but when all she had was a kettle, pot, and a single burner, it wasn't exactly ideal.

"It doesn't look right," Tony whined.

"What are you talking about? It's perfect," Zeke assured him.

"It is not! It's lopsided."

"Here's a secret about cooking you need to know. If something looks perfect, it usually tastes like crap," Zeke said confidently.

Elsie smiled from her cocoon of blankets on the couch.

"I'm serious!" Zeke exclaimed, obviously having been on the receiving end of one of Tony's skeptical looks. As he got older, Tony was harder to convince of the simplest things. She figured it was just a product of his inquisitive mind, but also a sign that he was getting wiser and wouldn't blindly believe her anymore just because she was his mom.

"I'd much rather eat a lopsided cake made with love than one baked by some famous chef who doesn't know or care about me," Zeke said. "Besides, hamburgers don't need to be perfect. We're gonna put them on the grill and they're gonna change shape anyway." Then, after a pause, "Let me put it this way, would you rather have a plate of French fries smothered in ketchup and so messy you can't eat them without getting the stuff smeared all over your face, or a perfect dollop of one perfect circle of ketchup on the end of each one?"

"Smothered," Tony said without hesitation.

"Exactly," Zeke said. "Look, if you wanted to be a professional chef, I might tell you to be more careful and to make sure each hamburger patty was exactly the same size. I might even buy a scale so you could measure to make sure each was the same weight. But as far as I know, that's not what you want to do...is it?"

"No," Tony said.

"What *do* you want to do?" Zeke asked.

Elsie smiled. She hoped Zeke was ready for her son's answer.

"I want to be a teacher."

"That's great, bub."

"And an astronaut. And I want to build really tall buildings, but make them bombproof so no one can make them fall down by crashing into them."

Elsie knew that last one came from the lesson he'd had in school about what happened in New York on September 11th.

"Oh, and I want to be an author, and discover aliens and make friends with them so they'll give us amazing technology and the cure to cancer."

Elsie wasn't surprised by her son's answers. He was into quite a few things at the moment, and she figured he had more than enough time to figure out what he wanted to do with the rest of his life. For now, she was thrilled he was so inquisitive.

"Wow. That's impressive," Zeke said, sounding completely sincere, which Elsie appreciated. "All those things take a lot of schooling."

"I like school," was Tony's response.

"Cool. So, back to my original point, unless you're disarming a bomb, you don't have to be perfect, bub. Lopsided hamburgers will taste just as good as perfectly round ones."

There was silence in the kitchen for a moment, then Tony asked, "Have you disarmed a bomb?"

"Actually, yes."

Elsie blinked in surprise. She hadn't known that about Zeke. She knew he used to be in the Army, but he didn't talk about that much. At work, he was all friendly smiles and concentrating on making sure the patrons and his employees were happy.

"*Really?!*" Tony asked.

"Yeah."

"Did it blow up?"

"Thankfully, no."

"Have you seen a bomb explode?"

Elsie wanted to tell her son to stop badgering Zeke. To not ask so many questions about something so serious. But her limbs felt as if they weighed a thousand pounds...and she was interested in Zeke's responses herself.

"Unfortunately, yes."

"But wasn't it cool?" Tony asked in confusion.

"Yes and no. The mechanics of it, sure. But the damage it did to the buildings and people around it wasn't cool at all."

Tony was quiet for a moment. "People got hurt?"

"Yeah, bub. My job in the Army was to find bad guys and make sure they couldn't hurt others."

"Did you like it?"

"No."

Zeke's answer was short and to the point. And there was so much anguish in that one word, Elsie pushed herself up onto an elbow so she could look over the back of the couch into the kitchen. Tony had hamburger up to his elbows and was staring up at Zeke with his hands frozen in a bowl of what she assumed was the raw meat he was shaping into burgers.

Zeke was looking down at her son, meeting his gaze head on.

She opened her mouth to tell Tony not to push, but he spoke before she could get a word out.

"So you changed jobs. And now you get to be a hero and not have to see people blow up."

Elsie saw Zeke's eyes close and his jaw tighten. Even as she watched, she could see him gather up his composure. He opened his eyes and smiled down at her son. "Something like that, yeah."

"You *are* a hero," Tony insisted. "I know what you do. You go into the forest and find people who get lost. There was that little kid a year or so ago. Her brother's in my class. He told me about it. How she was too young to know where she was or how to get home. She would've died. But you and your friends went out there and found her. Brought her home."

Zeke simply nodded.

"Right. That makes you a hero," Tony said matter-of-factly. "And you get to do another job too. Work with my mom. Making people happy. That's what I want to do. Have more than one job so I can do all the things I'm interested in."

"That's a great plan, bub," Zeke told him.

"Some of the kids at school think it's dumb," Tony said, looking down into the bowl.

"Why is it dumb?" Zeke asked.

"Because. They say you have to be one thing when you grow up. You know, a teacher, astronaut, truck driver. But you can't be more than one."

"You can be whatever you want, Tony. Look at your mom."

"My mom?" he asked in confusion.

"Yeah. She's a mom, a teacher, a waitress, a cook, a maid, a chauffeur, and even a doctor at times."

Tony rolled his eyes. That was another thing that was fairly new. He never used to do that, but as he grew older, he was learning the fine art of sarcasm and disrespect. Much to Elsie's dismay.

"None of that stuff counts. Except for the waitress thing. She's not really any of those other things."

"I beg to differ," Zeke told him. "Keep squishing, those burgers aren't going to make themselves. What was your last code word?"

Elsie approved of how Zeke was able to keep Tony on task but continue the conversation.

"Condone."

"And what does that mean?"

"To approve of something."

"Can you use it in a sentence?"

Tony once more rolled his eyes, but did as Zeke requested. "I don't condone you asking me all these questions."

Zeke laughed. "Good job, bub. Now—how did you learn what that word meant?"

Tony shrugged. "Mom told me."

"So, your mom *taught* you what it meant."

"Yeah, that's what I said."

"And you don't think she's a teacher?"

Tony stilled and looked up at Zeke. "Um...maybe she is?"

"All I'm saying is, you don't have to be pigeonholed into being only one thing. We all have many jobs. There's lots of things adults have to be. Accountants so we can manage our money, chefs so we can feed ourselves, teachers, waitresses, caregivers...the list goes on and on. And just because we don't get paid for all of the stuff we do, doesn't mean they aren't jobs and they're not important. So you wanting to be more than one thing is perfectly normal. Ignore those kids at school who try to tell you differently."

Elsie's eyes were full of tears. Zeke was...

He was amazing, that's what he was. She'd admired him from afar for quite a while now, as an employer, but learning more about him through what he was saying to her son was like seeing a completely different side of him altogether. He'd also encouraged her son more in thirty seconds than his father had done in nine years.

Just then, his gaze lifted from her son and met Elsie's across the room. "You're supposed to be resting," he scolded. But he was smiling when he said it, so Elsie didn't think he was upset in the least.

She gave him a small smile.

"Look, Mom! I'm making burgers!" Tony said excitedly.

"I see."

"Zeke and me are gonna make your noodles next," he informed her.

"Zeke and I," she corrected.

"That's what I said," Tony replied with a huff. "What now, Zeke?"

The man who'd somehow taken over her life chuckled and proceeded to tell Tony the next steps in hamburger making. She'd learned a lot about him in the last few hours. She already knew he was bossy and overprotective. She'd learned that firsthand that day when he'd told off the man who'd dared touch her ass, and he'd hauled her into his office, informed her they were now dating, and kissed her. Well, he hadn't actually *said* they were dating, but he'd inferred it.

Now she knew that Zeke was great with kids. Or at least her kid. He'd gotten out of the Army because he obviously didn't like what he was doing. And he was very good at winning arguments. Not that he and Tony were arguing, but he'd managed to turn her son's thinking around scarily easily. From past experience, Elsie knew that when Tony got his mind set on something, it was almost impossible to get him to deviate. And Zeke had managed to convince him that it was perfectly all right, and normal, to be interested in more than one profession.

She liked Zeke. A lot. Probably too much. He was her boss, and the last thing she needed was to get involved with him and have it go bad. If she lost her job, she'd be in big trouble. She was almost at the point where she had enough money saved to get her and Tony out of the motel. She not only needed first and last month's rent, plus a security deposit, but she needed to purchase everything that came with renting. Beds, pots and pans, furniture, bathroom stuff... the list went on and on. And all of that took money.

Elsie wasn't rich, not by any stretch of the imagination, but she was making it. On her own. Her ex had told her over and over again that she'd never amount to anything without him. That if she ever left him, she'd end up homeless since she had no education, no skills. To her shame, she'd believed him for a very long time.

"Else?"

She jerked at the sound of her name. "Yeah?"

"Stop thinking and go to sleep. We'll wake you up when your macaroni is ready."

She couldn't help but smile. "Okay," she mumbled, then flopped back down onto the incredibly comfortable couch cushions. Surprisingly, she felt herself fading off in just minutes. The sound of her son's happy chatter in her ears and Zeke's low rumble making her feel safe.

* * *

Zeke stepped into the living room to check on Elsie. Her cheeks were flushed, but her eyes were closed and she was breathing deeply and evenly. He'd check her temperature later; he didn't want to do anything to risk waking her up when she'd finally fallen asleep.

He'd been cognizant of her listening to his conversation with Tony earlier, and hoped she approved of what he'd said. He might like kids, but he didn't have a ton of experience with them. He figured it was better to treat Tony like a mini adult rather than talk down to him.

"You want to scoop out some macaroni for your mom?" he asked Tony.

The boy nodded and headed for the stove. He stared into the pot for a moment, then looked up at Zeke. "Is she gonna be all right?"

Zeke frowned. "Your mom? Of course."

"She's never sick."

Zeke stepped closer to the boy and put his hand on his shoulder. "She's tough, bub. And Doc Snow didn't seem too concerned. She just needs some sleep and to relax for a while."

"What would happen to me if she died?"

Zeke tightened his hand on Tony's shoulder. His first instinct was to say that Elsie wasn't going to fucking die. That he wouldn't let her. But he didn't want to dismiss Tony's fears either. He crouched down so he could look the boy in the eyes. "What's brought this on?"

Tony shrugged and focused on Zeke's shoulder. "I just...I don't have a dad. So if she dies, I won't be able to stay at the motel by myself."

Zeke struggled to come up with something that would reassure the boy, that also wouldn't be a lie. "Nothing is going to happen to your mom. She's strong and healthy. She simply has the flu right now. It happens. I'm going to make sure she has the best care possible. I'll also make sure she rests and doesn't try to overdo things until she's better again. With that said...I give you my word that if anything *does* ever happen to your mom, I'll do everything in my power to make sure you're taken care of."

Tony's chin came up and he met Zeke's gaze. "Promise?"

"Promise," Zeke said solemnly. "You aren't alone, bub. You've got me. And Rocky. And Ethan. And all the other guys. There are rules and laws, but we'll do whatever it takes to make sure you're safe. Okay?"

Tony nodded. "Okay. Do you think..." The boy's words faded, but then he looked at Zeke. "Did my dad leave because I was bad? Because he didn't like me?"

Zeke's stomach clenched. "No," he said without thought. "I don't know your father, or what happened between him and your mom, but I know without any shred of doubt that your dad isn't gone because of anything you did or didn't do. Sometimes relationships between adults just don't work out."

"Gabe's parents are divorced, and he sees his dad every other weekend. He even gets to spend summers with him," Tony said.

"That's good for Gabe, but again, there are lots of reasons why parents don't see their children. But I'll tell you this—your dad's missing out. You're a hell of a kid. Oh, shoot...don't repeat that word."

Tony smiled. "It's not that bad of a word," he informed Zeke.

"Even so. I don't think your mom would approve. As I was saying, you're an amazing kid. You take care of your mom. You notice things other kids don't. You learn really fast. I'm not sure anyone's picked up how to make hamburgers as fast as you did tonight. And you know a lot of words that most kids your age have never even heard. So your dad not being around is *his* loss, not yours." After a beat, he added, "Besides, he probably has hair growing out of his ears and boogers in his nose."

Tony giggled, and Zeke relaxed a bit. He brought a hand up and palmed the side of Tony's face. "And I think your mom's pretty amazing too. She's done a fabulous job of raising you all by herself. Don't you think?"

Tony nodded.

"Right. So...to recap. If something happens to your mom, you've got me and all my friends to have your back. All right?"

"Thanks, Zeke."

"You're welcome."

"Zeke?"

He stood and smiled down at Tony. "Yeah?"

"Would you wanna be my dad?"

Zeke's heart stopped beating in his chest for a moment at hearing that question. He hadn't thought about having kids...No, that was a lie. When he'd first gotten married, he'd been looking forward to starting a family. But that dream died, along with the trust and love he'd had for his wife.

But at Tony's question, and after spending the afternoon with him, the desire to have children hit him full force in an instant. And being this boy's dad meant Elsie would be a package deal.

Yeah, it was safe to say he was all for it.

"I mean, I know you aren't really. But maybe we can pretend?" Tony asked nervously when Zeke didn't immediately respond.

"I'm not sure about being your dad, bub, because that's mostly up to your mom...but I can be something better for now," Zeke said after a moment.

"What?"

"I can be your friend. We'll go camping and fishing, and if you have any questions, about anything, you can come to me and we'll talk it out. Yeah?"

Tony nodded. "Yeah."

There was more Zeke wanted to say, but he was perilously close to getting damn mushy. Which wasn't like him at all. "Now, how about we dish up that mac and cheese, get your mom settled, then taste our hamburger masterpieces?"

"Okay."

Zeke watched for a beat as Tony began to scoop some of the gooey, cheesy pasta into a bowl. He ruffled the boy's hair and headed for the couch. He half expected to see Elsie awake, and he was going over in his head what he'd say to her to explain that conversation with her son, but her eyes were closed and she was still fast asleep.

She'd kicked off the blanket and the T-shirt she wore was rucked up, showing him the pale flesh of her belly.

Zeke felt as if he'd been kicked in the head. All he could do was stand there and stare at her for a moment. Seeing all that smooth skin made his hands itch to touch her. Even with how skinny she was, her belly still had a tiny pooch. It was fucking sexy as hell, and Zeke wanted to put his lips there and kiss her awake.

Shaking his head, knowing she'd freak out if she woke to him touching her that way, he took a deep breath and went down on his knees next to the sofa. He reached for the blanket and covered her before putting his hand on her shoulder and shaking her gently. "Dinner's ready," he said softly.

Elsie went from asleep to awake in a heartbeat. She turned her head, her lips only inches from his own, and stared at him in confusion.

Not able to help himself, Zeke brushed her hair off her forehead. She was still warm, but he didn't think she was overly feverish, which was a relief. "Tony made your macaroni and it's ready. If you think you can eat? It'll be good to get some calories into you."

"Um, yeah. Okay."

She started to sit up, and Zeke put an arm around her upper back, helping her.

"It's probably time for another Tylenol too."

"How long was I asleep?" she asked.

"Not too long. Just long enough for Tony to master the art of knife cuts, pass the SAT, get a girlfriend, and graduate from high school," he teased.

"I know some parents might dream of the day their kids graduate and head out into the world, but not me," she said softly. "I dread that day."

"You're a good mom," Zeke replied.

She opened her mouth to say something else, but Tony interrupted them.

"Here you go, Mom. I made it extra cheesy, just the way you like it. And I did it all myself. Zeke taught me how to know when the noodles were done and I poured the milk in and measured and stirred."

"Thank you, baby. It looks delicious."

Tony beamed. "Wait until you see the hamburgers I made. I squished them and flipped them and everything!"

"Awesome," Elsie said.

Tony turned and ran back toward the kitchen.

"Pour another glass of Pedialyte for your mom, would ya, bub?"

"Okay."

"And grab two more Tylenol too."

"Got it!" Tony told him.

"I'm sorry I—"

"No," Zeke interrupted.

Elsie frowned. "You don't know what I was going to say."

"I do. And you have nothing to apologize for. Tony's good. I'm good."

"I just...it's been a long time since I had any help with him."

"Well, you do now."

"Thank you."

"It's not a hardship, you know. Tony's a great kid."

Elsie smiled. "Yeah, he is."

"You remember what I told you in the bar the other week?" Zeke asked.

"Um..." she hedged.

"I told you that we were happening," Zeke reminded her. "Which was hugely presumptuous. I get that. So I've been going slow. Trying not to spook you. But I haven't been doing a very good job of looking after you. That's gonna change, Else."

She stared at him with big eyes.

"Will you have a problem with that?"

"I'm not sure I have the time or energy to be in a relationship."

Instead of getting upset, Zeke was relieved she was being honest with him. "Being with me isn't going to be a burden, sweetheart."

"I have Tony," she said.

"Yes, you do. And we've already established that I like him. I have no problem spending time with both of you. I know you're a package deal. I actually *like* that. As long as I know you feel the same chemistry I do, everything else, we can figure out." Zeke waited, practically holding his breath. He wasn't above pushing her past her comfort zone just a touch to get her to take a chance on him, but he also wasn't about to force her to date him if it wasn't something she truly wanted.

"I'm a mess," she whispered.

"Life's messy," he retorted. He was still on his knees in front of the couch, and he didn't dare move as he waited for her answer.

She nodded slowly, and the weight on Zeke's shoulders suddenly felt ten times lighter.

"I feel as if I just won the lottery," he whispered.

The smile on Elsie's face was all the reassurance he needed that she felt the same way. Was it love? At this point, probably not. But it could very easily turn into that...fast.

"I had trouble getting the bottle open, but I finally got it," Tony said as he moved carefully across the living room with a glass filled to the brim with Pedialyte and two pills in his other hand.

Elsie took them with a small thank you and swallowed them down.

"I think we'll eat in here with your mom, if that's okay, bub," Zeke said.

"Awesome!" Tony exclaimed as he ran back toward the kitchen.

"He doesn't walk much," Elsie said dryly. "Not if he can run and get there faster."

Zeke smiled. He leaned closer and put his hand on her cheek. He loved touching her, Elsie's skin so soft against his calloused palm. He hesitated before his lips touched hers. "May I?"

"Yes. Anytime you want to kiss me, Zeke, you have my permission. Well, unless we're at work. That would be weird."

"Feisty, even when she's sick," Zeke murmured, then lowered his head. He brushed his lips against hers, resisting the urge to deepen the kiss. Now wasn't the time or place. Not when she was sick and Tony was there. But there was intimacy even in the brief touch, which he reveled in.

Zeke was a lover, not a fighter. He'd been a damn good special forces soldier, but in the end, he couldn't stomach the often senseless violence. He was a touchy-feely kind of man. Enjoyed holding hands, indulging in public displays of affection. But his wife hadn't liked any of that. Hell, she hadn't liked *him*. Not enough to be faithful. So he'd kind of buried that part of himself. Now, Elsie was bringing it back with a vengeance.

"Here you go, Zeke. I brought yours in for you," Tony said, holding out a plate with two hamburgers.

"Thanks, bub. That was thoughtful of you. I appreciate it."

The boy seemed to blossom at the compliment. He beamed at Zeke and ran back toward the kitchen to get his own meal.

"I'd love to know how many steps that kid gets in a day," Elsie said.

Zeke shifted until he was sitting on the floor with his back to the couch. Yeah, he could've gotten up and sat on the opposite end, but he liked being this close to her. Tony came back into the room and sat in the overstuffed chair perpendicular to the couch.

As they ate, Elsie asked Tony how his day went. They talked about school and kids Zeke didn't know. When Tony began to talk about camping, and how much he was looking forward to it, Zeke realized that what for him had been a one-day-soon kind of promise, clearly meant much more to the boy. He made a mental vow to find the time to take Tony camping sooner rather than later.

Elsie ate half her food, compared to her son polishing off both the huge hamburgers he'd made. Zeke would've liked to see her eat more, but her lids were drooping again. He encouraged her to finish off the drink—being dehydrated on top of having the flu wouldn't help—and as Tony carried their dishes to the sink, Zeke leaned over and picked up Elsie.

She didn't protest, simply lay her head against his shoulder and wrapped her arm around him. Zeke carried her back into his bedroom and got her settled on his bed once more.

"Sleep, Else. I've got things under control here."

"Tony's probably got homework," she mumbled.

"I got it."

"And he usually showers before bed."

"Okay."

"I try to get him in bed by eight-thirty. Wait, where is he going to sleep? We should really go back to the motel."

"No. I've got a guest room. He'll be fine in there."

"He hasn't slept in a room by himself in years...Make sure he's not scared, okay?"

"I will. I'll tell him he's welcome to come in here if he wakes up in the middle of the night."

"'Kay. Thanks. Zeke?"

"Yeah, sweetheart?"

She studied him for a moment, before saying, "Please don't hurt me. I can't take that, not along with everything else life's thrown at me."

"I won't. And I could say the same to you," Zeke told her.

She frowned at that. As if she hadn't even considered that *she* might be able to hurt *him*. "I won't," she said, repeating his words.

Zeke leaned forward and kissed her forehead once more. "Sleep well. I'll put a glass of water by the bed, if you wake up and get thirsty. I'll also put some more pills there. Just in case."

"Thanks."

"You don't have to thank me for taking care of you, Else. It's my privilege. Sleep well. I'll see you in the morning."

It took everything in Zeke not to crawl under the covers and take her in his arms. But he managed to control himself. Tonight was a new beginning for both of them. There'd be plenty of time for intimacy later.

He closed the door behind him and went back out to the living room. "Ready to get your homework knocked out, bub?"

"Yeah. I saw you have a ton of books. Do you think...maybe I can read afterward?"

Zeke was surprised by the question. He was going to suggest they could watch some TV, but he should've guessed Tony would be happier reading. The kid was smart as hell. He wouldn't be surprised if his reading level was well above what was normal for someone his age.

"Of course. I'm sure I've got something you'd like."

"Awesome!" Tony said.

"Oh, and you okay with sleeping in my guest room?"

Tony's eyes got wide. "I get my own room?" he asked.

Zeke grinned. So much for him being scared to be on his own. "If you want it."

"Yes! Yes! Yes!" Tony exclaimed, throwing a fist into the air.

"Come on. Homework. Reading. Shower. Then you can read a little longer after you get in bed."

In response, Tony ran over to where Zeke had put his backpack down when they'd arrived, ready to tackle his homework.

CHAPTER FIVE

"How're you feeling?" Zeke whispered. It was the next morning, and he'd gotten up from his couch several times in the night to check on his houseguests.

Tony had been excited to have a room to himself...at first. But he'd come out into the living room about an hour after he'd settled in the guest room with a book, admitting he was nervous. Zeke had sat in his room with him for about thirty minutes, and convinced the boy that there wasn't anything wrong with leaving the light on next to the bed.

Elsie had tossed and turned all night, if the tangle of covers on the bed was any indication. And every time he'd peeked into his room, she'd been in a different position. Zeke had no idea if that was how she normally slept or if it was because of the fever she still had. Regardless, every time he saw her in his bed, he wanted to join her. And every time, he forced himself to walk back into his living room.

Having this kind of reaction to a woman would normally get his guard up. Despite being affectionate, he still wasn't the kind of man to fall in love at the drop of a hat. But he'd known Elsie for over a year. He was constantly impressed by her work ethic and her ability to calm tense situations at the bar. That respect had turned to admiration, and then to something more.

It had taken someone putting their hand on her to make him pull his head out of his ass. But even afterward, he'd taken his time. His reticence had ended up hurting her. He wasn't so conceited as to think if he'd moved a little faster, she wouldn't have gotten sick... but maybe she wouldn't be *as* sick. Zeke wanted to think he would've noticed that she wasn't feeling well and would've made sure she took it easy before she was knocked on her ass.

Elsie was special. As was her son. He'd be an idiot to let them slip through his fingers. He'd show them both that he was a man they could count on...something they'd been lacking in their life so far, based on Elsie's comment about her cheating husband.

"Else," he said a little louder, when she didn't respond to his previous words. Zeke put a hand on her shoulder and shook her lightly. She was lying on her side, curled into a ball.

Her eyes popped open and she gasped, coming up on an elbow. "Tony?"

"No, it's Zeke. And Tony's fine. He's in the other room, eating breakfast."

Elsie groaned and fell back onto the mattress. "What time is it?"

"Around seven."

She made a noise in the back of her throat and tried to get up.

Zeke stopped her. "Hang on. Where are you going?"

"Got to get Tony to school," she said.

Zeke gently pressed her back to the mattress. "I've got it. I just didn't want to leave without telling you."

Elsie stared up at him with a look he couldn't interpret.

"What?" he asked.

"I...I'm trying to decide if I'm irritated or grateful."

Zeke couldn't help but chuckle. "Be grateful. But because I'm curious, why would you be irritated?"

Elsie closed her eyes, and Zeke couldn't help but reach out to rub her shoulder. It was as if she were a magnet, and he was helplessly drawn in whenever he got too close.

"It's been me and Tony for his entire life," she said.

"Your ex really didn't help with him at all?"

Elsie wrinkled her nose. "No. He said it was my job to raise him. He didn't want anything to do with stuff he deemed 'women's work.' Including his son."

"That's bullshit."

"I know."

"And for the record, I'm in no way trying to usurp your position as a mother."

"Usurp...that's a great word. Gonna need to make that our next code word," Elsie muttered.

Fuck. This woman slayed him.

"What's he eating?" she asked.

"Pardon?"

"For breakfast. What's he having?"

"I made him some scrambled eggs with lots of cheese, and I snuck in some chunks of ham I had left over."

"Protein. Good." Then she sniffed and frowned. "He usually gets something shitty from me. Like an overprocessed granola bar or something. He hates them, but he doesn't complain. I think he probably trades them for something better at school. He also comes home with food in his backpack sometimes. I pretend not to notice, but it's hard not to mention it."

Zeke himself decided not to mention the doughnuts he'd bought the day before, and how Tony was looking forward to eating one after he finished his eggs. "Look at me, Else," he ordered. He wasn't surprised she knew about the food Tony brought home. He also wasn't surprised she *didn't* seem to know how he was getting that extra food. He had a feeling she wouldn't be thrilled to know he was doing other students' homework so that *she* wouldn't go hungry.

"You're an awesome mom. Tony's happy, healthy, and smart. Cut yourself some slack, okay?"

She didn't respond, just stared up at him.

"The first thing he wanted to know when I saw him this morning was how you were doing. Before he started eating, he made sure there were enough eggs for me to make *you* some when you got up. You're raising a compassionate, inquisitive young man. I could never take your place in his life or heart. No matter what I feed him in the mornings."

"Thanks," she whispered.

"You're welcome. Now, since you're awake, why don't you sit up and take these pills. Feels like you still have a bit of a fever. I really would like for it to break completely today. If not, I'll call the Doc back."

"No, it's—"

"It absolutely *is* necessary," Zeke interrupted gently. "I know you aren't used to being taken care of, but I hope you *get* used to it, sweetheart. Because from here on out, you've got a champion."

She studied him, the look in her eyes a mixture of hope and skepticism. Zeke prayed he'd never do anything to make her doubt him.

"And I brought a fresh cup of Pedialyte. If you can, drink it all. Then sleep some more. When I get back, we'll see if you're up to eating and I'll make you whatever you want."

"I need to call Edna. I'm supposed to work this morning."

"I'll give her a call while I'm on my way back from dropping off Tony. But I'm guessing she already knows you won't be in. And... we'll have a talk about you taking that second job."

"No, we won't," Elsie said in a firm tone.

Zeke sighed. "I don't want to overstep, but—"

"Then don't." It was Elsie's turn to interrupt. "Look, I appreciate what you've done for me and Tony. But what I do for money isn't your concern. If I take four jobs, that's on me."

"Wrong. What you did in the past wasn't my concern. But what you do from here on out is one hundred percent my concern. I want a relationship with you, Else. And part of that, for me, means doing whatever it takes to make sure you're healthy and don't work yourself into the ground. Tell me honestly, you were never sick before you took that second job, were you?"

She pressed her lips together.

"Right. That's what I thought. This is also me being selfish. I want to spend time with you outside of On the Rocks. And while I think Tony's wonderful, I wouldn't mind spending just a little of that time with you alone. That means our only time to hang out with just the two of us is in the mornings, after Tony goes to school and before we head into work. If you're cleaning motel rooms or folding sheets and towels, we can't do that."

"I don't want to live at the Mangree forever," Elsie said. "I've almost got enough saved up for an apartment, as well as some basic household items. Without that second job, it'll be even longer before I can give Tony some normalcy in his life."

Zeke struggled with his instincts. He wanted to tell her he'd pay for whatever she needed, but she was a proud woman. There was no way she'd accept. And he couldn't blame her. "If I can figure something out—that wouldn't include me paying to get you guys into an apartment—would you consider it?"

Instead of dismissing him immediately, Elsie seemed to be thinking about his carefully worded question, which Zeke appreciated.

Finally, she asked, "Like what?"

"I don't know. Not yet. But I wasn't lying. I want to spend time with you. Get to know you better. I already know you're an amazing mother, an extremely hard worker, and you can charm even the most grumpy customer. But I want to know more. Everything."

"I'm not very interesting," she told him.

Zeke simply shook his head. "You're the most interesting and fascinating woman I've ever met...and that's before I've even gotten to know the woman you hide away from the rest of the world. Will you at least consider it?"

Elsie sighed. "You aren't thinking about moving us in here, are you?"

Zeke couldn't deny that he'd thought about doing just that. "Would you accept?"

"No."

Her answer was swift and firm. Damn. "That's what I thought. Can you trust me at least a little bit to help you? I know that's hard for you, but everything in me is rebelling at the thought of you working from seven in the morning to six at night. Eleven to six is long enough."

"You work longer hours," she retorted.

"I do. But I'm not a parent."

"If you were?"

A vision of Elsie holding an infant with her brown hair and his hazel eyes sprang into his head so fast, it almost made him dizzy. His words came out without thought. "If I had a child, nothing would keep me away from him...or his mother. I'd hire more help so I could be home with them."

His words seemed to break through whatever wall she'd put up between them. At least for the moment. Zeke had to remind himself that she wasn't operating at one hundred percent. She was sick, had a fever, and later would probably fight him on whatever he figured out in regard to her living arrangement. But for now, he'd take what he could get.

"I'll talk to Edna when I feel better," she said softly.

"Thank you," Zeke said. She hadn't actually said she'd quit, but he'd take what he could get. Leaning down, he pressed his lips to her forehead. She was still hot. Sitting up, he ordered, "Take the pills and drink the entire glass. I'll be back as soon as I can to check on you."

"Bossy," she muttered.

Zeke smirked. "Yup. It's best you get used to it now."

"Whatever," she said with a roll of her eyes.

He forced himself to stand and head to the door.

"Zeke?"

He turned. "Yeah?"

"Good luck with the drop-off line."

Frowning, he asked, "Why?"

"You'll see," she said with a small smile.

As much as he liked seeing her smile, Zeke was wary. He gave her a chin lift and headed for the door once more. How bad could it be? He'd go, drop Tony off, then come home. Easy-peasy.

* * *

"You have got to be kidding me," Zeke muttered under his breath.

Tony laughed from next to him.

"This isn't funny," Zeke grumbled. "This is taking *forever*. How long does it take for a kid to get out of a car and the next vehicle to pull forward? Oh my God—please tell me that woman isn't getting out to hug her kid goodbye," Zeke bitched.

"Mom hates drop-off," Tony said. "Says it's the seventh level of h-e-double hockey sticks."

"She's not wrong," Zeke agreed, watching in disbelief as it took another kid a full two minutes to grab her stuff from the back seat of the car.

Deciding to take his mind off the incredibly slow-moving line in front of him, Zeke turned to Tony. "So, you sleep okay last night?"

"Uh-huh."

"You sure? I know my guest room is different from what you're used to. There's no harm in admitting that you were uncomfortable."

"I wasn't. I mean, not really. I woke up once and was confused when I didn't see Mom in the bed next to me, but because the light was on, I realized where I was pretty fast."

"Good. And there's nothing wrong with sleeping with the light on," Zeke said.

Tony shrugged and looked out the window. "Only babies need nightlights," he mumbled.

"That's not true," Zeke countered. "You know I was in the Army." At Tony's nod, he continued. "Well, I saw some pretty awful stuff when I was overseas. People can be very mean to each other. Anyway, I had nightmares sometimes when I got back. I slept with my light on for six months after my last deployment, before I felt comfortable being in the dark."

Tony looked over at him. "Really? You aren't just saying that to make me feel better?"

"Really. And I won't lie to you, Tony. Ever. You're old enough to know what's what."

"Do you like my mom? Like, *really* like her?"

Zeke did his best to keep his face even. He wasn't sure he was ready to talk to Tony about his and Elsie's relationship, if it could be called that. He hadn't even taken her out yet. He wanted to, very much so, but they'd both been busy. Not to mention, he'd been trying to take things slow...like an idiot.

But he'd just promised not to lie barely a second ago. Also, they'd already kind of had this conversation back at the motel when he'd picked up the boy yesterday. If Tony needed repeated reassurances that he really did like his mom, he'd provide them.

He looked Tony in the eye and said, "Yes. I like her a lot."

"She likes you too," Tony said, looking back out the window.

"Yeah?" Zeke wasn't above probing for information. He might regret it, but he had a feeling he needed as much intel as he could get if he was truly going to win over Elsie.

"Uh-huh. She talks about you all the time. Says you're a good boss and that you care about your employees."

Zeke frowned at hearing that. He didn't exactly want to be seen as just Elsie's boss.

"And I heard her telling Miss Lilly that you have a nice butt. Whatever that means. A butt is just a butt. I don't know what's so nice about one over another."

Zeke grinned. He liked Lilly. She was down to earth and, after coming to town with a TV production company, had immediately befriended Elsie...which he wholeheartedly approved of. He hated what had happened to Lilly, being kidnapped by a co-worker. And was still relieved that she'd been found in time. She was putting that harrowing incident behind her, and she and Ethan were as happy as they could be.

Zeke loved that for his friend...and wanted the same for himself.

The fact that Elsie was gossiping about him with Lilly made him smile. He didn't think she'd bother if she didn't have some sort of feelings toward him. He could definitely work with that.

He finally shrugged. "I'll give you some advice, bub...don't try too hard to understand women. Just nod, agree, and move on."

"Why would I agree if they say something stupid?" the boy asked.

Zeke had a feeling he was just about to get into a conversation that was over Tony's head at the moment, but luckily, they were suddenly able to pull up another two car lengths.

Then, as another student got out of a car, she dropped her backpack and everything in it scattered on the ground at her feet.

"Oh for God's sake," he sighed under his breath.

"Zeke?"

"Yeah, bub?" he said, turning his attention back to Tony.

"Thanks for making me breakfast."

"You're welcome."

"And giving me money for lunch. But...don't tell Mom, okay?"

"Why not?" Zeke asked.

"I don't want her feelings to be hurt. She does a lot for me, but I know she doesn't have the money for a hot lunch. I usually get the free one for the poor kids."

Zeke closed his eyes for a second. Then he reached for Tony and squeezed his shoulder. "Your mom's lucky to have you," he said.

Tony bit his lip as he stared at him.

"I mean it. A lot of people would be embarrassed about the free-lunch thing. Or they'd be upset and bitter that they didn't have what other kids have. But you're more concerned about your mom's feelings. That's amazing, Tony. *You're* amazing."

"So you won't tell her?"

"Can't promise that, bub. Just as I told you that I wouldn't lie to you, I won't lie to your mom, either. But I *will* make sure she's okay with it."

Tony looked extremely skeptical at that, and Zeke couldn't help but chuckle. "I know, it won't be easy, since your mom's one of the proudest people I've ever met. She doesn't like to accept help. But she'll be all right with this. Want to know how I know?"

"How?"

"Because it's for you. She loves you more than anything in this world. And since we're kind of talking about this...no more doing other kids' homework for food...okay? That's not fair to them *or* you, even if the work is easy. I'll make sure your mom has enough to eat. Today and from here on out.

"You already know I like your mom. A lot. And I like *you*. I want to be involved in both your lives from now on. And by involved, I mean I'll be hanging out at your place and you'll be at mine. We'll go out and have some fun together, camping, hiking, maybe some bowling. We'll hang out with my friends, go to the library, even go out to eat together. Your mom's days of struggling are over, bub. I give you my word on that. You've both struggled for a while now, but not anymore. I promise."

Tony stared at him through eyes that seemed older than his nine years. "Don't promise that and then decide we're too much trouble."

Zeke's jaw tightened. "Has that happened before?"

Tony shrugged. "There have been other people who said they'd help me and Mom, but didn't. I'm not an idiot. I know that we had to move around a lot before we got here because we didn't have enough money. Mom never wanted to leave me alone after school, but it was hard for her to pay people."

Zeke hated that Tony was so aware of his mom's financial situation at such a young age, but he was also proud of how much he wanted to protect her. "You and your mom will never be too much trouble," Zeke said earnestly. "In fact, I'm guessing I'll probably have to worry about you guys deciding *I'm* too..." He paused, trying to come up with the right word. He couldn't think of something that fit.

Tony tilted his head. "Too what?"

"Overwhelming. Interested. Helpful. Cheerful. Take your pick."

"As long as you don't yell at Mom. Or me."

"I might get loud, but I'll never belittle you."

"Belittle?"

"Make someone feel unimportant."

Tony sat up in his seat and nodded. "Okay."

"Okay?"

"Yeah. Oh, it's almost our turn," Tony said, pointing out the front of the truck.

Zeke dutifully pulled forward, and when it was finally their turn, Tony opened the door and hopped out.

"Have a good day. Go ahead and take the bus home and I'll be there to pick you up. If I can't be there, I'll send one of my friends. You know...Ethan, Drew, Brock, or someone. Just be sure they tell you the code word. It's still austere until your mom tells you different."

"I know, Zeke. Jeez. Now *you're* holding up the drop-off line."

Zeke chuckled. Damn. The kid was right.

"Okay. Go on then. Learn something new today."

"Whatever." Tony grinned, then slammed the door. He turned

and hurried toward the doors at the front of the school. For a moment, Zeke watched him go, jerking in surprise when a horn sounded behind him.

Shaking his head at himself and how ridiculous he was being—he'd just mentally lambasted other parents for doing the same thing he was...holding up the line—Zeke pulled forward toward the street and went over the conversation he'd had with Tony. He and Elsie had clearly been through a lot together. He didn't want to come into their lives and mess with their dynamic. He simply wanted to be *part* of them. However they'd let him.

He'd always had the impression that it was frowned on in the Army to be too openly in love with someone. Soldiers were supposed to be tough. To keep their emotions in check. Zeke now suspected it was one of many reasons why he'd gotten out. He swore he'd never again put his heart on the line, not after his ex. But Elsie was making him realize he wanted someone to live for. Someone to take care of. He just couldn't admit it.

Before his ex, he'd loved making women smile. Making them feel worthy and cherished. He felt good when *they* felt good. When he married, he'd openly talked about his wife, how awesome he thought she was and how much he loved her.

He had a tendency to go overboard—or so his ex had insisted. She complained when he deployed, claiming he loved his job more than her. But when he returned, she'd flip the script and accuse him of smothering her, complaining that he barely let her breathe. Said it irritated her. Which he thought was ridiculous, considering how often he was gone.

His marriage was confusing and hurtful. Now he knew that, in reality, she wanted the best of both worlds. Wanted him gone so she could do what she wanted, when she wanted. To spend his money and see other men. When he was home, she wanted a handyman.

He should've seen the signs before he asked her to marry him. But he was too happy to have someone to love to realize his ex didn't even seem to like him all that much.

Elsie was different. While his ex gladly took whatever he gave her, and didn't appreciate any of it, Elsie was determined to do everything on her own. It made Zeke want to help her all the more. But she had her pride, which Zeke respected.

He'd do as much as Elsie would allow to help her and Tony live a more comfortable life. It might not be perfect, and he couldn't protect her from every shitstorm the world had a way of throwing around, but he'd damn well try.

CHAPTER SIX

Elsie stood with her co-workers in On the Rocks, listening to Zeke as he told them about the menu specials. It had been a few days since her stay at his house. Her fever had broken the second day, but he'd insisted she and Tony remain another night. She'd never slept as well, or felt as...free...as she did while she was there. It was blissful to have a room to herself. And a bathroom. As much as she loved her son, he was a restless sleeper. Every time he rolled over, she woke up, subconsciously worried that someone was trying to break into their motel room.

Stupidly (because where else would he be sleeping?), she didn't realize Zeke had been staying on the couch until after the second night, when she'd come out of his room feeling better rested than she had in weeks, and saw him there. He wasn't wearing a shirt, and the sight of his naked chest with its sprinkling of dark hair, his neatly trimmed beard covering the bottom half of his face, his hair mussed, an arm over his head while he lightly snored, made her want to snuggle up next to him and beg him to kiss her...and more.

The thought was hardly startling. Not only because of how much she'd come to love his platonic kisses over the last two days

—and he'd kissed her a lot. On the cheek, forehead, even on the lips—but because ever since that day a month ago when he'd declared that no one was allowed to touch her but him, she'd craved him in a way she hadn't wanted a man since she'd first been married.

Zeke was generally an easygoing guy. She'd observed him plenty at the bar over the last year. Even when someone got drunk and had to be escorted out, he never looked as if he was on the verge of losing his temper. She'd been scared when that man had grabbed her butt last month, but never in all the time she'd known him had Elsie ever been frightened of Zeke.

Her crush on him had only grown since that night. Embarrassingly so. When he'd told her that they were "happening," she'd been elated and nervous as hell. Then, as time went on and he didn't kiss her again, and seemed to go back to the friendly boss she'd always known, Elsie thought maybe he'd changed his mind.

After finding her sick, and coming to her rescue, it was clear he hadn't. If anything, he was trying to make up for lost time. For that long month after the kiss when he hadn't actively pursued her.

There was no doubt in Elsie's mind now that Zeke Calhoun was done messing around. She'd seen him every day since he'd dropped her and Tony back off at the Mangree Motel. He showed up in the mornings with treats from The Sweet Tooth for their breakfast. Then he hung out until it was time for them to go to work. She hadn't wanted to quit on Edna without notice, so he'd actually helped her clean the rooms and fold laundry.

The fact that they were hanging out so much should've been weird—he *was* her boss, after all—but Zeke made it seem normal. She'd never felt more comfortable with anyone as she did with him.

After her shift was over at the bar, Zeke usually followed her back to the motel. They picked Tony up and usually went back to his house, where he and Tony made delicious dinners. Zeke helped her son with any homework he had, then while Tony read a book, she and Zeke talked. As Tony's bedtime approached, Zeke took them both back to the motel, then they'd do it all over again the next day.

It was nice, but somewhat hard to get used to, sharing her life with someone else after so many years.

And just yesterday, Zeke had made an announcement to the entire staff that anyone who worked over four hours at a time was entitled to a full meal. Be it lunch or dinner. They could eat on their break, or take it home with them. All he asked was that they get the order in to the cooks at least thirty minutes before they wanted to eat or leave, so the cooks wouldn't have to worry about fitting in a rushed comped meal between the orders if they were busy.

As a result, Elsie hadn't gone without in order to feed Tony, which she'd done often in the last year. It was hard to believe that just a week ago, she'd worried about what she could make her son for dinner...and if she'd have enough left over for herself.

Zeke hadn't told her about that announcement beforehand— why would he? But she couldn't shake the feeling that giving free meals to his employees was partly because of her. She hadn't missed the way he frequently glanced at her little pantry in her motel room with his lips pressed together. And it was obvious he was going out of his way to feed both her and Tony. It was such a Zeke thing to do...make sure all of his employees had enough food to eat. Her son needed better meals than what he'd had for the last few months. And the money she was saving because Zeke was making them dinner every night would go a long way toward giving her the means to furnish a future apartment.

After Doug, she should be a lot more defensive and wary if a man barged into her life the way Zeke had. But there was something about him that made her *want* him around all the time.

Zeke called an end to the meeting with the employees and Elsie realized she wasn't sure what he'd said at the end. Mentally shrugging—Reina and the others would fill her in on what she missed—Elsie got ready for her shift.

While the bar opened at eleven-thirty, most of the business they did around lunchtime was for people coming in to eat. There was more money to make in tips in the evenings, and as much as Elsie needed and wanted that money, she had to be home with Tony. So she made do with working the day shifts. And tips aside, she preferred it, because she didn't do well with drunk men. They kind of scared her. Leaving the evening shift to the other waitresses was more than all right with her.

Throughout her shift, she was extremely aware of Zeke's gaze. Every time she looked up, he seemed to be looking back. It was a heady feeling. Elsie couldn't remember a time when she'd been the center of anyone's attention like she was Zeke's.

The door to the bar opened and three men walked in. Silas, Otto, and Art. Surprised to see them, Elsie headed over.

"Hi, guys. Everything all right?" she asked.

"Why wouldn't it be?" Silas asked. He was the youngest of the trio at sixty-nine. Otto was around eighty, and his white hair made him look stately instead of old. Art was the oldest at a little over ninety, but he was just as spry as his friends.

"No reason," Elsie said. "You guys just usually eat at the diner."

"We wanted a break today," Otto said with a grin and a wink.

"Make sure you seat us in your section, girly," Art said. "We've got questions."

Elsie stared at him in confusion for a second. They had questions? About what?

"Hey," a deep voice said from behind her, and Elsie jumped. She felt Zeke's hand on her back, steadying her. "Sorry. Didn't mean to scare you," he told her softly.

Looking up, Elsie was once more struck by how good-looking Zeke was. Some women went gaga over a man in a tuxedo, but she'd take Zeke just like this any day. Khakis, a polo shirt with the On the Rocks logo on the front, and the smell of his fresh, masculine soap surrounding her.

It wasn't as if this was the first time she'd seen him today. He'd come over and helped her fold sheets and towels for two hours before they'd left to get to the bar. But every time she laid eyes on him, she was struck anew by how attracted she was to this man... and didn't really understand what he saw in *her*.

"Yup, that's what we need to talk about," Art said.

Startled, and realizing she'd been staring up at Zeke for too long, Elsie blushed. "Sorry. If you'll follow me, I'll get you seated."

Zeke followed them to a table in the middle of the room, and when all three men were seated, he said, "It's good to see you guys here, but please don't embarrass Elsie. Ask your questions, but keep them polite. Okay?"

Elsie wanted to tell him it was all right. They could ask what they wanted. But everyone knew the three men were the biggest gossips in Fallport. She didn't really want to be on the receiving end of their curiosity. Now that she apparently was, she was grateful Zeke had her back.

"We aren't gonna embarrass anyone," Otto told him.

"Good. And, Silas...she's taken, so keep your hands to yourself," Zeke warned the older man.

All three men giggled like they were eight.

"He's got your number!" Art crowed.

"Guess that answers one of our questions," Otto mused.

"I wasn't gonna touch her," Silas grumbled.

"Don't you have inventory to do or something?" Elsie asked Zeke suggestively.

"Yup. Just makin' sure these three behave before I get started." Then he shocked the shit out of her by leaning down and kissing her briefly on the lips before tucking a piece of hair that refused to stay in her ponytail behind her ear. Elsie gaped as he turned to go back behind the bar.

"Wellll," Silas said, drawing out the word. "Looks like our guy finally made his move."

"About time," Art agreed.

"You've got yourself a good one there, missy," Otto added.

Elsie knew she was blushing again, but she couldn't exactly argue that last point. "All right, we all know you came in to get the deets, so let's just get it out of the way. Zeke and I are dating."

"Duh," Silas muttered.

"Haven't seen him take you out," Art said with narrowed eyes. "You guys work together, but that's not dating."

She didn't like that he seemed to be judging Zeke. Elsie straightened. "He's teaching Tony to cook. He's shared some of his favorite books with him. He comes to the motel and helps me fold laundry. He took care of me when I was sick last week, made sure I ate and stayed hydrated, and even got Doc Snow to come look at me. I don't want, or need, or have *time* for bowling or the movies or any of that. I'd rather sit on his back deck and listen to crickets than fit into whatever preconceived notion you guys have for dating. Now, I'll leave you gentlemen to decide what you want, and I'll be back in a bit to take your orders."

Not giving them time to respond, Elsie spun on her heel and headed for another table of guests. She was irritated just by the idea of anyone finding Zeke lacking. It wasn't anyone else's business what they did when they were together. If she was honest with herself, she was also irritated because she didn't like being the center of gossip. But mostly, she hated that someone who'd been nicer to her and Tony than anyone had in a very long time, was being talked about with even a hint of negativity.

By the time she'd finished with the table nearby, Elsie calmed down and realized that she'd overreacted. Art hadn't actually said anything bad about Zeke. Besides, from the vantage point of their normal spot outside the post office on the other side of the town square, all they *did* see was her and Zeke working.

Feeling a little silly for how she'd reacted, she went back to their table. "Sorry, guys, I—"

"Nothin' to be sorry about," Otto said. "I'm thinking your reaction was just what it should've been."

"Just as Zeke's was, to warn us about making you uncomfortable," Art added.

"Which we did. Sorry," Silas added.

A little surprised the gruff old men had apologized so readily, Elsie nodded. "Zeke's great," she told them. "We haven't been dating very long, but he's a really good guy."

"He is," Otto agreed. "I'm thinking I'm gonna try the special today. Meatloaf, right?"

Relieved the inquisition seemed to be over, Elsie nodded. "Yup. And from what I smell coming from the kitchen, it's going to knock your socks off."

"I'll have the fried chicken," Art told her.

"Thought you were supposed to cut back on the fatty foods?" Silas asked.

"What are you, my mother?" Art growled.

"No, but I'm behind eight hundred and forty-six to eight hundred and fifty-two. Can't have you dying before I can get ahead and beat your ass," Silas countered.

Elsie didn't realize she was frowning until Otto translated.

"Chess, honey. Art's up a handful of games and Silas can't stand it."

"Ah, I see."

"I'll have a side salad with my chicken," Art told her. Then motioned to Silas with his head. "For mother hen over there."

Elsie grinned and nodded as she wrote the order on her pad. "Silas? What can I get you today?"

"The soup any good?" he asked.

"I'd recommend the cream of potato over the vegetable," Elsie said.

"Done. I'll take that. And some fried okra too. And a side of ranch with that."

She wanted to giggle, but managed to refrain. "Right. And to drink?"

All three men requested sweet tea, and Elsie said, "I'll be right back with those drinks."

"Take your time," Silas called out. "We're enjoying the view."

She turned back to look at the older man and blushed when she saw his eyes glued to her ass.

When she'd first come to Fallport, it had taken Elsie some time to get used to the fact that the three gossips somehow seemed to know everything about everyone in town. But over time, she realized that they were harmless...and lonely. They got together every day to hang out and play chess outside the post office because they had no one at home anymore. She could relate. She might be busy from the time she got up to the time her head hit the pillow, but that didn't stop the urge to connect with someone.

She stopped by the kitchen and clipped the order to the wheel for the cooks, then went to the bar.

"You okay?" Zeke asked.

"Yeah."

"They being cool?"

She mentally sighed. Having Zeke as a champion was something she could get used to. Which both warmed *and* worried her. Dating her boss probably wasn't the smartest thing she'd ever done. If things didn't work out, it would make her job very uncomfortable. And since Zeke owned the bar, she'd have to be the one to quit. Finding another job she enjoyed as much as this one in a small town, and that paid as well, would be tough.

"What's going through your head?" Zeke asked with a tilt of his own, his eyes filling with concern. "You need me to have Tiana wait on them?"

"No, it's not that. They're fine. They're just curious."

"You sure?" Zeke asked. "I can go talk to them again. Probably should with the way Silas was eyeballin' your ass."

Elsie couldn't help but grin. "There's not much there to eyeball," she said with a shrug.

"You go right on thinkin' that, Else," Zeke said with heat in his eyes.

Elsie felt frozen for a moment. Zeke was a gentleman with her.

Always. That kiss in his office aside, he never pushed her. Never made her feel uncomfortable. But every now and then, he let the depth of his need for her show in his gaze. She swallowed hard.

"Let me guess, three sweet teas, right?" he asked, breaking the intense moment between them.

"Yeah."

Zeke grabbed three glasses from under the counter and began to fill them. It gave Elsie a moment to gain her equilibrium. She'd never been a very sexual person. Her ex hadn't exactly inspired her in the bedroom. It was nice enough at first, but his interest waned not too long after their marriage. When they *did* have sex, he didn't care about her pleasure. He always used lube because he said she was too dry. She'd suggested that if he spent a little more time on foreplay, they wouldn't need the extra lubrication, but he was too selfish and in too much of a hurry to get off to bother.

Elsie had a feeling that sex with Zeke wouldn't be anything like it was with her ex. He'd make sure she was more than ready, probably even insist she come before him. How she knew that, she had no idea, but with how considerate he was in his everyday life, she couldn't see him being a wham-bam-thank-you-ma'am kind of lover.

"Wish I knew what *that* thought was," Zeke said with a small smile as he placed the three full glasses of tea on a tray.

Feeling a touch braver than normal, and definitely stepping outside her comfort zone, Elsie returned his smile and said, "I was thinking that I like that you aren't afraid to touch me in public." Okay, so not very brave after all. And not exactly honest, either... but she figured it was far easier than telling him she was imagining what kind of lover he was.

"Never. I'm a touchy-feely kind of guy," he said, not looking uncomfortable with his admission. "I love holding my woman's hand. Touching that vulnerable spot at the small of her back when we walk. Kissing her so everyone knows she's taken. It's good to know you don't object."

Thinking back to her marriage again, Elsie realized Doug hadn't once held her hand. He'd told her in no uncertain terms that he didn't like public displays of affection. "I don't object," she told him.

"Good. My ex-wife hated it. Said I was always pawing her and that I might as well pee on her to mark my territory."

Elsie frowned. It was an interesting turn in conversation, but she wasn't going to let that comment pass without responding. "She was an idiot," she said firmly. "There's a difference between letting someone know you care and want to protect them, and being an overbearing jerk."

Zeke licked his lips, and Elsie couldn't help but let her gaze rest there. "True. Else, I—"

Whatever he was going to say was interrupted by the ringing of his cell phone in his pocket.

"Hold that thought," he said with a smile as he pulled it out. "You got Zeke," he answered.

And just like that, the easygoing, relaxed posture he'd had a second ago disappeared with whatever the person on the other end of the phone was saying. "Right. How long? Where? Shit. Okay. I need to call Reuben, but I'll meet you guys there. Bye."

Before Zeke spoke, Elsie knew he'd just been called out on a search.

"I need to go," he told her, already moving toward the end of the bar.

"I can call Reuben for you," she offered.

"Thanks. I'll take you up on that if you truly don't mind."

"I don't."

"If he can't come in, try Lance. Hank should be here around four. If he can't—"

"We'll cover the bar," Elsie told him. It wouldn't be the first time the servers had to pull emergency duty as bartenders. Most of them couldn't make anything complicated, but luckily the patrons were understanding when the Eagle Point Search and Rescue team got called out. That was the way of small towns. At least it was in

Fallport. Everyone knew that if it was themselves or a loved one who went missing, the team would have their backs.

"Thanks," he said a little distractedly. Zeke headed for the hallway and his office. He was back within a minute, and instead of going to the door, as she expected, he headed straight for her.

Zeke took her face in his palms and leaned close. It was an intimate gesture, one Elsie was getting used to.

"I don't know when I'll be back. Two hikers went missing on the trail out to Eagle Point Lookout. They were supposed to check out today, but when the front desk at the hotel didn't hear anything from them, their room was checked. Nothing's been packed. When the police tracked down their car at the trailhead, they'd left a note inside saying they'd planned to camp for a night."

Elsie reached up and grabbed his wrists. "Be safe out there."

Zeke nodded. "I will. Don't leave without grabbing something for you and Tony for dinner. Tomorrow's your last day working for Edna, right?"

She nodded.

"I'll try to get there, but I don't know what we'll find."

"I know, it's fine," Elsie reassured him. He could be gone for an hour or days. It all depended on what they found when they got on the trail of the missing persons. *If* they got on the trail.

"Tell Tony I'm sorry I'm not there to talk to him about chapter twenty-two tonight. We'll discuss it when I get back."

There. *That.* The fact that this man had places to go and things to do, and yet was still concerned about them eating and her son being disappointed that he couldn't discuss a book, was one of the many reasons she was falling for him. "I will."

"I'll be in touch when I can. Cell service sucks out that way, but I'll see what I can do."

"It's *fine*, Zeke. Go. Do your thing."

He nodded. "Are you really okay with me leaving?"

Elsie frowned, not sure why he was asking. "Of course. Why wouldn't I be?"

"Because we had plans tonight."

Their plans were to stop by Grogan's General Store before they headed to the motel to get Tony, then they were going to make homemade pizzas for dinner. Not exactly something that couldn't be postponed. "Zeke, someone needs you. Tony and I will be fine. We'll take a rain check on the pizza."

"She hated when I was deployed," Zeke said softly.

Elsie squeezed his wrists, knowing who he was talking about. She didn't like his ex very much.

"But...she hated when I was home too," he said with a shrug. "When I was gone, she bitched that I was leaving her when she needed me at home, not running off to save the world. Said I loved my job more than her."

"If she said that, she didn't know you," Elsie said confidently, putting a hand on his chest. "She was also an idiot," she told him. "Go. Do your thing. I'll see you when you get back. Just be safe."

"Thank you," Zeke said. "And I will." He stared at her for a beat, then leaned down and kissed her again. This time it wasn't a quick peck on the lips. It was hard, deep, and almost desperate. By the time he pulled back, they were both breathing hard...and Elsie was certain lube wouldn't be something they'd need in the future, if their relationship progressed that far. She really, *really* hoped it did.

Zeke took a deep breath, licked his lips as if trying to memorize the taste of her, then pulled her against him. His arms tightened in a hug before he let go and abruptly turned to leave.

Elsie watched him go, feeling proud of the job he did and worried at the same time. Then she took a deep breath and turned back to the bar. She needed to make some calls and do her part to make sure Zeke's business ran smoothly in his absence.

By the time she got back to Silas, Otto, and Art's table with their sweet teas, all three men were grinning from ear to ear. She held up a hand once she'd placed the glasses on the table. "Don't start," she warned.

"We wasn't gonna say anything," Art said.

"You weren't, but I was," Silas countered.

"I'm thinking *that* was a kiss," Otto said with a wink.

Elsie couldn't help but return the smile. He wasn't wrong. "Any other questions?" she asked cheekily.

"Nope."

"I think that covered it."

"No."

"Good. Your lunches should be out soon. Please spare a little patience as we wait for Reuben to arrive and take over the bar."

"Zeke get called out?" Otto asked.

"Uh-huh."

The three men looked at each other, and Elsie could practically see the wheels turning in their heads. They were obviously desperate for more information about who was missing, and from where. They might be gossips, but they had huge hearts and truly cared about the residents of Fallport.

"As I said, your lunches should be out soon. I'm guessing you can be back at your spots in front of the post office in twenty minutes. Tops," she told them.

"Thanks," Silas said.

Elsie nodded at him and the other two men, then checked on her other tables.

Zeke had told her that the trail to Eagle Point Lookout was a tough one. There were lots of elevation gains and it went on for miles, even beyond the lookout. If the missing hikers had gone off trail, it would be harder for them to be found. But if anyone could do it, it was Zeke and his team.

He'd be home soon, and if he could, he'd tell her and Tony all about what happened. Her son loved to hear his stories, and it was more than obvious he was coming to like Zeke as much as his mom did.

Remembering how Zeke had reminded her to take dinner home for her and Tony, she smiled. He treated her better than anyone ever had, and she would never take that for granted.

CHAPTER SEVEN

That evening, Tony had a ton of questions about where Zeke was and what he was doing. He was disappointed about not getting to read more of the book he'd left at Zeke's house, but understood that he was out helping someone who was lost. The cook at work had made her and Tony a giant serving of meatloaf to take home for dinner. And while it wasn't the same as eating it at the table in Zeke's house, it was still delicious and very filling.

The next morning, after Tony left for school and after she'd finished her last shift folding laundry for Edna, Elsie headed for On the Rocks. She half expected to see Zeke standing behind the bar, but it was Lance who greeted her when she entered.

"Any word?" she asked.

"From Zeke? Nope."

"Do you think they were out all night?" she asked.

Lance shrugged. "Probably." Then he turned back to the inventory he was taking before they opened for the day.

Intellectually, Elsie had known before she got to work that Zeke hadn't returned. He said he'd get in touch with her when he could, and her phone hadn't rung all night. She knew because she'd tossed and turned and checked the screen every time she'd woken up. Lance didn't seem worried about him, and neither did any of the other waitresses when they arrived.

To them, it was just another day.

But Elsie couldn't get Zeke out of her mind. Was he hungry? Had he been drinking enough? He had to be exhausted. And while summer was fast approaching, it still got kind of chilly at night. Had he been able to catch any sleep at all? Had they found the missing hikers? Were *they* all right? Zeke might've been a special forces soldier, but he was still human, and if something bad had happened, Elsie had a feeling Zeke would take it hard.

Standing at the bar twenty minutes later, as Lance poured the drinks for an order she'd just taken from a group of four men and women, Elsie inhaled yet another of the many deep breaths she'd taken since her arrival.

Search and rescue was what Zeke did. He was fine. He had to be.

Her shift was half over when the door to the bar opened once more. Glancing over, Elsie was ready to call out her usual greeting— but the words got stuck in her throat when she saw Zeke.

He looked rough. He had streaks of dirt on his face, the knees of his cargo pants were covered in what looked like mud and grass stains. His T-shirt had similar spots, but she'd never been as relieved to see anyone in her life.

"Zeke!" she exclaimed. She started toward him, but he was already on the move.

She vaguely heard her friends and co-workers greeting him, but the intense look in his tired eyes had her unable to look away.

He stopped before her and took her face in his hands, tilting it up so he could meet her gaze. "Hey. You good?"

Elsie frowned. Why was he asking *her* that? "Of course. Are *you?*" she countered.

"I am now," he told her.

Elsie was almost overwhelmed with emotion. He'd just come off of nearly twenty-four hours straight of being out in the wilderness. He was dirty, smelly, and obviously exhausted. And yet, instead of going home to shower, eat, and get some sleep, he'd come straight here. And his first question wasn't about how things had gone at the bar. If there had been any issues. It was to ask if she was okay. It was almost impossible to wrap her mind around such attention.

For her entire marriage to Doug, she'd never come first. From the moment she'd moved into his home, Doug had expected her to wait on him. Clean the house, make dinner, hobnob with his co-workers and clients. He rarely asked how her day had been when he got home from work. Simply complained that the house wasn't clean enough, or the meal she'd made sucked, or that she wasn't as attentive to his sexual needs as she should be.

When she'd had Tony, she put her *son* first in her life. She wouldn't have it any other way, and after leaving Doug, she'd continued putting all of her efforts into making sure her son was taken care of. That his needs were met before her own.

Which meant it had been a very long time since anyone had shown her the concern Zeke was at this moment.

"Else?" he asked, furrowing his brow in consternation at seeing the look on her face. "What's wrong?"

"Nothing," she said after swallowing hard. "Have you eaten? Did you find them? Are they okay? Did you get any sleep last night? What can I do to help you?"

His face gentled, and he brushed his thumb over her cheek. "You're doing it," he told her softly.

Elsie frowned. "That's not an answer," she complained. But she didn't give him a chance to respond to any of her questions. She pulled away and turned to the bar. "Lance? You still good to stay on as planned?" she asked.

"Of course. Hey, Zeke. Good to see you."

Zeke gave the man a chin lift, and even that made Elsie want to melt. What was it about that manly chin lift thing guys did to one another? Where did they learn it? Was it imbedded in their DNA?

Knowing her mind was getting sidetracked, Elsie forced herself to concentrate.

Looking at her watch, she saw that Tony should be getting off the bus at the motel soon. She turned to Zeke and pointed her finger at him. "Don't move," she ordered.

His lips quirked up. "Yes, ma'am. Wouldn't dream of it."

She knew he was amused by her, but she didn't care. She walked toward Reina, who was collecting plates of food from the kitchen. "Hey, you think you and Valerie will be okay by yourselves until the evening shift comes in?" she asked.

Reina grinned. "Let me guess. You want to go take care of Zeke."

"Someone has to. The man's been out there working his butt off trying to help others."

"Of course we can. Go. We aren't going to be slammed in the next couple of hours, and if we are, I'll call the others and see if they can come in early. They won't complain about extra tips."

That was very true. The evening shift made more tips than the daytime waitresses, but even if it was tempting for Elsie to switch shifts, she couldn't leave Tony to fend for himself in the evenings. Not that she wanted to. She treasured the time she got to spend with her son. Soon enough, he'd outgrow wanting to hang out with his mom, then he'd be graduating and moving on with his life. That both saddened and excited Elsie.

"I have to say," Reina remarked as she easily hefted the circular tray on her shoulder. "I never thought I'd see the day you gave up even one hour of your shift if you didn't have to."

She was right. Other than when she was sick, Elsie never called someone else in to do her shift. Even when she was in the darkest mood, she forced herself to work. Tony relied on her for everything, she wasn't going to let him down.

"I approve," Reina continued. "Zeke's awesome. As a boss and as a person. And you guys are so cute together," she added.

Elsie blushed. "Thanks."

"So no denial that you're dating?" Reina teased.

"No." It would be stupid to deny it. She and Zeke had been spending a lot of time together outside of work, and when they began showing up and leaving the bar together, as well, people had quickly put two and two together.

"Well, you go girl. Get some for the rest of us single ladies!"

Elsie laughed. Reina headed for her table with the food and Elsie went back to where Zeke was standing at the bar, talking with Lance. She overheard them discussing how the last day had gone and where the inventory stood.

"Okay, we're out of here," she said as she approached.

Both men turned to look at her "Are we?" Zeke asked, a slight grin on his lips.

"Yup. Lance can handle things here and Reina said she and Valerie were good."

"Guess she told *you*," Lance said with a chuckle.

"Guess so," Zeke agreed. Then he turned to her fully and asked quietly, "You sure? You don't have to leave early on my account. I'm just going to go home and crash."

It was just like him to be concerned about her losing a couple hours of pay and tips. And a month ago, she wouldn't have dreamed of leaving early. But Zeke was more important than money. "You gonna eat?"

He shrugged. "Not all that hungry."

"That's because you're probably dehydrated and overly tired. I'll drive. We can go get Tony, then go to your place. While you're showering, I can throw something together. Then you can get some sleep."

Zeke simply stared down at her.

Elsie had the sudden realization she was being a tad presumptuous. "If that's okay, I mean."

"It's more than okay," Zeke reassured her.

When he didn't say anything else, just continued to study her, Elsie shifted uncomfortably.

He took a deep breath and reached for her hand. "Come on. Let's go grab your purse and get out of here."

She let him tow her down the hall toward the break room in the back. She grabbed her stuff, and he took her hand again as soon as she was done. They walked back through the bar, toward the door.

"See you guys later!" he called out.

"Later!" his employees, and some of the patrons, shouted back.

Shortly after, Elsie was pulling up in Zeke's driveway. Tony was excited to see Zeke and had talked nonstop all the way home. Elsie could see that her man was fading fast.

Tony ran to the front door with the key Zeke handed him, and it was Elsie's turn to tow her boyfriend by the hand toward the house. They entered, and Elsie reached up and put her hand on Zeke's face. His beard scratched her palm and she resisted the urge to rub her hands all over him. "Did you find them?" she asked quietly. She'd asked earlier, but realized he hadn't responded. She hadn't wanted to ask when Tony was in the car, just in case the outcome wasn't positive.

He nodded. "They were cold, exhausted, and scared, but alive."

"Thank goodness."

"Yeah. They'd gone off the trail because they heard something and wanted to catch a glimpse of a bear or whatever it was and got turned around. Then they hiked miles in the wrong direction, farther into the forest. They would've been better off just stopping when they realized they were lost and waiting for someone to find them. It took all night and part of the morning to walk back to the trail, since they were so tired and had gotten so far off track, but all's well that ends well."

"I'm glad."

"Me too," Zeke agreed.

"Zeke, you want to read with me tonight?" Tony asked, poking his head into the foyer where Elsie and Zeke were still standing.

"Not tonight," Elsie answered for him. "Zeke's exhausted. He's been up all night hiking. How about you and me make us something for dinner, and we let Zeke shower and rest for a bit?"

"Can we have tacos?" Tony asked.

Elsie looked up at Zeke and lifted an eyebrow.

"I think I've got the stuff. The lettuce might be a bit wilted, but I've got cheese and tomatoes. Oh, the meat'll need to be thawed though."

"We've got it," Elsie reassured him. "Go. You stink," she teased.

Zeke chuckled. When Elsie dropped her hand from his face, he caught it in his and squeezed it tight. "Thanks," he whispered.

It occurred to Elsie then that Zeke was probably more like her than she'd realized. Taking care of everyone else, with no one to look after him when he needed it. Determination rose within her. She'd gladly take over that job.

He brought her hand up to his lips and kissed her knuckles before heading for the hallway and his bedroom. He tousled Tony's hair as he went by.

Elsie stared at his ass a beat too long before taking a deep breath. "You ready to see what we've got to work with for dinner, Tony?"

"Yup. After we eat, will you sit with me while I read?" he asked.

"You bet I will," Elsie told him, thrilled that for now, her son still wanted to hang out with her.

An hour later, Elsie tiptoed toward Zeke's bedroom. She'd heard the shower come on and turn off, and had given him as much time as she could to nap before waking him for dinner. But Tony was starving and the delicious smell of the meat cooking wasn't helping with his patience.

She cracked the door open and peered in. Zeke was lying on his bed in sweats and a T-shirt. One arm over his head, his mouth slightly open, and he seemed completely dead to the world. She took a moment to simply drink him in. It was almost scary how attracted she was to this man.

For a moment, she panicked when she pondered the depth of her feelings. What if he turned out to be like Doug?

But as soon as the thought popped into her head, Elsie dismissed it. Zeke was *nothing* like her ex.

She forced herself to enter the room. Remembering that he was a former special forces soldier, she decided it would probably be prudent not to startle him when she woke him up.

"Zeke?" she said quietly.

He didn't move.

She said his name again, this time a little louder.

Not surprised when he jerked awake, Elsie quickly said, "It's me, Elsie. Dinner's ready."

Zeke sighed and groaned as he nodded. He swung his legs off the side of the bed and stared off into space for a moment.

He was delectably ruffled. And Elsie kind of regretted waking him up. It was obvious he was still out of it. She held out her hand and he took it as he stood. Then he surprised her by pulling her close. Elsie inhaled deeply, loving his fresh clean smell from his earlier shower.

"Thanks," he said.

Elsie didn't know specifically what he was thanking her for, but she supposed it didn't matter, so she simply nodded against his chest. "You're welcome. Now, come on. Tony's gonna die if he doesn't get to eat in the next two minutes—his words, not mine."

She felt more than heard a chuckle move through Zeke. "Wouldn't want that," he muttered. He wrapped his arm around her shoulders and they left the bedroom together.

Zeke headed for the kitchen, but she steered him toward the table. "Sit," she ordered.

"You don't have to wait on me," he told her, sitting anyway.

"I know. I'm afraid if you serve yourself, you'll end up with all cheese and tomatoes and forget to put any meat on your taco in the state you're in."

"You're probably right. But as a side note...I neither expect nor want you to think this will be a normal thing."

"I know that too." And she did. In the limited time she'd spent with Zeke, not once had he ever made her feel like she was somehow beneath him simply because she was a woman. There hadn't been any defined roles in the short time they'd been hanging out together.

She got a plate ready for Zeke, and helped Tony make his four tacos. They sat at the table and Elsie listened to her son chatter on to Zeke about what he'd done in school that day, and what he'd read while Zeke was sleeping.

It was obvious Zeke was still groggy, but he nodded and said all the right things in the right place as Tony carried the mostly one-way conversation.

After they'd finished eating, Elsie refused to let Zeke help clear the table. "It's Tony's turn to do dishes tonight," she insisted. "Go back to bed."

"I feel bad," Zeke said. "I'm being a horrible host."

Elsie couldn't help but roll her eyes. "Whatever. We weren't the ones who were tromping all over the woods saving lives. Go, Zeke. We're good."

As a testament to how exhausted he was, Zeke simply nodded. He leaned over and kissed her briefly on the lips, then turned and went back down the hall.

Elsie stared after him for a long moment, so many feelings rolling through her. Pride. Exasperation that he'd let himself get to this state. Concern about what he'd done in the past when he'd gotten home from a long search.

But Zeke was an adult and obviously able to take care of himself. She just hated thinking about him being so tired, he couldn't even manage to eat something before he passed out.

The rest of the evening went by uneventfully. Elsie checked on

Zeke a few times, and he remained completely zonked. When nine o'clock came around, she knew she needed to get back to the motel. It was already past Tony's bedtime and he had school the next day. He'd gotten his homework done and had been happy to sit and read the book Zeke had loaned him.

"Go on out to the car while I check to make sure we have everything," she told Tony.

"Can I start it?" he asked excitedly.

"Sure."

Tony had an increased interest in everything that had to do with cars, ever since Lilly had shown him how to change their tire when they'd been stranded on the side of the road a couple months ago.

"Cool!" he exclaimed and ran for the door.

Smiling to herself at his exuberance, Elsie headed for Zeke's room once more. She had planned on waking him up to let him know they were leaving, but when she heard him snoring slightly, she didn't want to disturb him.

Spotting the clock radio on the table next to the bed, she set the alarm for nine the next morning. She wasn't sure how long he'd sleep, but figured he wouldn't want to be late for work. Elsie smiled at the fact that he had the ancient clock radio in the first place. He probably used his phone as an alarm, as most people did these days, but she didn't have his password.

Not able to help herself, Elsie leaned over him and gently kissed his forehead, as he did to her all the time. "Sleep well," she whispered. "I'm proud of you."

Zeke didn't wake, but sighed in his sleep.

Elsie forced herself to back toward the door. She took one more long look at the man who was stealing both her heart and that of her son, and closed the door behind her. She picked up Tony's backpack, checked to be certain everything was set to rights in the kitchen, locked the knob on the front door, and headed home for the night.

CHAPTER EIGHT

Zeke slept like the dead the previous evening. At thirty years old, he shouldn't have been as exhausted as he was after a search, but apparently his time away from the Army had softened him.

He vaguely remembered eating dinner with Elsie and Tony, but most of the night had been fuzzy. He'd woken up around seven feeling completely refreshed. Many times after a long, intense search like they'd had the night before, he'd come home and pass out right after his shower without eating. But this morning, his belly wasn't trying to eat itself and he didn't even have a headache.

All because of the care Elsie had shown him. She'd made sure he'd eaten and drank several glasses of water. She hadn't made him feel guilty that he wasn't spending time with her and Tony. In fact, she'd actually shooed him back to bed after he'd eaten as if he were a child.

Zeke smiled. Yeah, he could definitely get used to being taken care of by Elsie. He couldn't remember his ex ever doing something like that after he'd returned from a mission. And there had been plenty of times when he'd needed a loving touch desperately. Instead, she'd immediately started in on him, listing everything that needed doing around the house...and how annoyed she was that he hadn't been around to do it.

While watching the news earlier that morning, catching up on what he'd missed while in the forest over the last twenty-four hours, he heard a weird noise coming from his bedroom. When he went to investigate, Zeke realized it was the alarm on the ancient clock radio going off. He'd had the thing since childhood, and for some reason had hung on to it. Nostalgia, or maybe just him being crazy. But he couldn't remember using the alarm since he'd been in high school.

As he clicked it off, he realized Elsie must've set it for him. Another wave of warmth spread through him. It was such a tiny thing...but it was another way she'd taken care of him. It was nine o'clock, and she probably wanted to make sure he didn't sleep through opening the bar.

It was too early to go to work, but he needed to see Elsie. He'd called Brock when he'd gotten up, and he and Talon had picked up his car from the parking lot at the bar, bringing it to his house. He could've walked to work, as he didn't live that far from the square— nothing was too far from the center of town, really—but he was relieved to have transportation.

Without thinking about it, Zeke headed for his car. He stopped by The Sweet Tooth for a huge, sticky cinnamon roll for Elsie because he knew they were her weakness, and even popped into Grinders to get a caramel macchiato. He may not have been dating her for long, but her sweet tooth was hard to miss.

Now he was at the Mangree and he couldn't wait to see her.

Juggling the coffee cup and the bag with the cinnamon roll, Zeke knocked on the door.

"Who is it?" Elsie asked from inside.

Zeke smiled. He didn't like that there wasn't a peephole in the door, but he was glad she was being security conscious. Although, her question would alert anyone with nefarious intentions that there was a woman inside.

"It's me," he said. "And I think the code word is still austere, unless you changed it."

He heard her chuckle a second before the locks on the door were undone.

Then he was staring into her smiling face. And just like that, Zeke's day went from good to great.

"It's still austere. But you're right, I need to change it. And yes, we use the code word when someone comes to the door too. Since Tony is here on his own a lot, I've warned him over and over never to open the door to anyone. Even if they claim to be maintenance or a maid. Oh my God, is that cinnamon I smell?"

Zeke couldn't help but grin. "Yup. If you let me in, I'll give let you have this ooey-gooey cinnamon roll I picked up on my way here. And maybe, if you're *really* nice, I'll let you have the caramel macchiato too."

"Get in here," Elsie said as she reached for his shirt, grabbing a handful and pulling him inside the room. There was no way she could've moved him if he didn't want to budge, but since he wanted to be wherever she was, Zeke stepped into the room.

It hit him yet again how much he hated that this was where Elsie lived. There was nothing wrong with the place, per se. The room was clean and tidy. It was as safe as it *could* be for a motel, sitting next to the office. But it was still a motel, with cheap doors and even cheaper locks on the windows. It was also bland. Boring. And his Elsie was anything but.

"You didn't have to get these for me," she scolded, still reaching for the bag and cup.

"I know. Just as you didn't have to come over last night, feed me, put me to bed, and set my alarm."

The slight blush on her face made Zeke want to pull her into his arms and never let go.

"You would've done the same for me," she said with a shrug as she busied herself with the cinnamon roll. She put the bag on the circular table after pushing a few Matchbox cars out of the way, then went over to the milk crate on the floor and got two plates, two forks, and a knife.

She went back to the table, took out the pastry and cut it in half, putting a slice on each plate. Then she smiled at him and motioned to one. "Eat with me?" she asked.

Zeke had already eaten breakfast and certainly wasn't hungry, but he took the seat next to her and watched with heavy-lidded eyes as she forked a bite of the cinnamon roll into her mouth and moaned.

His dick twitched at the sound. He couldn't help but grin.

"What?" she asked.

"I'm not laughing at you," he reassured her. Deciding he needed to answer further, before he admitted he was getting an erection at hearing her moan over a breakfast pastry, he said, "I can't remember the last time someone cared enough about me to do what you did last night."

Elsie chewed and swallowed, took a sip of her coffee, then replied, "I didn't do much."

"Else, you fed me, made sure I rested. You *took care* of me. Hell, you even set my alarm. No one, ever, has done any of that for me before."

She met his gaze. "You were completely out of it when I left last night. I didn't know how late you'd want to sleep in, and I had a feeling you'd hate it if you were late to work."

"You're right. I actually woke up completely rested around seven. It took me a second to figure out what the obnoxious noise coming from my room was, when the alarm started going off."

Elsie laughed. "Yeah, I'm sure if you called a museum, they'd be happy to take it off your hands since it's such an antique. Anyway, I assumed you used your phone, but I didn't have the password to set it."

"Four, six, two, seven, six, nine," Zeke said without hesitation.

"What?"

"My password. It spells out Go Army, in case you forget the numbers."

Elsie stared at him in disbelief. "Did you just give me the password to your phone?"

"Yup."

"Why?"

"Why not?"

"Because! Zeke, your phone's private."

"I've got nothing to hide from you. Elsie...I went through a marriage that turned out to be full of secrets. I hated it. *Loathed* it. I swore that if I ever risked another relationship, I'd do whatever I could to make sure it was open and honest. No more secrets. And part of doing that is being willing to give you my password. You want to check my texts or emails, help yourself. Although there's not much to look at. Mostly me and the guys talking back and forth. And lots of junk mail in my inbox."

Elsie stared at him so long, Zeke began to get concerned. "Else? You okay?"

"I just...wow."

Zeke reached for her hand and brought it up to his cheek. He remembered her touching him like this the night before, and loved it. "No pressure, Else."

"One, one, one, one, nine, nine," she blurted.

"Pardon?"

"That's mine. I know it sucks, but I can never remember the stupid thing. I should've done what you did and thought up some word or something, but I didn't. And my phone is super cheap. It's one of those pay-for-the-minutes kind of thing. It's all I could afford when I got here. I don't text much, although now that I think about it, I probably *should* check my plan since I've been getting to know Lilly, and she texts all the time."

She was talking fast, as if she was uncomfortable. Zeke turned his head and kissed her palm, then lowered her hand and clasped it in his on the table. "I didn't tell you my password to make you feel as if you had to give me yours."

"I know," she said without hesitation. "I don't have anything to hide either."

Zeke liked that. A lot. His ex had been extremely protective of her phone and its contents, and had gone off on him in a big way the one time he'd asked who she was getting so many messages from.

"I'm sorry about your marriage," she said, as if she could read his mind.

Zeke shrugged and let go of her hand so she could continue to eat her cinnamon roll. "Thanks. I found out the hard way that she wasn't cut out to be a military wife. A few years after we got married, I discovered she'd been cheating on me from the very first deployment post-wedding."

"What a bitch," Elsie gasped.

Even that made Zeke smile. "Corinne hid her affairs pretty well at first. But as time went on, she got more and more lax about it... not that I noticed. I think she actually wanted me to find out toward the end. I was still in denial until I literally caught her in bed with someone. She threw all her lovers in my face when I confronted her, saying it was my fault she'd cheated. That if I wasn't gone so much, if I gave her the attention she needed, she would've been faithful."

"That's such bullshit," Elsie fumed. "Seriously. Blaming you for serving your country, for putting your life in danger. What a shitty thing to do!"

Amazingly, her reaction went a long way toward making Zeke feel better. "What about you? What happened with your ex? You mentioned him cheating as well. Is that why you left?"

Elsie shook her head, taking a deep breath and letting it out slowly. "That's why I *should* have left. But...he was mean," she said simply.

Zeke tensed. "Did he hit you?"

"No. But every day that we were married, he slayed me with his words. Made me feel as if I was stupid, not good enough for him, lacking in every way. I actually *was* ready to leave, but then Doug changed. Became more like the man I knew before we got married. I got pregnant with Tony and was so happy. But it was all a sham. He'd only been sucking up to convince me to have a child. His boss thought it would look better if he was a family man.

"After I had Tony, Doug went back to being the awful person he'd been before. He was back to yelling at me and telling me how stupid I was. I stayed for a while because I literally had nowhere to go and no means to support myself...and I knew leaving would mean Tony's life would get a hell of a lot more difficult without Doug's money and insurance. But he couldn't handle *any* part of child-rearing. Not the crying, the tantrums, the messes...anything. When he turned on Tony, I was done. He actually told his own flesh and blood that he was acting like a baby and if he wasn't careful, he'd turn out as stupid as his mom.

"I finally realized...if I stayed, I was dooming Tony to a life of trying to please a man who literally couldn't be pleased. I didn't want him to start believing his dad's criticism. So I got us both out of there. It wasn't easy. I accepted any job I could find and moved around a few times before coming to Fallport."

Zeke knew there was a lot more to her story, but she looked so distraught, he didn't push. "I'm glad you did. You and Tony are the best things that've happened to me since my divorce."

She smiled up at him. "Thanks. We think you're pretty darn wonderful too."

Zeke laughed. Then he put a finger under her chin and tipped her head up as he leaned forward. He kissed her then. Long and slow, trying to convey all the words he couldn't say to her yet.

When he pulled back, the dreamy look on her face almost made him drag her to one of the beds behind them. But this wasn't where he wanted to make love to her for the first time.

He also wanted to make sure Elsie knew deep in her bones that he wasn't manipulating her or taking advantage in any way. Wasn't helping her or hanging around just for sex. He simply enjoyed spending time with her. And Tony.

His resolve was tested when she licked her lips. "You taste like cinnamon," she blurted.

Zeke laughed. "So do you. With a chaser of caramel."

They smiled at each other before Zeke said, "Go on, finish up so we can get going. I want to make sure my bar survived without me for a day and a half."

Elsie rolled her eyes. "As if we couldn't keep things afloat for even longer." He loved her sass. When she finished her half of the cinnamon roll, she eyed his. "You gonna finish that?"

"Nope."

"Can I wrap it up for Tony? He'd love it as an after-school snack."

Every time she opened her mouth, Zeke fell harder for her. He knew how much she loved pastries from The Sweet Tooth. And also assumed she very rarely splurged. She could've easily polished off his half of the roll and her son would've been none the wiser. But instead, she thought about how much he'd love a surprise treat.

It made Zeke all the more determined to give both Elsie and her son as many treats as they could stomach in the future. "Of course you can," he told her belatedly.

She gifted him with a smile and stood up. She brought a small, beat-up plastic takeout container over to the table and shifted what he hadn't eaten into it. Then she threw away the bag, brought the silverware to the sink, washed it, and returned to the table.

"Okay, I'm ready."

"Do you think Tony would like to go camping with me this weekend?" Zeke asked.

Elsie looked taken aback for a second. Then she smiled. "Tony would love to do *anything* with you this weekend. But if you offer to take him camping, he'll be over-the-moon excited."

"I thought we could start out slow. Maybe set up a tent in my backyard. That way if he gets scared, or doesn't like it, we can come back inside," Zeke said.

Elsie's eyes misted. "Thank you."

"For what?"

"For thinking about that. I'm fairly certain, he's gonna love every second of it. Being dirty, peeing outside, eating hot dogs cooked over a fire. But he's never camped before. I'm not much of an outdoorsy girl. Not that we have the supplies..."

"You've given him *everything*, Elsie. Don't ever think that your love for him isn't enough."

She smiled, and Zeke couldn't resist. He stood and wrapped an arm around her waist. She met him halfway when he dropped his head.

He had no idea how long he stood there kissing her, but knew if he didn't stop, they'd be late. "I want you to stay at my place while we're camping. You can keep an eye on him, and I think, even though he'll be excited about sleeping in a tent outside, he'll feel better if you're close."

"Okay." Elsie's fingers traced a pattern on his chest. He wasn't sure she even knew she was caressing him. Goose bumps rose on his arm at her touch. If her fingers felt this good through the material of his shirt, he suspected having her hands on his bare skin would bring him to his knees.

"But no interrupting our man time," he said sternly, ruining the effect when he couldn't keep the smile off his face.

Elsie giggled. "I wouldn't dream of it. I'll sit inside and read romance novels, knit a scarf, and eat chocolate. How about that?"

"You know how to knit?" he asked.

"Nope. Don't have any romance books either. No room for them in here," she said without a shred of embarrassment.

"The library," Zeke said.

"What?"

"We'll go to the library. I should've already thought about it. We can get Tony and you library cards. Raid works there and would be happy to help."

"I don't have an address," Elsie said, for the first time sounding unsure.

"The hell you don't. The Mangree gets mail, right?"

She shrugged and nodded.

"I'm looking forward to seeing what kinds of romances you pick out," Zeke told her.

"Yeah? You read many?"

"I've read a few."

Elsie looked shocked. "Really?"

"Yeah. I picked them up when I was married, trying to figure out my wife. I thought I could get some tips about what women liked and make things better between us."

"And did you?"

"Pick up some tips? Yeah. But since Corinne was a bitch of the highest order, they had no effect on her."

Elsie giggled again. "All right then."

"And now we *really* have to get going if we're gonna open On the Rocks on time." He let her go so she could grab her purse and make sure all was right with the room. When she was ready, Zeke put his hand on the small of her back and followed her to the door.

She closed it firmly behind her and said, "I can drive."

Zeke was shaking his head before she'd finished speaking. "Nope. I've got this."

"Wait, how'd you get your truck from the bar?"

He opened the passenger door and waited until she'd climbed up into the seat before answering. "Some of the guys took care of it for me."

"Must be nice," she said quietly.

"It *is* nice," Zeke said, not letting the comment go. "And my friends are *your* friends, Else. You need something, anything, you call one of them. I'll give you all their numbers and you can program them into your phone when we get to the bar."

101

Elsie looked unsure.

Zeke leaned in, pulling the seat belt out and buckling it around her, not backing away when it snapped shut. "What do you think we're doing here, Else?"

"Um..." she said, frowning.

"We're dating. You're my girl—"

"Woman," she corrected immediately.

"Right, sorry. You're my woman, and I'm your man. That means you're in my circle now. You break a fingernail and need a file, if I'm not around, you call Ethan, Rocky, Drew, Brock, Talon, or Raiden."

"I'm not sure they'll be thrilled to go on a such a silly errand," she teased.

"Wrong. They'll be honored you asked them for help. That's how we are," he said. "We've all seen a lot of shit in our lives, and we know what's important. Friendship. Love. Loyalty. You have questions about any of that, talk to Lilly. She'll explain it."

With that, Zeke kissed the tip of her nose, drew back, and shut the door. He walked around the truck to the driver's side.

"You good?" he asked after he'd climbed behind the wheel. He couldn't really explain the way the team stuck together. It wasn't something they'd talked about, just something they did and who they were. No one hurt one of their own. And that included anyone in the future who ended up dating someone on the Eagle Point Search and Rescue team.

"I'm good," Elsie said quietly, probably still thinking about what he'd said.

After Zeke pulled out of the lot and headed for the center of Fallport, he was thrilled beyond measure when Elsie tentatively reached for his hand. He might've freaked her out a bit, but not enough for her to pull away.

Elsie Ireland was meant for him, and he was happy to remind her as often as needed that she and Tony had a champion, and a whole team at their backs.

CHAPTER NINE

That weekend, Tony was more hyper than Elsie had ever seen him. He was so excited for his campout, he could barely contain himself.

She stood at the window, watching as Zeke and her son put up the tent. Zeke was extremely patient, as always, letting the boy do most of the work, even though it took twice as long to make any progress that way.

Elsie sipped her tea and sighed. This was what she'd always wanted for her son. To be treated with respect. To have someone honorable to look up to and try to emulate. And she couldn't have chosen better than Zeke.

But a part of her, deep down, was still wary of deepening their relationship. During the six months she'd dated Doug before their marriage, he'd seemed pretty awesome too.

Shaking her head, Elsie knew she wasn't being fair. Zeke was the opposite of Doug in every way that mattered. She smiled into her mug. In particular, she loved how touchy-feely he was. He hadn't lied about that; he couldn't seem to keep his hands off her. He touched her arm while they were talking, pushed locks of hair behind her ear when they fell out of her ponytails; when they walked next to each other, he put his hand on the small of her back...and he kissed her constantly. Rarely deep kisses. Pecks on the cheek, or forehead, or her lips. And he held her hand as much as he could get away with. Not much at work, because they were always busy, but outside of the bar, he was always reaching for her.

"Good job, bub!" Zeke said, holding his hand up for a high-five.

Tony smiled and slapped Zeke's much larger hand.

Zeke handed him two sleeping bags, and her son crawled into the tent as Zeke came toward the house.

Elsie turned as he entered. He came straight for her. He took her mug out of her hand, put it on the table, then wrapped an arm around her waist, spearing his other hand into her hair as he leaned forward.

And proceeded to kiss the hell out of her.

All Elsie could do was hold on as he made her forget everything but the feel of his lips on hers. So much for the small pecks she was just thinking about. He angled his head, urging her lips to part, and his tongue tangled with hers over and over, wiping every thought from her head and filling her with longing.

When he finally lifted his lips, they were both breathing hard.

"You taste like cinnamon again," he said with a sexy smile.

He hadn't removed his hands, and Elsie felt surrounded by him. "I should, since I've been drinking cinnamon tea," she said, her words a little shaky.

"As much as I love showing your son the joys of camping, I have to say, I think I'd prefer to be inside hanging out with you."

There was nothing that could endear him to Elsie more than honestly enjoying being around her son. But she couldn't deny that the thought of having Zeke to herself for the night was thrilling. It had been a very long time since she'd had an evening without Tony, or even wanted one.

Her fingers curled into Zeke's shirt as she whispered, "Me too."

The smile he gave her was worth the slight feeling of betrayal she had at wishing she was alone with this man.

"You think Tony's gonna last all night outside in the tent? Or is he gonna bail?"

Elsie smiled. "He's probably going to be begging you to let him sleep in the tent every time we visit after tonight."

"So we're gonna be out there all night," Zeke said with a sigh. "I was kinda hoping he'd eventually want to come inside, so you and I could snuggle."

Elsie grinned. "Snuggle?" she asked. "I'm not sure I've ever met a man who uses that word, let alone wants to do it."

"You have now. I suppose I shouldn't admit this, but after those two nights when you were in my bed, I slept like a baby. My sheets smelled like you. Looking forward to tomorrow night, when they will again."

"I was going to sleep on the couch," Elsie informed him. The disappointed look on his face made her laugh. "I'm kidding," she said.

"You're mean." He tightened his hand in her hair. Then he sobered and got a serious look on his face. "You're quickly becoming an addiction, Elsie Ireland. One I have no intention of quitting."

She stared up at him, then opened her mouth to respond, but Tony chose that moment to poke his head inside and say, "Okay, Zeke, I got the sleeping bags set up. What's next? The fire?"

Without letting go of her, Zeke turned to look at Tony. "Yup. I picked up some bigger pieces of wood the other day, but we need smaller kindling to get it started. There should be lots of sticks around the yard. If you can gather some up, we'll be all set."

"On it!" Tony said, shutting the sliding glass door a little too hard in his exuberance to do as Zeke asked.

She would've reminded her son not to slam the door, but it was too late, he was already gone. "Sorry about that."

"About what?" Zeke asked.

"About him slamming the door. The last thing you need is him cracking the glass."

Zeke shrugged. "If he does, I'll just get it replaced. It's not a big deal." Then, after a beat, added, "What's that look for?"

"That door has to be expensive."

"Maybe. I have no idea. But in the grand scheme of things, cracked glass doesn't really matter. Tony being excited about camping and trying something new is more important than a door."

Yet again, Elsie couldn't help but marvel at Zeke's reaction. Doug had plenty to say anytime a young Tony damaged something in their house.

One particular instance came to mind, when Tony found a permanent marker and had drawn all over one of their kitchen cabinets. No matter how hard Elsie had scrubbed, she couldn't get the marks off. When Doug arrived home and saw the damage, he'd lost his mind. He'd screamed at Tony, making him cry, then turned his ire on Elsie. Telling her what a terrible mother she was for allowing their son to destroy something so expensive. He'd berated her for months after the incident, not letting her live down the fact that he'd had to replace the cabinet door.

"You're too good to be true," she said softly.

"Nope. I just know what's important and when I've got something precious. You and your son are worth way more than any material possession I own."

As if he knew she was getting emotional, Zeke deftly changed the subject, giving Elsie time to get control over herself and not start crying.

"Are you sure you don't want to camp with us? I could share my sleeping bag." He wiggled his brows suggestively.

"I'm an indoor girl," she reminded him. "Why do you think Tony's never been camping?"

"All right, but the offer stands. If you get jealous of all the fun we're having, feel free to join us."

"Right. Don't hold your breath, Zeke."

He chuckled. "Maybe *I'll* get scared and need to come inside and be comforted," he joked.

Elsie rolled her eyes. "Whatever. But for the record, anytime you need comforting, I'm here."

He got serious again. "I appreciate that. I've seen and done some pretty horrible things. I don't sleep well sometimes."

Elsie palmed his cheek. She loved touching him like this. It was intimate, even more so when he tilted his head and gave her some of his weight. "Thank you for your service, Zeke. That sounds trite, but—"

"Coming from you, it doesn't," he said, interrupting. Then he sighed. "I should probably get out there and make sure Tony's not making a pile of sticks bigger than he is."

"He's a little enthusiastic," Elsie agreed, semi-apologizing.

"Nothing wrong with that," Zeke reassured her. "My house is your house," he told her. "Feel free to eat and drink whatever you want. I'm going to lock this door behind me, I've got a key. I don't expect trouble, but there's no way I'm gonna leave you in my house behind an unlocked door."

"But you and Tony will be in the backyard. Without any kind of door between you and...whoever might come around."

"Your son is safe with me, Else," Zeke said seriously.

Elsie couldn't really follow his line of thinking. It was okay for him and Tony to be in the backyard, vulnerable to anyone who might want to approach—especially since he didn't have a fence around his yard—but it wasn't okay for her to be in his house with the back door unlocked? "I know," she said belatedly.

"I've already got a ton of snacks and drinks out there in the cooler with us, so we shouldn't have to come in for any reason, unless Tony gets uncomfortable. If that happens, I'll be sure to let you know that it's us coming in. Relax tonight, take a bath, do whatever you want. Enjoy your night off, sweetheart." Then Zeke pulled her to him and kissed her once more.

Elsie's dormant libido roared to life, and when he finally ended the mind-blowing kiss, she was more than ready to beg him to stay inside.

"Damn," he muttered as he slowly let go of her and took a step back. "You make it hard to walk away," he told her.

Elsie glanced at his crotch and grinned. "I see."

Zeke burst out laughing and shook his head at her. "This is gonna work," he said firmly. "You and me. We're gonna be good together."

Elsie couldn't disagree. She simply nodded.

His smile grew. "Best night ever," he said. "Getting to know Tony better, spending some time in the great outdoors, and you sleeping in my bed. The only way it could be better is if I was there with you. Sleep well, sweetheart."

Tingles ran through her, but Elsie managed to say, "You too."

He grinned and headed into the backyard. As he'd promised, he took the time to lock the door behind him, then turned and headed for where Tony had amassed quite a pile of kindling in the short time he'd had.

The more time Elsie spent with Zeke, the more she fell. Things were definitely looking up for her and Tony. For a while, she hadn't been sure if Fallport would turn out to be the right place for them; it wasn't as if there were a ton of opportunities for her work-wise, and small towns could be very unwelcoming to newcomers. But she'd found more than just a place to settle. She'd found someone she could see herself spending the rest of her life with.

With a smile, Elsie picked up her mug of tea and took another sip as she watched Zeke painstakingly teach her son how to build and start a fire.

* * *

Everything in Zeke wanted to go back inside his house, drag Elsie to his bed, and make long, slow, sweet love to her all night long. After Corinne, he hadn't thought he'd ever want to get seriously involved with a woman again. But already he couldn't imagine *not* being with Elsie. She was a bright light in his otherwise dull life.

Time with Tony also reminded him that he really *did* want children. Elsie's son was inquisitive, smart, and challenging. He asked a million questions and kept Zeke on his toes. He also soaked in every bit of information he heard.

Tony had listened intently as Zeke went over all aspects of building a fire. He taught him how to use a flint to get the flames going, and while it had taken the boy a bit to get the hang of striking the flint, the look of pride on his face when he'd gotten the fire started had been extremely rewarding for Zeke. He loved being the one to teach him a new skill.

They'd roasted hot dogs, made s'mores, pointed out constellations in the stars, and had finally settled into the tent for the night. The weather was perfect for camping, not too cold and not too hot. Man and boy lay side-by-side, and Zeke sighed in contentment.

"Zeke?"

"Yeah, bub?"

"We're safe out here, right?"

Coming up on an elbow, Zeke could just make out Tony's face in the darkness of the tent. "Of course. Why? What're you worried about?"

"It's stupid," Tony hedged.

"Why don't you let me be the judge of that."

Tony sighed. "It's just...that show that was here a while ago? They were looking for Bigfoot. What if he's real and he comes here and wants revenge on his hiding place being shared with the world?"

Zeke swallowed a chuckle. The last thing Tony needed was to think he was being laughed at. "You have absolutely no worries about Bigfoot coming to my backyard," he said honestly.

"How do you know? He could be out there now, watching us. Waiting for us to go to sleep."

"I'm thinking Bigfoot does whatever he can to stay away from humans."

"But, what if he wants revenge for those people trying to find him? What if he smells the hot dogs we made and he's hungry? And the fire might've drawn his attention. There's no fence around your yard. What if—"

"Easy, bub. Here's the deal...have you ever heard of *anyone* around here seeing Bigfoot?"

Tony thought about that for a moment before saying, "No."

"Right. If Bigfoot exists, I'm certain he's smart enough to stay the heck away from us humans. He might have a family to protect, and the last thing he'd do is come into our backyard and give us trouble. Because that would bring trouble down on him and *his* family. The forest has been a great hiding place for him for years and years and years. Just because that show came here to film, doesn't mean all of a sudden Bigfoot is gonna come walking through the downtown square. Can you imagine what Otto, Art, and Silas would do if that happened?"

Tony giggled, and Zeke relaxed. He wasn't sure he'd had the right words to reassure the boy they were safe.

"I have another question," Tony said.

"Shoot."

"What's the plural of Bigfoot? Bigfeet? Bigfoots?"

Zeke laughed out loud. "I have no idea."

"I'll ask Mom tomorrow. She'll know. She knows everything."

"Tony?"

"Yeah?"

"You and your mom will always be safe with me. You get scared, you come to me. I'll do whatever it takes to protect you. Got it?"

Tony was quiet for a moment. Then he said, "Okay."

"Okay," Zeke agreed. "You think you can sleep now?"

"Uh-huh."

"Good. You need anything in the middle of the night, just nudge me. I've locked your mom in the house, just to be on the safe side. Not that I think anything's gonna happen, but it's not smart to ever sleep with your door unlocked."

"Did you lock the tent?" Tony asked.

Zeke winced. He'd walked right into that one. "We're zipped in tight," he hedged.

"Okay. This has been an awesome night. I can't wait to go to school and tell Bridger all about it."

"Bridger? That's actually someone's name?" Zeke asked, managing not to laugh.

"Uh-huh. He has an ATV and he's always bragging that he gets to drive it everywhere. He thinks he's a big shot since he can drive."

A smile formed on Zeke's face. "I don't have an ATV, but I'm thinking you're old enough to learn to drive," he said impulsively.

The sleeping bag next to him rustled as Tony hurriedly sat up. "*Seriously?*"

"Yup. Although maybe not on roads. I'm guessing Simon, the police chief, wouldn't exactly like that too much. But I think you're tall enough to reach the pedals of your mom's car. We can go to the high school parking lot some weekend and see how you do."

"Cool," Tony breathed as he lay back down. "Zeke?"

"Right here, bub."

"I'm glad we're friends."

Four words had never hit him so hard. "Me too," Zeke said.

"Good night," Tony said.

"Night, bub."

Zeke stared upward at the top of the tent and listened to Tony's breaths even out. Instead of the awful memoires that often ran through his mind in the evenings, tonight, Zeke lay awake thinking about how blessed he was. He'd lived through some truly horrific things, but he felt as if he was finally being rewarded.

Tony was fun to be around, filling something in Zeke he hadn't even realized was empty. But he wasn't an idiot; he knew as the boy grew, he'd test his boundaries and probably be a pain in the ass sometimes. Though he also had a feeling the good times would way outshine the bad.

Then there was Elsie. He could picture her lying in his bed, holding a pillow to her chest as she curled on her side and slept...

He wanted this to be his future. Spending time with Tony, coming home to Elsie in his bed. They'd both had bad marriages, which he truly believed would serve them well in their budding relationship.

His thoughts turned to an idea he'd had the other day, when he'd brought Elsie breakfast at the motel. He'd already talked to Ethan about it, and his friend had been one hundred percent supportive. Maybe it was time to put the wheels in motion.

Edna at the Mangree had been awesome to both Elsie and Tony. But they needed a real home. Zeke hoped one day they'd move into *his* home, but in the meantime, he'd help the woman he was falling for, and her son, find a place of their own.

CHAPTER TEN

The next few days went by much like the previous week. Elsie spent her days working with Zeke, then he spent the hours after their shift ended with her and Tony. Most of the time they went to his house for dinner and to hang out. After years of uncertainty, Elsie was becoming more content by the day.

And every time she saw Zeke's head bent over Tony's homework as they sat at his table, she got teary. Zeke had spent more quality time with her son in a couple weeks than his own father had in four years. The bond between the two was obvious, and Elsie couldn't be more thrilled.

She was currently at On the Rocks, and the shift had been a normal one. Meaning, they'd been steady but not overly busy.

"Elsie? Grab your purse, we're going out for a bit. Lance, you good holding down the fort until we get back?" Zeke asked.

Frowning, Elsie looked at Zeke and said, "Where are we going? We can't just leave."

"Sure we can. Things are slow right now. Reina and Valerie are good. Come on, we want to be there when Tony's bus drops him off."

"Is something wrong?" Elsie asked as Zeke put his hand on her back and steered her toward the back offices so she could grab her stuff.

"Nope," Zeke said lightly.

"I don't like surprises," she grumbled as she took off her apron.

"Yes, you do," Zeke countered. "You liked it last weekend when Tony and I went out and grabbed you coffee and doughnuts for breakfast after we camped. You liked it when I taught Tony how to detail your car and you could see your reflection in the metal when we were done. You liked it when—"

"Okay, okay, fine," Elsie interrupted with a laugh. "I don't *usually* like surprises, but you're slowly curing me of that."

"Good. Come on, this'll be fun."

Shaking her head at Zeke's enthusiasm, Elsie wanted to protest. A "surprise" usually meant he was doing something for her and Tony. He never went overboard; he hadn't bought them anything crazy, like a new car, but it still felt weird for someone to go out of their way so often to make her happy.

When they headed out to the sidewalk along the square, Zeke lifted a hand and waved at Silas, Otto, and Art, who were in their usual spots across the way in front of the post office. They were constantly watching what was going on, and Zeke always waved to them when he left the bar.

He steered her to the parking lot and when they were settled, turned his truck toward the Mangree Motel.

"You gonna tell me where we're going?" she asked.

"Nope. Not yet," Zeke said with a small smile.

Elsie didn't even know why she'd asked. She'd learned quickly that Zeke was very good at keeping quiet about his surprises. He wouldn't spill the beans until he was ready.

They pulled into the parking lot at the same time as Tony's school bus. When the boy saw Zeke's truck, a huge smile formed on his face and he ran toward them.

"Hi! What are you doing here?" he asked.

"Code word?" Zeke asked, returning his smile.

"Enumerate," Tony recited dutifully. "Although since Mom's here, I technically don't need it."

"What's it mean?" Zeke asked, ignoring Tony's valid point.

Elsie merely grinned at the two of them.

Tony rolled his eyes. "To specify or count. And to use it in a sentence, I can't enumerate how many times I've told you that I don't need the code word when my mom is here."

Zeke laughed. "Good job, bub," he said, ruffling his hair. "I thought I'd take you somewhere special today. Your mom and I have to get back to work in a bit, but I think you'll like what I've got planned."

"Let's go!" Tony enthused, reaching for the handle to the back seat of the truck.

Soon, the three of them were on the road once more. Tony went on and on about school, Zeke encouraging him by asking pertinent questions. Elsie relaxed in her seat, happy to just listen. She couldn't believe she'd ever been wary of a relationship with Zeke. She shouldn't have been. He was amazing, never made Tony feel as if he was a third wheel, and he hadn't pressured her to move faster than she was comfortable.

If anything, Elsie wished he'd push a little more.

She wanted Zeke. So much. Wanted to do more than steal kisses wherever they could.

While Zeke was camping with her son, Elsie had spent the night in his bed. Surrounded by his intoxicating scent, she took the opportunity to pleasure herself, breathing him in and imagining *Zeke* touching her the entire time.

"Here we are," Zeke announced, bringing Elsie out of her own head. She looked through the windshield and saw they were at the Fallport Public Library.

"The library?" she questioned.

"Yup. Come on. Raid works here, he's expecting us."

Tony popped out of the back seat as Zeke came around to her

side. He took her hand in his and leaned down so his lips were by her ear. "Trust me," he murmured.

They'd had a talk about Tony's love of reading the other night. He wasn't interested in watching TV or playing video games like other boys his age, but could lose himself in books for hours. He'd been going through the selection of age-appropriate books Zeke had in his house at an amazingly fast pace.

Elsie had done her best to supply her son with enough books to keep him busy, but they didn't have a lot of space in the motel. She also hadn't had time to get to the library.

Tony practically bounced to the door and held it open for her and Zeke.

"Remember to keep your voice down inside," Elsie warned, knowing her son had a tendency to get loud when he was excited.

"I will," he said.

When they got inside, Zeke said, "Give your mom and me a sec, bub. The new releases in books appropriate for you are over there," he said, pointing to a section not too far away. "See if there's anything that grabs your interest."

"Okay," Tony said excitedly, taking off at a fast walk.

Zeke turned to her and said, "Before you get mad, let me explain."

"I'm not mad," Elsie interjected. "I should've brought him here before, or at least come in the morning before my shift, since I quit working for Edna. We even talked a little about getting him a library card, and myself too. I just haven't thought about it since then."

Zeke nodded. "Good to know. And there's a little more." At her questioning look, he continued, "You and I discussed how you don't like that Tony's by himself from the time he gets off the bus until you get home. Honestly, I don't care for it either. So, I called the school district, and I learned there's a bus that drops kids off two blocks from the library. And you know that Raiden works here. I talked to him as well...and he's more than all right with Tony coming here after school instead of going home. Raid has to be here anyway, since it's his job and all, and he said he'd watch over him until you came to collect him."

Elsie could only stare up at Zeke in disbelief.

"Are you mad?"

Elsie closed her eyes and did her best not to cry.

"Else? Talk to me."

She opened her eyes and blurted, "I want to kiss you right now."

He grinned.

"But I'm gonna refrain, because the kind of kiss I want to give you would be highly inappropriate in the middle of the library. And because my kid would probably think it was gross. Are you *sure* Raid won't mind? I don't think Tony will be a problem, but after a while, the newness of being here might wear off and he could get bored."

"We'll deal with that if it happens. Let's not borrow trouble. Besides, I think there are more than enough books to keep him busy for a very long time, and if he's ever bored, I'm guessing Raid will find something for him to do. Come on, let's go say hi to him, then we'll see if we can't find some books for Tony to take with him...and break the news that he'll be spending more time here."

Zeke started toward the checkout desk, but Elsie put her hand on his arm, stopping him.

"Seriously...just when I don't think you can get any better, you go and prove me wrong," she said softly.

Zeke moved closer and did that thing she loved, wrapping his hand around the back of her neck. "I'd move mountains to put that soft look on your face, Else. Believe me, this was no hardship."

"I don't need you to move mountains, Zeke. I just need *you*."

"You've got me."

They stared at each other for a long beat before he took a deep breath. "As much as I want to stay right here, we need to talk to Raiden, get Tony settled, and get back to work."

"I know," she whispered.

Zeke grinned. "You aren't moving."

"You aren't either," she countered.

"What does Tony think about sleepovers?" Zeke asked.

Elsie frowned in confusion. "Sleepovers?"

"Yeah, at a friend's house? Or maybe he'll want to go on an overnight trip with Talon and Rocky? I'm sure they'd be happy to take him on a short backpacking trip."

"He'd love that," Elsie said. "Why?"

Zeke leaned forward and whispered into her ear. "Because I want you. *Bad.* Without any distractions and without you worrying if your son will overhear us. I want to sleep in my bed *with* you. Show you how much I care about you. Wake up with you in my arms. I want to share a lazy breakfast in bed and then make love again."

Elsie's heart was racing by the time Zeke had finished speaking. "I want that too," she breathed.

"Thank fuck," he sighed.

Elsie shook her head. "Did you really think I'd say no?"

Zeke shrugged. "The first time we make love, I don't want it to be rushed. I want to be able to take my time. I want you to be able to make as much noise as you want. But I wasn't sure you'd be comfortable with Tony gone for the night. You two have been peas in a pod for a long time."

There he went again, being so damn considerate of her feelings. "I wouldn't be comfortable in letting Tony go with just anyone. But one of your friends? I have no problem with that. They're good men, just like you. And if you trust them, I know I can too. Even with the most important person in my life. When?"

He grinned at her enthusiasm. "I'll talk to them tonight and see when a good time might be."

Elsie nodded. Excitement and anticipation swam through her bloodstream. She wasn't precisely sure when she'd become so attached to Zeke. But she knew how. And it wasn't just because he was a good-looking man. He was. There was no doubt. But who he was *inside* had chipped away at the shields she'd erected. He'd been just as hurt by someone, but it hadn't hardened him past the point of being able to take a risk on another relationship. Thank goodness.

"I've never wanted a woman like I want you, Else," he said.

"Same," she told him.

Zeke nodded. "Right. It's gonna suck having to wait. But you're worth it. I'd wait as long as it took to be inside you. To have you looking up at me with those gorgeous brown eyes, giving yourself to me."

Elsie swallowed hard. "You aren't making this any easier."

He blew out a breath. "Yeah, sorry. I'll try to behave. Maybe."

Elsie couldn't help but shake her head. "It feels as if I'm a teenager again, trying to figure out how to make out with my boyfriend at my house without my parents hearing us."

Zeke laughed. "Come on. Let's go find Raid."

He intertwined their fingers and brought their clasped hands up to his mouth, kissing her knuckles before pulling her toward the checkout desk. He walked around it and toward an office in the back.

"Hey, Raid," Zeke said as he entered the office without knocking.

Raid had obviously seen them, because he didn't seem startled in the least at their entrance. Duke, his large black and tan bloodhound, lifted his head when Zeke spoke, then, seeing who it was, put it back down with a long, put-upon sigh.

"I see Duke's as excited to see me as ever," Zeke joked.

"I helped shelve books today, and he's tired from following me around," Raiden said with a shrug. "You're interrupting his nap."

"Sorry, Duke," Zeke told the dog. But the bloodhound didn't even lift his head to acknowledge his name.

"Are you sure it's okay for Tony to be here by himself after school?" Elsie asked.

"Wouldn't have agreed if it wasn't," Raiden said.

Of all Zeke's friends, Raid was the most...standoffish. Elsie wasn't sure that was the word she was looking for, but it would do. From talking with Zeke, she knew Raiden used to be in the Coast Guard as a dog handler. He and his canine partner spent their time searching for drugs on boats that were intercepted in the waters around Florida. Something had happened—Zeke hadn't said what—and he'd left the service and found his way to Fallport as a member of the Eagle Point Search and Rescue team.

The small town was lucky to have him, and no matter what had brought him here, Elsie was grateful.

She was sure the single women in town were just as thankful. Raid definitely wasn't hard on the eyes. He had red hair and a bushier beard than the others. His ears were a touch pointy and he had a long, narrow nose. He wasn't classically good-looking, but all of his features worked well together.

At the moment, he was wearing a red-and-blue plaid shirt and a pair of jeans. He looked like a mountain man, one of the heroes in some of the romance books she'd read. She idly wondered if he had an ax at home and if he chopped wood in his spare time.

Instantly, she wanted to roll her eyes at herself for stereotyping the poor man.

"Raid, I—"

Everyone in the room turned at the voice. A woman stood in the door. She was slight, around five-foot-four, but curvy. Her light brown hair was pulled back in a sensible ponytail. Her hazel eyes were focused on Raid as she entered the room, but as soon as she saw he wasn't alone, she came to a stop.

Duke, who'd literally been snoring loud enough to be heard on the other side of the library, sprang up and headed straight for her. His tail wagging a million miles a minute, as if he was being reunited with his most favorite person in the world.

"He's never greeted *me* that way," Zeke observed as Duke repeatedly nudged the woman's hand for pets.

"I'm sorry. I didn't know you had guests," the woman said, blushing slightly as she petted Duke, then turned to leave.

"Khloe, this is Elsie Ireland, and my friend Zeke Calhoun. We work on the SAR team together."

"Hi," Elsie said with a smile.

"Nice to meet you," Zeke added.

Khloe gave them a small smile. "I'll catch up with you later," she told Raid, giving Duke one last pet before leaving them alone.

As she left, Elsie noticed she had a pronounced limp. She couldn't help but wrinkle her brow in concern.

"She seems nice," Zeke said, giving Raid a look and not hiding his inquisitive tone.

"Is she okay?" Elsie said at the same time.

"She's cool," Raiden said gruffly, as Duke got resettled into his bed. "Just got hired the other day. Duke loves her already, which I don't get, considering he doesn't even *like* most people."

"Hmmm," Zeke said.

"Whatever. If he thinks she's good, she's good," Raiden said curtly. "And to answer your question, Elsie, she's okay. Said she has an old injury that never healed right." He stood, and Elsie was in subtle awe of his height. He seemed to tower over Zeke, who wasn't exactly short at six-foot-two. Raiden was six-eight, at least. Elsie felt positively tiny next to both.

"You tell Tony what's up yet?" Raid asked.

"Haven't had a chance. His eyes lit up the second we entered, and he's probably lost in a book already," Zeke said.

"Then let's go find him and tell him he doesn't have to read all the books right this second. He'll have every afternoon to read," Raiden said. "Duke, stay," he told his dog as he headed for the door.

Elsie stood back as Zeke told Tony that he'd be spending every weekday afternoon here at the library, instead of in the motel room. The joy in his eyes made Elsie want to cry and tackle-hug Zeke at the same time. She worried about Tony every afternoon, hating that he had to be a latchkey kid, and at a public motel at that. The relief she felt that he'd not only get to do something he loved after school now—namely, get lost in a story—but that he'd be supervised and safe as well was almost overwhelming.

"Your mom and I are gonna head back to work now, bub. You good?" Zeke asked.

In response, Tony surged forward and hugged Zeke hard. "Thank you," he said fervently.

"Don't thank me," Zeke said, hugging him back. "Thank your mom. She's the one who said yes."

Tony let go of Zeke and wrapped his arms around Elsie. "Thanks, Mom."

Elsie closed her eyes and enjoyed the moment. "You're welcome. But you have to be good," she warned. "If Raiden, or Khloe, or anyone who's here working says one word about you misbehaving, this privilege will be taken away. Understand?"

Tony nodded. He looked up at his mom. "How many books can I check out at a time?"

Elsie couldn't help but smile. She smoothed a lock of his too-long hair out of his eyes. "Let's keep is reasonable, huh? We still don't have a ton of room at home. Maybe three to start with?"

Tony's face fell, but he nodded. "Okay."

"I think that'll be plenty, especially since you'll be here every day," Elsie told him. "You can read while you're here, but I expect you to do your homework after dinner before you start reading again," she warned.

"Okay," Tony said.

Elsie had a feeling they'd butt heads over doing homework before reading in the future, but for now, she'd take his acquiescence. "Love you, Tony."

"Love you too, Mom."

She looked at her watch. "I'll be back to get you in about an hour and a half."

When Tony nodded and stepped back, Zeke stepped closer to Elsie and put his arm around her waist. "No talking to strangers, bub. If anyone makes you nervous, you walk away and go straight to Raiden. It's not rude if someone is making you uncomfortable, got it?"

"Yes, sir."

"And you aren't to go outside for any reason before talking to Raid."

"Okay."

"You can put your backpack in his office when you get here."

Tony nodded.

"And the most important rule..." Zeke said, letting his words trail off.

"Yeah?" Tony asked.

"If you read anything really good, write down the title and author so I can check it out for myself."

Tony grinned. "Will do."

"Awesome. Be good."

Tony nodded once more, then turned and headed toward the children's section of science fiction books. Elsie caught a glimpse of the woman who'd come into Raiden's office pulling a book off the shelf and holding it out to her son, smiling before chatting with him. Probably describing the book.

She might've been a little abrupt when meeting them, but it looked like she had no problem interacting with someone Tony's age.

"Thanks again," Zeke told Raiden.

"Of course. I'll talk to the other librarians and let them know what's up, in case I'm not here. They'll all keep their eye on him," Raid said, more to Elsie than Zeke.

"I appreciate it."

"No problem."

"See ya later," Zeke said with a chin lift toward his friend.

Raiden responded with a chin lift of his own and headed back toward his office.

Zeke held open the truck door for her, and the second he

climbed behind the wheel on his side, Elsie leaned toward him. She put her hand on his thigh and kissed his cheek.

Zeke turned toward her, and of course she went for it. Pressing her lips to his, she did her best to show him how thankful she was with that kiss. Her nipples hardened under her T-shirt and she squirmed in her seat.

She couldn't get Zeke's earlier words out of her head.

She wanted everything he'd mentioned. Wanted it bad. She'd spent the last nine years putting Tony first. She didn't regret one day of it...but having Zeke to herself for one night was quickly becoming her greatest wish.

"Damn, woman," Zeke said when she finally pulled back. He shifted in his own seat and adjusted his cock in his pants.

Smiling, Elsie sat back in her seat. "When were you going to talk to your friends again?"

"Not soon enough," he muttered. Then he smiled over at her. "I like seeing you like this."

"Like what? Frustrated and horny?"

His grin grew. "Happy. Carefree. Less stressed."

He wasn't wrong. Elsie felt less stressed right this moment than she had in a very long time. She still had plenty to worry about. But it felt as if she had a partner now. Someone she could lean on if she needed to. It felt good. Damn good.

"It's because of you," she told him.

Zeke immediately shook his head. "Nope. It's all you. Come on, let's get back to On the Rocks before Otto and the others spread a rumor that we've been kidnapped by Bigfoot."

Elsie giggled. "We're never going to live that show down, are we?"

"Probably not. Once it airs, Harry over at the general store is counting on an influx of tourists looking for Bigfoot, all desperate to buy the T-shirts, cups, and other shit he's making."

"I mean, I guess more people coming to town means more

money as well. But it's also an increased risk of people getting lost and hurt, isn't it?" Elsie asked.

Zeke nodded as he started the truck. "Yup. I'm guessing there will be a bunch of people tromping through the mountains for a while, but I think things will die down when no one finds hide nor hair of a legendary creature."

"You don't believe in Bigfoot then?" Elsie asked.

"You do?" he countered.

"Nope. But on the one-percent chance he's real...I say, let him live in peace. The world can be a harsh place. Especially for a Bigfoot. The government would probably want to study him. Then dissect him or something. I hope he stays hidden."

"Me too," Zeke agreed.

It didn't take long for them to get back to the parking lot behind the square. As he usually did, Zeke took her hand in his as they walked toward the front of On the Rocks.

"Thank you, Zeke," Elsie said softly as they approached. "No one's been as good to both me and Tony as you have."

"It's not a hardship making you guys happy," Zeke retorted. He stopped at the door, kissed the top of her head, waved at the three older men watching them avidly, then followed her inside.

CHAPTER ELEVEN

Elsie was a hard person to do things for. Zeke knew this, but it didn't dim his determination. She was largely uncomfortable with help unless it was in her son's best interest. Zeke had quickly learned that was his best chance in getting her to accept the things he wanted to do for her.

But he seriously hoped he hadn't overstepped in what he wanted to do next. It wasn't as if he was giving her anything himself...he'd just talked to a few people and arranged for something he hoped she'd accept.

Tonight they were going on a double date with Lilly and Ethan. Tony was spending the evening at Whitney Crawford's house. She owned the bed and breakfast where Lilly had stayed when she'd come to town for work, and Whitney had become a dear friend. She was happy to do them the favor of watching Tony, so Lilly could spend time with her only other close female friend.

And Ethan and Lilly had gone above and beyond to put Zeke's plan in motion. All they needed now was for Elsie to say yes.

They were spending the evening at the house Ethan had bought, which he and his brother had been working hard to remodel. It wasn't quite finished, but the two men had done a ton of work, so it was now livable.

"I'm excited to see the house," Elsie said from next to him as they drove. It wasn't far from the center of town—nothing in Fallport was. They'd just come from Whitney's after dropping Tony off. Her son had been happy for the change of venue, and Whit was planning on teaching him how to make homemade rolls before they grilled shish kebabs.

"Me too," Zeke said. He was more excited to hear what Elsie thought of their proposal, but that would come in time. Pulling into the driveway, Zeke was impressed. Ethan and Rocky had done so much work in a short amount of time on the old house.

Lilly came out to meet them, and she and Elsie hugged as if they hadn't seen each other in months rather than a day or so. It did Zeke's heart good to see Elsie so close with another woman. She needed friends. Deserved them. And Lilly was a great one to have.

"Hey," Ethan said as Zeke neared the front door behind the women.

"Hey," he echoed. "Everything good?" he asked.

"Yup. We're all set."

Anyone overhearing them would think they were talking about dinner. But Zeke relaxed a fraction. Ethan had needed to hammer out a few things with the owner of the apartment building where he and Lilly had lived, and it was good to hear that everything was set.

The couple gave them a tour of the old house. Zeke once more marveled at Ethan and Rocky's skills. The master bedroom was completed, as were the bathrooms. The kitchen was nearly finished, with just a few more cosmetic touches needed. The guest bedrooms were under heavy construction, and the office and living areas were well on their way—and a bit of a disaster—but Zeke had no doubt they'd be finished sooner rather than later.

Lilly served some wine for everyone and they talked about nothing in particular on the back deck as the roast Lilly had prepared finished cooking. When they moved into the dining room, settling down to eat, Lilly broached the topic that had brought Zeke and Elsie over in the first place.

"So...as you can see, Ethan and I have moved in," Lilly said. "Even though the place isn't done, I couldn't wait any longer. It feels like home already."

"It's beautiful, Lilly," Elsie said with a huge smile. "It's obvious how much work's gone into it."

"Right? I'm so impressed with Ethan and Rocky. They've worked really hard. I keep telling them they don't have to spend all their spare time here, since we've bought the house and can remodel at our leisure, but I think they're just as eager to see it completed as I am." Lilly smiled at Ethan.

"Need to get it done before our wedding," Ethan told her.

"You have a date?" Elsie asked.

"We just decided. We thought a Halloween wedding would be perfect. The weather should be cool enough that everyone won't sweat to death while standing outside in their fancy duds, but not cold enough that we'll all freeze."

"I love it!" Elsie enthused. "Congratulations!"

"Thanks," Ethan and Lilly said at the same time.

"We checked with both our families and it looks like everyone will be able to get time off their jobs and school and stuff so they can make it. That's a minor miracle in itself."

Lilly had a large family, and Elsie knew how important it was to her that all of them, along with Ethan's sister, could attend the ceremony.

"Now that we're moved in and getting settled, Lilly and I wanted to talk to you about something, Elsie," Ethan said.

Zeke could feel her curiosity and a bit of apprehension, so he reached out and put his hand on her thigh. Elsie glanced at him for a moment, then turned her gaze back to Ethan.

"Me?" Elsie asked.

"Yes. I still have about eight months left on my lease at the apartment. I'd recently signed for another year. Lilly and I don't need it anymore, since we've moved in here. It's not too far from the square and On the Rocks. My brother lives in the same complex too. The apartment isn't very fancy, to be honest; it's pretty rundown, but the plumbing is good and there's lots of hot water. Something I was always grateful for. The security is nonrefundable, whether I break or transfer the lease. I didn't have an issue signing because at the time, I figured I'd be there at least another year. Then I met Lilly..." Ethan smiled at his fiancée.

"Anyway, since I can't get my money back, I thought maybe you and Tony might want to move in? I've already talked to the landlord, and he's okay with transferring the lease. I reassured him that your son was a good kid, not a troublemaker. And Rocky's happy to keep an eye on him when and if you ever need him."

Zeke had kept his eyes on Elsie while his friend talked. It was hard to read what she was thinking from the look on her face. Her expression was blank...but her eyes conveyed longing as she stared at Ethan. It was almost painful to witness.

She didn't respond right away, so Lilly filled the silence.

"It's a perfect solution. I know Tony loves the pool at the Mangree, but he could have his own room at the apartment. The walls are kind of thin, but Ethan's neighbors are cool. It's a great starter place, Else. Please say yes."

Elsie swallowed hard once. Then again. She put down the fork she'd been holding in a tight grip and it clanked loudly on her plate. "I...Why?"

"Why what?" Ethan asked. "Why are we offering it to you? Because you deserve a break, Elsie. You work your ass off to provide for Tony. And we like you. You're not only going out with one of my best friends, more importantly, you're *our* friend. Let us do this for you. For you and Tony."

"I can pay rent—"

"Nope," Ethan said, as Lilly shook her head firmly. "The rent's already paid for the remainder of the lease."

"*What?!* I can't accept," Elsie said, shaking her own head. "That's thousands of dollars, you guys."

"Please, Else? Please let us do this for you," Lilly pleaded. "You work *so hard*, and you're a great person, a fantastic friend, and an even better mom."

"I don't know what to say," Elsie whispered, clearly overwhelmed.

"Say yes!" Lilly told her with a laugh.

"Also, I talked with the guys on the team, and they talked to some others, and we've collected quite a few things for the apartment. Beds, a table, a couch, two recliners, books, a bookcase for Tony's room, a couple of rugs, kitchen stuff, dressers...that sort of thing," Zeke told her.

Elsie turned her gaze on him. "You knew about this?" she asked.

"Knew?" Lilly asked, her eyes sparkling. "Who do you think set it all in motion?"

As he watched, Elsie's eyes flooded with tears.

For a second, Zeke was alarmed. Afraid he'd completely overstepped or even insulted her, completely blowing their relationship. She was a proud woman. Never once had she asked for help, even when she was going hungry so her son could eat. The last thing he wanted to do was make her feel bad about her situation.

He'd offered to pay the rent on all eight months left on Ethan's lease, but his friend wouldn't even consider it. They'd ended up splitting the cost...and it was just another reminder of how awesome his friends were.

When Elsie practically threw herself at him, Zeke closed his eyes in relief, even as he caught her.

Pushing back from the table so he could settle Elsie on his lap, he held her against him as she cried. His friends both smiled from across the table, Ethan reaching out to grab Lilly's hand as they silently let Elsie get her emotions out.

After a few minutes, Elsie lifted her head, wiped her eyes, and turned to look at their friends. "Thank you so much," she said, her gratitude clear in her voice.

"So you'll accept?" Lilly asked, obviously wanting clarification.

"I'd be stupid not to," Elsie admitted.

Everyone chuckled.

"You would. And I knew you weren't stupid," Lilly said with a wink. "We've been moving all the donated stuff in for the last week, so it's all ready for you and Tony. How's this weekend sound for moving the rest of your stuff in?"

"This weekend?" Elsie asked in surprise.

"No need to wait," Ethan told her. "We're all moved out and the place is empty. Well, not empty *now*, as there's lots of stuff in there, but you know what I mean."

"I, um...wow."

"That's a yes," Lilly declared.

"As long as we don't get called out, all the guys are planning on helping you move in," Zeke told her.

Elsie looked up at him and let out a small laugh. "It's not going to take seven of you to move me and Tony. We don't have that much stuff."

"Then it won't take that long," Zeke said. He loved having her on his lap. It was intimate, and he especially loved that when she'd been overwhelmed, she'd turned to him for support and reassurance.

As soon as he had the thought, Elsie seemed to realize where she was sitting. She blushed and tried to scoot off him and back to her own chair. Zeke held her still for a moment. "You okay with this?" he asked.

She held his gaze and nodded. "It's been my goal ever since I moved here to get a more permanent place for me and Tony. I didn't think it'd take this long. But things kept coming up. Tony would get sick and I'd have to pay for the doctor. He outgrew his clothes and needed new ones. My car needed fixing. It was one thing after another. If it was just me, I wouldn't mind staying at the motel for as long as it takes, but Tony deserves his own space. Deserves a place to live that's more than one room he has to share with his mom."

Elsie turned to look at Ethan and Lilly. "Thank you," she said softly. "If there's anything you ever need, all you have to do is ask. It's yours. I don't have much, but I can help clean. Do yard work. *Anything.*"

Ethan rolled his eyes. "As if I'd ask you to do yard work," he said in a huff.

"All we need is for you to be our friend," Lilly said. "Especially *my* friend. There are lots of people in town who still don't particularly care for me because of that Bigfoot show that's probably gonna bring a lot of crazy people to Fallport. I don't really care if everyone else likes me or not, but I can definitely use a friend."

This time, when Elsie attempted to get off his lap, Zeke helped her stand. She went over to the other side of the table and gave Lilly a long hug. Then she did the same with Ethan.

By the time she got back to her chair, her tears had dried and she was smiling. "This is so hard to believe," she said. "Tony's gonna be crazy excited. Wait—did you tell him already?" she asked Zeke.

"You think he'd be able to keep it from you if I did?" he asked.

Elsie laughed. "Good point. No. The kid can't keep a secret to save his life. Which I'm glad about. It helps me figure out when something's up with him."

Zeke reached over and squeezed her hand.

"Right, so now that *that's* done, let's finish eating so I can show you where Ethan and Rocky are going to build me a she-shed in the backyard," Lilly said.

"A she-shed?" Elsie asked.

"Yup. A place I can work on editing my photos and videos."

"So you're doing it? Going to officially open a photography business?"

"Talked to Nissi today. She's a lawyer in town. Got the paperwork going for the LLC," Lilly confirmed.

"Yay!" Elsie exclaimed.

"That deserves a toast," Zeke said, holding up his glass of wine.

The others all raised their glasses as well.

"To new living digs. New business. Good friends and good food," Zeke said.

They all clinked glasses, and Zeke couldn't help but feel excited about the future. Things were going great with his own business, the search team was doing good, and his relationship with Elsie was better than any he'd ever had.

He'd reached a place in his life when it seemed as if all his hard work and heartache was paying off. He'd had some shit things happen to him in the past, but everything was looking up.

* * *

Elsie stared at the apartment building from the passenger side of Zeke's truck. He'd brought her by after they left Lilly and Ethan's house, just to show her which apartment was hers.

The complex wasn't fancy. Like Ethan said, it looked somewhat rundown. But not as much as the Mangree. And in Elsie's eyes, it was perfect.

"What d'ya think?" Zeke asked.

Looking at her watch, Elsie saw they had thirty minutes before they'd told Whitney they'd be back for Tony. Undoing her seat belt, she scooted over and climbed onto Zeke's lap.

He immediately reached for the lever of his seat and pushed it back, giving her more room so the steering wheel wasn't digging into her back. The position was awkward, and Elsie had a feeling her knees would be screaming at her way before she was ready to move, but for now, she was quite happy to be right where she was.

She wrapped her arms around Zeke's neck and scooted even closer. His cock was pressed against her core, and he gripped her hips tightly.

"This was all your idea, wasn't it?"

Zeke shrugged.

"The apartment, the donations...everything."

"Ethan was moving out, I knew you were looking for an apartment. It just seemed like perfect timing."

"I'm guessing he probably wasn't planning on moving out of his apartment until the house was done," Elsie said dryly.

"When you and I became a thing, I made a vow to myself that I'd do whatever it took to make your life better, Elsie. This is just part of me keeping that promise."

She studied him. Because she was in his lap, they were eye-to-eye. Sometimes his eyes seemed more blue, and other times the green stood out. Tonight, in the dim illumination from the lights in the small parking lot, they seemed more gray. But as always, she could read the sincerity in his expression.

"You scare me," she admitted.

Zeke blinked in surprise and his hands loosened a fraction around her hips. He opened his mouth to say something but she kept talking, not giving him a chance.

"My life's been hard. But I'm not unique. Everyone goes through hardships. I think I've had a bit more than my fair share. From my parents dying, to my relationship with Doug, to Tony having heart surgery as a baby, to moving here as a single mother with nothing but a high school education and no skills. But I didn't even mind all that. I had Tony, and he kept me going. Then you gave me a job, and I realized that I actually like what I do. I know being a waitress isn't exactly the career most people strive for, but I enjoy talking to people and making them happy, even if it's just bringing them food and drinks.

"But I never expected *you*, Zeke. Through you, I've gotten a little more stability. I've gotten support. I've gotten to know Lilly and Ethan, and I'm guessing I'll get to know your other friends better if we stay together."

"We're staying together," Zeke said without hesitation.

Elsie smiled at him. "I don't know what I'm trying to say, other than…I'm so glad you're in my life. And Tony's. All he talks about now is camping, books, and something about you teaching him how to drive…?"

"It's me who's glad you're in *my* life, Else," Zeke countered. "I was just going through the motions before you arrived. It took me a while to see what was right in front of my face, but now that I have, I can't imagine you and Tony not being around."

Elsie's heart felt as if it was going to burst. Somehow Zeke had redeemed her faith in men. Made her see that not everyone was like her ex. Maybe they clicked so well because he'd been through a failed relationship, just as she had.

Leaning forward, Elsie kissed him.

And just like that, sparks ignited. What started as a short "thank you" kiss flared into much more. Elsie ran a hand into his hair, clutching a fistful as he caressed her tongue with his own. One of Zeke's hands eased under her shirt and pressed against her lower back, his warm palm bringing her closer. The other inched up the front and palmed one of her breasts.

Elsie arched her back, which pushed his cock harder between her legs. She began to undulate against him, rocking her hips restlessly as she angled her head to deepen their kiss. She was desperate for more. To feel his bare skin against her own. She not only wanted this man, she *needed* him. Felt as if she'd die if she didn't get him inside her.

"Fuck," Zeke muttered as he pulled his lips from hers and thunked his head against the seat back.

Elsie's pulse was hammering in her chest and she could feel how wet her panties were. His hand was curled around her bare breast now, as he'd pulled the cup of her bra down. And even as he otherwise sat still under her, his head back and his eyes closed, his fingers continued to play with her nipple.

She shivered and couldn't help but press even harder against his cock as a small whimper escaped.

His eyes opened at the sound and he stared into her eyes. "So beautiful," he whispered.

"Zeke," she pleaded, not sure what she was even asking.

But he seemed to know. His fingers tightened on her nipple, even as his other hand moved to her ass. He jerked her against him, hard. "Take what you need, beautiful."

It was Elsie's turn to close her eyes. "Zeke..."

"Move against me," he urged. "That's it. I want to see you come."

It was then Elsie realized how close she was to doing just that. Zeke had read the clear signs her body was giving him. She'd practically given her ex a road map and he *still* never came close to making her come.

Her hips began to thrust more urgently, and his fingers didn't stop their erotic play on her nipple and breast. He'd gently tease her one second, then pinch hard the next. She didn't know what to expect, and it only heightened the eroticism of the moment.

A part of Elsie knew what they were doing was highly inappropriate. They were sitting in the parking lot of her new apartment complex, making out, and she was dry-humping him as if she were back in high school making out with her boyfriend before having to go home to meet curfew.

"Stop thinking," Zeke ordered. "Just feel."

"But you...This isn't fair."

"The hell it isn't. I get to see you come for the first time. There's *nothing* unfair about that."

Elsie might have continued to protest, but she felt too good. Too happy. Too relieved that she would finally be able to give Tony a home. At least a place that was more permanent than a motel. And because she wouldn't have to pay rent for eight months, she could save a ton of money in the meantime, giving her and Tony their first small taste of financial security.

She felt more excited about her future, and Tony's, than she had in a very long time. And she had Zeke to thank.

She opened her eyes and looked into Zeke's as she continued to rub her clit against his rock-hard cock. Even through their clothes, it felt incredible. It had to be hurting him, but nothing showed in his eyes but lust. For her.

"Take what you need, Else," he said.

So she did. Not taking her gaze from his, Elsie rocked herself against Zeke, faster and faster, until she was on the verge of coming. Her breath hitched and a small groan left her throat. Her legs began to shake as the orgasm approached.

Zeke pinched her nipple once more and dipped his fingers beneath the waistband of her jeans. Clutching her ass, he jerked her against him even harder than before, over and over, aiding her movements.

That was all it took. Her mouth opened, but no sound escaped beyond heavy breaths when she flew over the edge. She couldn't keep her eyes open as pleasure swam through her entire body.

Zeke leaned forward and buried his nose in the space between her neck and shoulder, and she held him tight as she shook.

When the overwhelming feelings finally began to subside, Zeke lifted his head just slightly. His fingers gently caressed her nipple, the touch so different from only seconds earlier. He moved his other hand back to her hip, holding her against him.

"So damn gorgeous," he murmured against her skin.

Elsie shivered at the feel of his warm breath on her neck. "Should I be embarrassed about that?" she asked softly.

"Fuck no," Zeke said, lifting his head. "It was one of the most beautiful experiences of my life. If you apologize, I'm gonna cry."

She smiled at him and took a deep breath. His hand moved then, pulling the cup of her bra back up and over her breast. It would've made her blush any other time, but at that moment, Elsie couldn't find the energy to feel anything but satisfied and replete.

Zeke shifted under her, and she realized he was still just as hard as he'd been moments earlier. Proving he was completely in tune with her thoughts, he said, "Don't worry about that. It'll go down. Maybe. Eventually."

Elsie couldn't help but giggle.

He smiled. "I love that sound." Then he pulled her against him, and Elsie gladly let him. She rested her cheek over his heart, listening to it thump over and over. They sat like that for a minute or two until her thigh started to cramp.

"Shoot. I need to move," she said as she sat up.

Even before the words were out, Zeke had lifted her and helped her back into the passenger seat. "You okay?" he asked.

"Yeah. I'm fine. I guess I'm not as limber as I used to be. I'm getting old, you know."

He rolled his eyes. "You're only thirty-three."

"Yup, old," she quipped.

Zeke put his hand on her cheek. "You're amazing," he said.

Elsie gave him a somewhat shy smile. Now that she wasn't lost to her lust or on his lap, she felt a little self-conscious about what she'd done.

"Nope. None of that. What just happened was natural. And beautiful. And so damn hot, it was all I could do not to come in my pants. We aren't going back, Else. Only forward."

What could she say to that? "Okay."

"Okay," he confirmed. "How about we go get Tony and let him know that he'll soon be getting his own room?"

Elsie nodded.

"We'll bring him by so he can see it on the way back to the motel. You're going to have to make sure he understands that he can't open the door to anyone without hearing the code word. He'll need a real key too. Do you think he's responsible enough not to lose it?"

"I think if we make him understand the importance of it, and how his safety and mine depends on him not losing it, he'll be fine."

It wasn't until she was done speaking that Elsie realized she'd said *we*...not I. To her amazement, that didn't worry her. Which was just another sign that she'd made a good decision to be with Zeke.

"Sounds like a plan," he said. Then he put his hand palm up between them, and Elsie gladly laced her fingers with his. They held hands all the way to the bed and breakfast.

It was getting close to Tony's bedtime, but because she was feeling so mellow, Elsie wasn't worried about it. They thanked Whitney, told Tony the good news once they were all back inside the truck, took her son by the apartment complex, then Zeke headed to the Mangree.

Tony was definitely excited about moving. He asked Zeke and Elsie a million questions and she did her best to answer all of them. She'd sent her son inside their room so she could say goodbye to Zeke.

They stood in front of his truck, and he hugged her tight.

"Thank you for accepting Ethan's offer," he told her.

Elsie's arms were around his waist and they were pressed together from hips to chest. She could feel his semi-hard cock against her belly. She longed to see it. To help him ease the pressure. This wasn't the time or place, but it was coming. No pun intended. She couldn't wait.

"Thank you for setting it all up."

"Anything you need, I'll move heaven and earth to provide," he said simply.

For the hundredth time that night, Elsie wondered what she'd done to deserve him.

"I'll bring some boxes over tomorrow before work," he told her. "You can start packing your stuff so the guys can pick it up and get it moved this weekend."

"Again, it's not going to take long," she said with an uneasy laugh. "Or even more than one vehicle."

"Material stuff doesn't make someone rich. It's the kind of life you lead. And you, Else, are rich beyond measure. All you have to do is look at that son of yours to know that."

He wasn't wrong. Her lip trembled.

"Don't start crying," he warned with a small smile. "Tony will freak out, wanting to know what I said to make you cry."

"Then stop being so awesome."

Zeke laughed. Then he leaned down and gave her a sweet, long kiss that made her toes curl once more. "I'll see you in the morning."

"Can't come soon enough," she reassured him.

"You make it really tough to leave you," he grumbled as he dropped his arms from around her.

Elsie couldn't agree more. The more time she spent with Zeke, the more she wanted to spend.

"You want a caramel macchiato tomorrow?" he asked.

"You don't have to stop to buy me anything," she said.

"Not what I asked," he told her.

"Then yes. Please."

"You got it," Zeke said. He took two steps back, then muttered, "Fuck it," stepped back toward her and kissed her once more. Long, hard, and a little desperate, before tearing himself away and stalking around his truck to the driver's side.

Elsie ran her tongue over her lips and watched as he started the truck.

"Inside, Else," he said after he'd rolled his window down.

Nodding, she gave him a small wave that was probably dorky, though at the moment she didn't really care, and headed for the door to her room.

She waved once more right before she shut the door behind her and put on the chain and turned the deadbolt.

"Are we really gonna move this weekend?" Tony asked.

Elsie turned to look at her son. "Yup. Are you sure you're okay with that?"

"Yes! Why wouldn't I be?" he asked.

"Well, there's no pool at the new apartment."

"I don't care. I'll have my own room!" he exclaimed.

It took way longer than usual to get him settled down enough to fall asleep. When his soft snores finally filled the dark room, Elsie let herself truly soak in everything that had happened during her evening.

She and Tony would finally have their own place.

She'd made the first move toward making her and Zeke's relationship more intimate.

And it had been...glorious.

Life was changing for her and her son, and Elsie couldn't be more content.

CHAPTER TWELVE

The day had been completely hectic, but one of the best Elsie'd had in a very long time. She took a deep breath and a brief moment to look around her new apartment.

She and Lilly were in the kitchen, along with Drew, who'd volunteered to help with snacks. Zeke and the rest of his friends were all in the living room, playing some kind of card game with Tony. It seemed to be a combination of the old classic War, with shades of Go Fish thrown in.

Zeke and Tony had teamed up and were playing one hand together, while Ethan, Rocky, Brock, Tal, and even Raiden sat around the coffee table. Good-natured insults were being thrown back and forth and everyone was laughing and having a great time. Duke, Raid's bloodhound, was lying on his back, snoring, ignoring the craziness going on all around him.

Almost everything in the apartment had been donated by people in the community. The coffee table, the dishes, their beds... hell, even the towels in the bathroom.

In the past, Elsie might've been embarrassed that she was the recipient of so much charity, but at the moment, she was just too happy to have a place to call her own.

"Elsie," Lilly said, catching her attention.

Turning, Elsie looked at her friend, still smiling—and looked right into the lens of a camera.

"Stop that," Elsie scolded without heat.

"Sorry, couldn't resist," Lilly said.

"Go take pictures of *them*," she ordered, gesturing toward the loud card game going on in the other room.

"You okay finishing up in here?" Lilly asked.

"What am I, chopped liver?" Drew asked, overhearing her question. "Elsie and I have this. Shoo."

Lilly laughed, nudged Drew with her elbow, and wandered out into the other room.

The apartment wasn't very big, the kitchen really too small for three people anyway. But to Elsie, who'd made do in a single motel room, the amount of space she now had seemed like a luxury.

"You holding up okay?" Drew asked.

She glanced at him. Elsie didn't know a lot about the man. Zeke had mentioned he'd been a police officer before quitting, becoming a member of the search and rescue team. He was the oldest member at forty-five, had black hair and a trimmed beard, like most of the other guys. His full-time job was accounting, and he was apparently very good at it, staying extremely busy the first few months of the year, before he had time to relax a bit more.

Elsie liked him, as she did all the other guys. They were fun to be around, and they'd more than proven time and time again that they were absolute professionals when it came to finding missing people in the forest.

"Yeah. This is...it's a little overwhelming," she said. "But good."

Drew nodded. "I'm glad. Zeke likes you a lot," he said.

Elsie raised a brow, surprised he'd gone there. "I like him too," she replied honestly.

"His ex really did a number on him," Drew added.

Elsie wanted to joke that he was acting a lot like Otto, Silas, and

Art by gossiping, but he was being so serious, she kept the comment to herself.

"She made him doubt himself," Drew went on. "While he was off putting his life on the line and dealing with the worst of humanity, she was fucking anything that moved. She had no respect for him or the Army. After everything was signed and the divorce was done, he quit. I'm sure he was more than ready to get out after the things he'd seen and done, but he admitted it was also partly so Corinne didn't get any more money from him."

"Wow. That sucks."

"Yup. I'm telling you this because we've all heard Zeke say many times over the last few years that he was done with women. That he wasn't ever going to get into a situation like he'd been in with his ex. He threw himself into making On the Rocks the best he could, had no problem working long hours. Then he hired you...and everything he thought he wanted was turned on its head."

Elsie wasn't sure Drew was insinuating that was a good thing or not.

"You're good for him," he said, reading her mind. "You've brought him out of the shell he's been living in for years. You've shown him that not all women are like his ex. He's happier. More content. He still works a lot, but it's not all-consuming like it was before. So thank you."

Elsie shook her head a little. Couldn't believe Drew was *thanking* her. "I was in the same boat he was," she explained. "My ex did a number on me too. Zeke's proven that not all men are assholes like Doug, a man who didn't even want his own son. I never thought I'd find someone who cared about Tony as much as I do. But Zeke does. He isn't pretending to tolerate him, or just putting up with him to get me in bed. Look at them," she said, turning to glance at the men huddled around the coffee table.

Zeke had his arm around Tony and they were whispering together. Her son threw his head back and laughed at that moment, and it did Elsie's heart good to see it.

"I'm not the smartest woman in the world, but even I know he's not pretending to enjoy spending time with my son."

"He's definitely not," Drew agreed. "The two of you have made him happier in the last couple months than I've ever seen him."

His words made Elsie feel good. Really good. "What about you?" she asked, belatedly feeling guilty for talking about Zeke behind his back. "Anyone you're interested in?"

Drew snorted. "No."

Elsie blinked. "Well, that was short and to the point."

Drew shrugged.

"I don't know you very well, and I hope that changes. But from where I'm standing, you and the rest of the guys are all pretty amazing. A woman would be very lucky to have you at her side."

Drew didn't comment, simply turned back to the bags of snacks they'd been working on putting in bowls.

"You remind me of me," Elsie said softly to his back. "I want to be the first to say 'I told you so' when you meet someone."

"I highly doubt that's gonna happen, but if it does...I'll be happy to hear you say it," he told her.

Elsie wanted to hug him, but she got the impression he was more than done with the subject. So with a shrug, she got to work next to him, opening bags of junk food.

* * *

That night, after everyone had left, after getting Tony settled into his new room, and after hanging out with him as he wound down by reading a chapter in the newest book he'd checked out from the library, Zeke sat on the couch with Elsie. She was curled up against him, her head on his chest, her arm around his belly, knees against his thigh.

"I love your house," she said out of the blue. "But it feels really nice to have you at *my* place and be able to do this."

"Yeah," Zeke agreed. He was more than relieved to have her out of the Mangree Motel. Elsie had cried when she'd said goodbye to Edna. The older woman could be gruff, but she'd looked after both Elsie and Tony while they'd been living there. He'd even overheard Edna tell Elsie that she could bring Tony back to swim in the pool whenever she wanted, which was quite the offer, because the woman was notorious for chasing people away who weren't paying for a room or a space in the RV park behind the property.

When the team had solicited for donations for the apartment, once people heard who it was for, they'd gladly offered items to give to her. She'd touched more people than she knew. She might be a relative newcomer to Fallport, but her positive attitude, friendliness, and obviously hardworking personality had won people over.

"Tony had an amazing time tonight. He was on cloud nine being around all the guys," Elsie said. "I'm so thankful for you all. I'm sure everyone had better things to do than hanging out with a nine-year-old after all our stuff got moved in."

"You might not be as thankful when he starts repeating some of the words he heard tonight," Zeke said dryly.

Elsie chuckled against him. "Believe it or not, he's heard most of them before. I'm not exactly Miss Prim and Proper. Besides, he knows better than to say those kinds of things at school or around others. He sometimes slips with me, but since he's generally polite, gets good grades, and is a damn good kid, I can't complain when he says the occasional bad word."

"You're a remarkable mom," Zeke said, something he reminded her of often.

Elsie shrugged. "Maybe. I've made lots of mistakes with him. But hopefully he knows that I love him more than anything else in the world and all I want is for him to be happy."

"He does," Zeke said. "You know what he said to Ethan tonight when he was leaving?"

Elsie shook her head.

"He thanked him for letting his mom have his apartment. Said you worked your butt off and deserved a place where you didn't have to share a room with your kid." Zeke heard Elsie sniff and pulled her closer. "He might only be nine, but you've taught him right from wrong, compassion, empathy, and he's able to appreciate the little things in life. He's not spoiled and loves his mama. I'm not sure what else a mother could want from her kid."

They sat in silence for a minute or two before Elsie said, "I think Lilly took a million pictures tonight."

Zeke chuckled. "Yup."

"She showed me a few. They're really good. The light in here isn't great and yet somehow the shots she took look as if they were done in a professional studio or something. She said she'd print some off and give them to me."

"That's cool," Zeke said.

"You don't get it," Elsie said softly after a moment.

"What don't I get?" Zeke asked.

"I don't have many pictures of Tony. A few from when he was younger, but cameras and printing pictures isn't something I could afford. My ex never cared about that sort of thing." She paused and took a breath. "The pictures she took tonight, and that she took at his birthday party, are the first I've had of him since he was a baby."

Zeke's heart broke for her. There were so many things he took for granted. "We'll get you some frames so you can put them up," he told her.

Elsie squeezed his belly. "I wasn't telling you that to make you feel sorry for me," she said. "I just wanted to express how grateful I am that Lilly didn't even hesitate to take pictures."

"I don't think you could've stopped her," he said, grinning. "And I could never feel sorry for you, Else. You have more goodness in your life than people who have ten times the material possessions you do."

"I know," she whispered.

Zeke kissed the top of her head. "And not to change the subject, but did you hear the discussion about camping that Tony had with Rocky and Brock?"

She lifted her head. "The one where they were making fun of you camping in your backyard and insisting on taking him on a 'real' camping trip?"

"That's the one," Zeke said. "I have a confession."

"Yeah?" she asked.

"I kind of put the guys up to that. I hope that's okay."

"Of course it is. I trust all your friends with him. But why?"

Her words made Zeke's heart beat faster. She'd said it so nonchalantly. She trusted his friends with the most precious thing in her life. She hadn't even hesitated. Her trust meant the world to him.

"What? What'd I say?" she asked, looking concerned.

"You *can* trust them. They'd never do anything that would put Tony in danger."

"I know," she said softly. "Zeke, you guys are heroes. In both your past occupations and what you do now. You don't hesitate to tromp out to the woods to look for anyone who gets lost. Kids, older people, stupid tourists, even escaped convicts and pets. There's no way you, or any of the others, would do anything that might get my son hurt. He's definitely not going to get lost when he's hanging around with members of the best search and rescue team in the state. Maybe the entire east coast. Besides that, hanging out with guys is a dream come true for him. He's wanted male companionship his entire life. Well...since he's realized he's different because his dad isn't around. Of course I trust all of you."

"Well, it means the world to me, and them. Anyway, I kind of suggested they ask Tony if he wanted to go camping with them next weekend...because I want you to myself."

She stared up at him.

"We talked about this, about Tony having a sleepover so we could have some time alone. I figured this would be perfect. The apartment is a step up from the motel, but I don't want to make love to you for the first time when your son is on the other side of the wall from us. The walls are way too thin here for you to enjoy our first time without feeling self-conscious or worrying about what Tony might hear. So I arranged for us to have a night to ourselves. Are you mad that I didn't talk to you about the camping trip first?"

It took her a moment to answer, and Zeke held his breath waiting for her to respond.

"I'm not mad," she said, and Zeke's breath let out in a whoosh. "But I *am* kind of nervous now."

"About what?" Zeke asked in surprise.

"It's been a while for me," she admitted. "And I've never been all that good at sex."

"Bullshit," Zeke said without hesitation.

Elsie raised a brow in surprise.

"Sorry. I just...that's your ex talking. You've told me how negative he was. How he always put you down. Forget everything you ever heard from him. I have no doubt that you're going to blow my mind."

At her skeptical look, he grabbed her hand on his belly and boldly moved it lower. "Feel that? I've been that way for what feels like weeks. And trust me, I learned a long time ago how to control my urges. But every time I get around you, smell you, listen to you interact with your son, see your smile, I get hard. You have nothing to worry about, sweetheart. Promise."

Instead of a shy smile or a nod, a mischievous look crossed her face and her hand tightened on his cock. Zeke groaned, every muscle in his body tensing.

"I never did return the favor from the other evening, did I?" she asked.

Zeke couldn't help but remember how gorgeous she'd been, sitting on his lap, grinding against his cock, getting herself off. She was absolutely stunning in the throes of passion, and he couldn't wait to see it again.

He grabbed her wrist and stopped her caress of his dick.

Elsie pouted, and it was absolutely adorable.

"I want to wait," he told her. "I want to be deep inside you when you make me come for the first time."

She shivered against him.

"You're special to me, and I want to make sure you know how much I appreciate and care about you. This isn't about sex, Elsie. Not for me. It's about more. Much more."

"For me too," she said.

Zeke brought her hand up to his mouth and kissed the palm, before putting it back on his belly, covering it with his own.

"I'm...I'm not on anything," she told him.

The blush on her face was surprising. They were adults, and talking about birth control shouldn't be embarrassing, but it somehow still was.

"I'll take care of it," he told her.

"Please tell me you aren't going to go to Grogan's General Store and buy condoms," she pleaded. "It would be all over Fallport that we're having sex if you do."

Zeke grinned. "I'm guessing people are going to know anyway," he said. "Or at least assume. Is that going to bother you?"

"No," she said without hesitation. "I'm proud to be your girl-friend. But that doesn't mean I want to advertise what we do behind closed doors."

"Agreed," Zeke said. "I'll take care of it in a way that won't have Otto and the others spreading the word I bought condoms."

"Just the part about you spending the night at my apartment, right?" she asked with a smile.

Zeke chuckled. "Not much I can do about that. Anyway, Rocky and Brock will pick up Tony Saturday morning. They'll hike out to one of the more popular camping spots, spend the night, then bring him back early Sunday afternoon."

"So we'll have a full twenty-four hours together?" she asked.

Zeke smiled. "Yeah. And luckily, your boss already gave you the weekend off so you could get settled into your new apartment."

"Lucky me," Elsie said with a smile. Then she sat up and moved over him, straddling him like she'd done in his truck.

Zeke's cock hardened even further in his jeans. This was now one of his favorite positions, and he made a mental note to make love to her like this in the very near future.

She wrapped her arms around him and scooted as close as she could get. "Today has been one of the best days of my life. Thank you, Zeke."

"You're welcome, sweetheart."

"So...we can't make love since Tony's down the hall, but do you think we could christen this couch with some making out?"

"I think that can be arranged," Zeke told her with a smile.

The next half hour was a lesson in control for Zeke. He'd never wanted a woman more than he wanted Elsie. They'd shifted on the couch until she was under him and he had one hand under her shirt, cupping her breast, and the other tangled in her hair, holding her still for his kisses. One of her hands had slipped under his waist-band and was clutching his ass, the other holding his arm, her fingernails digging in.

Zeke knew he had to stop or he wouldn't be able to. And based on how she was writhing beneath him, it was obvious Elsie wasn't going to be the one to put on the brakes either.

He took a deep breath, but didn't move his hands. He loved the feel of her tit in his palm. So lush and full. Her nipple was hard, and his mouth was practically watering at the thought of feeling it on his tongue.

"Else, we need to stop," he said.

The little whine that escaped her mouth was fucking adorable.

"I know," she said after a moment. "But for the record? I like this. A lot."

"Same," he told her.

"And...I'm thinking that my ex was an idiot."

Zeke chuckled. "He was. But about what, specifically?"

She looked into his eyes and her fingers stroked his arm. Zeke had no idea if she knew she was petting him, but he wasn't going to bring her attention to the fact in case she stopped. He loved her hands on him.

"He never made me feel like this. Ever. So I'm thinking the issue with our sex life was with him, not me. Which means I'm not frigid. Not even close. If things between us are as hot as I believe they're going to be, you might have a problem on your hands."

Zeke chuckled. "A problem?"

"Yeah. I'm gonna want *this* a lot."

At the word "this," she pressed her hips up against his cock, making goose bumps break out on Zeke's arms. He leaned down and kissed her hard. Lifting his head just enough to speak, his lips brushing against hers with every word, he said, "Anytime you want to make love, all you have to do is say so. I'm yours, Else."

"Even if I want a quickie at work?" she asked not so innocently.

"Fuck, woman. You're gonna kill me," he said.

"Is that a no?"

"Hell no, it's not a no! I'm yours. Any time. Any place."

She smiled up at him. Then she got serious. "I'm scared, Zeke."

"Of what?" he asked, pushing up a bit to give her some room. But she didn't let go of him. Her fingernails dug into his butt, making it clear she didn't want him to pull too far away.

"I have a lot to lose here. My job. This apartment. Tony already loves you and your friends..."

Zeke did his best to control his emotions. "Nothing that happens between us will affect any of those things."

"You can't promise that," she said.

"The hell I can't. Look, I have no idea what the future holds, but even if things don't work out between us, you're still gonna be fine. You and Tony. But I'll tell you right now, I'm gonna do everything in my power to make sure things *do* work between us. I'm not an idiot. I know when I've got something beautiful and amazing, and you, Elsie Ireland, are one of the best things to ever happen to me. I'm not going to fuck it up."

"I feel the same about you. I just can't help but worry."

"We can't change the past. We've both got baggage. The best thing we can do is put that shit behind us and concentrate on the here and now. You aren't Corinne, and I'm not Doug. Period. We make our own way. Fresh slate."

"I like that."

"Me too. Now, I'm gonna get up and get going before you ravish me on your couch."

She giggled, and because Zeke hadn't removed his hand from under her shirt, he felt the jiggle of her flesh against his palm. It took everything he had to slowly let go of her. They both sighed as they disentangled their hands and sat up. Zeke pulled her against him and held her for a long moment. At five-foot-five, she was petite against his six-foot-two frame, but most of the time he didn't even notice her short stature. She was larger than life in his eyes.

He grabbed her hand and walked toward the front door. He let go long enough to put his shoes on that were sitting in the small foyer, then pulled her close again. He couldn't resist kissing her one more time. They were both panting by the time she pulled back.

"Thanks again for today. For everything."

"You're welcome. After you get Tony off to school, try to relax before coming to work."

"You aren't coming by?" she asked with a cute tilt of her head.

"No. But not because I don't want to see you. If I have you alone, I'm gonna want to make love to you. And I don't want to rush. I want to wait until Saturday, when I have all the time in the world to explore. To learn every inch of you. If you need me though, don't hesitate to call."

Elsie blushed, but she nodded. "This anticipation...it's frustrating, but kind of fun."

Zeke groaned. "If that's what you want to call it. I'll see you tomorrow, sweetheart. Sleep well."

"I will."

"Good night," he said, kissing her forehead and forcing himself to turn to the door. Ethan had replaced the locks, adding an extra deadbolt. "Make sure to lock these behind me," he ordered.

Elsie rolled her eyes. "As if I was going to leave the door unlocked," she sassed.

"Brat," he teased.

"Thanks for caring," she said seriously.

"I more than care," Zeke blurted. It was a bit too soon to say the words, but she had to know this wasn't a casual fling for him. At the way she bit her lip and looked at him with her heart in her eyes, he was sure she felt the same way.

"See you tomorrow," he said, pulling the door open and heading down the short concrete walkway toward the stairs.

He heard the door shut behind him and took a deep breath as he walked toward his truck. The day had been perfect. Elsie was perfect. He couldn't wait for next weekend. To make her his in every way.

CHAPTER THIRTEEN

Elsie was nervous.

It was silly. She wanted this. Wanted Zeke.

But as they stood in the parking lot together, waving goodbye to Tony, Rocky, and Brock as they headed out for their camping trip, all of a sudden, Elsie wasn't so sure about what she and Zeke were planning.

She'd thought Doug was going to be it for her, and look how *that* turned out.

Not to mention, she had Tony to worry about. If he got any closer to Zeke and his friends, he'd be devastated if they were taken away from him.

Hell, who was she kidding? He'd be devastated *now* if things didn't work out between her and Zeke.

Just as she was beginning to talk herself out of spending the night with him, he said, "Come on."

Looking up, Elsie saw him motioning to his truck, not to the stairs that would lead them back to her apartment.

"Where are we going?" she asked.

"Not sure. I'll figure it out when we get there."

Elsie frowned in confusion. "I thought we were going to go upstairs and...you know."

"We were. But you're stressing. So I thought we could just hang out together for a while."

And just like that, Elsie's reticence melted away. "I'm okay," she said softly.

"I want you, Else," Zeke said matter-of-factly. "But I want you to be just as turned on and excited as I am. There's no rush. I'm not going anywhere. If we don't make love this weekend, that's okay. We'll wait."

"But the whole point of Tony going camping was to get him out of the house so we could have time alone."

"We're still spending the day together," Zeke insisted. "Nothing, short of you kicking me out, will keep me from hanging out with you on our days off. But I want you relaxed, not anxious. So, come on, get in the truck. We'll find something to occupy our time for a while and take your mind off whatever it is that's making you nervous."

Zeke was such a good man.

"I don't have my purse."

"Since you're not paying for anything today, you won't need it," Zeke said.

Elsie rolled her eyes. "Fine, but I have other stuff in there that I might need."

"Like what?"

She shrugged. "I don't know. Chapstick. Keys to the apartment. Tissues. *Stuff*."

Zeke chuckled. "Right. I should've known better than to ask what's in a woman's purse. Will you stay put while I run up and grab it? Or are you gonna bolt on me?"

Elsie rolled her eyes. "Bolt? What am I, a feral dog?"

"In some ways. So I'm treating you with care. A few minutes ago, I thought you were gonna suggest going with your son and the guys, even though you hate outdoorsy activities, just so you wouldn't have to be alone with me."

Elsie immediately felt bad. He wasn't too far off. She *had* been panicking. All the things Doug had filled her head with for so long crept in, making her wonder what she was doing. How she thought she could have a normal relationship.

She stepped into Zeke's personal space and wrapped her arms around his waist as she looked up at him. "I won't lie. I had a moment there when I definitely had second thoughts. But it was more because of me, not you. I'm good now."

Zeke leaned in and rested his forehead on hers as his hands clasped together at the small of her back. "I said it before, but I'll say it again, you need more time, all you have to do is say the word. I've waited this long for you, I can wait as long as it takes for you to be one hundred percent sure about me."

And that right there solidified Elsie's decision. Zeke wasn't going to turn on her the second they made love. He wasn't going to become a completely different man after he'd had her, tossing aside Elsie and her son. She knew that. "I don't want to wait," she said simply.

Zeke's hazel eyes locked onto hers. He licked his lips. "You're incredible," he said softly. "Tough down to your core."

Elsie shook her head. "I'm really not."

It was Zeke's turn to roll his eyes. "Whatever. Now, go get in my truck, woman, while I grab your purse. You need anything else while I'm up there? Want me to grab a bottle of water or anything?"

"You planning on taking me on a hike?" Elsie asked.

Zeke looked confused. "No. You'd hate that."

"Then I don't need water," she said with a small smile.

"Right." Zeke returned her grin, kissed her hard and fast on the lips, then gave her a small push toward his truck. "I'll be back in a sec."

Elsie was still smiling when she climbed into the truck and closed the door. She watched as Zeke made sure her apartment—

man, those words were so awesome, *her apartment*—was locked, then jogged down the stairs toward her.

It seemed the longer she knew him, the more gorgeous the man got. Just thinking about having him all to herself later, in bed, made goose bumps break out on her arms. But he was right, she needed a bit more time. It felt weird to say goodbye to her son, then go upstairs and get naked. Besides, she loved spending time with Zeke.

She wasn't sure where they were going, as there wasn't all that much to do in Fallport, but she was game for whatever he decided.

Zeke got into the truck and put her purse on the seat between them. "You ready?" he asked as he started the engine.

"Ready," she agreed.

* * *

Five hours later, Elsie couldn't believe she'd thought there wasn't anything to do in Fallport. Zeke had outdone himself in entertaining her.

First, they'd stopped by Grinders and he'd gotten her a caramel macchiato. Then they'd gone next door to Fall for Books, the used bookstore on the square. It was right down from the bar, but she'd never been there. As soon as she entered, Elsie was in heaven. There were books stacked literally everywhere. On the floor, haphazardly on every shelf, even in the walkways. She'd ended up with a grocery bag stuffed full with paperbacks that Zeke insisted on paying for. When she'd started to protest, he'd leaned down and said, "Else, at twenty-five cents each, I think I can afford to spend five bucks on my woman."

He had a point. So she'd given in, excited to bring her new treasures home and put them in the bookcase someone had donated to the apartment.

Then Zeke took her to the dog park, Barks a Lot, where she spent a solid forty minutes or so playing with the doggies that were visiting. Afterward, they went back to the square, where Zeke dashed into Sunny Side Up to grab them some lunch while she talked to Art, Otto, and Silas.

The three men were just as ornery and hilarious as always, and by the time Zeke returned, she'd told them all about Tony's camping trip, admitted that she'd never been bowling, Hawaii was her dream trip, and that, when she was eight, she'd found a snake in her yard and kept it as a pet...for a week, until her mom had found it in her closet. It had escaped the shoebox she'd been keeping it in while she was at school.

How the men were able to get her to talk about that stuff, she had no idea, but she now understood a little better why they were the undisputed kings of gossip in Fallport.

Zeke had then brought her to Caboose Park, so named because there was a red caboose parked in the middle of a large field that kids could play on. They'd eaten lunch there, and Elsie couldn't remember ever laughing so much.

At no time during their day together had Zeke made her feel like he was irritated at not being back at her apartment, having wild sex. Yet another contrast with her ex. Early in their marriage, before he stopped wanting her at all, Doug complained that she didn't put out enough.

By the time Zeke pulled into the parking lot of the apartment complex, Elsie was completely relaxed.

He turned off the engine and looked over at her. "What's that look for?" he asked, studying her grin.

"That was fun," she told him.

Zeke winked. "I'm glad. You're mostly right in that Fallport isn't exactly excitement central. But as long as you aren't looking for high-end restaurants, museums, or a huge mall, there's always something to do."

"Let's hope Tony thinks that when he gets older," Elsie said with a small chuckle.

Zeke returned her smile, then pushed open his door. He walked around the truck and took the bag of books Elsie had just gotten out of the back seat. Then he shut her door and grabbed hold of her hand. They walked up the stairs toward her apartment.

After entering, Zeke put the books down on the small table in the dining area. Then he turned to Elsie. "Ball's in your court, sweetheart. You need some more time, I can head on out. I'd like to come back tomorrow morning and make you breakfast though."

Just the thought of him leaving made Elsie's stomach hurt. But knowing he was perfectly willing to give her some space after they'd already pretty much made plans to spend the night together made her fall for him all the more.

In response, she took a step forward and plastered herself against him. "Were you able to buy condoms?" she asked. "I mean, without old man Grogan and half of Fallport knowing what you were doing?"

Zeke chuckled, the sound vibrating through Elsie. "I went to Walmart. Although I had to abort the mission twice. Once, because right when I was about to go down that aisle, Sandra—you know, the woman who owns the diner—appeared out of nowhere and started talking to me. Then, after she went on her way, I was heading for the aisle again when a group of teenagers swooped past me and I swear set up shop in front of the condom display for half a year, talking about which were the least uncomfortable and wondering what the biggest size was."

Elsie giggled.

"Right? There was no way I was gonna interrupt that. So I walked around and picked up a bunch of shit I didn't need. Finally, on my third pass, the aisle was clear. I grabbed what I wanted and got the hell out of there. Oh—and I almost blew it when I got in a line behind Simon."

"The police chief?" Elsie asked.

"The one and the same. No way was I going to put boxes of condoms onto the conveyer belt in front of him. I like and respect the man, but there was no need for him to know our business. So I switched lines. Took about twenty extra minutes, but it was worth it."

"*Boxes?*" she asked, zeroing in on the plural part.

Zeke's arms tightened around her. "Yeah. I was positive one box wasn't going to be enough. Not with how much I want you."

Tingles shot through her. "I have another question," she said.

"Shoot. I'm an open book for you, sweetheart. Ask whatever you want, whenever you want."

"So I guess you were still able to get what you needed even though those teenagers probably bought all the big sizes, huh?" She managed to ask that with a straight face, but couldn't hold it as Zeke's eyes widened.

"Oh, she likes to tease...good to know," Zeke said with a huge grin. "For your info, there were plenty of the Magnum extra-larges left. Guess those boys wised up."

Sex had never been like this before. Not that they were having sex yet, but Elsie had never joked around like this in the past. It was more of an uncomfortable moment when she asked whoever she was dating if he had a condom, and he frowned, grumbled and moaned, but eventually pulled one out of his wallet. And Doug hadn't bothered with condoms. Hadn't bothered with asking her *anything* about what she wanted in regard to birth control.

"What was that thought?" Zeke asked quietly.

Shit. She'd been lost in the past for a moment. That happened more and more often around Zeke. She was constantly comparing him to her ex, with Zeke coming out on top every time.

"I was just thinking how not awkward this is," she said honestly. "I'm not sure I've ever been with a guy who was so nonchalant about birth control."

"You want more kids?" Zeke asked.

"Yes." It was an easy question to answer. "But I'm not sure that'll ever happen. There's no way I want to bring a child into my situation right now. It's too uncertain. And kids are expensive."

"I've told you before, and I'll say it again, your old life is done.

No more scrounging for food. No more living in a motel. No more working your ass off only to be able to afford dinner for Tony and not yourself," Zeke said sternly.

His words made Elsie feel good. But that didn't mean she was ready to let him be her sugar daddy. No way. "I appreciate that, but you know that's not how life works," she told him.

He nodded. "You need more time for me to prove myself to you. Prove that I'm not your asshole of an ex. That I'm all in. I get it. This isn't a fling for me, Elsie. I'd decided I was done with women. After what Corinne did, I was *done*. Then you kind of knocked me on my ass. You're everything I've ever wanted. Loyal, hardworking, funny, beautiful, and a damn good mother. I always wanted children. But I'm more thankful than I can say that I didn't have any with Corinne. It's probably going to freak you out, but I have to admit I *can* see myself having kids with you."

Elsie swallowed hard. He wasn't wrong. She *was* kind of freaked out.

"But not right now. You need time for me to show you that I've got your back. To let it sink in that your life, and Tony's, is different now. No matter how long it takes, I'll be here."

"How did we go from talking about condoms to me having children?" Elsie asked.

"No clue. But the bottom line is, you want me to wear condoms, I'll wear them. With no complaints. No weird faces. I'll do whatever it takes to protect you, both physically and mentally."

"It's hard for me to believe this is real," she admitted.

"It's real. *We're* real," Zeke reassured her. "Now...do you want me to go?"

"No."

Elsie hadn't realized how tense Zeke was until his shoulders lowered at her answer. "Thank you."

He'd worked hard today to put her at ease. Making her smile. Making sure she was relaxed. And Elsie realized at that moment— she hadn't worried about Tony since he'd left. In the past, anytime he was away from her, she was nervous until he got home. But today, even though he was going out into the woods with men she trusted but didn't know particularly well, she wasn't concerned. She wasn't sure if that made her a bad mom or not.

"Come on, let's get those books set up on a bookshelf. Then we can watch a movie or something," Zeke said.

Elsie caught his hand as he went to walk away. "Aren't we going to..." Her words trailed off.

"Make love? Have sex? Fuck? Yes to all three. But I want you one hundred percent on board with that before it happens. There's no rush. We'll hang out, chill, figure out what to have for dinner."

"Okay," she agreed.

"Okay."

Elsie let him guide her into the other room, where he got her settled on the couch. Then he grabbed the bag of books he'd bought, placing it on the coffee table in front of her.

For the next two hours, they did just what Zeke suggested. It felt weird to be just sitting and doing nothing, her life had been too busy for a long time. With Zeke right there by her side, Elsie didn't mind so much. The day had been perfect. *Zeke* had been perfect, up to and including his willingness to give her space if she needed it.

But as the minutes ticked by, she knew space wasn't what she wanted. She wanted Zeke. It was still a foreign concept to have a man be so in tune with her needs. The more time she spent with him, the more she *wanted* to spend with him. Some people might think it was weird to spend every day working with a man, then be perfectly content to spend the evening and next morning with him too. But not Elsie.

While Lilly was her friend, Zeke was her *best* friend. She felt as if she could tell him anything and he wouldn't even blink. She wanted to be that for him in return. While they had crazy chemistry, she wanted to know this man inside and out.

She knew a little about his time in the Army, and about his drug-addicted parents, but craved to know more.

"How'd you find yourself here in Fallport?" she asked.

Without hesitation, Zeke lowered the sound on the TV and turned his attention to her. She appreciated that when she or Tony was speaking, he always looked them in the eye, to let them know he was listening.

"You heard what I told Tony about one of my last assignments. It had all just gotten to be too much. I used to love what I did, but I'd started to dread being deployed. Not only because of what was happening at home with my wife, but because I didn't trust my superior officers anymore. It wasn't a good situation. So I got out when my reenlistment came up. I was kind of at a loss as to what I was going to do when Ethan got a hold of me. I'd met him a few times, as special forces teams tend to run across each other here and there, even work together occasionally. He heard I was out and wanted to know if I had any interest in joining the search and rescue team.

"He actually tried to make Fallport sound unappealing." Zeke chuckled. "Probably so I'd know what I was getting into. He said it was a tiny town, in the middle of nowhere, with no malls, no movie theaters, only one elementary, middle, and high school, and the trails we'd be working were overgrown and not well marked. I was intrigued by the job, and being in the middle of nowhere actually appealed to me after all I'd been through. I moved here without a second thought, and I've never been disappointed. What about you? What brought you here?"

Elsie shrugged. "I might not like being out in nature, but I love small towns. Quiet streets. Trees and mountains. Being away from the city. I also liked living in Virginia, just not the northern part near Washington, DC, which is where I lived with Doug. After I left him, I struggled to get by. First I stayed with a friend. Then I wandered around a bit, trying to find a place I liked for Tony, where we could settle. After a couple years of looking...I found Fallport. Of course, once we got here, I was so low on money I didn't really have a choice *but* to stay," she said with a small shrug.

"Well, I for one am thrilled that you're here. Both of you."

Elsie snuggled up next to Zeke, loving the feel of his arm around her shoulders.

"Did you tell your ex where you went?" he asked.

Elsie nodded. "Yeah. I didn't kidnap Tony, if that's what you're thinking," she said a little defensively.

"That never crossed my mind. I was just thinking about how much your ex has missed out on when it comes to his son."

"He really has," Elsie agreed. "He always knew our whereabouts, just in case he wanted to see Tony. And I wrote him when I got here and gave him the address of the Mangree Motel. He's never replied. Never shown even a little interest in seeing Tony since we left all those years ago."

"It's his loss," Zeke told her. "Tony is amazing."

"He is," she agreed. Then she shook her head. "How do you do that? We started out talking about you and then ended up once more talking about me and Tony."

"You're much more interesting than I am," Zeke said.

"That's definitely not true. How'd you come to own the bar?"

"It's not a very exciting story," Zeke hedged.

Elsie sat up. "Well, now I think I *need* to know. Especially with you sounding so reluctant to tell me."

"I'm not reluctant, it's just..." He sighed. "Fine. I was suckered by Art and the boys." At Elsie's surprised look, he continued, "I was bored. There's only so much hiking in the woods and working out I could do before going crazy. I'd stopped by the post office to get my mail, and the three musketeers were there, as always. Art told me the guy who owned the bar was moving. Said it was a shame, since he hadn't had any buyers for the place and it would probably just close down. Silas threw in his ten cents and mused that there was a guy up in Roanoke who was thinking about buying it and turning it into an oxygen bar. You know, where people sit around and inhale scented oxygen and shit? Then Otto muttered something about the guy who owns the Cellar maybe buying it."

"The pool hall? That place is kind of dangerous, right?"

"Yup. I played right into their hands and went to talk to the owner that day. A week later, I was the new owner of On the Rocks. My days of being bored were officially over, and those three guys still claim to this day that they saved the entire downtown area by talking me into buying it."

"They weren't exactly wrong. I can't imagine the vibe of the square if it became a rough place like the Cellar, or if it became a yuppie oxygen bar," Elsie said with a giggle.

"I was thinking about adding a smoking station," Zeke said with a completely straight face. "Putting it in the corner, and starting out with cotton-candy- and cherry-flavored smoke."

"Shut up," Elsie said.

He lunged forward, and Elsie wasn't prepared for his tickle attack. She did her best to fend him off, but she was laughing too hard. She found herself on her back on the couch, with Zeke hovering over her.

"You don't like my idea? I'm the boss, you have to like *everything* I suggest."

"Not when it's stupid," she told him.

Zeke's fingers dug into her sides once more, and Elsie couldn't remember when she'd laughed harder in her life. But then the teasing tickles changed. Morphed into gentle caresses, and Elsie realized Zeke was lying between her legs, pinning her down, his fingers touching the bare skin of her sides.

Zeke pushed her shirt up, baring her belly, and he leaned down, placing a gentle kiss on the small bump.

"So. Damn. Sexy," he said under his breath, warm puffs of air brushing against her skin.

"Zeke..." Elsie whispered as she grabbed hold of his shoulders. Not to push him away, simply to have something to hang on to when fire raced through her body as suddenly as if she were engulfed in a flashover.

He looked up, and the heat in his eyes seemed to burn her alive.

"I want you," he said softly. "More than I've wanted anything in my entire life. Let me love you?"

How could she say no to that? She couldn't. Not when she wanted him just as badly.

"Yes," she whispered.

CHAPTER FOURTEEN

Almost as soon as the word left her mouth, Zeke was standing and pulling her up with him. He had a firm hold on her hand as he led the way to her bedroom. The nervousness Elsie had felt earlier was gone, as if it had never been.

This was right. One of the most right things she'd ever felt in her life. She wanted to be with Zeke. Wanted to touch him and be touched in return. She knew with no doubts that making love with Zeke would be nothing like it had been with her ex. Doug had only been about *him*. Getting himself off, not caring if Elsie orgasmed.

Everything Zeke did was with Elsie's well-being in mind. From her workload at the bar, to getting Tony settled in after school at the library with Raiden, to making sure she ate healthy meals. Making love would be no different. In fact, she had a feeling she'd have to work twice as hard to make sure he took his turn in receiving pleasure, and didn't just see to her own.

Zeke had brought in his overnight bag earlier, not wanting to bring it inside when Tony was there. Another way he constantly looked after both her and her son's best interests.

The first thing he did after closing her bedroom door was go to his bag and pull out a box of condoms. He placed it on the small bedside table next to the queen-size bed, then turned to look at her.

Elsie fidgeted, wondering what she should do next. But she shouldn't have worried. Zeke lifted his arms, grabbed the material of his shirt behind his head and pulled it off. Leaving him in nothing but his jeans. He then unbuttoned his pants, but didn't push them off.

She stood stock still and stared at the most beautiful man she'd ever seen. A sprinkling of black hair covered his chest and got a little fuller as it disappeared into the front of his jeans. He had a tattoo of a shield with a skull in the middle on his left pectoral. There were words written underneath it. And while Elsie had never been the kind of woman who was turned on by tattoos, she had to admit, on Zeke, it fit.

Seeing where her eyes had gone, he said, "*De Oppresso Liber.* That's what it says. It's the Green Beret motto."

"What does it mean?" she asked softly, still staring at him from across the room.

"To free the oppressed. We fought for those who couldn't fight for themselves."

"Like me," Elsie said.

Zeke immediately shook his head. "No. You've done a hell of a job fighting for not only yourself, but Tony too. You don't need me."

"I'm thinking you're wrong about that," she said, more to herself than him.

Zeke lifted an arm. "Come here, Else."

For just a second, she was overwhelmed by this man. He was amazing. He had his flaws, but for the things that mattered, he was perfect. She felt so out of her league.

Longing flashed across his face, so brief she almost missed it, before he turned to pick up the shirt he'd just dropped on the floor.

The thought that he was going to leave got her feet moving. In seconds, she was plastered against him.

"Are you sure?" he asked, as he dropped his shirt once more.

"I'm nervous that I'm not going to live up to your expectations, but I'm sure that I want to try."

Zeke snorted. "The only expectation I have is that I'm going to lose it way too fast once I get inside you."

The images his words invoked made Elsie shiver.

"So that's why I'm going to take my time. Learn every inch of you before we come close to getting that far. Lift your arms."

He was both bossy and tender at the same time. Elsie loved the juxtaposition. She raised her arms and felt Zeke's hands at the hem of her shirt. She thought he'd quickly remove it, but instead, he inched the material up slowly. His fingers brushed against her sides as they moved upward.

When he had the shirt off, Zeke simply stared at her. Elsie couldn't help but arch her back a bit. The desire and reverence she saw in Zeke's eyes made her preen.

"Damn," he muttered under his breath, seconds before he reached for her. But instead of touching her breasts, he went for the fastening of her jeans. He knelt as he slid the material over her hips. Once again, his fingertips brushed her skin as he removed her clothes. She stepped out of the jeans and his gaze ran back up her body. His hands gripped her hips and he stayed crouched in front of her.

Elsie expected him to stand, and when he didn't, she raised a brow. "Zeke?"

"Shhhh. I'm memorizing the moment," he said in a deep tone she barely recognized. If she had any doubts about whether or not this man was truly attracted to her, they were completely obliterated as he gazed at her nearly naked body.

Elsie'd had a baby. And she had proof in the form of a belly she couldn't get rid of no matter how hard she tried. She also had stretch marks. They'd faded a bit over the years, but they were still evidence that she'd had a child. Her breasts were saggier than they probably should've been at her age.

But as Zeke knelt in front of her, licking his lips, Elsie felt more beautiful than she ever had. She could see the clear bulge in his pants, and that made her feel even more desirable.

This man wanted her. And she definitely wanted him back.

Just when she was about to reach for his arm to pull him up, Zeke's chin lifted and he stared up at her. "I don't know where to start," he admitted.

Elsie couldn't help it. She laughed. "I'm thinking us getting on the bed would be a good place," she quipped.

His lips quirked upward. "Yeah," he agreed, then stood. But he didn't lose bodily contact with her as he did so. His hand palmed her side, his thumb brushing against the skin of her belly and his fingers gripping her tightly as he turned them. He pushed her gently backward until her knees hit the mattress and she sat.

"Scoot back," he ordered.

Elsie had read some books where the hero was dominant. She wasn't so sure she'd like that sort of thing. But when Zeke told her what to do in that low, raspy voice of his, she understood why the heroines in those books were so willing to do whatever the heroes asked.

She moved backward, keeping her eyes on Zeke as she did. He shucked his pants off, pushing his underwear down at the same time. Elsie couldn't tear her eyes away from his cock. He wasn't much longer than average, but holy crap, he was *thick*.

Zeke grinned as he crawled onto the bed on his hands and knees. She lay back as he continued forward and blurted, "I was kidding about the extra-large condoms earlier, but you're huge."

His smile widened. "We'll fit," he said confidently.

Elsie gave him a skeptical look.

"We will," he insisted. "You were made for me. Besides, I'm gonna make sure you're soaking wet before we go there. Guarantee when we get to that point, you won't be thinking about anything other than wanting me inside you."

"I'm not sure whether or not to give you shit about being overly confident and conceited, or if I should be concerned over what's about to happen."

"Don't ever be worried about anything we do together," Zeke said immediately. "Whether we're in bed, in the car, at work, or hanging out anywhere else. You're always safe with me."

"Zeke," Elsie whispered, feeling overwhelmed.

Without taking his gaze from hers, Zeke curled his fingers around the elastic of her underwear. She lifted her hips to help him remove them. He threw the scrap of cotton to the side before moving his gaze downward.

He took a deep breath and moved along her body until he was lying between her legs. She had to spread them to give him room. He couldn't seem to take his eyes from her pussy. Elsie wasn't a fan of the completely shaved look. It took too much maintenance, and she didn't have time for that. But she did keep herself trimmed down there. Zeke seemed to approve.

Realizing she still had her bra on, Elsie arched her back and reached for the clasp behind her. The position was awkward, but she managed. She threw her bra off the side of the bed, and when she looked back down, Zeke was now looking at her boobs.

She did her best to swallow the chuckle that wanted to escape. Straight men were the same all over the world. Boobs always seemed to fascinate them.

"You're beautiful," he said reverently. "And all mine."

"Are you mine in return?" she asked. If any other man had said that, she would've set them straight. She didn't "belong" to anyone. She was her own person. Period.

But hearing Zeke say those words in that low, rumbly voice of his as he gazed on her in admiration, made her want to claim him right back.

"Damn straight I am," he said. Without another word, he lowered his head.

At first, he simply nuzzled her, inhaling deeply, as if learning the shape and feel and scent of her. Then he looked up again from between her legs. "You ready?"

Elsie laughed a little nervously. "Yes?" It came out more of a question than an answer.

Zeke grinned. He rubbed his beard against the sensitive inner skin of her thigh, making Elsie squirm. Then he apparently decided to quit messing around and got to work.

At the first touch of his tongue to her clit, Elsie jerked in his grasp. It had been a very long time since anyone had gone down on her. But the memories of any past lovers were obliterated as Zeke blew her mind.

He used his fingers, tongue, and lips to make her forget anyone and everything but him. The feel of his beard against her skin was one of the most sensual things she'd ever felt. The sounds he made as he feasted on her were borderline obscene. Guttural moans, long slurps, deep grunts, and even a murmured expression of ecstasy now and then, all serving to ramp up her pleasure.

It wasn't long before Elsie was rocking her hips. Her thighs widened and her fingers sank into his hair, holding him to her tightly as she soared higher and higher.

Her reaction seemed to excite him. He locked his lips over her clit, eased two fingers inside of her, and began to finger-fuck, sucking hard on her sensitive bundle of nerves.

Generally, the orgasms Elsie had given herself over the years had been pleasant. Not overwhelming, not anything particularly memorable, but nice.

This was anything but "nice." The pleasure that rolled through her body was almost painful in its intensity. She'd never felt anything like it. Her entire body locked as waves of bliss rolled through her.

She thought Zeke would lift his head and get on with their lovemaking after she came...so it shocked the shit out of her when he didn't stop sucking on her clit.

"Zeke!" she exclaimed. "Too much! I can't..."

But he ignored her, and in fact his fingers sped up their thrusts in and out of her body, his tongue thrashing against her clit.

One orgasm rolled into another, and Elsie's stomach actually hurt from clenching so hard. Her thighs shook uncontrollably and it was hard for her to catch a breath. Every nerve ending in her body seemed to be on fire. Her fingers gripped Zeke's short hair so tightly, she had to be hurting him, but she couldn't let go. Needed to hold onto something to keep from shattering into a million pieces.

He finally lifted his head, and Elsie took a much-needed deep breath. Even his warm exhalations on her clit made little shivers of pleasure race through her body.

"Holy crap," she whispered.

"I knew it would be like this," he said softly. "You respond so perfectly."

"Only to you," Elsie blurted.

"*Fuck yeah*," he crowed.

She didn't even care that she was stroking his ego. Hell, he deserved it. She'd never come as hard as she just had. She wasn't even sure she'd one hundred percent enjoyed what he'd done, based on the extreme intensity alone, but she couldn't deny she felt incredible in the aftermath.

Lifting her head, she looked down her body and saw Zeke hadn't moved from between her legs. One hand was resting on her belly and the other was gently stroking her pussy. His thumb was sliding through the moisture he'd wrung from her as if he were a conqueror enjoying the spoils of war. She squirmed a little when he didn't move.

"Zeke?"

"Yeah?"

"Are we...I want you."

"And I want you," he said immediately. "But I don't think you're wet enough yet." Then he lowered his head.

"Oh, shit!" Elsie cried as she went from being relaxed and boneless to being right on the verge of coming once more.

Apparently, he was serious about making sure she was wet enough to take him without any issues, because he made her come a third time. She could feel how soaked she was. Zeke's face glistened with her juices. He licked his lips as his fingers eased in and out of her body lazily.

When he moved upward, Elsie was sure he was finally going to make love to her—but instead, he stopped when his head was even with her chest. The hand between her legs never stopped its gentle caress as he took one of her nipples in his mouth, supporting his weight with his elbow.

Elsie was overwhelmed with sensations. She'd never been the object of so much attention. Foreplay in the past had consisted of being fingered and her giving the guy she was with a blow job. This was...

She didn't know what this was.

Zeke sucked her nipple and her back bowed. She wasn't sure if she wanted more or wanted him to stop. Her hand landed on the back of his head and she inhaled sharply.

"You're so damn perfect," he said as he blew on the stiff tip. "So sensitive."

Elsie could only moan.

"Can you come from me sucking on your tits?" he asked.

Elsie stared down at him. The word "no" was on the tip of her tongue, but she reconsidered. She had a feeling this man could make her come simply by looking at her. Her body didn't feel like it was her own anymore. Zeke owned it. Owned *her*.

"How about we find out?" he asked without giving her time to come to her wits and answer.

The next twenty minutes or so were spent with Zeke experimenting, finding out what she liked, what might push her over the edge. And while she may not have been able to come with just attention to her breasts and nipples, with the addition of his fingers between her legs, she managed one more thankfully not-as-overwhelming orgasm.

When she stopped shaking, Zeke lifted his head and stared at her. The confidence and pride in his eyes shook Elsie to her core. Suddenly, it wasn't enough to lie back and take. She wanted to give him some of the same pleasure.

She sat up and put a hand on Zeke's chest, pushing him backward. He went willingly, since there was no way she could overpower this man. But instead of scaring her, that thought turned her on even more. He was letting her take control for the moment, but there was no doubt who was in charge in this bed.

* * *

Zeke lay back, the heady scent of Elsie in his mouth, on his fingers, permanently embedded on his very soul. She'd been so damn responsive, he hadn't been able to get enough. He'd pushed her hard, but instead of shutting down, Elsie seemed to open up to him more and more. He felt even closer to her now than he already had.

She knelt over him, her breasts hanging down, making him want to suck on them all over again. She straddled one of his legs, and he could feel her wetness against him. God, he'd never seen anything as beautiful as when he'd pushed her over the edge. He could've spent all night between her legs, making her orgasm over and over and over, licking up the proof of her pleasure. As it was, he could feel her juices in his beard, and it made him want to sit up and pound his chest in some sort of over-the-top Neanderthal way.

His thoughts scattered when she lowered her head. Her hair brushed against his belly and he quickly brought a hand up and caught it in his fist. He wanted to see her take him. The sight of her tongue coming out to lick the head of his dick was as carnal as anything he'd ever seen or fantasized. Even more so because of the shy, lustful look she aimed his way as she licked her lips, then took as much of him into her mouth as she could.

A long, drawn-out groan escaped, but Zeke refused to close his eyes. One of her hands grasped the base of his cock, moving up and down in tandem with her mouth as she bobbed on him.

Fuck, he was seconds away from coming, but there was no way he was going to stop her. He reached down and wrapped his hand around hers at the base, squeezing hard, cutting off the premature orgasm.

"Keep going," he rasped when his actions made her pause.

The smile that curled her lips was sexy as hell.

Zeke bent one knee and moved it outward. Since Elsie was straddling his other leg, he couldn't move that one. Her free hand cupped his balls, and another groan escaped Zeke's lips. Her movements were untried, somewhat unsure, and he'd never had a better blow job than this one.

He held on as long as he could, but he knew this was going to be over before he was ready if he didn't do something.

Taking a deep breath, Zeke sat up, pulling Elsie's mouth off him. The loss of her warmth was almost painful, but Zeke knew it was only a matter of time before his cock would be buried deep in the hot, wet core between her legs.

He pulled her face up to his and kissed her. He could taste himself on her tongue, just as she had to be able to taste herself on his lips. The moment was carnal and intimate.

Without lifting his lips from hers, Zeke rolled them and reached for the box of condoms on the table next to the bed. More than thankful he'd had the foresight to open the damn box before placing it on the table, he still fumbled trying to get a packet out.

He finally tore his mouth away and kneeled to hover over her. Elsie was on her back, legs spread, a lazy smile on her face. Her chest was blotchy pink from her earlier orgasms, and he had a hard time looking away from her to see what he was doing.

He spread his knees, pushing her thighs even farther apart. Her pussy glistened with her earlier orgasms, and even as he watched, a bead of come leaked out from between her lower lips. It was all Zeke could do not to lean close to lick it up.

He rolled the condom down his length, wishing he didn't have to use it. But he'd promised to take care of his woman, and that was exactly what he would do. Though coming inside her, filling her with his seed, making a baby, was something he definitely wanted in the future. The thought didn't even freak him out. He'd known from that first kiss that he wanted a permanent relationship with Elsie.

"Now, Zeke. Please," she whispered. Her hands moved to his hips and her thumbs brushed against his hip bones. It was an innocent touch, but it still made his dick twitch with impatience all the more.

Zeke scooted forward, stretching Elsie's legs to the limits. She lifted them and wrapped them around his waist. As if Zeke's cock had a homing beacon, the head notched between her legs without him having to guide himself.

Reaching down, he took the base of his cock in his hand and used her juices to lubricate the tip.

"You ready?" he couldn't help but ask.

In response, Elsie chuckled. "If you can't tell how ready I am for you, we've got a problem."

Smiling, Zeke pushed the head of his cock inside her.

He had to grit his teeth not to come right then and there. He wasn't even all the way inside and it felt as if she were strangling his dick.

They both moaned.

"Yes, Zeke. More!"

"I don't want to hurt you."

"You aren't. I need *more*. Please!"

He'd wanted to make her beg, but now that she was...Zeke found he didn't enjoy it as much as he thought he would. He didn't want her to have to beg for *anything*. Even his cock.

He moved slowly, aware of how tight she was and how thick *he* was. He pushed in a bit, then pulled back, feeding his cock to her in increments.

After a few small thrusts, she apparently lost patience and pushed her hips up on his next slide. He sank far deeper than he'd been before, and knowing he was a goner, Zeke didn't stop. He pushed all the way inside her welcoming sheath.

"Yes!" she exclaimed. "God...I'm so full. Holy crap, Zeke. You feel amazing...More. Please, more. *Move!*"

He was as gone as she was. Nothing could've stopped him from thrusting at that moment. Zeke had meant to take this slow and steady. But he couldn't stop himself from pulling back and sliding back inside her, hard. The friction was delicious, and he knew from this moment on he'd crave this. *Her.*

The gentle lovemaking he'd planned was thrown out the window as he fucked her like an animal. Her tits bounced up and down on her chest with each thrust. Her hands grabbed his ass and she dug her fingernails in as he rocked his hips faster and faster.

Sweat beaded on his forehead as the orgasm he'd managed to hold back earlier surged forth once more.

It was the long, high moan from Elsie that pushed him over the edge. To Zeke's surprise, he felt himself coming. He hadn't meant to come before she'd exploded one more time, but he couldn't stop it. She was too tight. Too hot. Too wet. Too *everything.* The sounds his cock made as he tunneled in and out of her body were loud and lascivious, their bodies slapping together with each thrust. He'd never been so turned on in his life.

He shoved himself inside her as far as he could get and threw back his head as he came. Warmth surrounded his cock from his come inside the condom, and it was all he could do to hold himself up. His cock didn't soften all the way when he was done. He wasn't quite ready to go again, but he was more than content to keep his dick buried deep within her body.

Looking down, Zeke saw Elsie was smiling up at him.

"Hey," she said softly.

Shifting slightly, Zeke reached between them and gathered some of her juices with his thumb and began to massage her clit.

Elsie jerked against him, and he grunted at the feel of her inner muscles clenching his cock. "Zeke, I'm...Holy crap, this is..."

He loved that she couldn't seem to form a coherent sentence. He pressed hard against her clit, needing her to come one more time. "I'm sorry," he told her.

"For what?" she asked, even as her hips jerked upward.

"For coming before you."

Elsie looked surprised. "Um, did you forget all the orgasms you gave me before?" she asked.

"They don't count. I mean, they do, but that was to make sure you could take me. And for the record, that's gonna happen every time we make love."

"I'm not sure I'll survive that again," she panted.

"You will. And I'll do my best to make sure you come first when I'm inside you in the future, but I'm not sure how successful I'll be. You feel so damn good. My cock fits perfectly inside you, Else. We were made for each other. But I feel cheated that I missed feeling you come around me. Gonna rectify that now. And I'm gonna want *this* every time too."

"*Zeke*," she moaned.

"That's it," he urged, stroking her clit harder. "Come all over me, sweetheart. Let me feel it."

She gasped and her thighs tightened around his hips as her body began to shake. She let out an adorable little screech as she flew over the edge.

The feeling of her tightening around his cock was indescribable. It was almost painful, but in the best way.

It was official. Zeke was addicted to this woman.

He moved his hand from between her legs and lowered his body over hers as she came down from her latest orgasm. They were both sweaty and flushed. Elsie's hair was mussed on her pillow, and he knew there was most likely a huge wet spot under where they were laying.

He'd never felt as close to another human being as he did with Elsie right that moment.

He pressed his lips to the side of her neck, almost too overwhelmed to look at her. He felt her turn her head and kiss his temple, the gesture so intimate and loving, he closed his eyes to memorize the moment. Her hands caressed his back, and her legs wrapped around him. They were as intertwined as two people could be, and he still wanted to get closer.

He'd never had this. His ex had always pushed him away as soon as the sex was done. Zeke hadn't even known he'd *needed* this until right this moment.

He didn't want to move, but knew he had to ditch the condom. Sighing, he lifted his head and looked down at the woman who owned his heart. "I need to get up for a second."

She nodded and slowly dropped her legs from around him.

Gritting his teeth, he pulled out of her body. He hated to leave her. Hated to separate from her for even a moment. He got out of bed, not feeling self-conscious at all as he headed for the small bathroom.

He was back within moments. But not knowing if she'd prefer to sleep alone, for him to go home, he couldn't help but feel uncertain about what would happen next.

He shouldn't have been. Elsie had scooted under the sheet, and, as he approached the bed, she lifted it, welcoming him back to her side. Zeke breathed out a relieved breath when Elsie immediately plastered herself against him once he lay back down. Her arm went across his stomach, one of her legs hitched up and over his thigh.

Wrapping his arm around her, Zeke sighed in contentment.

"I'm not sleeping on the wet spot," she said softly.

Zeke chuckled. "Noted."

"Not that it's time for bed, but I'm not ready to move yet. Is that okay?"

"Me either. This is perfect."

They were both silent for a long moment before Elsie lifted her head. She scooted up so their faces were even. Then she leaned down and kissed him. It was a long, slow kiss. One full of promise, and so intimate, Zeke felt as if he'd been stripped raw when they finally broke it off to take a breath.

Elsie moved down and rested her head back on his shoulder and squeezed him tight. "For the record?"

When she didn't continue, Zeke asked, "Yeah?"

"I liked that. A lot."

He chuckled. "Me too."

He felt her smile against his chest.

They dozed a bit after that. Then got up and took a shower. Together. Which was hilarious, because the shower definitely wasn't big enough for both of them. They ended up making love with Elsie leaning over the bathroom counter while Zeke took her from behind. Then they got cleaned up—again—and cooked dinner.

Afterward, they lay on the couch, and Zeke went down on her once more. He couldn't get enough of her taste. The feel and sight of her orgasming in his arms, under his tongue. He carried her back into the bedroom and did what he promised to do earlier but hadn't had the patience for. He learned every inch of her body, as she did his.

They fell asleep in each other's arms.

It had been a very long time since Zeke had slept so deeply. Usually visions of the things he'd seen and done in the military haunted his dreams. But that night, he slept more peacefully than he had in years.

CHAPTER FIFTEEN

By the time Sunday night came along, Elsie was sore but completely satisfied. She never expected things between her and Zeke to be as...explosive...as they'd been. He was true to his word, making sure she'd had several orgasms before he ever came close to making love to her. And it was definitely making love. There was no doubt there were strong feelings on both their parts.

Elsie was optimistic about their future. She'd always assumed she would spend the rest of her life alone. She'd raise Tony until he was old enough to either go to college, or move out after he graduated high school and got a job. But now, she saw Zeke right there with her. Maybe they'd have children together, maybe they wouldn't. But whatever happened, she wanted him by her side, and Elsie had no doubt he felt the same.

Tony had come back to the apartment jazzed up and excited about his camping trip. He'd talked nonstop for a full hour, telling her and Zeke everything he, Rocky, and Brock had done. He'd looked like he'd been rolling around in the dirt and smelled like a sweaty little boy. He only agreed to take a shower once he was satisfied he'd told them all the important things he could remember about the trip.

It had been hard to say goodbye to Zeke Sunday night. Even after only one night in his arms, Elsie was addicted. But she wasn't ready to have sleepovers with him while Tony was there, and he agreed. Especially since the apartment was so new to her son.

The next couple days were great. Tony was happy to have his own room, still riding high from his camping trip with "the guys," and was thrilled Zeke was hanging out with them every evening.

Elsie was feeling mellow and content. The amount of money in her bank account, while small, was still more than she'd ever had before—thanks to Ethan and Lilly's generous gift—her son was as happy, and the stolen intimate moments she and Zeke indulged in made her feel as giddy as a teenager. They hadn't made love again, but the looks she saw on Zeke's face when she caught him staring at her at work were enough to make her blush.

The staff noticed the change in her and Zeke's relationship— the few who hadn't already—and were thrilled for them both.

Everything had been going so well, it took Elsie by surprise when she picked up Tony at the library after work on Wednesday, and he was in an awful mood. He was grouchy, not answering any of her questions, and actually snapped at her when she asked what he wanted for dinner.

It was completely out of character, and by the time they were home, and he'd stomped into his room and slammed the door, Elsie was firmly worried.

This wasn't like him. Not at all.

After work, Zeke usually gave her a little time to get settled in after the day before he came over. It gave mother and son some time alone to talk about school and life in general before he arrived. Sometimes he brought dinner, other times he or Elsie cooked.

When Zeke knocked on the door that night, and Tony still hadn't talked to her, Elsie was beside herself.

"What's wrong?" he asked as soon as she opened the door.

"It's Tony."

"Is he hurt?"

Hearing the concern in Zeke's voice helped Elsie calm down a fraction. She took a deep breath. "No. But he's not himself. He's extremely moody. He barely said two words to me on the way home and when we got here, he shut himself in his room and hasn't come out since."

"Hormones," Zeke said with a nod.

"He's only nine!" Elsie countered.

"Nine going on fourteen," Zeke said.

"Will you talk to him?" Elsie asked, dismissing the hormones remark. She wasn't ready for a teenage boy yet. It was way too soon. She wanted her little boy to stay a little boy a touch longer.

Zeke gave her a look she couldn't interpret. "What?"

"Will you talk to him?" she repeated. "See if you can find out what's wrong? Maybe he'll talk to you."

Zeke continued to stare at her.

"If you don't want to, that's okay," she said quickly.

"It's not that. I just...You trusting me to find out what's wrong... it means a lot."

"Zeke, he loves you," Elsie said. "Of *course* I trust you. You've been nothing but a positive influence in his life. There's no guarantee he'll tell us what's wrong, but maybe while I'm making hamburger casserole, you can get him to open up."

Zeke stepped into her space and took her face in his hands. "Means the world to me that you trust me with him."

Elsie took hold of his wrists. Being this close to him made her hormones spring to life. But this wasn't the time or place to think about sex. "*You* mean the world to me," she said softly.

"You guys want to spend the night at my place this weekend?" he asked, seemingly out of the blue.

"Um...yes?"

"Good. My walls are thicker than the ones here. And the guest room is across the house from mine. But there's no pressure. Okay?"

Her pussy spasmed. "You would no sooner pressure me to do something I didn't want to do than ignore a call to search for someone lost in the woods," she told him. "And I can't think of anywhere I'd rather be this weekend than with you."

"You think Tony will be okay with both of us staying in my room?" he asked, running a thumb over the apple of one of her cheeks.

"Yes. I don't think our relationship is what's bothering him."

"Okay. We'll take things slow. If he seems to be upset about us spending more time together, we'll back off. Figure something out."

Once again, Elsie wondered how she'd gotten here. How she'd somehow managed to attract a man as wonderful as Zeke.

"I'm gonna go see what's up with Tony. You good?"

"Now that you're here, yeah. You'll tell me what he says?" she couldn't help but ask.

"Of course," he said, sounding surprised. "I'd never keep anything about your son from you."

"Thank you."

"You don't have to thank me for that," he said. He leaned down and kissed her. It wasn't a peck, but it wasn't a full-blown, precursor-to-sex kiss either. It was perfect for the moment. "Be back soon."

"Take your time," she told him as he headed into the small living area of the apartment.

Elsie watched him go, relieved he was there, and hoping Tony would tell him what was bothering him. It felt good to share parenting duties. Having someone she could trust felt amazing.

Shaking her head, she left the small entranceway just inside the apartment door and headed to the kitchen to make dinner for her boys.

* * *

186

Zeke knocked on Tony's door softly. "Hey, bub. You in there?"

"Yeah."

The boy's response wasn't very enthusiastic. But Zeke cracked his door open anyway. He saw Tony sitting on his bed, his back to the headboard, his feet flat on the mattress, his arms around his knees.

Zeke went inside the small room and shut the door behind him. He went to the bed and sat on the edge. "Tough day?" he asked.

Tony shrugged.

"You know, sometimes it helps to talk about what's bothering you," he tried again.

The boy let out a huge sigh, then looked up at Zeke, his eyes full of sadness. "Why are some people such jerks?"

"If scientists could figure out why some people are mean and others are sweet and nice, the world would be a much better place," Zeke told him.

Tony frowned.

"Talk to me, bub. Your mom's worried about you. It isn't like you to be grumpy."

To Zeke's surprise, he didn't have to push any more than that.

"Remember that kid I told you about? Bridger?"

"The one who has the ATV, right?" Zeke asked.

"Uh-huh. He was bragging again at school today. Telling everyone he got to drive it around last night on his property. Then he started making fun of me. I don't even know *why*. I never bother him at all. He said that I'll never get to drive an ATV because my mom's so poor. He made fun of me for living in a motel for so long, saying I was pathetic for being so excited to be in an apartment. I guess he overheard me talking to Gabe or something." Tony met Zeke's gaze again. "I didn't care that he was talking shit about me, but when he started in on Mom, I got really mad."

Zeke felt the urge to teach this Bridger kid a lesson in humility himself. But he remained calm. "What'd you do?"

"Nothing," Tony said sadly. "I told him to shut up and walked away."

"That had to be a hard thing to do," Zeke said.

Tony frowned. "I thought you'd tell me it was the *right* thing to do," he said.

"It was," Zeke agreed. "But that doesn't mean it was easy. Sometimes doing what's right is the hardest thing ever. What would've happened if you got in a fight with this Bridger kid?"

"I would've gotten in trouble," Tony mumbled.

"Exactly. Which would make your mom sad. And worried. And maybe you would've gotten a reputation for being a troublemaker in school. Teachers would look at you differently. Maybe other bullies would decide that they want to pick on you too. You'd take up smoking at age eleven. Get a tattoo at twelve. Move out at thirteen, live the life of a deadbeat."

By the time he stopped speaking, Tony was smiling. "You're weird," he told him.

Zeke smiled back. "All I'm saying is, doing what's right instead of what you really want to do is the responsible thing. And it makes you the better man."

"I guess," Tony said.

"I'm proud of you," Zeke told the boy. "Your mom is one of the hardest-working, nicest, and most-loving people I know. She'd do anything for anyone, even if it meant giving away her very last dollar. And you know firsthand that she was willing to go hungry so you could eat. Anyone who makes fun of a person like that is stupid. And pathetic.

"But I'll tell you this...if in the future, there comes a time when you need to defend yourself against this Bridger person, you do it. Boys like him need to be taught a lesson. He's probably going to always be a bully. Spoiled people sometimes are. Everything they have is given to them. They don't have to save up, sacrifice, or work for the things they want. And if you get in trouble, so be it."

Tony's eyes went wide. "You won't be mad?"

"Nope. Not if you're defending yourself or protecting your mom, or anyone else who needs it. Here's the thing, bub. There will always be people bigger, stronger, and more powerful than some. If those people use their strengths against others, they deserve to be taken down a peg. You understand?"

"I think so."

"I'd much rather you be a protector than a bully," Zeke told the boy. "Not that I want you to go around knocking kids down for fun or anything. Because that's not cool either. But sometimes you have to remind those bullies that there are people in the world who won't put up with their shit."

"That's what you did," Tony said. It wasn't a question. "In the Army. You took down the bullies."

Zeke nodded slowly. "Yeah, I guess it is. You know what?"

"What?"

Zeke was pleased that Tony sounded a little less down. He wasn't sure if he'd said anything Elsie would approve of, but what was done was done. "I told you before that I'd teach you how to drive. You still want to do that?"

Tony's eyes widened and he nodded enthusiastically.

"How about now?"

"Now?" Tony asked in confusion.

"Yeah."

"But it's a school night."

"It is. But we aren't going to be staying out all night drinkin' and smokin'," Zeke teased.

Tony giggled. Then sobered. "I'm only nine. Too young to drive."

"Yup. But so is Bridger, and his dad lets him drive that ATV," Zeke said.

Tony sat up straighter. "I'm not sure Mom's gonna let me."

"Leave your mom to me." Zeke reached out and put a hand on Tony's leg. "You're a good kid," he said. "It sucks, but there will always be people like Bridger in the world. You're getting to an age in school where bullies are starting to be meaner to people. You find those kids—the ones who are made fun of, who are different, who get cornered on the playground, who are learning to hate school because they feel as if they have no support—and you be extra nice to them. Be their friend. Trust me, being nice will make you happier. I've never met a happy bully," Zeke told him. "The saying 'sticks and stones will break my bones but words will never hurt me' is a big fat lie. Words *can* hurt. But being a friend can go a long way toward making those words not hurt as much."

Tony nodded.

"Right, so you want to change or anything before we head out for your first driving lesson?" Zeke asked.

"No, I'm ready," Tony said, dropping his legs and scooting off the side of the bed.

"Okay, give me a minute to talk to your mom and we'll go."

"Awesome. Zeke?"

"Yeah, bub?"

"Thanks."

"You're welcome. Anytime you want to talk, anytime you need me for anything, I'm here."

The boy nodded, and Zeke stood. He wasn't sure what he was going to say to Elsie to make her all right with taking her son out to drive...but he'd think of something.

He exited Tony's room and went into the living area. As he expected, Elsie's eyes were on him as soon as he stepped into view. He went straight to her. He backed her up until she was leaning against one of the counters in the galley kitchen.

"Is he all right?"

"Yeah. A kid at school was being an asshole. It got to him."

Elsie sighed. "Why are kids so mean? I mean, I swear it seems as if they're turning nastier earlier and earlier. It used to be it wasn't until they were in middle school that the cliques and stuff really started."

"No clue. But you should be proud of him. He wasn't upset that the kid was mean to *him*," Zeke said.

"He wasn't?"

"Nope. This particular kid was talking trash about *you*. And that's what put him in a funk."

Elsie's expression was pure dismay. "I stayed in that motel too long—" she started.

"No."

"No what?" she asked, looking up at him.

"Don't do that. Don't take this on your shoulders along with everything else you're carrying. Tony's got more love in his life than most kids. The two of you have spent a lot of quality time together, time other kids don't get because they're sitting in front of a TV, or playing a video game, or on their mobile devices. You and Tony are not only mother and son, you're friends."

"True," she said softly.

"Right, so...I kind of promised Tony something. And I'm not sure you're gonna be too happy about it," Zeke told her.

"Oh, Lord. What?" she asked.

"In my defense, he first talked to me about it when we were in the drop-off line. Which really is the seventh level of hell."

To Zeke's relief, Elsie chuckled. "Agreed."

"Anyway, he was telling me about this Bridger kid having an ATV and bragging about driving. I wanted to make him feel better...and I told him I'd teach him to drive a *real* car." He held his breath as he waited for Elsie's reaction. When she continued to stare up at him, he said, "So, to help him feel better after a hard day at school, I suggested we go out this evening and give it a try."

"He's nine," Elsie said after a moment.

Zeke chuckled. "That's exactly what *he* said. I'm not going to head to the interstate and take him on a joy ride," he said. "I thought we'd go to the high school parking lot and drive in circles for a while. But I'm thinking I should probably start him out on your car, instead of my truck."

"That's probably smart."

Zeke blinked in surprise at her reply. "You aren't pissed?" he couldn't help but ask.

"No."

"Why not?"

"Are you going to let him get hurt?" she asked instead of answering his question.

"Hell no."

"Right, so that's why I'm not upset. I mean, you'll need to make sure he doesn't think he can take my car joy riding in the future whenever he feels like it, but I can just imagine how excited he is right now. And since I can't buy him an ATV, or even a freaking bicycle, you spending time with him, teaching him how to be safe in a car, is probably the most exciting thing he's done in his life so far."

This woman. She never reacted the way he thought she would. He put his hands on her waist and said, "Hop up onto the counter, Else."

She furrowed her brow in confusion, but did as he asked.

Zeke helped by lifting as she jumped up. He stepped between her spread legs and leaned in, meeting her gaze head on. "You don't need to give Tony a bike. Or material things. He just needs love. And he's got that in spades. Getting to know him has been an incredible experience. He's gonna be one hell of a man."

"That's the best compliment I could ever receive," she replied.

"Thank you for letting me be a part of his life."

"Thank you for *wanting* to be a part of his life," Elsie countered.

Zeke grinned. "I'm not planning on being gone too long. Probably less than an hour. But it'll mean he's in bed a little later than usual. And is he gonna starve to death if we put dinner off that long?"

Elsie giggled. "No. But you might have him eat a snack on the way to learning how to be a race car driver by age eleven."

Zeke shook his head and chuckled. His Elsie was funny. "Right. *You* gonna starve to death if we put off dinner?"

"No."

"Uh-huh. You wouldn't admit it anyway," he said with a shake of his head.

"Zeke, I'll be here at home. In my kitchen. With a pantry full of food—which feels amazing, by the way. I can grab something if I feel peckish before you get back. Seeing my boy smile is worth putting off dinner. Thank you for making him feel better."

"He would've pulled himself out of his funk without me," Zeke said.

"Yeah. But it would've taken a lot longer, and I would've worried about him all evening," Elsie countered.

"Is it okay?"

Zeke turned to see Tony standing in the entry to the hall that led to the bedrooms. He was biting his lip and looked worried.

Before he could say anything, Elsie beat him to it.

"Yes. But if you're going to do this, you need to listen to everything Zeke says. And don't think you can drive crazy fast. ATVs don't go all that fast, and a car is a lot more powerful. And you are never, *ever*, allowed to drive on your own until you're sixteen and have your license. Oh, and it's probably best if you didn't brag about driving my car at school. I know that'll be hard because you're going to want to put Bridger in his place, but Zeke could get in trouble if people find out that he let you drive."

That last part was a bit of a stretch, but Zeke wasn't going to contradict Elsie. It was cute how Tony was nodding his head dutifully, but Zeke had a feeling if he didn't get on with this, Elsie would come up with a hundred other warnings and rules for Tony.

"I'll be careful," Tony told his mom. Then he looked at Zeke. "Can we go now?"

Zeke chuckled. "Yeah, bub. You know how to start your mom's car?"

The boy rolled his eyes. "Duh. You stick the key in and turn it. Mom lets me do it all the time."

"Okay, take the keys and head out. Start 'er up and I'll be right there." Zeke felt Elsie tense against him, but he didn't let go of her.

"Cool!" Tony exclaimed. He ran toward the kitchen, grabbed his mom's keys sitting next to her purse, and headed for the door.

"All right, maybe I've changed my mind," Elsie muttered as the door slammed behind Tony.

Zeke didn't waste time. He pulled Elsie's ass to the edge of the counter, wrapping one arm around her waist and tangling a hand in her hair. When she looked at him in surprise, he spoke.

"Your trust in me means everything," he said softly. "I'm well aware that kid is the most important person in your life. You'd kill to protect him. As would I. He's safe with me, Else."

"I know. If I had the slightest doubt about that, there's no way I'd be okay with this crazy idea of yours."

Zeke chuckled. "What? Teaching a nine-year-old to drive is crazy?"

She rolled her eyes. "You know it is."

"There are plenty of kids even younger than him who are driving. Farm kids have to learn how to operate tractors and trucks and other vehicles. He'll be fine."

"Okay, but we don't live on a farm," she countered.

"Being picked on is no fun. And even if he can't brag about what he did, *he'll* know. I want him to feel special. And this was the first thing that came to mind when he told me about this Bridger kid bragging about his ATV."

"It's fine. Now, get going so you can get back. It's a school night and I'm sure Tony has homework."

"You know he'll finish it in like fifteen minutes," Zeke said. "Kid's smart as hell." He tightened the hand in her hair and pulled her head back a fraction. "Kiss me, then I'll get going."

Zeke lowered his head, and Elsie's lips met his with the same lust he felt coursing through his veins. The weekend couldn't come fast enough. He needed her under him again. Over him. On her knees in front of him. In his shower. It didn't matter how they made love, he only knew he craved her.

They were both worked up by the time he forced himself to let go. He helped her off the counter, then couldn't help but lean down for one more kiss. "Damn, woman," he said when he stepped back. "Maybe Tony can learn to drive by himself and we can stay here."

Elsie laughed. "Go," she ordered. "And if you get stopped by Simon or one of the other Fallport officers, leave me out of it."

It was Zeke's turn to chuckle. "Of course." He brushed a knuckle down her flushed cheek, then turned for the door.

Minutes later, he was sitting in the passenger side of Elsie's car in the school parking lot, instructing Tony on how to drive. They'd moved the seat all the way forward and he was sitting on a scrunched-up blanket Elsie had in the trunk so he could see over the dash.

"Good. Okay, so normally you'd use one foot for both the gas and the brake, but for now, you can use your left foot for the brake and right for the gas. Go ahead and push on the gas. Just a little." When the car started to move, Zeke grinned. "Awesome! You're doing it, bub!"

Tony had an intense look of concentration on his face as he went about three miles an hour through the huge parking lot.

Zeke snuck a picture on his phone to show Elsie. He was adorable, and keeping Elsie's comment in mind about her lack of pictures of her son, he wanted to share this moment with her.

"All right. We need to turn around. Turn the wheel a little my way. Good. Now harder. Yes! You've totally got it."

Too much speed seemed to freak Tony out, so they never really went any faster than about ten miles an hour, but after thirty minutes, the kid seemed to have the hang of the gas, brake, and turning. They'd made several circles in the huge parking lot, and Zeke couldn't have been more proud of the kid.

After he stopped the car and put it in gear, Tony turned to him with a huge smile on his face. "That was amazing!" he said.

"You did great, bub! You're a natural," Zeke praised.

Tony took a deep breath, looked like he was going to say something...but then looked out the windshield instead.

"What's wrong?" Zeke asked.

"Nothing. I just...this has been the best day ever," Tony said. He turned to look at Zeke. "I wish you were my dad."

Zeke blinked. He hadn't expected that, and wasn't sure what the right thing to say might be. But Tony continued, not giving him a chance to respond.

"I know you're not, but I still wish you were. Mom doesn't talk about him, but I can't help but wonder why my real dad didn't want me."

Zeke reached out and put his hand on Tony's shoulder. "We talked about this, bub. Because he's an idiot."

"Do you know him?" Tony asked.

"No. But anyone who meets you, and doesn't want to be your friend, is an idiot," Zeke said a little harsher than he probably should have.

He took a deep breath. He and Tony had already had this conversation, but he didn't mind repeating it as many times as the boy needed to hear it. "Relationships can be tricky," he said. "Your mom and dad's relationship not working out had *nothing* to do with you, it's all about him. Some men aren't cut out to be fathers, just as some women aren't good mothers. But he's the one missing out, Tony."

The boy nodded and sighed. "It's fine. I don't need him. I've got you. And Rocky, Ethan, Drew, Brock, Tal, and Raid. Brock is gonna teach me how to change the oil in the car. And Drew says I'm smart enough to be an accountant like him if I want to. Camping with Rocky and Brock was awesome, and I love Duke. Raid lets me hang out with him while I read at the library. And Tal's accent is awesome. He told me all the girls love it. And Ethan's gonna help me with my project for the science fair. We're gonna make a thingy that gives people a shock when they touch it. Not enough to hurt, but it'll be hilarious to see people's reactions." He grinned at the thought. "Anyway...I don't need my real dad. I've got you guys."

Zeke couldn't help but be touched. "Yeah, you do, bub."

"I love you, Zeke."

Zeke inhaled sharply at hearing those three words. Could his life be any better? "I love you too."

Tony, of course, didn't seem to feel the moment was as meaningful as Zeke did. "I'm hungry. Can we go home now?"

Zeke chuckled. "Yeah, kid. I'll teach you some rules about driving as we head back to your apartment."

"Cool. Are you staying for dinner?"

"Yup. That okay?"

"Uh-huh. Are you spending the night?" Tony asked.

Zeke wanted to say yes, but he needed to feel the kid out first. "Not tonight," he said carefully.

"Okay. But in case you're wondering, I'm all right with you staying. You like my mom, right?"

Zeke snorted. Like wasn't the word, but he nodded anyway. "Yeah, bub. I definitely like your mom."

"And you're dating?"

"Yup."

"When people are dating, they have sleepovers. So you and Mom should do that."

Zeke wanted to laugh. So much for worrying if Tony would be all right with staying at his place that weekend, and if he'd be concerned when he and Elsie shared a room. "How about this weekend?" he asked. "You want to come stay at my house?"

"Yes!" Tony said happily. "Mom too?"

"Your mom too."

"Good. Can we make a fire and have s'mores again?"

"If you want, sure."

"Awesome!"

Tony was a pretty laid-back kid. Yeah, he'd had a tough day, but luckily he'd been able to bounce back fairly quickly. Zeke attributed that to how Elsie raised him. He wasn't spoiled, he was empathetic and smart as hell.

Later that evening, after Tony had talked nonstop about his driving skills and the sleepover at Zeke's that weekend, and after he'd done his homework then settled in his room with a book, Zeke took Elsie in his arms by the front door.

It was later than Zeke normally left, and it was taking everything in him to make himself walk out the door. He was addicted to this woman, and wasn't ashamed to admit it. She made him happy on a level he hadn't experienced...ever. The feelings he had for her went way deeper than anything he'd felt in the past. The love he'd thought he had for his ex seemed small and insignificant compared to his feelings for Elsie.

"I haven't seen Tony this happy in forever," Elsie said. "I don't think he took a breath for a full ten minutes as he went over every second of his time with you tonight."

She wasn't wrong. "I love hanging out with him. He's fun," Zeke said.

Elsie merely shook her head. "He adores your attention," she said with a shrug. "Thank you for being so good to him."

"How could I not?"

"You'd be surprised. Some adults just don't like hanging out with kids."

"Then they're missing out," Zeke said.

Elsie nodded. "He sure sounds okay with us coming over this weekend."

"I was a little worried when he brought it up, but he reassured me that when people were dating, they had sleepovers."

Elsie laughed. "I'm relieved. I mean, he's nine, not four, but still."

"This is going to work out," Zeke said firmly.

"I hope so," Elsie whispered.

"I know so. Sleep well and I'll see you at work tomorrow."

"You want to come over in the morning?" she asked shyly.

"Want to? Yes. But you're having brunch with Lilly. There'll be times when a quickie is exactly what I want...but right now, I can't imagine not having a few hours to explore what we have together."

Elsie blushed, but she didn't protest.

"And now you're thinking about quickies, aren't you?" he asked with a grin.

"Can't *not* think about it," she complained.

Zeke leaned down and kissed her. He kept it short, didn't back her up against the wall and show her exactly how amazing quickie wall sex could be. But he hadn't lied. The more he touched her, the more he wanted to take his time and explore.

"I'll see you at the bar tomorrow. Let me know if you need anything."

"What would I need?" she asked, genuinely curious.

Zeke briefly thought about his ex. She was constantly texting him with shit she wanted him to do. Stop at the store. Fix something at the house. Elsie never asked him for anything...other than his time and affection. She was literally a dream come true.

"I don't know. But I'm always just a phone call away if you *do* need something."

"All right. Thanks."

Zeke kissed her on the forehead, then backed toward the door. The words "I love you" were on the tip of his tongue, but he held them back. He gave her a smile, and she returned it. Then he opened the door and headed out to his truck.

The night had been good. Really good. He hoped he'd been able to help Tony navigate the uneasy road to adolescence just a little. If nothing else, he'd made him smile. Teaching him to drive had been fun, but the boy had a ways to go before he'd be street-ready. That hadn't been the point, though. Spending time with Tony, making him feel special, bonding with him...that was the point.

And bonus, the kid had flat-out told him he approved of him dating his mom. Being all right with sleepovers was definitely a stamp of approval.

Zeke couldn't help but think of how the boy had said he loved him. Tony and Elsie Ireland had tunneled their way under his skin and into his heart so deeply, Zeke could hardly remember a time when they weren't a part of his life.

This was what love was. He thought he'd loved in the past, but he was wrong. The feeling of wanting to be with Elsie and Tony all the time was almost overwhelming, but in a good way. They'd all lived difficult lives before making their way to Fallport. Now, all Zeke could see was a bright future ahead of them.

CHAPTER SIXTEEN

Elsie couldn't keep her eyes off Zeke the next day. She'd lain awake forever the night before thinking about her life. About Zeke. She was in love with the man. He'd more than shown her he could be trusted with her heart, and with her son's.

She was finally starting to believe the words Zeke had said more than once. That her life would be easier now that he was in it. When he'd first made the claim, Elsie had mentally rolled her eyes. It was a bold statement. But he'd proven time and time again that he wasn't just placating her or trying to get her into bed. There had been plenty of times they could've had sex. Mornings after Tony had gone to school. Quickies here and there. He'd been clear that wasn't what he wanted from her.

But it was the care he'd taken with Tony the night before that made it clear she'd fallen head over heels for him. Elsie still wasn't thrilled with the thought of her nine-year-old driving, but she trusted Zeke. She'd been alarmed at the tales Tony had told after they'd returned last night, but Zeke had taken her aside and quietly explained that Tony hadn't gone above ten miles an hour, and the zooming he'd demonstrated with his frantic arm movements had only been in his imagination.

Zeke was treating both her and her son as if they were the most precious things in his life. Elsie couldn't remember ever feeling this safe with a man. It was heady. And scary. Zeke could hurt her more than Doug ever had.

Brunch with Lilly that morning had been fun. They'd gone to Sunny Side Up and Elsie had insisted on paying. She felt like a millionaire with all the money she was saving. That wasn't even close to being true, but she definitely felt comfortable enough spending thirty bucks on a meal, and it was the least she could do for her friend.

Lilly had told her that old man Grogan was almost done finalizing the design for the shirts he wanted to sell to all the Bigfoot hunters who would surely descend on the town when the *Paranormal Investigations* show Lilly had worked on aired. She'd also updated Elsie on the progress Ethan and his brother had made on the house.

And of course, she'd managed to discreetly pry into Elsie and Zeke's relationship. Since Elsie kept her personal life private at work, for the most part, it felt good to be able to talk about him with her friend.

She'd been a little worried about how quickly things were moving between her and Zeke, but Lilly just laughed, reminding her how fast her own relationship with Ethan had gone. It made Elsie feel a lot better. Looking at Lilly and Ethan, it was clear they were deeply in love and their relationship, no matter how fast it had started, was clearly working out. It gave her hope that if her friend could make it work, so could she and Zeke.

After brunch, Elsie had walked over to On the Rocks to start her shift. It might be the fact that she'd finally admitted to herself she was in love with Zeke, but everyone around her seemed to be in a fantastic mood. Elsie, Valerie, and Tiana joked with all the patrons, Reuben didn't complain for once about having to do an inventory of the alcohol so Zeke could make the weekly order, and even the people who came in for lunch were smiling and left larger-than-usual tips.

So when three-thirty rolled around and the door to the bar opened, Elsie was still smiling, ready to greet another regular.

She was completely unprepared to see the man who entered.

She blinked, sure her eyes were playing tricks on her. After the door shut behind him, it took a minute for her eyes to adjust after the harsh mid-afternoon sun was blocked again. By then, the man had walked closer, stopping almost in her personal space.

"Hello, Elsie," he said. "Long time no see."

Elsie didn't respond. She couldn't. She was so shocked, she couldn't get one word out.

She felt more than saw Zeke step up to her side. His hand landed on the small of her back, and just having him there made her mentally sigh in relief.

"What? Nothing to say?" the man asked. His eyes went to Zeke, and he frowned when his gaze traced down to Zeke's arm around her.

"Don't tell me you're dating," he said.

Elsie swallowed hard. "It's been a long time. What brings you to Fallport, Doug?"

At the sound of her ex's name, Zeke's fingers pressed more firmly against her back. She was just as surprised as Zeke to see him. It had never been her intention to hide herself or her son, and she hadn't...though she'd always suspected Doug wouldn't care *where* they were. And the fact that five years had passed since she'd seen or heard from him proved she was right.

"I've missed you. And our son. Where is he, anyway?"

Elsie frowned. "School."

"I thought he'd be out by now," Doug said.

She resisted the urge to roll her eyes. Even when Tony was a toddler, Doug hadn't bothered to learn anything about their son's routine. He didn't know what time he ate, took naps, or even when he went to preschool. The only time he really noticed Tony was when he cried, annoying Doug.

"Anyway...I missed you, Elsie. I've been thinking about how good we were together. Want to see if we can't patch things up so you can come home, and we can be a family again."

Elsie almost laughed in his face. He hadn't missed her. And home? She hadn't thought of his house in the DC area as home in a very long time. "You should've called," she told him. "It would've saved you a trip."

Once more, Doug's gaze shifted to Zeke before he looked at her again. This time, she could see a calculating look in his eyes. One she'd gotten used to seeing when she lived with him, but hadn't missed in the five years since. "I wanted to see my *wife*," he emphasized. "Reconcile. I admit I wasn't the best husband, but I've realized how much I love you and miss you. I want to try again."

Elsie opened her mouth to tell him there wasn't a chance in hell of her going back, but Zeke spoke before she could.

"Elsie is *not* your wife."

"That's how I still think of her," Doug said with a smarmy smirk.

"I don't think of you as my husband," Elsie told him. "In fact, I don't think about you at all."

"Don't be that way," Doug cajoled. "You've always been so defensive."

She stiffened at the implied criticism.

"Elsie, honey, we need to talk," he continued. "Alone," he added, looking meaningfully up at Zeke—way up, since he was so much shorter.

"Give us a second," Zeke said. And without waiting for Doug's reply, he took Elsie's hand and led her a few feet away, turning his back on her ex.

Before he could say anything, Elsie insisted, "I didn't know he was going to show up today. I didn't contact him."

"I know," Zeke said.

But he sounded...off. Elsie couldn't figure out exactly what was wrong.

Then she wanted to laugh. What was *wrong* was that her ex was here, calling her his wife, and saying he missed her and wanted to get back together. No wonder Zeke wasn't exactly happy right now.

"You want to talk to him?" Zeke asked. "Because if you don't, I'll kick his ass out."

Elsie sighed. She did *not* want to talk to Doug, but she also knew him. He was relentless. And stubborn. And he was obviously here for a reason. He wasn't going to go away until she heard him out. It was better to let him have his say now than try to put it off.

She shook her head. "I'll talk to him."

Zeke stared at her for a long moment. She could see a muscle in his jaw ticking as he clenched his teeth. "Okay. You want me to be there?"

She did. Oh, how Elsie wanted Zeke to have her back. But whatever Doug wanted to say probably wouldn't end well. Certainly he wouldn't paint her in a good light. She truly hadn't done anything wrong since leaving her ex, but she didn't want Zeke to hear the hurtful shit Doug would probably fling at her. It could make Zeke do something he'd regret. Doug wouldn't hesitate to push his buttons, then press charges if Zeke lost his temper.

No. She couldn't risk it. Doug was not his problem to solve.

"It's okay. I'll hear him out and then he'll probably leave."

"All right."

Zeke took a step back, and Elsie instantly wanted to blurt out that she'd changed her mind. That she wanted him by her side. But she straightened her shoulders. She could do this. She'd made the mistake of marrying Doug in the first place. She had to deal with this herself.

Still...she couldn't help but feel a smidge of disappointment. Which was completely irrational. But she didn't really *want* Zeke to give her a choice. Wanted him to simply insist on staying with her.

God! Doug wasn't back in her life for two minutes and she was already rattled.

When she turned back to Doug, he still had a smirk on his face. As if he thought he was winning the first round of whatever this situation was. Elsie had always hated that superior, righteous look he got when he thought he was getting exactly what he wanted.

"You can use the back office," Zeke told her.

Elsie felt his fingertips on the small of her back briefly before he stepped away. A shiver went through her when he left her with Doug. It was what she asked for, what she said she wanted, but the reality was already hitting her in the face.

She was going to be alone with the man who'd made her life a living hell.

Her walk was stilted as she led Doug down the hall toward the office. The second the door shut behind them, she turned to her ex and asked coldly, "What do you want, Doug?"

"Just what I said. I want to get to know my son. See if we can make a go of things again."

"You can see Tony. I've never hidden him from you. But as far as you and me go, we're done. Forever."

"Still overly emotional, I see."

Elsie winced. He hadn't been here more than five minutes and he was doing what he always did. Using his words to try to tear her down. Make her feel like she was worth less than him. She'd worked extremely hard to overcome the doubt and worthlessness he'd made her feel for years. To forget the way he'd stomped her self-esteem into the ground time after time.

She wasn't going to let him do it again.

"I'm not overly emotional," she said firmly. "You're just being an ass." It felt good to stand up to her ex. She'd never done it before, had always walked on eggshells around him. But he'd come to *her* workplace, to Fallport, after five years of silence. She wasn't the same person she'd been when they were married.

"You know what?" she suddenly decided. "I changed my mind.

I'm not doing this now. I'm at work. I'm busy. If you truly want to have some sort of relationship with your son, that's fine. But we'll discuss it later."

She walked toward the door, intending to open it so he could leave. But Doug stopped her, grabbed hold of her arm.

She rounded on him. "Let go of me!" she hissed.

He did. Immediately. "We need to talk."

"Fine. But not right now."

"Why not?" he whined.

He'd done *that* a lot in the past too. Whined to get his way. When that didn't work, he'd berate her. Make her feel awful for not being the kind of woman he seemed to want. But no more. She wasn't going to deal with his shit. Not now. Not ever again.

"Because you didn't give me a head's up that you were coming to Fallport. I need time to process."

"Right, because it's always about *you*," Doug sneered.

Elsie straightened. "Now? Hell yeah, it is. You came here, I didn't invite you," she reminded him. "And for the record, we aren't reconciling. No way in hell."

"I love you, Elsie."

She rolled her eyes. "Right. Which is why I haven't heard from you in five years. Cut the shit, Doug! You shouldn't have come."

He narrowed his eyes. "You won't keep me from my son," he threatened.

Elsie's blood ran cold, but she kept all emotion from her face. "I'm not trying to. But if you even *think* about trying to get custody, a judge will have something to say about you not so much as *calling* your son for five years."

"I don't want custody," he said in a rush.

Of course he didn't. Elsie barely suppressed the urge to roll her eyes again.

"I just want to see him. Talk to him. A boy needs a father figure in his life."

Tony had plenty of father figures in his life...starting with Zeke. But she didn't say that. "Fine. We'll talk later," she said firmly.

"When? How will I find you?"

"This isn't DC, Doug. It's Fallport. I'm assuming you're staying at the hotel at the edge of town?"

"Of course. There wasn't anywhere else," he told her.

There was the Mangree, which was much closer, but she didn't point that out. "I'll be in touch."

"I want to see Tony," Doug insisted for the millionth time.

"So you've said. But I need to talk to him first. Explain things."

"What *things*? I'm his dad. That's all he needs to know."

Elsie shook her head. Doug didn't get it. Never would. She really didn't want him back in Tony's life. He'd disappoint the boy, just like he'd done to her. And if he thought he could belittle their son and talk to him the way he had to Elsie when they were together, he was dead wrong. "I'll be in touch," she repeated, motioning toward the door with her hand, praying he'd just leave already.

She held her breath, sighing in relief when he glared at her once more, then finally stomped out of the office like a toddler having a temper tantrum.

Elsie sagged, her shoulders slumped. Standing up to Doug felt good, but it had also taken a lot out of her. She took a few minutes alone to get her anger and resentment toward the man under control.

She needed to see Zeke. Needed his reassurance that everything would be all right. That there was no way Doug was going to try to get custody of her son.

She walked back into the bar, looking around for a minute before frowning.

"You looking for Zeke?" Reuben asked from behind the bar.

Elsie nodded.

"He left."

She froze at that. "What?"

"After you went into the office with your ex, he left," Reuben repeated.

Elsie was stunned speechless. She couldn't believe he left without talking to her first. Yes, he was a grown man and didn't need her permission to do anything...but considering how protective he was, she would've thought he'd stay until Doug was gone, make sure she was all right.

It hurt.

A lot.

She was head over heels in love with the man and if the situation had been reversed, if Corinne had come into the bar, telling Zeke she wanted to get back together and that she missed him, there would be no way in hell Elsie would've left before speaking to Zeke, making sure he was okay.

"Did he say anything before he left?" Elsie asked.

"He didn't look happy," the bartender said with an apologetic shrug. "But no, he didn't say where he was going or why he left."

"Okay."

"You don't look so hot either," Reuben went on. "You're a little pale. Why don't you go on and head out. It's not busy right now. We can handle things, Elsie."

Normally, she wouldn't leave work early, but right now she was grateful. She needed to think. She was worried about her ex's motives. She wanted to talk to Zeke about everything, but he'd up and *left*, so that wasn't an option.

A part of her understood why he'd probably taken off. It was a lot to ask of him, stepping aside so she could talk to Doug alone. She knew it went against his instincts. But another part of her was extremely hurt. And confused. So she gave Reuben a nod. "Thanks. I think I *will* take off. If you're sure..."

"I'm sure," he said, offering a kind smile.

It didn't take Elsie long to say goodbye to the others and grab her purse. She'd go pick up Tony. Come up with an excuse as to why she was at the library so early. Figure out what to make for dinner...

Figure out how to tell him his father was in town and wanted to see him.

She *definitely* needed to figure out how to help Tony proceed with caution with Doug...when she knew all her son wanted was a dad.

She wanted to hope that Doug *had* come to his senses. But she couldn't. She knew her ex. He had an agenda. She'd bet everything she owned on that...which wasn't very much, but that wasn't the point.

Doug was going to hurt Tony. Elsie knew it. And she had no idea how to keep it from happening.

She'd never bad-mouthed Doug to his son. Didn't want to be "that" person. If Tony wanted a relationship with his father when he got older, she didn't want to give him any preconceived notions of what he was like. He'd have to form his own opinions, based on how Doug treated him. But that didn't mean she wanted to leave her son open to the disappointment and heartbreak she knew his father could inflict.

Sighing, Elsie rubbed her temple. She had a raging headache. And heartache. She had no idea what tomorrow would bring, but she'd take things one day at a time. Eventually, she'd talk to Zeke. Figure out why he left without a word.

But first, she needed to figure out what her ex wanted and why he was here. Needed to protect Tony. Everything else could wait.

* * *

Zeke paced his house, his adrenaline making him crazy. He couldn't stop thinking about what had happened. One second he'd been on top of the world, excited about spending the weekend with Elsie and Tony, and the next her ex was there, talking about how he still loved her and wanted her back.

What the fuck?

He'd needed some space. Needed to think.

He couldn't lose Elsie. *Wouldn't*. But it wasn't just up to him. And while he trusted her, a small part of him—the part still devastated by Corinne's betrayal—wondered...*would* she go back to her ex?

He was keenly aware of how badly Tony wanted a dad. He'd hoped he might be able to take on that role officially one day...but Doug's sudden appearance sent him reeling and might've blown that thought to smithereens.

Thinking about Doug calling Elsie his *wife* made him so angry he could barely see straight. It was ridiculous and irritating and inappropriate.

And he kind of wished Elsie had protested a little more.

He loved her so much. And while his insides had been twisted in knots, witnessing how calm *she* was about seeing her ex had hurt.

When she'd insisted on talking to Doug alone, Zeke had been devastated. She didn't want him to have her back. Didn't want him around.

It was shades of Corinne all over again.

He'd left the bar. Didn't really remember much about what he'd said to Reuben before taking off. His only goal was to get some air. Some space.

But as the afternoon turned to evening, he'd started to think a little more clearly.

He was still upset—evidenced by his continued pacing—but he was slowly starting to wonder if he hadn't made a huge mistake.

He had no idea what Elsie and Doug had talked about. But the woman he'd come to know had nothing good to say about her ex. Had never admitted a single regret about leaving him, or that she'd consider taking him back. And according to Elsie, Doug was cruel at every turn, always using his words against her.

Jesus...

He was an idiot for not staying. For not demanding to know what her ex wanted. It had been years since she'd left him, and not once had her ex tried to reach out to her or see his son. Why now? What if he was there to take Tony away from Elsie?

How was she feeling? Was she scared? Pissed? She was probably extremely upset after she got done talking with Doug, only to find Zeke had simply left.

Shit. He'd screwed up so bad.

When Elsie likely needed him most, he'd deserted her.

That one decision could've ruined all the trust he'd worked so hard to earn.

Zeke wanted to call her. Wanted to go over to her apartment. But he wasn't sure what he should say. "Sorry I was being a tool and left without making sure you were okay? How'd things go with your douchebag ex?"

How the hell did he apologize after such a huge fuck-up?

He was still kicking his own ass and trying to figure out what in the world he was going to do next when his phone rang.

For a second, Zeke had the desperate hope that it was Elsie calling. That she'd be fine and explain what had happened with Doug as if he hadn't left her alone to deal with the emotional backlash she must be feeling.

But reality kicked in immediately. No, there was no way Elsie would want to talk to him right now, not after the way he'd treated her.

When he looked down—he saw the call *was* from her, after all.

His heart beating fast, Zeke answered.

"Else?"

"It's Tony," a small voice said.

"Tony? What's wrong?" he asked urgently.

"It's Mom."

"What about her? Where is she? Is your father there? Are you all right?"

"She's here, and no, my dad isn't. She told me he was in town though. Is that true?"

"Yeah, bub. It is. I met him today."

"She told me he wants to see me. But I think that's weird. Isn't that weird? I mean, why now? I asked her but she didn't have an answer. Said it was up to me if I wanted to spend time with him and how much."

Ignoring his question—because it *was* weird; it was definitely weird—Zeke asked, "So, what's up with your mom? Why are you calling?"

"I thought everything was okay. But she wasn't talking a lot. Then after dinner, she said she was going to bed. She *never* goes to sleep before me. I tried to go in but her door was locked. And I heard her crying. I don't know what's going on, Zeke! I'm scared. Her phone was out here and you said I could call you whenever I needed to."

"I did say that, and I'm glad you did. I'm on my way."

"Really?"

"Yeah."

"Okay."

The immense relief Zeke heard in the boy's voice made his heart hurt. The kid was more than scared. He was terrified. Probably confused as well, considering what was going on with his father. "What's the code word this week?" Zeke asked.

"Lament."

Zeke couldn't help but smile. "And what does it mean?" he asked as he grabbed his keys and headed for the door.

"To feel sad for. I'm lamenting that I can't make my mom feel better."

Now Zeke's heart felt like it was breaking.

"I'm gonna fix this," he told the boy. "Don't open the door until I say the code word."

"I won't. Zeke?"

"Yeah, bub?"

"You'll make Mom feel okay again, right? Will you tell her that I promise not to leave her to go live with my dad? I figure maybe that's why she's sad. Maybe she's scared now that he's here, that I'll leave her because I've wanted a dad for so long."

Zeke took a deep breath before he responded. "I'll tell her, but I doubt that's why she's sad."

"Why then?"

Knowing he had to be honest, Zeke said, "I messed up today, bub. I hurt her. I didn't mean to, but I was shocked to see your dad here and needed some time to deal with that."

"I don't understand."

"I know you don't. But I'm going to fix it."

"Promise?"

"Promise."

"Good. Because I don't like to hear her cry."

This kid was killing him. Making Zeke understand *exactly* what he'd lose if he'd fucked up irrevocably. If he couldn't get Elsie to forgive him for leaving her with her ex without a word.

"Me either."

"Don't do it again," Tony warned. "We don't need you around if just you're gonna make her sad."

It was a weird feeling to experience both pride and guilt at the same time. He was proud of Tony for sticking up for his mom, and upset for putting the boy in the position to have to do so. With *him*. The man who should've stayed by her side from the second Doug made his appearance.

"I understand. And I give you my word that it won't happen again."

"Okay. Have you left yet?"

Zeke smiled. "Yeah, bub. I'll be there in probably less than five minutes."

"Good. But don't speed, because if you get a ticket it'll take you longer than five minutes."

"I won't. Thanks for calling me, Tony."

"See you soon. Bye."

"Bye."

Zeke hung up and took a deep breath. Then another. He wasn't happy that Elsie's ex was here, apparently wanting to make a second go at a relationship. But now that he'd had some time to think, he knew there had to be more to the man's visit than simply wanting Elsie back. Doug hadn't been in her life for five years. Hadn't lifted a finger to get to know his son or help her out. People like that don't suddenly change without a reason...or without a motive.

Zeke loved Elsie. Whatever was going on, they'd figure it out together.

Determination filling him, he pressed a little harder on the gas. He needed to fix what he'd done. The sooner the better. He just prayed Elsie would give him a chance to make things right.

CHAPTER SEVENTEEN

Zeke stood outside Elsie's bedroom door. He could tell Tony had been crying as soon as he'd seen the boy's face. Just another way he'd fucked up. Zeke had taken the time to hug him tight, and reassure him again that he'd make his mom feel better. He'd asked Tony to stay out in the living room, finding a movie on the TV for him to watch. Zeke was sure he was too distraught to pay much attention to it, but he was grateful for some time to make things right with Elsie without Tony overhearing.

He knocked on the door and heard Elsie's muffled voice say, "I'm fine, Tony. Just tired."

"It's Zeke," he told her. "Please open the door. I want to talk."

"Go away, Zeke," she said a little more forcefully. "We don't need to talk right now."

The hell they didn't. But Zeke wasn't going to have this conversation, wasn't going to grovel, through a closed door. He'd come prepared, since Tony had told him Elsie had locked herself in the bedroom. He stuck the stretched-out paper clip in the small hole in the knob and within seconds, quietly cracked the door open.

Thank God for cheap locks that were easy to pop.

He eased the door open wider and went inside, his heart immediately sinking further.

Elsie hadn't turned the light on. She was sitting on the floor, near the far side of the bed. Her back was against the wall and her legs drawn up. There were tear tracks on her face, and even as he entered, more tears spilled over her eyelids before she rested her cheek on her knee and looked away from him.

"Seriously—go away, Zeke. This day's been bad enough without you making it worse."

Zeke flinched, but ignored her request and walked over to where she was sitting. He lowered himself to the floor in front of her and put his feet on either side of her hips, the inside of his thighs touching her legs as he scooted closer.

Her tears fell faster. "I can't do this right now," she whispered.

"You don't have to do a thing. All I need you to do is listen to me," Zeke said.

Elsie closed her eyes and put her cheek back on her knees, turning her face away once more. She tightened her arms around her legs, her entire body shutting him out.

Her actions hurt. A lot. But Zeke understood. He shouldn't have left her with her ex. Shouldn't have left without talking to her, making sure she was all right.

"I shouldn't have left," he said quietly, wanting to reach out. Wanting to pull her into his arms. But he stayed where he was, his legs touching hers, close enough to smell her shampoo.

"When I first got married...I was so excited. I had the whole world in front of me. A beautiful wife. A career I was good at. The hope of a family. But within a year, all my hopes and dreams for the future was crumbling at my feet. Instead of support from my wife, she gave me disdain every time I deployed. I never got any letters or emails while I was away. When I came home, she gave me the cold shoulder for at least a week. I guess to punish me for leaving... not that I had a choice."

He took a deep breath. "It was one of the guys in my unit who told me about her affairs. We were overseas, in the mountains, tracking down a terrorist. It was nighttime, we were lying in the dirt, hadn't eaten a real meal in a week. We were dirty, hungry, exhausted, and the terrorist had managed to give us the slip. I made a comment about how I wished I was home, how nice it would be to lie in bed with my wife after a huge dinner...and he just blurted it out.

"He told me that Corinne hadn't been faithful. That he knew of at least four guys on base she'd been with since we'd gotten married. It was no wonder she was in a bad mood when I got back from deployment. I was interrupting her parties."

Elsie didn't look up, but Zeke heard her sigh. He hoped that was a good sign.

"I have no idea how he knew...maybe guys bragged about screwing her, I don't know. But it was embarrassing and demoralizing to hear about her infidelity from someone else. I felt like a huge chump. Why wasn't I good enough? Was I that bad of a husband that she had to turn to others? Was the sex that bad?

"I wracked my brain, trying to figure out what I'd done wrong and how I could fix it. And I didn't want to believe it. I'd half convinced myself that my teammate was wrong, or lying for some reason, until I got home early that last time and caught her in bed with an eighteen-year-old private. Even then...even though I'd caught her red-handed...I told her I wanted to go to counseling. To fix our marriage."

Zeke paused for a moment and swallowed hard, the memory swamping him.

"What'd she say?" Elsie whispered. She'd turned her head. Her gaze was fixed on his chest, but he'd take it.

"She told me I was a joke. That she had no idea why anyone would want to stay married to me. She'd only said yes when I asked because she knew I'd be gone a lot and she wouldn't have to work if she married me. I had government housing, a steady paycheck...she could live an easy life. I realized I had been a means to an end all along. She'd never loved me. Just put on a helluva show while we were dating—and I bought it hook, line, and sinker. I couldn't fix something she hadn't wanted in the first place."

Elsie put her hand on his calf and squeezed.

Zeke sighed. "You're nothing like her. *Nothing*. But somehow, when your ex walked in and was all eager to get back with you...and you wanted to talk to him without me, it threw me back to when I was married. I was suddenly feeling...unsure. About us. I guess I needed to think. I was so *pissed* at him. I still am. Why should he get to come here after years of nothing and get to spend time with you? Or Tony, for that matter? I *hated* thinking about him alone in the office with you.

"But after I had time to think, I knew I'd messed up. I *left* you there with him. What if he'd hurt you? Said awful things? Shit—*did* he hurt you?"

Elsie shook her head.

Zeke sighed in relief. "I'm sorry, Else. I shouldn't have left without talking to you. Making sure you were okay. I don't know what's going on. But you know what? I don't give a shit. I'm not giving you up without a fight. That asshole might want you back, but as far as I'm concerned, he lost the right to be with you. He had you once and fucked it up. He doesn't get a second chance, not if I have anything to say about it. I *know* you don't love him, and there's no way in hell he can still love you. He hasn't bothered to contact you or Tony in years. That's not love." Zeke's voice had risen, but he couldn't help it.

"I'm scared," Elsie admitted softly.

Not able to keep himself from touching her anymore, Zeke shifted closer until her knees were against his chest and he wrapped his arms around her. She ducked her head onto his shoulder and shuddered. Her fingers let go of her knees and clutched his sides. The position was a little awkward, but Zeke didn't care. She was letting him touch her—he hadn't fucked up totally.

"I'm here. I'm so sorry for abandoning you."

"I was just as shocked as you," Elsie said into his shoulder. "Before I left him, I went online and bought a divorce from a legal site. I didn't ask him for *anything*. I didn't sneak out in the middle of the night. I even said he could visit Tony whenever he wanted. I gave it to him when he got home from work...one of the rare nights he actually came home at all. Told him I was leaving and we could both move on with our lives. He wasn't happy. Said some pretty nasty things, but he eventually signed the papers when I told him I'd ask a judge for half of everything and disclose his affairs if he didn't."

Elsie sniffed, otherwise silent for a beat. "He gave me a single day to gather our stuff and get out, and I rushed to get Tony and myself away from him. I kept him updated on where I was living over the years, and when I got here, I sent him the address of the Mangree, but I never heard from him. Until today."

She lifted her head, and her bloodshot eyes and the wetness on her cheeks slayed Zeke even more. "I won't go back to him. *Ever.* Tony is his son, and if he truly wants a relationship, I won't deny Tony that. But Doug coming here out of the blue like he did and claiming he wants me back and calling me his wife...it scares the shit out of me. I don't know what he wants, but I know it can't be good."

"We'll go see Nissi O'Neill in the morning. From everything I've heard, she's a damn good lawyer," Zeke said.

"What if he wants Tony?" Elsie whispered.

"He's not getting him," he replied firmly.

"Zeke, I lived in a motel. Tony's on the free lunch program. I'm not going to look like a very good prospect, compared to Doug."

"You have a full-time job. You're in this apartment now. Tony is happy and healthy. Besides, where's Doug been for the last five years? He hasn't seen his son, hasn't given you a dime in financial support."

"What if he wants to take him?"

"He's *not* taking Tony. In fact, your son asked me to make sure you knew he wants to stay with you."

"He did?"

"Yes. He loves you, Else. You're the only parent he's really known. He might be curious about his dad, but he's not going to want to leave Fallport and live with him full time."

"You don't know Doug," she said. "He's incredibly manipulative. Sneaky. He's got something up his sleeve."

"Well, we've got Simon on our side. And Nissi, once we go see her tomorrow. And the rest of my friends. Tony's not going anywhere. But...where do *we* stand? Can you forgive me for my momentarily lapse of judgement?"

Zeke held his breath as he waited for her response.

"You hurt me..." she whispered, not meeting his gaze.

"I know. And that kills me," he said.

"I wasn't done," Elsie said.

"Sorry. Go on."

"You hurt me. But honestly...I hurt you too. I should have refused to speak to Doug alone. And I get it, Zeke. Corinne really did a number on you, and I don't blame you for needing some space to think."

"It won't happen again," Zeke vowed. "I'm not going to let my ex-wife fuck with my life anymore. Losing you would destroy me, Elsie. I need you. I can't promise not to make mistakes in the future because I'm human, but I swear to you, on everything I am, that I'll talk about whatever's bothering me."

"What if he really thinks he can win me back?" she asked.

"Do you love him?"

"No!"

"Then it's a moot point *what* he thinks. Nissi will make sure everything is good with your custody of Tony. Doug will either learn to be happy with shared custody or he'll just disappear again. Either way, I'll be by your side the entire time, and when...*if*...you're ready, I'll propose, and you'll marry *me*."

Her eyes widened. "What?"

"I love you, Elsie. That's why that ass saying he wanted you back hit me so goddamn hard. I love you so much that just the thought you might go back to that douchebag sliced my heart to ribbons."

"Zeke..." she whispered.

"I want to marry you. Want to spend the rest of my life with you. Anything I have is yours. I'll never neglect you. I want to have another child with you, if that's something you might consider. Tony will always be your firstborn, and if you both agree, I'd love to look into adoption. I know all of that is sometime in the future. But I need to make sure you know that today shook me. Badly. Made me realize exactly how much both you and your son mean to me."

A small smile crept across Elsie's face. "Did you just propose?"

Zeke chuckled. "No. When I do, you'll know. And there won't be any huge questions between us. But I *did* just let you know as clearly as I can what my intentions are. I won't let you down again like I did today. I should've had your back, and I left you out there swinging. Please tell me you can forgive me."

Elsie met his gaze. "I'm not usually a crier. My life's been too hard to be crying about every little setback. But I admit today was overwhelming. Doug showing up, you leaving, talking to Tony about his father being here, worrying about Doug's motive. It was just too much. But you should know...tomorrow, when I was more myself, I was going to go into work and give you a piece of my mind. Tell you how disappointed I was that you'd up and left."

Zeke breathed out a sigh of relief. "Yeah?"

"Uh-huh. So yes, I forgive you. I'm so sorry for asking to talk to Doug alone. That won't happen again. I need you just as much as you need me, Zeke. And I don't blame you for reacting the way you did. I would've done the same thing if I'd been through what you have. It hurt; I can't deny that. But you being here right now goes a long way toward making me less upset."

"Tony called me."

Elsie blinked. "He did?"

"Yeah. He was scared and worried about you."

"Shoot. I didn't want him to see me crying."

"He knows that. Which was why he was worried. How about we get up, you wash your face, and we go out and reassure Tony that you're good?" Zeke suggested.

Elsie nodded. "Zeke?"

"Yeah, sweetheart?"

"I love you too."

The words were barely a whisper, but Zeke's heart seemed to swell ten times at hearing them. "I know."

Elsie smirked. "You do?"

"Yeah. There's no way you would've forgiven me so easily if you didn't. And you wouldn't have let me hold you like I am now. But thank you for giving that to me. I don't deserve that gift after what I did today, but I'm gonna take it anyway."

"I can't do this again," she warned quietly.

Zeke didn't have to ask what "this" was. He knew. "You won't have to. No matter what we find out tomorrow, next week, a month from now, you've got me. And we'll both try harder to communicate when we're upset."

Tears formed in her eyes again, and Zeke prayed they were tears of relief. Her next words confirmed it.

"I love you." Louder. Certain.

"And I love you."

Zeke pulled her to him once more, then awkwardly climbed to his feet, taking her with him. He walked with her to the bathroom, got a clean washcloth from the cabinet and handed it to her.

"No more tears, Else. We're in this together. Whatever your ex has up his sleeve, we'll roll with it. Tomorrow, we'll see Nissi and she'll find out what she can. If we need more firepower, so to speak, I've still got some connections from my time as a special forces soldier. Doug's not getting Tony. Not legally, and your son definitely isn't going to willingly go with him long-term. He's a smart kid.

Even as much as he craves a father, he's not gonna buy into Doug's shit."

"I hope not."

"He won't. Take your time. I'm gonna go out and make sure Tony's okay."

Elsie nodded. "Are you staying?"

Zeke stilled. "Do you want me to?"

She nodded.

"Then I'm staying," he said firmly.

"Okay."

"Okay." He leaned down, kissed her forehead, then forced himself to leave.

What Zeke really wanted to do was take her to bed and hold her tightly. He knew how close he'd come to fucking up the best thing that had ever happened to him. The fact that she'd so graciously accepted his apology said a lot more about her than him.

He also couldn't help but love that she'd planned to confront him tomorrow. Her apology and willingness to fight for what they had went a long way toward reassuring him the future he saw for them was within their grasp.

As he'd told her—never again. It went against everything he'd learned in the Green Berets about always questioning someone's intentions, especially after his experience with Corinne, but as far as he was concerned, Elsie was the exception. He'd never doubt her again. And she wouldn't doubt him. He knew that down to the bottom of his soul.

* * *

Elsie stared at herself in the bathroom mirror. She looked like hell. Her eyes were swollen and red, her face was blotchy...but she couldn't help but smile.

Zeke loved her.

It seemed like a miracle.

Yes, he'd disappointed her today. But she'd done the same. And she hadn't lied, she'd planned on confronting him tomorrow. Zeke was worth fighting for. The fact that he hadn't made her wait, had come over the moment Tony called for help, was proof enough.

Now that she and him were all right, she needed to check on Tony. Apologize for worrying him. Thank him for calling Zeke when he was worried and upset.

The one thing she wouldn't do was tell him horror stories about his father. Doug was an ass, but she didn't want to taint Tony's upcoming interactions with him. He was still his father, and if there was a chance that Doug was here because he truly wanted a relationship with his son, she wouldn't do anything to sabotage it.

Besides, Tony was smart, as Zeke had said. She was fairly sure Doug would eventually show his true colors. And if Tony compared his biological father to the men he'd been hanging out with lately, Doug would surely fall short.

While she might not want to come right out and say all the bad things she was thinking about Doug, that didn't mean she wouldn't warn Tony. She wanted him to be cautious when dealing with his father, but not turn him against him before Doug had a chance to do the right thing. Time would tell what would happen.

Elsie was still worried about Doug trying to take their son away from her, but she felt better now that Zeke was going to go with her to see the lawyer. She was a different person than she was five years ago. She wasn't going to let Doug run roughshod over her anymore. Not like she had in the past.

She couldn't stop thinking about how Zeke had sort of asked her to marry him. To be honest, she would've said yes and gone down to the courthouse tonight if he asked. Doug had never apologized for anything he'd ever done. At least, never apologized and truly meant it.

The sincerity and fear in Zeke's voice when he'd begged her to forgive him had made it an easy decision.

Taking a deep breath, Elsie pushed off the counter and headed for the door. She approached the living room, then stopped, watching unnoticed for a moment. Zeke was sitting on the couch with Tony. He had his arm around her son and their heads were almost touching as they talked. Zeke was reassuring him that she was fine and would be out soon. He wanted to know how school had gone and if Bridger was still giving Tony a hard time.

Zeke was going to make an incredible father. Hell, he was already a hundred times better than Doug had ever been.

She must've made some sort of sound, because both Tony and Zeke's heads came up and turned in her direction. Tony sprang up from the couch and ran toward her. Elsie let out a small *oof* as her son hit her. She took a step back to stay upright, Tony's arms around her waist and his head resting on her chest.

"Mom! Are you okay?"

"I'm good, baby," she said, stroking his head. "I'm sorry I worried you."

Tony lifted his head and looked up at her. "I want to stay with you," he blurted. "I told Zeke to tell you. Did he?"

"Yes, he did."

"I want to get to know Dad, but that doesn't mean I want to leave you."

"Okay. I'm glad to hear that. I love you, kid."

"I love you too. No one will make me go with him, will they?"

"No." That came from Zeke. He'd stood and was standing nearby, watching them.

Her son turned his head to look at Zeke. "Promise?"

"Promise," he said without hesitation. "You aren't a baby anymore. You have a say in where you want to live."

"Okay." Tony took a deep breath and stood back. "Now that you're good, I'm gonna go read. Is that okay?"

Elsie wasn't even surprised that Tony took Zeke's words as gospel. He didn't even question his promise.

"You want a snack?" Elsie asked.

"No, I'm fine. But...maybe can we have waffles in the morning?"

he asked.

"Of course we can."

"You okay with me staying tonight?" Zeke asked.

Tony turned to him and nodded. "Yes! Are we still going over to your place this weekend?"

"If you want to," Zeke said easily.

"I want to," Tony told him with a huge smile. Then the boy ran over to Zeke, hugging him tight before turning to head to his bedroom.

Elsie took a few steps until she was in front of Zeke and did as her son had, hugging him tightly. Zeke turned them without letting go and slowly shuffled back to the couch. He eased them down, and Elsie never wanted to be out of this man's arms. She'd experienced a huge range of emotions today, and she felt drained and exhausted as a result.

But as she sat next to Zeke, and as he held her, she felt a contentedness she'd rarely experienced wash over her. This was what she wanted every day for the rest of her life. Ending each one in his arms.

"You hungry?" he asked quietly.

Elsie shook her head against him.

"Thirsty?"

"No."

"What do you need?" he asked.

"This," she said firmly. "You."

"You've got me."

Eventually Elsie fell asleep, only waking when she felt herself being picked up. "I can walk," she mumbled.

"I know," Zeke said, not putting her down.

Cuddling into the man she loved, Elsie let him carry her to bed. He put her down, then began to unbutton her jeans. He got them off before he undid her bra under her T-shirt. He didn't remove her shirt or underwear, but got her settled under the covers. "Be right back," he said, then kissed her lips gently.

Elsie watched him go into her bathroom. When he came back out, he was in nothing but a pair of boxer shorts. He climbed under the bedding, and she curled into him as he wrapped an arm around her.

Elsie waited for him to make a move to do more than just lie there, but he didn't. "Zeke?" she asked.

"Yeah?"

"Do you want to...you know?"

"Make love? Yes. But I need to just hold you even more."

All right then. How could she complain about that?

"I'm gonna make today up to you," he whispered after a moment.

Elsie was half asleep, but she managed to say, "Nothing to make up for."

"You're wrong, but that's okay. I'm going to do it anyway."

Deciding to let it go, Elsie simply nodded against him. "Thank you for being here."

"No place I'd rather be," he reassured her. "Sleep, sweetheart. We've got a long day ahead of us tomorrow. Getting Tony off to school, seeing the lawyer, and unfortunately, you're going to have to call Doug to try to find out what the hell he's doing here."

"You'll be there with me?" Elsie asked.

"Of course."

Those two words made any stress she had about the next day fade away. She didn't know what tomorrow would bring, but Zeke would be at her side whatever happened. Today had been difficult, but in the end, it made her and Zeke closer.

"You're not sleeping," Zeke scolded gently.

"Sorry. Love you."

Zeke tightened his arms around her for a moment. "Love you too, Else."

She fell asleep not too much longer after that and dreamed of sitting next to Zeke, with Tony on her other side, as they all looked down on a small infant bundled in a blanket in her arms.

CHAPTER EIGHTEEN

The next morning, after getting Tony to school, Elsie tried not to stress about going to see the lawyer. Waking up with Zeke was heaven. For most of her adult life, she'd been on her own. Yes, she'd been married, but it wasn't as if Doug helped her with the house or Tony. While she'd been in the shower, Zeke had gotten Tony up, started the waffle batter—letting Tony do the mixing—started a load of laundry, and put all the dishes he'd used to make breakfast into the dishwasher.

Elsie was surprised, though by now, she shouldn't have been. Zeke had merely kissed her lightly on the way to take his own shower, not considering anything he'd done out of the ordinary.

Tony had been extra helpful that morning as well. Elsie supposed it was because he was still worried about her and didn't want to do anything that would make her sad. Once again, she counted her lucky stars that she had such a good kid.

But now they were pulling into a parking spot outside the lawyer's office. Nissi's office was located on the east side of the square, between the bowling alley and Sunny Side Up. Elsie had seen it of course, but hadn't given it a thought since she didn't have a need, or the money, for a lawyer.

"Relax, Else. This is going to be fine."

"I'm not sure about this," she said in a fretful tone. "I'm just now feeling as if I'm getting ahead of my finances."

"Look at me," Zeke said firmly.

Elsie took a deep breath and did as he asked.

"I fucked up yesterday. I failed at the first test of our relationship."

Elsie snorted. "Zeke, you were at my apartment not even four hours after Doug showed up, spewing his crap. I'm not sure I would say that's a failure."

"Glad you see it that way, but the fact remains that instead of sticking by your side, I left you to the wolves, so to speak. That's not going to happen again. Starting this morning."

"I can't let you pay for this," she told him.

"Why not?"

"*Because.*"

"I love you. I love Tony. Your ex is a douche. If he has any funny business in mind, it's best to stop that shit now. I'm actually being selfish here, Else. Because the sooner your ties to that fucker are squared away, the sooner I can officially make you mine. Please let me take care of you both by paying for Nissi and making sure your ex doesn't find any loopholes that might take either one of you away from me."

"I'm not going anywhere," she told him seriously.

"Good. I love you and I want you to be happy. You *and* Tony. And right now, making sure you're protected and your ex doesn't pull anything would make *me* happy. So that's what I'm doing."

"You're too good to me," she said softly. "I'm not sure I can handle it."

"You can. And you better get used to it, because I'm not gonna stop making you happy anytime soon. Now, let's get this done, yeah? I want to have as much info as we can get before we see your ex again," Zeke said.

Elsie couldn't argue with that. She'd thought about Doug a lot. What he was doing here. What he wanted. And so far she couldn't think of anything that was good. Zeke pushed his door open and Elsie did the same. He met her on the sidewalk and they walked into Nissi O'Neill's office hand-in-hand.

A secretary greeted them, and Zeke briefly explained the situation and why they were there. Even though they didn't have an appointment, the woman told them Nissi would see them.

Fifteen minutes later, Elsie sat in a chair in front of the lawyer's desk with her hands clenched in her lap, taking deep breaths. The woman was beautiful. She had black hair with curls Elsie would die to have, flawless brown skin, and her dark eyes were empathetic and shone with intelligence as Elsie finished explaining the entire situation with Doug. What their marriage was like, the divorce agreement she'd bought online before she'd left him, and even how she was scared he'd use her living in the Mangree Motel and her lack of funds against her.

Zeke had stayed mostly silent as she talked, which Elsie appreciated. He didn't try to mansplain anything, just let her speak without interrupting.

Nissi leaned forward and put her elbows on her desk. "Why do you think he's here?"

"I don't know. But the only thing I can think is that it has to do with Tony. Doug doesn't really like me. I'm sure he's not actually looking to get back together. I'm not opposed to letting him get to know Tony, but on my son's terms, not his. He hasn't tried to get in touch with us at all in five years. And he had my contact info the whole time."

"Okay," Nissi said. "In the state of Virginia, both parents are responsible for child support. It doesn't matter if they're married or not. They're both obligated to pay for things like health and dental care, childcare costs, and other expenses that come with raising a child. Being married or divorced doesn't absolve him of those responsibilities."

"But the divorce agreement stated that he didn't have to pay that stuff," Elsie said.

"That's technically true. However, if he now wants to be in Tony's life...he's going to need to step up and provide some support. He can't just waltz into his life and decide to be a father now, while still expecting *you* to pay for everything."

"I don't care about the money," Elsie said.

"I do," Nissi said as she leaned forward. "Look, you and your son have rights. Even though Doug is Tony's father, that doesn't mean he can come here after five years and start demanding things from either of you. Money doesn't make up for his lack of interest or caring, but it can help with things that Tony might need in the future."

She wasn't wrong. Elsie nodded.

"Here's my card," Nissi said, holding out a business card to Elsie. "I want you to call me if he does or says *anything* that makes you uncomfortable. Understand?"

Elsie nodded, feeling a huge burden lift from her shoulders.

"On your way out, please see my assistant to fill out some paperwork. Including anything about Doug you can remember...his birthday, social security number, etcetera, will be helpful, and will save me some research. We'll do very comprehensive due diligence before presenting Doug with any terms regarding shared custody. And in the meantime, I'll be in touch." She stood and held out her hand to Elsie.

Elsie shook it and asked tentatively, "Um, how much is all this going to cost?"

Nissi grinned. "You'll get the friends and family discount."

She blinked in surprise. "I will?"

"Yup. I'm assuming, since Zeke has had a hand on you the entire time you've been here, that you're together?"

Elsie side-eyed Zeke a little shyly, then nodded at Nissi.

"The Eagle Point Search and Rescue team found my mother a few years ago, when she wandered out of the house and into the woods. She had dementia, and I was utterly frantic when I found she was missing. These guys stayed out all night until they'd located her. Then kept her safe and warm when she was too frightened to budge, until she trusted them enough to get her home. They could've passed her on to the paramedics at that point, but one of them—I'm sorry, I don't remember who—stayed with her even at the hospital, holding her hand until I could get there.

"I owe Zeke, and all the members of the team, a huge debt of gratitude. Once we figure things out and have a custody agreement signed and in the books, we'll figure out money. Okay?"

Elsie couldn't believe this woman was going to basically work for free until a settlement was signed. But she'd be an idiot to disagree. "Thank you," she said fervently.

"You're welcome. And I haven't even met your ex, but I'm thinking you've traded up," Nissi said with a wink.

Elsie couldn't help but smile at that. "I definitely did."

"Be careful," Nissi warned, getting serious. "I have no idea why your ex is here, but I've been involved in a lot of divorces and child-custody cases, and most aren't exactly cordial."

"She'll be safe," Zeke said.

Nissi's gaze went to him and she nodded. "Good. We'll talk soon," she told Elsie.

Taking that as her cue this first meeting was done, Elsie thanked her once more and turned toward the door. It took about twenty minutes for her to fill out and sign all the official paperwork to hire Nissi, and when they stepped outside, Elsie took a deep breath.

"You okay?" Zeke asked.

She turned to him. "Surprisingly, I am. Did you really find her mom in the woods?"

"Yeah. She passed about a year ago, but I'll never forget that case. We were lucky to find her when we did. She wasn't on any trail, but was bushwhacking through the briars and undergrowth. She was covered in scratches. When we tried to approach, she became hysterical, so we decided only one of us should attempt to calm her. The others hung back so I could get close, but it took quite a bit of time to convince her to trust us and that it was all right to leave the woods."

Elsie leaned into him, putting her hands on his chest. "I already thought you were pretty amazing, but now I'm even more impressed."

Zeke chuckled. "Just doing my job," he told her.

Elsie rolled her eyes. "How'd I know that's what you would say?"

"Because you're smart," Zeke said matter-of-factly. "Now, since we have about an hour and a half before I need to open the bar, you want to head over to Grinders and get a caramel macchiato? Maybe we can grab a cinnamon roll from The Sweet Tooth and hang out in The Circle until it's time to open."

"I'd love that. I know I should probably call Doug, but I'd much prefer to hang out with you."

"And, of course, Otto, Art, and Silas," Zeke joked, using his head to gesture to the three gossips settling into their spots in front of the post office.

Elsie chuckled. "Them too."

"All right. Let's do it. I'm proud of you," Zeke told her.

"For what?"

"For being strong. For not freaking out about this entire situation with your ex."

"Oh, I'm freaking out," she said. "But I've learned that being overly emotional never really solves anything. Like last night," she said dryly. "I should've just called you and not let my doubts fester."

"Agreed. Don't hesitate to call me out on my shit in the future," Zeke said. "Although I'm going to do my damnedest not to do something that stupid again."

"It goes both ways," Elsie said. "If I do something insensitive or that irritates you, please tell me. I mean, I don't want you to be a dick about it, but if I mess up, I want to know."

"Deal." Then Zeke leaned down and took her lips with his. It wasn't a chaste kiss either. It was long, deep, and by the time he pulled back, Elsie wanted to go back to her apartment, or his house, instead of getting something to eat and drink.

Grinning as if he knew exactly what she was thinking, Zeke took her hand in his and towed her toward Grinders.

* * *

Zeke wasn't exactly surprised when Doug Germain walked into On the Rocks later that afternoon. He'd expected the man to come back. He had to have an agenda, and Zeke was more than happy to get on with it, to figure out why the man was in Fallport.

But this time, he wasn't leaving Elsie alone with the man.

Over breakfast, Zeke learned that when Elsie had gotten married, she hadn't changed her name. And when Tony was born, Doug didn't give a damn if the boy had his last name or not. Odd, considering he needed a child to pull of the family man image. But Elsie decided if her husband didn't care, she'd give him *her* name.

Zeke couldn't imagine not wanting to claim his wife *or* his son in that way. He wasn't so old fashioned that he would demand his wife take his last name, but he'd at least have a conversation about it, which it didn't sound like Doug cared enough to do.

Without having to ask, Talon had come over from the barber shop to hang out at the bar for the day. Zeke's team now knew the basics of what was going on, and he was glad to have his buddy at his and Elsie's backs.

Doug walked into the bar with a smirk on his face. As if he knew his appearance the day before had rocked Elsie's world, and he didn't care. He waved off Reina, who greeted him and offered to get him a seat.

He walked up to where Elsie was standing next to the bar and said, "We didn't get a chance to talk yesterday, and since you didn't contact me, here I am."

Zeke hated this for Elsie, but he was proud when she nodded. "I'm not surprised you felt it was all right to come to my workplace, interrupt me, and demand I talk to you. But since Zeke is such a good boss—and an even better boyfriend—he's graciously granted us the use of his office again. You have twenty minutes."

Doug's lip curled. "How magnanimous of him," he said under his breath.

Zeke had told Elsie he would stay silent...if Doug behaved himself. But since her ex had lobbed the first volley, he felt justified in responding. "It is," he told the other man. "I'm guessing you don't allow or enjoy people barging into your place of business and demanding your time. Especially your exes. I'm granting you twenty minutes to talk to Elsie, but that's it. I suggest you get to the point so I don't have to interrupt and kick you out."

Doug glared at him before giving Elsie a look. "Nice. This is the best you could do?"

In response, she turned and headed down the small hallway toward the office.

Doug looked a little thrown by her non-reaction, but quickly followed.

Zeke shut the door behind them—and Doug turned to look at him in surprise.

"You didn't actually think I was going to leave her alone with you again, did you?" Zeke asked.

"Actually, yes. We have things to talk about that don't concern you."

"That's where you're wrong. *Anything* having to do with Elsie and her well-being very much concerns me."

Zeke recognized the moment when Doug decided to change tactics. He turned his back on him. "It's good to see you, baby."

"Cut the crap, Doug," Elsie said. "What do you want? Why are you here?"

"I missed you—" her ex began.

Elsie rolled her eyes. "Please. That's not true and we both know it. You were relieved when I left."

"Things were rough between us for a while," Doug conceded. "But I've been thinking recently, and I hate that I haven't been a part of your life. Or our son's. I want to rectify that."

"Being part of my life is out of the question," Elsie said firmly.

Zeke could see Elsie was holding onto her patience by a thread. He was ready to step in if needed, but so far, his Else was doing just fine.

"Now, get to the point, please."

"Right...fine. I'm sorry about how things ended between us. You were always the best thing in my life and I just didn't see it. Things were tough at work after you left, and it kind of consumed my life. But everything's more stable now. I'm at a place where I'm ready to be a better father."

"Better? Doug, you've *never* been a father to Tony."

Doug's face got red and his fists clenched. Elsie had never said her ex was violent, but Zeke wasn't going to take any chances. He stepped around the man and leaned against the desk at Elsie's side. If Doug made a move toward her, Zeke would make sure he regretted it.

As if he could read his thoughts, Doug took a deep breath and took a step back. "I *tried*," he whined. "But when I got home from work, I was so tired. And he cried a lot. Was so...clingy. I wasn't emotionally ready to be a dad."

"But you are now?"

"Yes."

"For how long? A week? Two? Tony deserves better than having you in his life for a week or so every five years. If I'm going to let you be part of his life, you have to be in it for the long haul," Elsie said, her tone hard.

But Zeke knew those words cost her. The last thing she wanted was Doug back in her life, even peripherally. But the man was

Tony's father, and she didn't want to prevent him from seeing his son if he truly had decided to make a change.

"I will be," Doug said.

"Why now?" Elsie asked quietly.

"He's ten. He needs a man in his life," Doug said.

It was all Zeke could do not to roll his eyes.

"Shit, Doug—you don't even know how old your own son is! He's not ten, he's only nine. And he *has* a man in his life. Several of them."

"You've been getting around, huh?" Doug asked, sneering.

Elsie gasped, and Zeke shoved up from his relaxed position against the desk. But she stopped him from beating the shit out of her ex simply by putting a hand on his arm.

"Of course that's where you went with my comment," Elsie said with a shake of her head. "Not that it's any of your business, but I haven't dated anyone until Zeke and I started seeing each other. But I also haven't lived in a bubble, Doug. Fallport's a great town. There are a ton of awesome people who live here. Including men. Men who've stepped up to teach Tony the things his *father* should've been around to do. But even if I *had* been dating people in the last five years, it's no business of yours. Should we talk about how many women you've slept with since I left...or while we were still together?"

It was obvious Doug wasn't going to go there. "You're right. I'm sorry."

Silence descended between the pair. And it wasn't a comfortable one. Finally, Elsie broke it. "I went to see my lawyer this morning. Just to make sure our divorce agreement is rock solid. As is my custody of Tony."

"We were good once. We can be again—" Doug began.

But Elsie refused to let him continue. "No."

"But—"

"No, Doug. Not only no, but *hell no*. We're done. More than done."

"Even if we are," he continued, not conceding, "Tony doesn't deserve to live like this."

"Like what?" Elsie asked sharply as she glared at her ex.

Doug shrugged. "You're a waitress, Elsie. I can give him so much more than you can."

"I don't want your money," she said. "I never did. All I ever wanted was your time and your love. But you weren't able to give me *or* Tony either of those things."

"I just want to do what's right for my son," Doug said.

But to Zeke, he didn't exactly sound sincere.

Elsie shrugged. "I'm glad. Because I do too," she said.

Doug sighed. "I want to see Tony. Want to spend time with him."

"Why?"

"Why? Because *he's my son*."

"He's been your son for years, and you didn't want to see him even before we left," Elsie returned.

"Well, I want to now."

It was Elsie's turn to sigh. "I'm not opposed to that—but on his terms, not yours."

"What does that mean?" Doug asked, seemingly genuinely perplexed. "He's a kid. He should do what he's told."

"He *is* a kid, but he's nine years old. He knows what he likes and what he doesn't. I've never forced him to do anything, and I'm not going to start now. You can see him as long as Tony is agreeable."

"You said you weren't going to keep him from me," Doug argued, frustration and anger easy to hear in his voice.

"And I'm not. He's actually excited to get to know you. But if you do *anything* to scare him, hurt him, or make him feel bad about himself, my generosity will end."

"Your generosity," Doug said with a hint of sarcasm. "Give me a break."

"I hold all the cards here," Elsie clarified. "You're the deadbeat father. The one who hasn't bothered to reach out to his son in five years."

Zeke could practically see the steam coming out of Doug's ears. "You're different," he said after a moment...and he clearly didn't mean it in a good way.

Elsie nodded. "If you mean I'm not willing to put up with your shit anymore, you're right. You treated me like crap, Doug. You belittled me constantly. Told me what a terrible parent I was. An awful wife. Called me stupid. It took me a while to figure out that was just your way of attempting to control me, but now that I have, I'm not ever going back to being that person."

"I gave you everything," Doug seethed. "You were *nothing* before you met me."

"Wrong. I was *me*. A person with feelings, hopes, and dreams, which you did your best to destroy."

"Yeah, I can see you've really fulfilled any dreams you've had," Doug said, his remaining calm obviously slipping. "You're a waitress in a rundown bar in the middle of nowhere. You lived in a *motel*, Elsie. If I wanted custody, I would win in a heartbeat."

Zeke was done listening to this asshole.

But apparently, so was Elsie. She took a step toward Doug and pointed her finger in his face. "I dare you to try," she said, offering a small laugh that wasn't humorous in the least. "Seriously. First, Tony's not a baby. He'll gladly tell any judge that he doesn't want to leave Fallport. He has friends here. Loves his school. And I might've lived in a motel, but Tony never went hungry. He had a roof over his head. And yeah, I'm a waitress. A damn good one. I love what I do, and I'm not letting you belittle me or anything I had to do to take care of my son. Also, there isn't a judge in the state who would grant you custody, not after learning you didn't contribute a penny to Tony's care over the years, no matter *what* the divorce paperwork says.

"If you're here to try to take him from me, you're going to fail, and you might as well go back to DC. If you're here because you honestly want to have some sort of relationship with your son before it's too late, I'll support that. But mark my words, Doug, the second I sense you have ulterior motives, you're done. *Done*."

"I don't like this new Elsie," Doug retorted.

Elsie laughed again. "I don't care."

"When can I see Tony?" Doug asked. "I want to see him today."

Elsie nodded.

"When does he get out of school?"

"You can meet us at Caboose Park around four-thirty," Elsie told him.

"I don't want you hovering over us while we get to know each other," Doug said.

"Too bad. There's no way I'm leaving you alone with him until *he's* comfortable with that."

Doug and Elsie stared at each other for a long moment, before he finally nodded. "Fine."

"Fine. Do you need directions to the park?" she asked.

Doug snorted. "As if this backwater town is big enough to need directions to anything. I'll find it." Then he turned and headed for the door without another word. He slammed it behind him, as if needing to get the last word in.

The second the door shut, Elsie sagged.

Zeke caught her in his arms and held her tight. Elsie was shaking. "Easy, Else. You were incredible."

"I don't like this."

"I know. But you said everything right. He knows that he's got a huge hill to climb in regard to his son, knows you won't put up with any of his shenanigans, won't let him talk down to you. You hold all the cards, and he's well aware of that." Zeke tipped her chin up and smiled down at her. "You were awesome," he said softly.

Elsie returned his smile. "I have to admit, that felt really good. But honestly?"

"Yeah?" Zeke asked when she didn't continue.

"I'm not sure I would've been able to say any of it without you here."

"Yes, you would've," he countered.

Elsie shook her head. "No. I knew he wouldn't want to say or do anything that would seriously piss you off. He's always been that way. Around others, he's nice and polite, but in private, he feels as if it's okay to say whatever he wants. Thank you."

"You never have to thank me for having your back. I'm only sorry I left you to him yesterday."

Elsie shook her head. "No. We're done with that. We've moved past it. You need to stop beating yourself up about it."

Zeke knew that would never happen, but if it made his Elsie happy, he'd at least try.

"Thank you for letting me take a couple hours off in the afternoon to make sure Tony's good with him," she said.

"Of course. But you know that I'm not going to let you go by yourself, right?"

Elsie frowned. "*Let me?*"

"Sorry, that came out wrong. I don't trust him. And you just said it yourself, when he gets you alone, he's gonna get nasty. And that shit's not going to happen. Not on my watch."

"But your bar..." she said, letting her words trail off.

"What about it?"

"If you leave early, you'll have to pay Hank, Lance, or Reuben to come in."

"And?" Zeke asked.

"I have no idea how long Doug's gonna be here. It could cost a lot in the long run."

Zeke took Elsie's face in his hands. "You and Tony are more important than money. Than this bar. I don't care if I go broke, I'm gonna have your back for as long as you need it."

"Zeke," she whispered.

"Don't get emotional over me being the kind of man you should've had all along," he ordered.

"Then stop being nice!" she countered.

"Never." Zeke lowered his head. The kiss started out slow and easy, but quickly morphed out of control. It had been too long since he'd had her, and his cock throbbed in his pants. Zeke didn't think he'd ever get enough of Elsie. When he was around her, she was like gas to his flame.

Taking a shuddering breath, he pulled back. When she licked her lips, it was all he could do not to throw her on his desk and take her right there and then.

"I love you," she whispered.

"And I love you. You think he's gone yet?" Zeke asked.

Elsie chuckled. "I'm guessing yes. On the Rocks isn't his kind of hangout."

"Good. I need to go out and talk to Talon. Bring him up to speed on what your ex is up to."

"What *is* he up to?" Elsie mused with a small shake of her head.

"I don't know. But I'm not getting warm and fuzzy feelings."

"Me either. He's going to hurt Tony," Elsie said softly.

"Tony's not stupid," Zeke countered. "Yes, he's excited his dad is here and to get to know him, but he's not going to put up with his shit. You know how I know?"

"How?"

"Because he's got a hell of a mother who's taught him what unconditional love is. And he's got me. And Ethan. And Rocky, Tal, and the rest of my team. Hell, the entire town of Fallport, for that matter."

"I hope you're right," she said.

"I am. Now...I'm thinking after the park, if Doug wants to, we can let him take Tony to dinner at Sunny Side Up. We can let them talk in a booth while we eat nearby. Then we'll all—meaning you, me, and Tony—go to my house and make a fort in the living room and watch a movie and have popcorn. Get our weekend started. That sound okay?"

Elsie's eyes filled with tears once more. "You're being nice again," she complained as she blinked furiously to keep her tears from falling.

"You'll get used to it," he said. "You still want to stay the night?"

"Yes."

"Can I have you guys all three nights? I'll even take him to school on Monday. I know you hate the drop-off line."

"So do you," she countered.

"Yeah, but I'm willing to do whatever it takes if it means I get to hold you in my arms three nights in a row. And spend time with Tony."

"I'd like that. But I want to make sure it's okay with Tony before I say yes."

Her respect for her son was just another reason Zeke was madly in love with this woman. "Okay."

"Zeke?"

"Yeah, sweetheart?"

"Tell me it's going to be all right. That Doug isn't going to turn my and Tony's lives upside down."

"He won't. You aren't on your own anymore, Else. He tries to pull anything, he'll be in deep shit."

"Okay."

"Okay."

They went back out on the floor, and Zeke was glad to see Elsie quickly get into the swing of her serving duties. He kept his eye on her for a while until he was reassured that she really was all right. She was strong, there was no doubt. She hadn't taken any shit from her ex, which Zeke was extremely proud of. But he still couldn't shake the feeling that the man had an agenda. What that was, he didn't know, but Zeke would keep his eyes and ears open to make sure whatever it was didn't hurt the woman and the boy he loved.

CHAPTER NINETEEN

The next week went extremely well as far as Elsie and Zeke were concerned. Every day, she fell more in love with the man. But just because things with her relationship were going well, didn't mean Elsie had let down her guard when it came to her ex. With each day that passed, she was more sure Doug was up to something. He'd *never* taken so much time off work, as far as she knew. For him to do so now was out of the ordinary, and it had all of Elsie's internal alarms blaring.

She and Tony had spent last weekend at Zeke's house, and she couldn't remember ever hearing her son laugh so much. Zeke was attentive, but didn't spoil him. School had gotten out for the year the previous Tuesday, and Zeke kept Tony busy with a list of chores the boy attended to each morning, before spending time with his father. Luckily, Tony seemed excited about each and every one—especially when Zeke worked right alongside him. He was blossoming under the man's attention.

Doug, in the meantime, was going all out to win Tony's affection in a very different way. He'd gone overboard, in fact. He spent time with him every day...but he'd also bought the boy way too much stuff already. A bicycle, an Xbox game console, toys, books, even a ton of clothes. Elsie had asked him to stop, insisting Tony didn't need material things, but of course her ex didn't listen.

Doug had been on his best behavior with their son, as well. He still snuck in little digs about Elsie every now and then, but he'd surprisingly kept them to a minimum.

Every night, Elsie sat with Tony in his bed and they talked about the day, including how he felt about Doug. It was obvious he'd made significant strides with the boy. The gifts had definitely helped, and Elsie couldn't help but feel jealous. She hated not being able to give her son the things his father had. But she did her best to tamp down those feelings. Tony was happy. That was what mattered.

That night, they were back in the apartment. As much as Elsie wanted to spend every night in Zeke's bed, she didn't want to confuse Tony. And she knew every time they stayed at his place, it got harder and harder to leave. Tony had his own room and Zeke had helped him paint it the other night. It felt more like a home than the apartment did, which made Elsie feel guilty. It wasn't that long ago they'd been living in the motel and moving into this apartment had been a dream come true.

"Mom?" Tony asked as they sat on his bed together.

"Yes?"

"Dad asked me something tonight, and I wanted to talk to you about it."

Elsie was instantly on alert. But she managed to nod anyway. "Shoot."

"Now that school's over, he wants me to come stay at his house for two weeks, in Washington, DC. He said he'd take me to see all the monuments, and we could visit the White House where the President lives, and maybe go up in the Washington Monument."

It was suddenly hard for Elsie to breathe. She'd been allowing Doug to have more time alone with Tony, but she wasn't sure about him taking their son all the way to DC.

"He said I'd have a room to myself and that there's a little boy who lives next to him who's my age," Tony said.

Elsie looked down at her son. His brown hair was messy and in need of a cut. He'd taken a bath earlier, and his hair was still drying. He looked up at her with big hazel eyes. "You want to, don't you?" she asked.

Tony shrugged and looked down at the book in his lap, the one he'd read for a bit after Elsie said good night.

"Look at me, Tony," she said.

Her son raised his head and met her gaze once more.

"Be honest with me. Has Doug said anything—anything at all— that's upset you?"

Tony shook his head, but having known her son for nine years, Elsie could tell he was lying. "Tony," she warned in her mom voice.

Her son sighed. "Sometimes he says mean things about you. But I don't listen to that. He doesn't know you. How come you don't ever say bad things about *him*?" Tony asked.

Elsie swept a lock of hair off his forehead. "It's no secret that your dad and I don't get along anymore. We did once. I loved him, and I think he loved me. But we grew apart. I respect the fact that he's your father. I want you to make your own decisions about him and not be influenced by anything I tell you. That's not fair to him or you."

Tony nodded. Then asked, "How come Dad didn't give you money so we could move out of the motel and into an apartment before now?"

Elsie wanted to groan. Out of the mouths of babes. "I don't know. But let's get back to you visiting DC. My only concern is *you*. Do you feel comfortable enough with your father to go with him for two weeks?"

"I think so."

"You need to be sure. Because once you leave, it'll be...complicated if you change your mind," Elsie warned.

"If I hate it, can I come back?" Tony asked.

Elsie hugged her son tightly. "I would never force you to stay somewhere you weren't comfortable or happy. Remember when you were in the second grade, and you went to a friend's house to spend the night and called me in the middle of the night?" she asked.

Tony nodded. "You came and got me. Even though it was dark and really, really late."

"Exactly. The same thing will apply here. Even though you aren't just across town, if something happens and you want to come home, all you have to do is call me and I'll come get you."

"He's nice most of the time," Tony said quietly. "He gives me presents."

Elsie nodded. She hated that Doug's bribery had worked, but their son was only nine. She wasn't exactly surprised.

"I think I want to go," Tony said.

"Then we'll figure it out." Elsie wanted to throw up, but she refused to be that parent. The one who made her son afraid to try anything new. And the bottom line was that Doug *was* Tony's father. He might be a jerk to her, but from what she'd seen over the last week, he seemed to be enjoying getting to know Tony. She shouldn't be surprised, Tony was a good kid. He won over just about everyone he met.

"Thank you, Mom," Tony said and hugged her. "I don't want to live with him forever. Just visit."

"Thank goodness. I need you around for a while longer," Elsie teased. "Who else will take out the garbage and put the dishes away for me?" Her voice was a little flat, but she didn't think Tony noticed.

She needed to talk to Doug. Make sure he understood that this trip was a temporary thing.

As Tony began to read out loud, Elsie's mind wandered. She couldn't help but remember how amazing last weekend had been with Zeke. He'd made love to her so sweetly and tenderly. But he'd also shown her what had been missing in her marriage to Doug —passion.

Zeke turned her on more with one look, one innocent touch, than she could've imagined. Sleeping with him, next to him, in his arms, was one of the most satisfying things she'd done in a long time. He was generous with his loving, always making sure she came at least once before even considering taking his own pleasure. She'd been nervous about making love with Tony in the house, but after her son's long days of spending time with first his father, then Zeke, he fell into a deep sleep every night.

All in all, things in Elsie's life were going well...except for the questions surrounding her ex. But as long as Tony was excited about the trip, Elsie would hide her misgivings and do what she could to make her son feel as safe as possible.

Starting with getting him a phone. She didn't really want her nine-year-old to have a cell already, but Tony had been begging for one for at least a year. Most of his friends had one. His trip to DC seemed like an appropriate time to be granted the responsibility... and to give him a way to call her. Every night. So she could check on him.

After Tony finished reading the chapter, Elsie kissed him on the head and said good night. She gave him thirty minutes to fall asleep, then called Zeke. She didn't want Tony overhearing her conversation.

"Hey, sweetheart," Zeke said as he answered.

"Doug asked Tony if he wanted to go visit him in DC for two weeks," Elsie said, without even a hello first.

"What?"

"I told him if it was what he wanted to do, he could. But I'm flipping out, Zeke!"

"Breathe, Else," he ordered.

Elsie realized she was practically hyperventilating. She forced herself to slow her breathing.

"When?"

"I don't know. I need to talk to Doug, I guess," she said.

"We need to get Tony a phone," Zeke said.

Elsie couldn't help but chuckle at that.

"What? What's funny?" Zeke asked.

"Nothing. But I'd just decided the same thing. I want him to be able to call me whenever he needs. I told him we'd come and get him anytime, no questions asked, if he wanted me to."

"Of course we will," Zeke said.

"What do you think?" Elsie asked.

There was silence on the line for a moment, and Elsie's stomach dropped.

"One part of me thinks this is a good thing. I'm impressed Doug has stuck around this long and seems to honestly be trying to be a father to his son finally."

"And the other part?" Elsie asked.

"Wants to lock Tony up and tell Doug there's no way in hell he's taking him out of Fallport."

Amazingly, his words made Elsie feel a lot better. "Me too," she agreed.

"If you want to fight this, I'll stand by your decision. A week isn't nearly enough to make up for the five years he neglected both of you," Zeke said.

"I know. But...Tony's excited about this. He's never been to DC, and of course Doug told him he'd take him to the freaking White House. I could say no, but if there's even a five percent chance this trip will help create a bond between Tony and his father that will last a lifetime, I'd be a terrible person to do so."

"But you'd be human," Zeke said gently.

Elsie closed her eyes. God, she loved this man. She opened her eyes and stared sightlessly across her bedroom. "I haven't spent more than a few nights away from Tony since we moved to Fallport," she admitted.

"Well, I'm a bit older than nine, and I'm definitely not as cute as your son, but I can make sure you aren't lonely while he's gone."

Elsie couldn't keep the smile from forming on her face. "Yeah?"

"Uh-huh."

"Thanks," Elsie said after a quiet pause.

"I'm awed by you," Zeke told her. "You have every reason to keep Tony from your ex. He's never treated you very well, but you haven't let that keep you from being the bigger person and letting him get to know Tony."

"I'm still not sure this is the right decision," Elsie said. "What if this trip is a disaster?"

"Then Tony will see firsthand Doug's true colors. That's not necessarily a bad thing."

"And if he gets hurt in the process?" Elsie asked.

"If Doug says or does something stupid, Tony will have both of *us* to help him understand that it's not him, it's because of the kind of person Doug is. He'll be okay, Else."

"I hope so."

Conversation veered from her ex to more mundane things. Work, what they needed to get at the grocery store, things like that. When Elsie yawned for the fourth time, Zeke said, "You feel better now?"

"Yeah. Talking to you always makes me feel better," she said.

"Good. I'm comin' over for breakfast," he informed her.

"Okay," she agreed immediately.

"Good thing you didn't protest. I hate that I'm not with you right now," Zeke said. "I need to make sure you and Tony are both all right."

Had anyone ever put her first like Zeke did? The answer was definitely no. "We're okay," she told him.

"And I'm gonna make sure in the morning. You want your usual from Grinders?"

"Zeke, all those drinks get expensive. Do you know how many books I could've bought with the money you've spent on my caramel macchiatos?"

"Do you like them?"

"You know I do."

"Then it's worth it. And if you want a book, you just let me know. I can get it for you on my account."

"I'm sure you don't want a bunch of romance books on your account," she said with a laugh.

"You still don't get it," Zeke sighed.

"Get what?"

"I'd bend over backward to get you whatever you want or need. I love you. I want you to be happy. If that means spending five bucks on a coffee, that's what I'll do. If that's buying a romance novel and being sent emails about romance books for the next twenty years, it's not a problem because your happiness is more important to me than an aversion to spam mail. If you'd feel more comfortable if we drove up to DC and spent the two weeks Tony's with Doug in a hotel, so we can be near him, say the word."

Elsie couldn't talk through the lump in her throat.

"I know when I've got something good, Else, and even then, I almost lost the two best things in my life when I didn't bother to *talk to you* when Doug first arrived. It won't happen again. I'm Team Elsie from here on out. Period. Full stop. Do not pass go, do not collect two hundred bucks."

"All right, you have to stop being so amazing," Elsie managed to say.

"I'll stop. For now. Tony's the luckiest kid in the world to have you as his mom," Zeke said.

"You're not stopping," Elsie said with a half laugh, half sob.

"Right. I'm hanging up now. I'll see you in the morning."

"I love you, Zeke."

"I love you so much it hurts, Else. Good night."

"Night."

When Elsie clicked off the phone, she felt a lot better. It felt good to know that Zeke wasn't exactly convinced of Doug's motives either. That she wasn't simply being an overprotective, paranoid mother.

She didn't want Tony to get hurt, but she also wanted him to be able to make decisions for himself.

Elsie fell asleep with Zeke's words swimming in her brain, and more determined than ever to do whatever she could to make sure Tony was prepared for anything Doug might throw his way.

CHAPTER TWENTY

The next morning, Elsie was surprised when Zeke didn't show up at the crack of dawn. But she should've known something was up, because when he did finally knock on the door, he came bearing gifts. He'd somehow managed to get hold of a cell phone for Tony before he arrived, even though most of the stores were still closed.

"Zeke, it's too much," Elsie protested.

"Did you forget what I told you last night?" he asked.

"No, but for the first time in my life, I can actually afford something like that for Tony."

Without hesitation, Zeke pressed it into her hand. "I know you can. But I wanted to do something for him *and* you. Please let me."

How could she make him take it back when it was the exact kind of phone she would've gotten for Tony herself? It wasn't terribly fancy, was one of those pay-as-you-go cells. It didn't have internet capability, it was strictly for making calls and texts. The perfect starter. It was only a matter of time before Tony would want something fancier, but she knew he'd be over-the-moon excited about having *any* kind of phone of his own for now.

Elsie also heard the excited tone in Zeke's voice. Doug had been showering the boy with so many gifts, she wasn't surprised Zeke wanted to get him something as well.

She held the box out to Zeke. "No, you give it to him."

"Are you sure?" Zeke asked.

"Yeah."

Zeke swooped down and kissed her. Hard. "I love you," he said firmly.

"Love you too. Go on. If he's gonna get to his friend's house on time, he needs to finish eating and have time to examine his phone."

"He'll be on time," Zeke said with a shrug. Then, looking as eager as Tony did on Christmas morning, he headed into the apartment to greet the boy.

As it turned out, Tony *was* late. But man and boy were so distracted by setting up his phone and exclaiming over how cool it was, Elsie didn't have the heart to disturb them.

When Zeke returned from dropping Tony off to spend the morning with a school friend, Elsie immediately recognized the look in his eyes.

He locked the apartment door behind him and strode toward her.

Elsie smiled and met him halfway. Their lips touched, and Zeke didn't hesitate to pick her up. Wrapping her legs around him as he turned to the hall, Elsie deepened the kiss as he carried her into her room.

As if they'd planned it, the second her feet hit the floor, they both began to strip. Clothes went flying and within twenty seconds, they were lying on her bed. Her hands gripped Zeke's hair tightly as he dipped his head to her chest.

When he went to slide down farther, Elsie pulled him back up. She pressed on his shoulder and he obliged her, rolling to his back. Straddling his thighs, Elsie grabbed hold of his cock and began to stroke.

Zeke groaned and thrust into her hands. Within seconds, he

was hard as a pike. He reached for the drawer next to her bed and brushed her hands away before rolling the condom down his cock. Then he gripped her hips and urged her up until she was hovering over him.

"Fuck me, Else," he ordered.

"Bossy," she breathed, moving even as she said it. The tip of his cock met the soaking-wet folds between her legs, and she sank down on him in one fluid movement.

They both moaned as he bottomed out inside her.

"Move," he begged.

He didn't need to ask her twice. Elsie hadn't done this very often, but with Zeke's help, she was soon riding him as if her life depended on it. The feel of him so deep inside her every time she lowered herself was breathtaking. But she also loved how every inch of him scraped along her sensitive insides when she pulled back.

It was obvious Zeke was enjoying the view, as well. His pupils were dilated and his gaze went from her breasts bouncing up and down on her chest to where they were joined.

Then he moved one hand, pressing his thumb hard against her clit.

Elsie's muscles tightened.

"Keep moving," he ordered.

"I can't!" she gasped. Her up-and-down motion stopped as she began to rock instead, back and forth. The feel of his thumb on her extremely sensitive bundle of nerves was almost too much. All her body weight was on him, his cock deep inside her body, and Elsie couldn't help but lean back to give him more room to stroke. She braced her hands on his thighs behind her and let out a long, low cry.

"Damn, you're so gorgeous," Zeke said. "Love the feel of you squeezing my cock."

"Less talk, more action," Elsie gasped.

Luckily, Zeke was in the mood to comply.

The feel of him inside her as she came, filling her almost too full, was indescribable. She loved when he went down on her and made her come, but this was almost overwhelming.

The second she began to recover from one of the most intense orgasms she'd ever had, Zeke sat up, eased her onto her back, and began to fuck her. Hard.

It took her breath away, and unbelievably, Elsie felt another orgasm welling up inside her. She came a second time seconds after Zeke slammed into her one last time, holding himself still as he came. They were both sweating and exhausted by the time he fell on top of her, holding up some of his weight at the last second.

"Good Lord, woman," he panted after a moment. "You almost killed me."

"I think that's my line," she mumbled.

Zeke got up on an elbow and brushed a thumb over her lips. "That was staggering," he said quietly.

"Yeah."

"No, seriously. Anytime you want to be on top in the future, I'm one hundred percent in favor of that. Seeing you riding me, my cock buried deep inside your body, feeling your muscles flutter against me...God. It was awesome."

Elsie couldn't help but smile. "For me too," she agreed.

Zeke took a deep breath, then said, "I need to take care of the condom. Don't move."

"Don't think I could even if I wanted to," she told him honestly.

She didn't even mind the cocky grin on his face. He'd earned it.

The second Zeke disappeared into the bathroom, Elsie's phone began to ring. She was going to ignore it, but now that Tony had a phone, she knew she'd never be able to ignore her phone ever again. When she picked it up off the bedside table, she scowled when she saw it was Doug calling.

The last person she wanted to talk to was her ex, but she knew from experience he wouldn't stop bugging her until she answered.

"What do you want, Doug?" she asked in lieu of a greeting.

"Well, good morning to you too. Someone woke up on the wrong side of the bed this morning," he said.

That wasn't the case at all, and if Doug knew she was still recovering from two intense orgasms, he probably would've fallen over dead. Zeke returned then, climbing under the sheet and pulling her into his arms. If she had to talk to her ex, doing so in the arms of the man she loved made it not quite so distasteful.

"Seriously, what's up?" she asked.

"Did Tony talk to you?" he asked.

Elsie stiffened. "About what?"

"About him coming to DC with me for two weeks."

She didn't want to do this. Not now, not ever. But this was part of being a parent. A parent who was divorced. "Yes."

"And?" Doug asked.

Elsie sighed. "I'll allow it, but I swear to God, Doug, if you do anything to upset him, you'll never get to spend time with him again."

"Jesus, I'm not going to say anything. I just want to get to know him without his mommy hovering. Let him grow up already."

Elsie clenched her teeth. Zeke stroked a hand up and down her arm, but his touch wasn't making her feel better.

"When?" Doug asked.

"I'm not sure."

"I was thinking there's no time better than the present," Doug said.

Elsie stiffened. "I was thinking more toward the end of the summer."

"Come on, Elsie. Don't be a bitch about this. He's excited to see me every day and I want to foster that. Besides, all the good stuff is going on now. By the end of the summer, the festivals and stuff will be over. I've also got a big project coming up in a month or so and I won't have the time that I do now."

Elsie had just started to be all right with the idea of Tony leaving for two weeks. She *never* expected it would be so soon.

Doug's impatience was also making the hair on the back of her neck stand up, but she couldn't put her finger on why.

"I don't know, Doug."

"Come on, Elsie. I've done everything you've asked me to. I've talked to my lawyer and he's been in touch with yours. I'm going to pay the back child support. I'm *trying*. Throw me a bone here."

"I need to think about it. I'm not going to make a decision right here and now."

Doug sighed in exasperation. "You always overthink things," he complained. "But whatever. I'll be picking Tony up later. I got him something."

"You need to stop buying him things," Elsie scolded for what seemed like the hundredth time. "All he needs is to spend time with you. You don't need to bribe him with expensive gifts."

"*Someone* needs to," Doug said.

Elsie winced. Her ex always seemed to know exactly what to say to hurt her the most.

"I thought we'd spend the afternoon at my hotel. I bought him a Nintendo Switch, and he can play that while we hang out."

Elsie sighed. "What about dinner?"

"I'll get him something from McDonald's."

Elsie wanted to complain *again*. Every time Doug had Tony for a meal, he fed him fast food. It wasn't healthy. But he just made fun of her when she brought it up.

"Make sure he's home by seven."

"Seven? That's too early. It's summertime, give the kid a break. I'll bring him home by eight. And I'm gonna want an answer about him coming back to DC with me soon, Elsie. Talk to you later."

He hung up before Elsie could get another word in.

"So much for enjoying our post-orgasm high," Zeke said with a sigh. "Give it to me. What'd he say?"

Elsie didn't even hesitate. She told Zeke everything.

"He's a dick," Zeke said. "But...maybe it's not a bad thing for Tony to go now. It's kind of like a Band-Aid. Ripping it off and getting the trip over now would prevent you from worrying about it for the next however many weeks until it's scheduled."

"True," Elsie mused. "I just can't help but wonder why he's being so insistent."

"Yeah, me too."

Taking a deep breath, Elsie nodded. "Okay. If Tony says he wants to go, I'll let him."

Zeke hugged her tight.

"Why does my heart feel as if it's breaking?" she whispered.

"Because Tony's getting older. It's always hard to let them go. To let them spread their wings."

Elsie nodded. She supposed Zeke was right. "You wanna know one good thing about this trip?"

"What?"

"We can spend as much time together as we want without having to worry if we're scarring my son for life."

Zeke chuckled and tightened his hold. "Very true. You'll stay with me?"

"You could stay with *me*," she countered.

Without hesitation, Zeke shrugged. "Fine by me."

"Seriously? I was kidding. Zeke, your house is way better than this place."

"As long as you're there, I don't care where we stay," Zeke said.

It was a good answer. Elsie threw a leg over Zeke's belly. "I'm done talking about my ex and about my baby leaving. I'm thinking I want to see if I can get that orgasm high back."

"Yeah?" Zeke asked.

"Uh-huh. But first, I want to please you," she said.

"You always please me," Zeke said promptly.

Elsie smiled. "I think I know a way I can please you just a little more." With that, she scooted down, pushing the sheet away as she went, until her head was even with his crotch.

Even before she took his cock in her hand, he was hardening.

"Tell me if I do this wrong," she said.

"Sweetheart, there's no way in hell you can do anything wrong. I'm about to blow just thinking about your mouth around me."

Smiling, Elsie lowered her head, determined to show her man how much she loved and appreciated him. He'd supported her more than anyone ever had. At work, with Tony, with the shitty Doug situation, and simply being there for her when she was worried or frustrated. She wanted to return the favor even a fraction.

By the time they'd both orgasmed again, Elsie felt as if every bone in her body had been liquefied. She'd brought Zeke to the edge, but he hadn't let her push him over. He'd insisted on being inside her when he came, but before making love to her, he got her off with his fingers and tongue, *then* fucked her long, hard, and thoroughly.

They lay in her bed, the sheets pushed off to the side, naked as the day they were born, and Elsie had never felt more comfortable or at ease.

"You really think letting him go is the right thing to do?" she whispered.

Zeke immediately rolled into her and put his hand on her cheek. "I don't know. But you're right, if Doug is serious about wanting to be in Tony's life, we have to give him that chance. I told you before, if he fucks it up, that's on him—and we'll be here to make sure Tony's okay."

Elsie nodded. Zeke was right. All she could do was let Tony make decisions about his father...and be sure he knew how much she loved him, that she was there for him no matter what.

"Come on. We need a shower," Zeke said.

"What, you don't want to go to work smelling like sex and sporting sex hair?" she asked.

"Men don't get sex hair," Zeke said with a frown.

Elsie's gaze went to his head and she laughed. "Um...right. Okay."

Zeke smirked. "And to answer your question, no I don't.

Because that might embarrass you. And I'd never do anything to make you feel uncomfortable."

Once again, Elsie's insides tumbled and rolled. "You're too good to me," she said softly.

"No such thing. Let's get moving. I'll even let you be under the spray first."

Elsie chuckled. The shower in her apartment was so tiny, only one of them could be under the water at a time. It was just another reason why spending two weeks at Zeke's house was preferable while Tony was away. He had a bigger shower.

"I love you," she said when he pulled her upright and headed for the bathroom.

"Love you too."

The words were said almost off-hand. As if he'd told her a million times. It made Elsie feel good that he was so comfortable saying them. She hoped she *did* get to hear them a million times... and he'd still feel that way days, months, years in the future.

CHAPTER TWENTY-ONE

Three days later, Elsie was standing in the parking lot of her apartment complex waving to Tony, who was in the back seat of Doug's car. They were heading off to Washington, DC—and Elsie was *not* okay.

Everything had moved so quickly. When she finally agreed to let Tony go, Doug made all the arrangements. Zeke had let Tony borrow one of his suitcases, and he'd filled it to the brim with clothes and some of the new toys his dad had bought him.

He'd been excited to leave...right up until it came time to actually get into Doug's fancy Mercedes. It seemed to hit Tony that he was really leaving.

Doug had been surprisingly patient while Elsie did her best to reassure her son. She'd hugged him tight, reminded him that he had the cell phone so he could call whenever he wanted. That seemed to make him feel better.

She was still waving as Doug pulled out of the parking lot, when she felt Zeke's arm go around her waist and pull her against him. The car blurred as her eyes filled with tears, but she didn't let her smile slip or the tears fall until the Mercedes was far enough down the road that Tony wouldn't be able to see her.

Then she turned and buried her face in Zeke's chest.

"Shhhh, you're all right," he soothed.

But Elsie didn't feel all right. She wanted to jump in her car and chase down Doug. Wanted to yank Tony out of the car and barricade them in her apartment. It was a ridiculous thought...but she couldn't shake the feeling she'd just made a huge mistake.

"He agreed to sign the papers, right?" Zeke asked.

Knowing what he was talking about, Elsie nodded. "Yeah, Nissi talked to his lawyer this morning. She just has a couple more things to check into, then everything will be finalized."

"That's good," Zeke commented.

Elsie nodded against him. Doug agreeing to sign the papers granting her full custody *was* a good thing. Especially when the new agreement was much more fair to Elsie, including a nice chunk of child support. Doug had also agreed to pay back child support from the last five years. It would put a healthy amount of money into Elsie's bank account, which was almost overwhelming, considering how little she'd had in there for years.

Elsie looked up at Zeke. "I just don't understand, why now? It makes no sense."

"I don't know."

Zeke had done an amazing job of keeping his thoughts about her ex to himself, especially when Tony was around. He might not like Doug, but he was taking Elsie's lead in not badmouthing the man. It just made Elsie love him all the more.

"Come on, you didn't eat breakfast, and if you're going to get through your shift today, you need sustenance," Zeke said, steering her back toward the stairs leading up to her apartment.

Elsie wasn't hungry. Not in the least. But she knew Zeke wouldn't be happy until she ate something. He was always taking care of her, and it meant the world.

Glancing up, Elsie caught movement in the window of the

apartment down from her own. It was Rocky, who gave her a wave when she spotted him. Ethan's brother, his twin, lived in the same complex. Another person who was always looking out for her.

It was an odd feeling after being on her own for so long. Now, wherever she went, she had a protector looking over her shoulder. Some women might've been irritated. Might've taken exception to the hovering, but not Elsie. She embraced it. Because looking out for her meant they were looking out for Tony as well. And she had no problem whatsoever with that.

Looking at her watch when Zeke opened her apartment door, Elsie sighed. It had been exactly four minutes since she'd last seen her son, and it already felt like four hours. The next two weeks were going to be excruciating. She wanted to send him a message, call him to hear his voice. But he'd literally just left. Besides, the cell reception on I-480, the road leading to the interstate, sucked. She knew that better than most people. When she'd had a flat tire coming back from Roanoke, stranding her and Tony late at night, she hadn't been able to call for help. She was extremely lucky Lilly had driven by and stopped.

Thinking about her friend made Elsie smile. Lilly had already arranged for them to have dinner tonight at her house again. Throughout the next two weeks, she'd also planned to come to On the Rocks for lunch, scheduled a girls' night out at the bowling alley, and even a morning trip to A Cut Above for manis and pedis. Lilly was incredibly thoughtful, so it wasn't a surprise that she wanted to help take Elsie's mind off missing Tony.

Elsie was able to eat enough to satisfy Zeke, but the tiny meal sat like a lump in her stomach. She had no idea how she was going to get through the next two weeks without going stark-raving mad. There had been times in the last five years she'd fantasized about having a night to herself. To not have to answer a million questions. To not have to try to be as quiet as she could in the motel room so she didn't wake her son.

But now, with two full weeks stretching out before her, it felt... weird. Wrong. And she didn't like it.

Zeke came up behind her in the kitchen. She was standing in front of the sink, staring off into nothingness. He wrapped his arms around her and put his chin on her shoulder.

"Tony's gonna be fine," he whispered.

"I know," Elsie said, not sure she truly believed what she was saying.

"He's a smart kid. He's even starting to get annoyed by all the things his dad is buying. The other night, he told me that the new stuff was cool, what he really wanted was to go on a hike with his dad. Or go fishing. Or have him teach him how to unclog a toilet."

Elsie couldn't help but chuckle at that. "The last thing Doug's gonna do is teach Tony anything about a toilet. He's got a house-cleaner or handyman. When something goes wrong with the house or his car, or anything else, he simply calls someone to take care of it."

"Not surprised. My point is that I have a feeling this trip is going to open Tony's eyes to the true nature of your ex. I'm thinking he's going to be more than happy to come home at the end of two weeks."

Elsie should've felt bad about hoping Zeke was right. It wasn't that she was afraid Doug would talk Tony into wanting to live with him full time. She just didn't want Tony to be swayed by the life-style Doug could give him...one she certainly couldn't.

She turned in Zeke's arms and squeezed him tightly. "He's been so happy lately," she said. "Hanging out with you and your friends has been a dream come true for him."

"I like being around him. He's smart and funny and pretty damn insightful. He's kind, too, which you don't always see in someone his age. You're raising him right, Else."

Nothing pleased Elsie more than someone saying good things about her son. "Thanks. Although I'm still not sure teaching him to drive is the best idea. Maybe when he gets back, you can help him learn how to ride that bike Doug got him? I know Tony was hoping his dad would teach him, but of course he didn't."

"Already on my agenda. Although the bike is way too big for him. A ten-speed isn't exactly appropriate for him to learn on. I've already ordered a smaller one."

"Of course you have," Elsie said, shaking her head. For the hundredth time, she thought about how lucky she and Tony were to have this man on their side. To have him love them. "I'm sorry I'm so maudlin," she said. "I'll get better. Promise I won't be a Debbie Downer for the entire two weeks he's gone. I'm looking forward to spending time with you."

"I know you are. And I want you to feel exactly how you feel. Don't pretend to be happy when you aren't. Don't agree to do something with me if you don't feel like it. We'll take each day as it comes."

"Okay. Thank you," Elsie whispered.

"You don't have to thank me for looking out for you," Zeke said. "You want a coffee from Grinders this morning?"

"I shouldn't," Elsie said. "I'm getting a little too addicted to those things. I'm guessing all that sugar is going straight to my hips."

Zeke's hands slid down and he palmed her butt cheeks. "You don't hear me complaining, do you? Besides, you're still too skinny."

Elsie rolled her eyes. Leave it to Zeke to want her to put on weight instead of losing it, as most men would.

He leaned down then, kissing her gently, reverently. It was so sweet, Elsie wanted to cry.

"You want to take the day off work?" he asked after lifting his head.

Elsie frowned. "What? No. There's no way I want to sit here and think about where Tony is and what he's doing and what Doug's saying to him."

"Right. Then let's get going. We'll get you your coffee, and maybe stop by The Sweet Tooth and grab a doughnut."

Elsie rolled her eyes again. She wanted to tell him that she in no way needed a doughnut, but just thinking about the delicious pastries Finley Norris made at the bakery had her salivating. She might not feel like eating, her stomach might be in knots, but there wouldn't ever be a time Elsie turned down anything from Finley's shop.

Zeke chuckled as if he could read her mind and gently nudged her out of the kitchen. "I'll finish the dishes. Go change and get what you need to head out. Oh, and pack a bag for tonight. I'm taking you straight to my place after work."

Shivers ran through Elsie at his bossiness. She'd spent plenty of time at his house, but this would be the first time they'd be there alone. A flash of excitement went through her at the thought. She loved her son. Missed him terribly already. But for the first time since she'd agreed to let Doug take Tony for two weeks, a sense of anticipation flowed through her veins.

"While I love that look on your face, we don't have time for any hanky-panky right now. We've got coffee and treats to pick up, and a bar to open," Zeke told her.

"Hanky-panky?" Elsie asked with a chuckle.

The smile on Zeke's face was so damn sexy, it made her feel hotter just seeing it.

"Go, Else. Before we're both late opening the bar and Otto, Silas, and Art have something else to gossip about."

Elsie laughed at that. The three men who sat outside the post office every day were worse gossips than the ladies who hung out at the beauty shop.

"I'm going, I'm going," she told him. Elsie headed for her room. The next two weeks were going to be hard, but she had no doubt whatsoever that Zeke would make them better. Without him, there would be no way she'd be able to cope. Now, she felt as if she'd have the strength.

Taking a big breath, Elsie did her best to pull on her big girl panties and get on with her life. Tony would be back in two weeks and things would go back to normal. Hopefully Doug wouldn't mess things up with his son, but if he did, Tony had her and Zeke. He'd be fine.

* * *

Tony sat in the back of his dad's car, worrying his bottom lip. The second they pulled away from the apartment, his dad changed. He wouldn't talk to him at all, and every time Tony asked a question, his dad ignored him.

They'd been sitting in silence for ten minutes. As they passed the Walmart and his dad's hotel, nearing I-480, Tony had a growing pit in the bottom of his stomach. The trip had seemed so exciting, but now he was second-guessing leaving his mom.

Tony thought this would be like the camping trip he'd taken with Brock and Rocky. The two men had been a blast, making him laugh, answering all his questions, and they never treated him like he was a pain in their butts. They hadn't cared when he got dirty, had eaten too many s'mores, or that he got scared in the middle of the night.

But right now, he felt as if his dad was mad at him...and Tony hadn't even done anything wrong.

Pulling out the phone Zeke had gotten him, Tony saw there were no bars, meaning there wasn't any cell service. He wanted to text his mom and ask her to come get him. But if he did that, he knew his dad would get pissed for sure.

A loud popping noise sounded seconds after they got onto I-480, and the car swerved a little bit on the road. Tony wanted to laugh, since his mom's car *also* had a flat tire on this road, that night when they'd been on the way back from Roanoke.

His dad swore. Not softly or under his breath either. Tony had a feeling his mom wouldn't be happy if she knew his dad was talking like that in front of him.

Pulling over to the side of the road, his dad looked into the back seat after he turned off the car. "Stay put."

"I know how to change a tire," Tony said excitedly, taking off his seat belt. "Lilly taught me. Then Zeke let me practice, and I even went to Brock's car place and he let me use the lift thingy to help—"

"I said, *stay put*," his dad replied in a loud, mean voice, talking over him.

Tony froze. He stared into the front seat at his dad.

"Understand me? Do *not* get out of the car. The last thing I need is you getting in my way while I take care of this."

Tony swallowed hard and nodded. He'd never heard his dad sound like that before. It was kind of scary. Tears welled in his eyes as the door slammed after he'd gotten out. Tony looked down at his fingers and the phone he was still gripping tight. He wished he had cell service. He'd totally call his mom, or better yet, Zeke.

Zeke wouldn't let his dad be mean to him.

Tony wasn't stupid. He understood that his mom didn't like his dad. He'd also heard some snarky comments his dad had made about her when she wasn't around. But he'd been so nice to *him*. Buying presents. Taking him out to eat for fast food.

As he sat there, struggling not to cry, something clicked in Tony's head.

Buying things wasn't love.

How many times had his mom told him that while he might really like the French fries from the fast food restaurants, they weren't good for him? And when Tony got mad about it, she'd hugged him and said while she'd love to give him everything he wanted, sometimes what he *needed* wasn't the same thing.

He hadn't understood then, but sitting in the back of his dad's expensive car, after being yelled at and treated as if he was stupid, Tony began to get it.

He wished he hadn't agreed to spend time with him. Who cared about a bunch of stupid statues? He should be enjoying summer with his friends. But...he'd thought his dad truly wanted to spend time with him.

Now he didn't know *what* his dad wanted, but Tony didn't think it was to get to know him better.

It took a long time for his dad to change the tire. Tony heard lots of swearing and there was banging and clanking going on. He got up the courage to peek out the window and saw that his dad wasn't changing the tire right. He didn't have the jack under the jacking point. He'd put it in the middle of the car instead of closer to the tire. Tony would've been able to show him where it should've gone, but his dad thought he knew better just because he was an adult.

It was obvious he had no idea what he was doing, but he couldn't call anyone since there was no cell service.

Tony sat and stewed. Fine. It served his dad right that he was having a hard time. His mom always told Tony there was nothing wrong with asking for help when you needed it. In fact, it was stupid not to ask for assistance, or ask questions, when you didn't understand something.

By the time his dad got back in the car, he was sweaty and in an even worse mood. He was muttering under his breath as he started the engine, slammed the car into drive, and spun his tires pulling back onto the road.

Tony made sure his seat belt was fastened and decided not to remind his dad to put his on. But even though Tony hadn't said a word, his dad began to yell at him anyway.

"You need to listen better. When I tell you to do something, you *do it*. Don't argue with me. Your mother's an idiot, always has been. She's spoiled you. Turned you into a brat. I knew she'd fuck you up, and I was right. Never should have married her. Who knows if you're even mine? She was probably fucking around on me."

Tony's teeth clenched, trying so hard not to cry. He didn't say a word, just watched the miles go by as his dad went on and on about how much he hated his mom. How stupid he thought she was...how awful he thought his *son* was.

Eventually, despite his efforts, a tear fell—and his dad saw it in the rearview mirror.

"What are you crying about?" he sneered.

"Nothing."

"Suck it up and be a man. Jesus, you're pathetic!"

Tony took a deep breath, baffled. He couldn't believe how...*mean* his dad was being! He wasn't like this before. He couldn't help but wonder if it was something he'd said or done that had changed his dad's attitude so much.

But...no, he hadn't done anything wrong. All he'd done was sit in the back seat and be quiet, just like his dad asked.

Knowing he hadn't done anything to deserve such anger, Tony decided as soon as he had cell service, he was sending a message to his mom.

He immediately felt better. She'd come get him. Zeke too. They wouldn't let his dad swear at him anymore.

They drove for another ten minutes or so before his dad put on his blinker to pull off the road. Looking up, Tony saw that they weren't even on the interstate yet. They were pulling into the rest area that was about a mile before I-81.

"Why are we stopping?"

"Because."

Tony pressed his lips together. Staying quiet was the best plan at this point.

After his dad parked, well away from the little building that housed the bathrooms, he turned to Tony and said, "Go pee. I've got to make a phone call."

Wanting to tell him that he didn't need to go, since his mom had made sure he went before he left not too long ago, Tony did as he was told. He unbuckled his seat belt and walked toward the building.

It wasn't until he was halfway there when he realized this was the first time he'd ever been to a bathroom in a rest area by himself.

His mom *never* let him go in by himself. She always walked him up, then stood outside the door to make sure he was all right. He'd been a little embarrassed in the past, feeling as if she was treating him like a baby, but now, as he looked around at all the strangers going in and out of the building, a wave of unease swept over him.

Stranger danger. All these people were strangers, and any one of them could kidnap him. He'd read about little kids being snatched off the street. His mom had even talked to him about it. Said that if anyone ever tried to get him into their car, he should fight as hard as he could to get away. He knew better than to fall for the "I'm looking for my puppy" ruse. But what if someone snatched him from the bathroom?

Deciding he didn't want to go inside after all, Tony turned around and headed back to the car. His dad might be a jerk now, but at least Tony knew him.

As he approached the Mercedes, Tony heard his dad talking on the phone. He was standing outside the car, leaning back against the driver's side door, so he didn't see or hear Tony approaching. It wasn't hard to overhear his conversation—and what he heard made Tony freeze in terror.

"Right. We're about to get on eighty-one now. We should be at the rest area before Roanoke in about an hour and a half. I'll send the brat in to pee again and when he gets back to the car, I'll go in. That's when you can take the car...No, I don't care how you fucking kill him—just that he's fucking *dead*. Dump his body somewhere it'll be found, but not too soon. I want his fucking mother to suffer, wondering where he is and what happened to him.

"You'll get your damn money. As soon as I cash in the life insurance policy. Yes—twenty thousand. But you have to make it look like a carjacking gone wrong. If anyone suspects anything.... Right. No, I don't give a shit. He's a pain in the ass. I just need him gone so I can get the money...no way am I paying that fucking bitch child support. Yeah. An hour and a half. I'll leave the keys in the ignition. Make sure to get rid of the phone you're using as soon as it's done. I don't want anyone tying me to this. Fuck you! I'm not going to double-cross anyone. You'll get your damn money."

Tony's eyes felt huge in his face and he thought he might throw up. His dad wanted someone to steal his car with him in it? And kill him for *money*? He wanted to make his mom suffer?

His mind was reeling. But he was smart enough to realize that if his dad knew he'd overheard his phone call, he was in deep shit.

He quietly jogged backward, putting more space between him and the Mercedes. By the time his dad turned around and saw him, Tony was slowly walking toward the car once more, his eyes on the ground.

"It's about time," his dad bitched. "Get in the car and don't fucking touch anything. I'll be right back." Without waiting to see if Tony did as ordered, his dad strode toward the building and the bathrooms.

For a second, Tony just stood beside the car. Frozen in fear. If he got in the car like his dad ordered, he was going to be killed.

Moving stiffly, he walked around to the other side of the vehicle. He looked into the driver's side and saw his dad's key ring sitting on the seat.

Tony moved without thinking.

He opened the driver's side door and sat down. He reached down and tried to find the lever under the seat that would move it up. To his dismay, he couldn't find it. It wasn't where it was in his mom's car.

Knowing he didn't have time to figure out how to move the seat, Tony scooted as far forward on the cushion as he could. Luckily, he could just reach the pedals.

He stuck the key in the ignition and turned it. The engine started right up. He'd seen his dad put the car in park before, and even though he'd used a lever between the seats instead of by the steering wheel, Tony figured out how to push the button and move it down to the R.

He pushed on the gas pedal and the car moved backward.

He couldn't believe he was doing this! He was going to be in so much trouble. But he couldn't just sit there and let his dad kill him! He needed to get to his mom. And Zeke. They'd protect him.

He looked down and moved the lever up to the D and pressed on the gas. The car shot forward jerkily. Taking a deep breath, Tony told himself to take it easy. He couldn't bring attention to himself. If anyone found out he was driving, he'd get arrested. And he didn't want to go to jail.

Pressing a little harder on the gas pedal, Tony shook in fear as the car picked up speed. He had to get out of there. Get back to Fallport.

There was a narrow gravel path between the east and west lanes of I-480. The place where police usually sat and waited for speeding cars to go by, so they could peel out after them and hand out tickets. Concentrating as hard as he could, and trying to remember everything Zeke had taught him about driving, Tony managed to get his dad's car turned around using the gravel lane and headed toward Fallport.

He was shaking in fear, but he'd gone this far. He couldn't stop now. He was sitting at the very edge of the seat. His back hurt and his hands were sweaty on the wheel, but the farther he got from the rest area, the more relieved he became.

It seemed to take forever to get back to Fallport, but thankfully there weren't many cars on the road. Still, the longer he drove, the more he worried.

He knew what he was doing was bad. *He'd stolen a car*. He didn't have a driver's license. But his dad had hired someone to kill him.

Kill him!

Tony began to cry. He couldn't help it. He was so scared. And worried. He didn't know what was going to happen. Would anyone believe him? Would he have to go back with his dad?

So many questions ran through his mind, and the only thing he could think to do was get to his mom. He had no idea what time it was, but he hoped she was at work.

He passed a few cars once he got into the outskirts of town, but he was so close to safety, he wasn't going to stop. He passed the fast food restaurants, the motel where he used to live, the car place where Brock worked.

The sight of the square made Tony's tears fall faster.

He pressed too hard on the brake and the car lurched. Tony's head flew forward and hit the steering wheel with the abrupt stop, but he barely noticed. He put the car in park, opened the door, and practically fell onto the pavement. The car was literally in the middle of Main Street, but Tony didn't care.

As more tears fell from his eyes, he ran around the car toward the door to On the Rocks. His legs felt like jelly and he was shaking so hard, it took him two tries to grab the handle of the door, but once he had it, he pulled it open and raced inside.

CHAPTER TWENTY-TWO

Zeke was sitting at a table with the rest of the Eagle Point Search and Rescue team. Simon Hill was there, as well. Some people might think the chief of police had a cushy job since Fallport wasn't exactly crime central, but the man worked extremely hard to make sure his citizens were safe. He was in his mid-fifties and was in incredibly good shape. He took pride in his appearance and was always seen jogging on the streets of Fallport. Women seemed to think he was good looking, but Zeke wasn't exactly the best judge of that. He had short brown hair with hints of gray, brown eyes, and had never been married.

He was currently giving the team a rundown of the budget city council would be voting on. There was an increase for the search team, which was a welcome relief. It seemed as if each year they were busier and busier. And with the airing of the *Paranormal Investigations* show, more people were expected to come to Fallport to see if they could catch a glimpse of the elusive, legendary Bigfoot.

Zeke's gaze swept across the room to Elsie, smiling at the sight of her. She'd been at On the Rocks for almost two years, and he was kicking himself for not seeing what was right under his nose sooner. She was his reward for everything he'd seen and done in his life. He didn't deserve her, he knew that. But he wasn't giving her up. Ever.

Nothing was more important than Elsie. *Nothing.* Relationships were hard work. They weren't all sunshine and roses. But he vowed to do whatever he could to make sure she and Tony were happy and healthy. They were everything important in his life.

"Happy for you, Zeke," Ethan said.

He turned his attention back to the table, not ashamed in the least that he'd been caught staring at Elsie like a lovestruck fool. "Thanks," he said, smiling wider.

"What are you two going to do to stay busy while Tony's gone for two weeks?" Rocky asked with a grin.

"I'm sure we'll think of something," Zeke quipped.

Everyone chuckled.

The meeting over, Simon began to pack up the spreadsheets he'd brought when the door to the bar flew open.

Habit had Zeke turning to see who'd entered. He blinked in surprise to find it wasn't one of the regulars. It was a kid.

Zeke was standing before it even registered in his brain that the kid who'd entered was Tony.

"*Mom!*" Tony yelled hysterically.

One second he was standing inside the door, and the next he was across the room. The tray Elsie had been carrying fell to the floor with a crash as she opened her arms to her son, who had fully thrown himself at her.

"What the fuck?" Drew muttered.

That was what Zeke wanted to know. No one else had come in with the boy, and he was supposed to be halfway to Roanoke by now. Zeke rushed over to Elsie and Tony. She'd crumpled to the floor with her son in her arms. She was rocking back and forth as Tony cried uncontrollably.

Zeke went to his knees beside her and wrapped his arms around the most important people in his life. "What's wrong?" he asked.

Elsie's brow was furrowed and she looked to be in almost as much distress as Tony. "I don't know," she said. "He hasn't said."

"Doug's car is sitting in the middle of the road," Talon called from the doorway of the bar.

"Any sign of Doug?" Brock asked.

"No."

"*Fuck!*" Rocky exclaimed.

"Did *Tony* drive here?" Simon asked.

In response to that question, Tony cried even harder. "I d-don't wanna go to j-jail!" he sobbed against Elsie's chest.

"Can you get them into the office?" Raiden asked Zeke quietly.

He looked up at his friend and teammate, nodding. He couldn't think. He couldn't imagine what was going on or what had happened. He was extremely grateful his friends were here.

"Drew, I need you to go move the car," Simon said.

"On it."

"If there's anything amiss, don't touch it," the police chief warned. "Otherwise...I'm thinking it's best if you take it to the impound lot behind the station."

Zeke had no idea what the man was thinking, and at the moment, he didn't care. Tony's cries were breaking his heart in two. He wrapped his arm around Elsie's waist and arm. "Come on, sweetheart. Let's get you guys off the floor and into the office so we can figure out what's going on."

She nodded and allowed him to help her stand. Tony clung to her like he was two years old instead of nine, but Zeke knew Elsie wouldn't have let him go for anything. She staggered a bit after she was on her feet. Zeke kept his arm around her, and wrapped the other beneath Tony's butt, taking some of his weight, careful not to pry him off his mom's chest.

They shuffled toward the office, Zeke unconcerned about his business. He had good employees; they'd keep things moving. If not, he'd simply close. Elsie and Tony were more important. And he wasn't surprised in the least when his entire team—minus Drew, who was moving the Mercedes out of the middle of the road—and Simon all crowded into the office behind him and Elsie.

Zeke steered her toward the small loveseat and sat next to her, not willing to let go of either of them. "You're safe, Tony," he said, rubbing the boy's back. "I need you to take a deep breath and talk to me."

To his surprise, the kid did just that. He didn't let go of his mom, and he didn't lift his head, merely turned it so his cheek was against Elsie's chest.

"That's it. Deep breaths. Good." Zeke brought his hand up and palmed Tony's head. "Can you tell us what's going on? What happened? Why are you here? Where's Doug?" It was probably too soon to be pushing him so hard, but Zeke needed to know what the hell was going on so he could fix it.

"Am I going to jail?" Tony asked.

Zeke frowned. "No. Why would you think that?"

Tony's eyes skimmed the room and stopped when he saw Simon. "Because the police are here. And I know I'm not supposed to drive. You told me it was illegal."

"You aren't going to jail," Zeke said firmly.

"But I stole Dad's car," Tony whispered.

"Where is he?" Zeke asked. Starting to shake slightly herself, Elsie seemed happy to let him ask the questions, which was a relief.

"At the rest area. I guess."

"Right. Okay, can you start from the beginning? What happened? Why'd you take the car and drive back here?" Zeke asked.

Tony didn't look convinced he wasn't going to get in trouble, but he began to explain.

"I was excited to go with Dad, but as soon as we left, he changed. He wouldn't talk to me. Told me to be quiet. He got a flat tire and I wanted to help him change it, but he yelled at me. Told me I'd just get in the way, and that Mom was stupid and she turned me into a brat." He took a shuddering breath. "I was really confused and upset. I wanted to call Mom right then, but I didn't have any bars on my phone. Before we got to the interstate, Dad stopped and told me to go pee. I didn't really have to, but I could tell he was mad, and I didn't want to make him madder. So I went."

"By yourself?" Elsie demanded.

Tony nodded. "I got scared though. There were lots of strangers around. So I went back to the car. Dad was on the phone. I don't know who he was talking to, but he said a lot of mean things about me...then he told whoever it was that he didn't care how he killed me." Tony's tears started again. "He said he wanted you to suffer, Mom. And talked about life insurance."

The entire room went cold. Zeke saw red. The only thing keeping him from racing out to find Doug right that second was Tony's sobs. He was scared to death. And when he heard Elsie's gasp, he knew the only place for him was right here. Protecting them and making sure that piece of shit Doug Germain didn't get near his family ever again.

"Are you *sure* that's what he said?" Simon asked.

Tony tensed, but nodded.

"Maybe you misunderstood...?"

Tony's lips pressed together and he shook his head harder. "He told the man to take his car with me inside at the next rest stop, and that he didn't care where my body was dumped. He said I was a pain in the ass. He never cared about me! He only pretended to!"

Zeke knew Tony was right. And he was pissed at himself for not suspecting something, being more cautious. It was bizarre that the man had shown up out of the blue, suddenly wanting to be in his son's life, but for Elsie's sake, and Tony's, Zeke hadn't protested too much. He didn't want to do anything to rock the boat. Their relationship, as deep as it was, still felt new in some ways.

Lesson learned. It wouldn't ever happen again. Elsie and Tony's well-being came first, even if it meant they got upset with him.

"What happened after you heard him on the phone?" Simon asked. "Does he know you heard him?"

Tony took another deep breath, wiping away his tears. "I don't think so. His back was facing me. I walked backward really far, so he didn't know I was so close. Then he said he was going to pee and told me to get in the car. I knew if I did, and we got to that next rest area where he said the person on the phone was supposed to steal the car, I'd be in big trouble. I didn't really think. I saw the keys on the seat and just left."

Tony looked up at Zeke. "I couldn't find the lever to move the seat up," he said, his voice trembling, his eyes brimming with more tears.

"It's okay, bub. Your mom's car is older and has a lever. I'm guessing Doug's Mercedes has an electric button." Zeke was doing his best to stay calm. Both Elsie and Tony needed that from him right now. But inside, he was a mess. He was itching to find Doug and fucking kill him.

"You did *awesome*, Tony," Ethan told the boy.

Tony glanced at him shyly. "I did?"

"Yes. You didn't panic. You did exactly what you needed to do to get safe."

"All I could think of was getting back here. To Mom and Zeke."

Zeke's heart melted. He *wanted* to be Tony's safe place. Wanted to have the right to call him his own.

"We've got a big issue," Simon said quietly.

Everyone turned to look at the police chief. He subtly nodded his head at Tony, indicating he was reluctant to speak in front of the boy.

"Why don't you take Tony and see if Max will make him one of his special hamburgers and fries," Zeke told Elsie.

She frowned and shook her head.

"I'll take him," Talon said. He knelt in front of the loveseat and touched Tony's arm. "I don't know why you Americans call them *fries*. They're chips."

Tony wasn't quite ready to be placated with the bribe of French fries. Elsie rarely let him eat the greasy treat, and in any other circumstance, he would've been all over the offer.

Simon took a step toward the loveseat. "Tony, you aren't in any trouble," he told the boy. "In fact, I'm going to put your name in for Hero of the Year."

Tony's eyes widened. "You are?"

Hero of the Year was an annual award the city of Fallport gave out. The person chosen was celebrated at the Pickleport Festival the town had every summer. It started out as a celebration of all things dill pickle, but now included homemade crafts, silly contests, and lots and lots of pickle-flavored goodies. It was ridiculous, but the townspeople embraced it, and each year Pickleport grew larger and larger. The recipient of the Hero of the Year award got to ride on a float, wear a sash, and generally be treated like royalty for a day.

"Absolutely. I can't think of *anyone* who's ever been braver than you were today. And you're right, you're too young to drive, but you did it to protect yourself. Not only that, but you didn't even wreck!" Simon said with a smile.

"That's because Zeke taught me," Tony replied quietly.

Simon glanced at Zeke and shot him a small grin before looking back at Tony. "Well, he did a great job. I'm proud of you, and I'm sure Zeke, your mom, and everyone else is too."

Tony seemed to perk up a little at the praise. Then he frowned. "What's going to happen to my dad?"

"I don't know," Simon said honestly. "But no matter what, you and your mom will be safe. Do you believe me?"

Tony looked from Simon, to Zeke, to the rest of the men standing in the office, then at his mom. His gaze came back to Zeke. "Do you promise?"

"Promise what, bub?" Zeke asked.

"To keep me safe? To make sure someone doesn't kill me so Dad can get money?"

"Tony, I give you my word as a man, as your friend, and as a former Army soldier, that you'll be safe. And I'll go even further and tell you that your *mom* will be safe too. No one will hurt either of you. Ever. Want to know why?"

"Why?" Tony asked.

"Because I love you. And your mom."

"I love you too. I wish *you* were my dad," Tony whispered.

"In all the ways that matter, I am, bub," Zeke said without thought. He glanced up at Elsie. He was definitely overstepping, but to his relief, the only thing he saw in her eyes was love.

Tony took a deep breath, sat up on his mom's lap, and turned to Talon. "You won't leave me?"

"Never, mate."

Tony nodded and climbed off Elsie's lap. She reluctantly let him go. He immediately reached out a hand for Talon's. Tony was at the age where he felt holding hands was a bit too babyish, but it was obvious he needed that connection at the moment.

Zeke met Talon's gaze and nodded at him in thanks.

Talon lifted his chin in response. Man and boy left the office and headed for the kitchen. Drew returned then and joined the rest of the team in the office.

As soon as he shut the door behind Drew, Ethan said, "What the *fuck?*"

Simon held up a hand. "Listen. All of you. I know you want to go and find this asshole and drag him back to me to throw in jail, or worse, but we have a problem."

Zeke felt Elsie stiffen next to him. He gathered her into his arms and held her tightly as Simon spoke.

"Solicitation of murder is extremely difficult to prosecute. It generally takes concrete, irrefutable evidence. Clear intent, money changing hands to prove the person is serious, among other things," Simon said.

"And a nine-year-old boy overhearing a phone conversation isn't exactly rock-solid evidence," Rocky said with a sigh.

"Exactly."

"But...can't we track his cell phone call?" Elsie asked. "And Tony said something about insurance. I didn't sign any documents for any kind of life insurance on him," she insisted.

"Those things are circumstantial, not evidence of Doug hiring a hitman," Simon said.

Zeke felt sick. He understood what the police chief was saying. Doug was going to get away with hiring someone to kill his own son.

"So, what? We just sit back and wait for a hitman to come to Fallport and try to take Tony out?" Brock asked, incredulous.

"That's *bullshit*," Raiden barked. His bloodhound, who never left Raid's side, picked up his head at the agitation in his owner's voice.

"No, we aren't going to sit back and wait," Simon said calmly. "I have a plan."

"I'll do whatever it takes to make sure Tony's safe and to take my ex down," Elsie said firmly.

Unease rolled in Zeke's gut. She would too. Elsie would literally put her own life on the line for her son. He both loved and hated that.

"So, Tony stole Doug's car," Simon said. "It's gonna take him a while to get transportation out of that rest stop. I don't know if he'll call the cops or not, but I'm guessing *not*. He won't want to have to explain anything about what happened, in case it comes back to bite him in the ass. I'm thinking he's gonna show up here acting all frantic, with some sort of story for Elsie."

She nodded. "He knows I was planning on calling Tony every day."

"Right. So he doesn't have a lot of time. He needs to tell you his version of what happened. He doesn't know Tony's here. He might suspect this is where he'd go, but if he shows up...and you act like you haven't seen your son and don't know what's going on...I'm guessing he's going to pretend it was a carjacking like he originally planned. With Tony inside. All while hoping Tony wrecked the car and got hurt or killed."

Elsie's breath hitched, but she didn't cry. She stared at Simon with determination in her eyes. "What do you want me to say?"

"Wait—" Zeke began, but Simon ignored him.

"I think you just act like you would if what he was saying was true. You don't let on that Tony's here, safe and sound. Cry, scream, and say you're gonna call the cops. *Me*."

Elsie nodded. "Then what?"

Before Simon could continue, Elsie's phone rang in the pocket of her apron. She stiffened as she pulled it out. "If it's him, should I answer?" she asked. But even as she asked the question, Zeke saw the name on the screen wasn't her ex, but Nissi O'Neill's.

"It's my lawyer," she said.

"Go on and answer it," Simon said.

"Hello?" Elsie said into the phone. "Hi, Nissi. Do you mind if I put you on speaker? Zeke's here, and I'd like him to hear whatever we talk about. Okay, hang on...there."

"Good afternoon, Zeke," Nissi said.

"Hello."

"Right, so I'll get to it. I realize you're at work, Elsie. But I thought this was something you should know immediately. I was going over the final paperwork for your agreement and had been waiting for a background check on Doug. We do it on everyone, just in case. Well, something interesting came up."

"Yes?" Elsie asked.

"Did you know there's a one million dollar life insurance policy on Tony?"

Elsie inhaled. "A million dollars?"

"Yes. It surprised me too. Insurance policies on children aren't very common, but they exist. Mostly for smaller amounts, like ten thousand dollars or so, to help pay for a funeral or something. But a million dollars? Not so much."

"I didn't know."

"Your signature is on the paperwork," Nissi told her.

"I didn't sign anything. I would *never* sign something like that," Elsie insisted.

"There's more."

"More?" It was Zeke who asked the question.

"Yeah. There's also a policy on *you*, Elsie."

Zeke shouldn't have been surprised. And yet, he still was. "How much?" he asked.

"Five million."

"*Fuck!*"

The reactions of the other men in the room were just as violent, but they were surprisingly silent about it.

"Oh my God. Seriously?" Elsie asked.

"Yes."

"I didn't sign *anything*," Elsie repeated.

"I'll call the insurance company," Nissi told her. "Tell them your signature is fraudulent. Don't worry, I'll take care of this."

"Thank you," Elsie whispered.

"As a side note...it's not illegal to have a life insurance policy for a divorced spouse under certain circumstances. And of course, he's allowed to have one on his son. But *neither* are valid without your legal signature. We'll definitely get cracking on figuring out if he signed your name himself, or had someone else do it, or if the agent who created the policy is crooked...whatever might have happened."

"Okay."

"If you need anything, just let me know."

"I will."

"Thank you, Nissi," Zeke said.

Elsie clicked off the phone and looked up at Zeke. "I would *never* sign something like that for Tony."

"I know you wouldn't," he soothed.

"What an asshole!" Elsie fumed.

Zeke blinked in surprise. He expected her to get upset. Possibly even break down. And she *was* upset, but she was more mad than distraught.

Elsie looked at Simon. "I'll do anything to make him pay," she told him.

"Good. Because there's more to my plan than you pretending to be upset that Tony's missing," Simon said.

Zeke frowned. He wasn't sure he wanted to hear whatever the chief was about to propose.

Simon didn't hesitate to continue. "We send Tony into the mountains with a few of you guys. Y'all know the land like the back of your hand. And if anyone can protect him, it's you. That'll serve to distract Tony from what happened, and get him out of view just in case whoever Doug hired comes looking for him. In the meantime, Elsie plays along with whatever Doug tells her when he gets in touch. We need to get everything he says on tape. Elsie can wear a wire, try to get him to incriminate himself. At the very least, we can catch him lying his ass off about what happened to Tony."

Zeke wasn't okay with the police chief's plan. Not at all. "No," he said firmly.

"I'll do it," Elsie said at the same time.

"Else, it's too dangerous," Zeke said. "He's got a five million dollar policy on you. If he can't get his hands on Tony, what's going to prevent him from going after *you* to get the money?"

"What's the alternative? We let Doug hire someone to kill Tony?" Elsie asked.

"That's not happening," Zeke insisted.

"You heard Simon. There's no evidence against him. No one is going to take a nine-year-old's word about what he heard, even with Doug lying about his disappearance. Good lawyers will tear him to shreds. I won't let that happen to my son. I want to do this. I *need* to do this."

"For what it's worth...I think it might work," Ethan mused. "Her ex is conceited. And arrogant. And greedy and obviously desperate. I'm sure if Simon digs, he'll find a reason he needs that money. Gambling. Drugs. Something."

"What if he decides one million isn't enough and goes after Elsie?" Zeke retorted.

"I'm not helpless," Elsie insisted. "Besides, I'd much rather him come after me than Tony."

"Don't say that," Zeke fumed. "Don't *ever* say that! I've just found you, I can't lose you now!"

"You won't lose her," Simon said. "We'll have officers covering her. The plan is for her to talk with him, not necessarily meet with him. But if that happens, the wire she'd be wearing also has a tracking device. We'll know where she is at all times."

"You can't guarantee he won't do something rash," Zeke insisted, glaring at the chief.

"You're right. I can't. But if he wants that money, whatever he comes up will have to look like an accident. He's not going to outright kill her."

Zeke shook his head. He couldn't take that chance. The thought of not waking up to Elsie's beautiful brown eyes sent a shaft of fear through his entire body.

Elsie turned on the couch and put her hand on his cheek. "I have to do this, Zeke. If there's even the slightest chance it'll keep Tony safe, I have to do it."

"We don't know what Doug's plan is," Zeke argued, grasping at straws. "He might not even come here. Might not even let you know what happened."

"In that case, we'll figure something else out. But I know him, and Simon's right. He's going to come, and he's going to try to figure out a way to get that life insurance money."

Zeke turned to look at Simon. "I want to be in on this. Every step of the way."

Simon frowned. "I'm not sure—"

"Then the answer's no," he said firmly, relieved when Elsie didn't protest.

Simon sighed. "Fine."

"He's not an officer, but he's got a hell of a lot of combat experience," Drew said, telling the police chief something he already knew.

"And I want Rocky with me," Zeke insisted.

"Now wait a minute—" Simon said.

"No. If Raiden, Drew, and Talon are taking Tony into the mountains, and Ethan and Brock are here in Fallport making sure there's no blowback on Lilly or anyone else in town, and watching for strangers possibly looking for Tony, I want Rocky with me to have Elsie's back."

"All right—but I don't want either of you going off half-cocked. I give you my word my officers and I will have this covered. Targeting one of Fallport's own is unacceptable. It's bad enough we had to deal with that unpleasantness from the murder of that TV show guy. I don't want anything else to happen. The most exciting thing I want going on in Fallport is everyone guessing who'll win the annual pie bake-off at the fall festival."

Zeke studied Simon, and seeing the sincerity and determination in his eyes, finally nodded. "Fine."

"It's probably a good idea to get Tony out of town as soon as possible. The fewer people who see him, the better," Brock said.

"I'll go talk to Art and the other guys at the post office," Rocky said. "They had to have seen Tony pull up in that Mercedes. We need to make sure they keep their mouths shut."

"Thanks," Zeke said. He had no doubt when Art, Otto, and Silas heard what was going on, they'd rather die than tell anyone. They were notorious gossips, but they were extremely loyal to those who were kind to them, and to their town. And Elsie had never been anything but friendly and giving. They'd definitely keep their mouths shut once they knew the basics of what was happening.

"I need to go talk to Khloe," Raiden said. "Let her know I'll be out of pocket for a while. She'll need to take over at the library."

"I'll update Tal about what's going on," Drew said, heading for the door.

"Don't let Tony overhear," Elsie warned.

Drew nodded. "I'll take care of your son," he told her. "You have my word."

She nodded, and Drew left the room.

Soon, after more reassurances, it was only Zeke and Elsie left in the office.

"I know we need to go and talk to Tony, but are *you* okay?" Zeke asked softly.

Elsie nodded, but said "no" in a small voice. "I can't believe Doug hired someone to kill our son. It's crazy, Zeke! It's like one of those murder shows on TV or something, except it's our life."

"He's not going to get away with it," Zeke said. "Between Simon, his officers, your bravery to stand up to him—and the fact that you're dating a former Green Beret who's friends with a bunch of badass former special forces soldiers—I'd say you and Tony are in good hands."

"I'm scared," she whispered.

"I'd be worried if you weren't," Zeke told her. "But I swear to you, Elsie, he's going down."

"I know."

"I wish you'd reconsider. Let Simon and the rest of us handle this."

She shook her head. "You know as well as I do that Doug's never going to say anything incriminating in front of you guys. He thinks I'm stupid. I don't know what he's planning, but he'll brag about what he did at some point. I know him. He won't be able to stop himself from pointing out what an idiot I am. The more he talks, the better the chance he'll say something that can be used to put him in jail."

"You aren't stupid," Zeke said.

Elsie smiled. "I know. And honestly, one of the only reasons I'm certain I can do this is because I know *you've* got my back."

"Damn straight, I do." Zeke leaned in and kissed her. It was brief, but full of all the stress and worry he had in his heart about what might go down in the next day or so. "Whatever happens, your job is to stay alive. I mean it, Elsie. You fight. You give as good as you get. Tony needs you. *I* need you."

She nodded. "Okay."

"*Fuck!* I wish I could just hunt him down like I used to do to terrorists and take care of this fucking situation quickly," Zeke seethed.

Elsie shook her head. "That's not who you are," she said.

He gave her a look. "When it comes to your safety, and Tony's, that's *exactly* who I am."

She stared at him for a long moment before inhaling deeply. "That should disturb me...but it doesn't. Come on. I need to make sure Tony's all right. He's probably still terrified, even if he's excited about going camping again with the others."

"You're amazing," Zeke told her.

Elsie shook her head. "No. I'm a mother who will do whatever it takes to protect her child."

"That too. I love you, Else."

"And I love you. I have no idea what we'd be doing right now if it wasn't for you and your friends."

"It's a moot point because you've got me, sweetheart. Come on. Let's go find Tony."

Zeke's stomach was still in a knot and the hair on the back of his neck was standing straight up. He had no doubt that Doug would make his move soon. He'd want to regain the upper hand in the situation, even though he had no idea what exactly the situation *was*.

He was going to fail, and spend the rest of his life in prison for daring to hurt what belonged to Zeke.

Elsie *was* his. As was Tony. That wasn't a very modern sentiment, and was probably frowned on by most of the free world, but fuck it. He didn't care. Zeke had been through hell in his life, and now that he'd found Elsie and Tony, he wasn't going to let anyone hurt them.

His resolve bolstered, Zeke put his hand on the small of Elsie's back and led her from the office. The next couple of days were going to be tough, some of the toughest he and Elsie had ever had, but no matter what, they'd come out on top. The alternative was unthinkable.

CHAPTER TWENTY-THREE

Elsie felt nauseous. Doug called twenty minutes after Tony had left with Raiden, Drew, and Talon to hike into the forest surrounding Fallport and lay low for a few days. The call was being recorded, thanks to something Simon installed on her phone, so they'd have evidence of every single illegal thing Doug was saying and doing. He'd been frantic on the phone, saying someone had stolen his car with Tony inside.

It hadn't been hard to cry at hearing Doug's made-up story. Just knowing this was what Doug had planned to happen to her baby all along was enough to make her almost hysterical. He'd claimed he'd called a police officer he knew, but also told her he had "connections" and was "dealing with the situation," which, if this whole thing had been real, certainly wouldn't have satisfied Elsie.

But because she was playing a part, she begged Doug to find her baby and bring him home safe and sound. He'd told her he'd be in touch as soon as possible with updates.

She was disgusted Doug hadn't even bothered to tell her about Tony's supposed disappearance in person. He was a slimeball. A dickhead. A slithering excuse for a human being—and she was ashamed she'd ever once thought herself in love with him.

Later that night, when she was lying in bed with Zeke, trying to sleep and failing, her phone rang again. Zeke wasn't sleeping either, and he handed her phone to her with a murmured, "It's Doug."

Every muscle in Elsie's body stiffened, but she took a deep breath and answered it, putting it on speaker so Zeke could hear what Doug had to say as well. "Hello? Doug? Did you find him?"

"No. But there's been a development," Doug said.

"What? What's happening?" It wasn't hard to sound panicked. Elsie felt as if her heart was going to beat out of her chest.

"I got a call from the guy who stole my car. He said he's got Tony and he'll give him back, but we have to meet him tomorrow morning at the rest area where my car was taken. The one right before eighty-one."

"Thank God!" Elsie said. "We can call the police and get them to come—"

"No! No police!" Doug said. "The guy swore if he saw even one cop, he'd kill Tony and bury him somewhere we'd never find him."

Even though she knew her son was safe and sound, she couldn't help but break down at the images Doug's words evoked.

Her ex went on, "And he said you have to be there too."

"Me?" Elsie asked. "Why?"

"He says Tony's crying for you, begging for his mom."

Oh, her ex was *such* an asshole. Turning this around on Tony, trying to tug on her heartstrings to get her to do what he wanted.

Zeke had grabbed a notepad and scribbled something on it while she'd been talking to Doug. Elsie read it, nodded, then asked, "What does this guy want for returning Tony to us?"

"Ten thousand dollars."

Elsie inhaled sharply. "Ten thousand? Doug, I don't have that!"

"You could ask your *boyfriend*," Doug snarled.

Elsie rolled her eyes. "Tony isn't Zeke's responsibility. Besides, even if he wanted to help—which he would—all of his money's tied up in his bar, which is barely making ends meet," she lied. "And I'm going to bring Zeke with me tomorrow."

"No!" Doug said immediately. "The guy was adamant it's just us. Did you not hear me, Elsie? You wanna get our son killed? I've got the money. I'll pay whatever it costs to make sure Tony's safe."

Elsie wanted to scream at her ex that he was a goddamn liar. She wanted to confront him about the life insurance policies. Basically, she wanted to tell him that he was a despicable human being. But in order to make sure Tony was safe, and to get the evidence Simon needed to put Doug away, she had to keep her mouth shut. "Okay, okay. What time is the meeting? What's the plan?"

"I'll come pick you up in the morning. We'll head to the rest area, get Tony, and I'll bring you back."

"I'll be ready."

"Good. I'll be at your apartment at seven. Don't be late, like always."

There was Doug's true personality coming out. He couldn't resist a chance to take a dig at her, even now.

"I'll be ready," she repeated.

Zeke held up the pad of paper again with another question.

"Do you have a car? I mean, since your Mercedes was stolen?" Elsie asked.

"I rented a Ford Mustang. It's black."

Elsie's teeth clenched. His son was supposedly kidnapped, and he'd gone and rented a luxury car to replace his Mercedes. What a colossal asshole!

"All right," she managed to say.

"See you tomorrow," Doug said, then hung up without giving her a chance to respond.

Elsie stared at Zeke, her heart in her throat. She was breathing hard, and it took every bit of control not to leap out of bed and go on an epic rant against her ex.

"You did so good, Else," Zeke told her.

His words were all it took for her anger to morph into worry and fear. "What do you think he's got planned? I mean, it's not like Tony is going to be at the rest area."

"Clearly nothing good. But we aren't going to have to find out. We need to call Simon and get things rolling. He can have people ready at the rest area by the time you get there."

"But Doug said not to contact the police. If he sees them, he'll freak out."

"They won't be in uniform," Zeke soothed. "But it's not too late to call this off. You already know I don't like it. I don't want you alone with Doug. He's obviously desperate, and desperate men are dangerous."

"I don't want to be alone with him either. But I told you before, I'd do anything for Tony. *Anything.* Even get in a car with my asshole of an ex and try to get him to say something incriminating. This is my chance to get him out of our lives for good. If I don't do this, there's a chance he'll keep popping up years down the line. And he'll never stop trying to get money via unscrupulous means... namely, killing me or Tony. I have to do this, Zeke. You won't let anything happen to me."

"No, I won't," he said fervently.

"I knew he had something up his sleeve," she said, devastated. "I knew he wouldn't come to town to get to know his son. I just *never* imagined..."

"This is not your fault," Zeke said with a shake of his head. "Don't take his asshole-ness on your shoulders."

"But Tony was so excited to have his dad here," she went on. "I put my misgivings aside to give him a chance to have a relationship with Tony, but that was so stupid! He had everything he needed in a father figure with *you.* I should've told Doug to fuck off. That he'd had five years to get to know his son and hadn't bothered. Hell, not five years, he'd had *nine* years; he didn't care about our son when he was living under his own roof!"

Zeke moved, rolling over until Elsie was under him. He braced himself on his elbows and put his hands on either side of her neck,

297

his hold gentle but firm. "Okay, first—you seeing me as a father figure for Tony means the world to me. I'd do anything for that kid. Hearing him say he loved me today would've been the second best day in my life so far, if we hadn't been in the middle of a fucking clusterfuck. And for the record, the *best* day in my life was the day *you* told me you loved me."

Elsie sniffed as her eyes filled with tears. She was overly emotional lately, but she had a pretty good reason to be, so she didn't really care.

"Second, you *weren't* stupid. You were putting Tony's well-being before your own, which you always do. Not only that, giving people a second and third chance is part of who you are. You wouldn't be the woman I loved so much if you were bitter and closed off. I'm not happy about you being alone with Doug—but you're right. He's not going to be able to keep his mouth shut about what he's done. He's too conceited. He's gonna think he won as soon as you get in his car. I just need you to be *extremely* careful. Don't push him too far, Else. If he thinks for one second you're double-crossing him, I have a feeling he's not going to take it well."

"I'll be careful," she promised.

Zeke stared down at her for a long moment before he sighed. "I really want to lock you in the closet and forbid you to come out until Doug's been taken care of," he said softly.

Instead of pissing her off, his words calmed her. "I know. But you aren't going to do that."

"No, I'm not," he told her. "But I have to say, I've never been as scared as I am right this moment. It doesn't feel right, letting you put yourself in this position. My entire life has been spent protecting people. I've never dreamed of a scenario like this. Letting someone I love knowingly walk into danger when everything within me is screaming to send you into the forest to keep you safe, like we did Tony."

"I'm scared too," she told him. "But I'm more pissed off. I can't spend the rest of my life looking over my shoulder, wondering if someone is coming for me or Tony. Being with *you* has given me the strength to do this. You've helped me realize that everything Doug ever said about me was a result of *his* insecurities, not mine."

"Damn straight," Zeke said.

"I love you. So much it's terrifying. But you supporting me in this...it means everything to me. Not only that, if anything goes wrong, I know you'll be there to fix things. To make sure I'm safe."

"I will," he said, resolution clear in his voice.

Elsie ran her hands up Zeke's sides. The fact that this man was here with her, loved her, was scared for her, absolutely gave her the strength to stand up to Doug once and for all. "As much as I want to stay right here and have you love my fears away, we need to call Simon. Let him know what's up and figure out this wire and tracker thing," she said softly.

"Yeah," Zeke agreed. But he didn't move.

Elsie couldn't help but smile. She picked her head up and kissed him gently. "There's no way Doug's gonna win," she whispered. "Not when I've finally got everything I've ever wanted."

"When this is over, we're getting married," Zeke declared quietly. "Then we're ditching the birth control. I want to give you another baby. Show you how a real father and husband is supposed to act."

A shiver ran through Elsie. She should be irritated that he was *telling* her what would happen, instead of asking. But she couldn't be upset, because everything he'd said, Elsie wanted with every fiber of her being. "Okay."

The serious look on Zeke's face smoothed out and his lips twitched. "Okay?"

"Yes."

"Good." Then he kissed her, deeper and longer than she'd kissed him a second ago, before lifting his head and shifting off her. Elsie could feel his hard cock against her thigh as he moved, but he didn't acknowledge it. He simply held out his hand and helped her up. "Get dressed, Else. We have a takedown to plan."

* * *

Precisely at seven the next morning, a black Mustang pulled into the parking lot of Elsie's apartment complex. She hadn't slept much. After calling Simon, him coming over to Zeke's house, going over what she should say to Doug and what the courts needed to convict him of solicitation to murder, what she should do and say if her ex got suspicious, going to her apartment with Zeke, and lying awake for most of what was left of the night, Elsie was running on pure adrenaline.

Rocky had come down to her apartment an hour ago, and he and Zeke were ready to join Simon and the deputy who would be following her and Doug. Two other officers had already left in unmarked cars to set up at the rest area.

"Rocky and I will be no more than five minutes behind you," Zeke reminded her for the hundredth time. "I'll be with Simon, and Rocky will be with the deputy in the marked car. We'll all be listening to what's going on with you and Doug."

"I know," Elsie told him. And she did. They'd talked about all the worst-case scenarios over and over. The discussion hadn't lessened her anxiety, but knowing help would be minutes behind went a long way toward making her feel better. No matter what Doug had planned, she could hang on for five minutes until the cavalry arrived.

"I love you," Zeke said, the fear in his shaky voice almost overwhelming Elsie.

She took a deep breath to get control over her emotions and hugged him tightly. "I love you too. This is going to work. Doug's gonna run his mouth, we'll get it on tape, and then we can get married and have babies."

She heard Rocky snort behind Zeke, but ignored him.

"Damn straight, we are. Now go. Before Doug feels the urge to come up here."

Elsie rolled her eyes. "No way in hell would he do that. He's never in his life held a door open for me or gone out of his way to be a gentleman."

"Fucker," Rocky muttered, while Zeke simply shook his head.

Elsie went up on tiptoes once more to kiss Zeke, then forced herself to turn and head for the door. The second it closed behind her, she felt an almost overwhelming sense of dread. But she stiffened her spine. She could do this. For Tony.

She walked down the stairs to the parking lot and climbed into the passenger seat of Doug's rental.

"You're late," he grumbled as soon as she shut the door.

Wanting to tell him to fuck off, she merely said, "Sorry."

When he didn't say anything else, just started driving out of town, Elsie asked, "Did you hear back from the guy who has Tony? Is our son all right? Have the plans changed for today?" She remembered Simon telling her that she needed to get Doug to talk as much as possible about his concocted plan, for the recording.

"No, I didn't hear anything else. As far as I know, the plan's the same."

"So he'll be at the rest area when we get there? With Tony?"

"I don't know," Doug bitched. "All I know is what I told you already. That the guy said to come to the rest area with ten thousand bucks, and we'd get Tony back."

"But will he have him there? Or will he have coordinates or something where we're supposed to go get him?"

"Fuck, Elsie. I don't *know!*" Doug told her.

She pressed her lips together, knowing she needed to back off. When her ex got pissed, he got mean. Well...meaner than usual. The last thing she wanted to do was goad him into doing something rash. She could practically hear Zeke in her mind, telling her to go easy.

The uncomfortable silence in the car continued as Doug pulled onto the road that led to the interstate. She had around twenty minutes until they arrived at the rest area. I-480 cut through the Appalachians to get to I-81, the main artery running north to south

301

in Virginia. Trees lined both sides of the road and made cell service sketchy, if not impossible.

She was more than aware of how desolate the area was after getting that flat tire a few months ago. Thinking about her son driving Doug's Mercedes all the way from the interstate back to Fallport, alone, on a road with basically no cell service, gave her hives. He'd been lucky he hadn't wrecked.

She attempted once more to talk with Doug, to see if she could get him to open up, but he was unusually close-lipped and quiet. It made Elsie extremely nervous.

She took a deep breath, then let it out. As she did, Doug happened to look over at her.

"What the fuck is that?" he barked.

Jerking in fright, Elsie looked out the window and didn't see anything out of the ordinary. "What? Where?" she asked in confusion.

Doug reached over and grabbed the sleeve of the blouse she was wearing. She'd purposely worn a slightly baggy shirt to cover the small recording device hooked to her bra.

When Doug jerked violently on her shirt, Elsie heard a ripping sound as the neckline stretched and the stitches in the shoulder tore. She brought a hand up to protect the device in her shirt, but it was too late.

When she looked down, she saw a wire sticking out of the ripped material of her neckline.

"*Fucking bitch!*" Doug roared.

His arm was moving before Elsie could protect herself. He slammed his fist into her face, and she screamed as pain exploded. He'd hit her right in the left eye, and it immediately began to swell.

While she tried to recover from the unexpected blast of pain, Doug reached inside her shirt and ripped the device off her bra.

"A *wire*? You've got to be fucking kidding me!" he seethed, fury making his voice shake.

"It's not what you think!" Elsie cried out, trying to remember what Simon had told her to say in case this happened.

"Right. Sure it's not! What is it then? Enlighten me," Doug growled, throwing the small box with the wires into the back seat.

Elsie had no idea if it was still recording or not, but she prayed it was.

"I'd already told the police chief about Tony missing before you called about the kidnapper. He came over last night and...and I just found myself blurting everything you'd told me. I was scared, Doug! Our *son* is missing! Chief Hill insisted I wear it so we could catch the kidnapper. Since the guy said no police, this was the next best thing we could think of!"

"You're a fucking moron!" Doug shouted, throwing his fist once more. Elsie managed to jerk away so he only clipped her shoulder. "There *is* no fucking kidnapper!" he yelled.

"What?!" Elsie asked in fake confusion. "What are you talking about?"

"*Tony* stole my fucking car! I'm sure he crashed the damn thing. It was a Mercedes, for God's sake! There's no way he could've handled the power under that hood. He probably ran off the road and crashed. Hell, I haven't seen any sign of my car, so he might've even gotten on eighty-one. I don't know—and frankly, I don't give a damn."

Elsie flinched at the hatred in his tone.

"All I care about is finding his goddamn *body* and cashing in! I only agreed to have a fucking kid because my idiot boss thought all his employees should have families."

"I know about the life insurance," she blurted.

In response, he threw back his fist and punched her again. "Doesn't matter. I'm *getting* that money. Call it compensation for putting up with you and that brat for so fucking long."

"Fuck you!" Elsie shouted. She was done putting on a submissive front, she didn't care how much she pushed him. "No one's gonna find Tony's body because he made it back to Fallport safe and sound. He's hidden somewhere you and your low-rent hitman won't ever find him!"

"Fuck! *Shit!* Dammit!" Doug bellowed, pounding the steering wheel.

Elsie huddled against the door, keeping her eyes on her ex, vowing not to let him hit her again. "What was your plan once we got to the rest area?" she taunted. "Obviously, Tony wasn't going to be there."

"My guy is gonna take *you* instead," Doug told her in a deceptively calm tone. "If you know about the insurance, you know that you're worth five times what the fucking brat was. He'll take you, kill you, like he was going to do to Tony, and I'll get paid a shitload more."

Elsie shook her head. "You're a fucking asshole," she retorted.

"Don't talk back to me, bitch," Doug warned.

"Why not? You've done nothing but talk down to *me* since we got married. But *you're* the damn idiot now. You aren't going to win, Doug. You screwed up. Big time. You should've continued to forget about us. Now your greed will be your downfall."

The look her ex shot her was so furious, so utterly evil, Elsie visibly flinched.

She realized, too late, that she'd finally poked the bear a little too hard.

Doug yanked the steering wheel to the right.

He was pulling off the road. They were literally in the middle of nowhere...and of course Elsie's cell phone wouldn't be of any help. The only saving grace to this situation was that help was literally minutes behind them.

"Stupid, huh? I'm going to enjoy beating the shit out of you. I've wanted to do this for fucking years. The bruises and broken bones will all fit the plan. When your body is found, everyone will assume the carjacker beat you to a pulp."

He slammed the car into park as soon as it stopped on the

shoulder of I-480. He clicked his seat belt off and lunged, his hands going for her neck.

Thank God Elsie had already removed her own seat belt. She swiveled and lifted a leg, kicking out at Doug. There wasn't a lot of room in the sportscar and she wasn't able to get enough force behind her kick to do much beyond shove him back in his seat. Doug swore and hit her in the face once more.

Desperate, knowing Doug was on the verge of hurting her badly enough she wouldn't be able to fight back, Elsie fumbled behind her for the door handle.

With Doug's evil laughter ringing in her ears, she found the handle and pulled it just as he lurched forward again. She fell backward out of the car, landing on the dirt and gravel at the side of the road.

There were no cars going by. It was as if she and Doug were the only people on the planet. Glancing into the car at Doug's expression, she knew he was going to kill her. Right then and there. He wasn't going to wait until they got to the rest stop, or for whoever he'd hired to do his dirty work for him.

She did the only thing she could do. She sprang to her feet and fled into the forest behind her. Doug's swearing and threats followed, but she tuned them out. Her only thought was to get away. To find a place to hide.

CHAPTER TWENTY-FOUR

Simon swore viciously next to him, and Zeke stiffened. Something was obviously wrong. He'd had a bad feeling about this plan from the moment Simon suggested it, but Elsie was determined to do whatever she could to keep Tony safe.

And his old Army teammates might call him weak for agreeing, reluctantly, to the plan, but Elsie having the power and control she'd never had while married to Doug was important to her. Therefore, it was also important to him.

Zeke was driving his own truck, even though Simon had thought it was a bad idea. But Elsie wasn't the only one who needed to feel in control. He needed to be the one on Elsie's tail. And with Zeke driving, Simon was able to concentrate on listening to what was happening inside Doug's vehicle via the wire Elsie was wearing.

But as Simon continued to swear, Zeke knew he'd fucked up —*again*. Knew they should've gone about this differently. Should've come up with a safer plan. Tony was safe, but if something happened to Elsie, neither he nor Zeke would ever recover.

"What?" he barked. "What's happening?"

"Well, Doug's a fucking idiot, for one. He discovered the wire, and apparently removed it, but it's still running. Still recording. He's fucking going down," Simon swore. But his brow was intensely furrowed and he didn't look happy in the least.

"He found the wire?" Zeke asked, pressing harder on the gas pedal. He'd told Elsie that he'd be five minutes behind her, but the lack of traffic on the road required they back off a bit farther than he liked to avoid being spotted. What he wouldn't give for an old-fashioned traffic jam about now.

"Yeah. He's said more than enough to put himself away. Keep your shit together—but it sounds like he hit her," Simon said.

Zeke swore sharply and pushed his vehicle to the limit, trying to make up the extra space he'd put between him and the woman he loved.

"If the sound of the engine is any indication, he's pulling over," Simon informed Zeke. Then, seconds later, "Someone's getting out. By the sound of Doug's swearing, it's Elsie." Another pregnant pause. "*Shit*."

Zeke's blood ran cold at the police chief's exclamation. "What? Damn it, Simon, *what?*"

"I can't hear either of them anymore," he answered.

At that, Zeke took a shuddering breath. "Good girl," he rasped. He was by no means happy, but Elsie running into the woods on the side of the road was the best thing she could do...as long as Doug didn't catch up to her.

The forest was *his* domain. He was as comfortable there as he was behind the bar at On the Rocks. It didn't matter how far or where Elsie ran into the trees, he'd find her.

"She doesn't have the wire on anymore," Simon said. "Which means we can't track her." The police chief sounded pissed and worried.

"I can," he said, his voice confident.

Simon glanced at Zeke and nodded. "You're right. When we get there, you and Rocky go after Elsie. My deputy and I will take care of Doug."

He didn't need to tell him that. Zeke's first responsibility was to Elsie. Always and forever. That didn't mean if he ran across Doug while on the hunt for her, he wouldn't do what needed to be done. Doug had better pray the police got hold of him before Rocky or Zeke did.

Both former special forces men knew several ways of killing a man without leaving a mark. If they found him before Simon, Doug was a fucking dead man.

Determination rose within Zeke as he flew down the road, looking for the Mustang. Elsie and Tony's nightmare was ending today...and Doug's was just starting.

The sight of the black car parked haphazardly on the side of the road was a relief. As was seeing Rocky and the deputy already stopped behind it, the two men just getting out.

Simon swore and grabbed the "oh shit" handle above the window on his side when Zeke barely slowed as he neared the cars. He slammed on the brakes at the last minute, gravel spewing as he screeched to a halt. He threw the truck in park and was out of his seat before the vehicle stopped rocking.

Just as he took a step toward the forest, Doug reappeared.

Zeke didn't know who was more surprised. Elsie's ex, or the deputy who immediately pulled his weapon and pointed it at him.

"Put your hands up. Now!"

Doug was stupid enough to ignore the command and turned to run back into the forest.

Simon gave chase and impressively tackled the asshole within seconds, taking him to the ground, planting him face first into the ground as he yanked his hands behind his back and secured him.

Without a word to Simon, Zeke headed for where Doug had exited the trees. His Eagle Point Search and Rescue teammate was on his heels as they followed the very clear trail left in the woods by Elsie's flight. Branches were broken off and the ground disturbed where she'd fled. Looking down, Zeke saw both her footprints and Doug's.

All he could do was pray Elsie had outrun her ex. There was no guarantee Doug hadn't caught up to her immediately, hurt or killed her, then exited the woods, heading back to his car.

Elsie had desperation and adrenaline coursing through her veins. And Zeke knew she'd fight like a mother bear protecting her cub if it came down to it. Which is exactly what she was doing. Why she'd been with Doug in the first place.

"That way," Rocky said, pointing to the right.

The path Elsie had taken in the woods wasn't a straight one. She'd veered left and right, probably doing her best to throw Doug off her trail.

"Elsie!" Zeke yelled, praying she wasn't still running. She'd had a head start on him. She could be more than a mile in front of them. And if she was still running, she'd get farther and farther away.

They got to a point in the woods where Doug's footprints stopped and Elsie's continued.

"There's no sign of an altercation," Rocky said, reading Zeke's mind. "Looks like this is where he gave up and went back to the car."

Nodding, Zeke pressed forward. He yelled Elsie's name again.

Silence greeted him, but he wasn't discouraged. Doug hadn't gotten his hands on her. According to Simon, he'd hit her in the car, but his Elsie had the strength and determination to get away. She'd done the best thing she could've done in the situation she'd been in.

Run from the person trying to hurt her.

And she'd fled into the woods. Zeke's home away from home.

It was only a matter of time before he found her.

* * *

Elsie's side hurt, but she didn't dare stop running.

She didn't hear Doug anymore, but that didn't mean he wasn't behind her. And if he caught her, she had no doubt her ex would kill her. The look in his eyes before she'd fled had been proof.

She'd had no other choice but to run into the forest, but the longer she ran, the better she felt. While she wasn't a nature girl, Doug *loathed* anything to do with being in the outdoors. She had the upper hand, however slight, and despite her left eye practically swollen shut and her face and shoulder throbbing from where he'd hit her, her legs worked just fine. As long as her lungs held out, she could stay ahead of Doug.

She stopped for just a moment to try to catch her breath and glanced behind her. The trees were getting thicker, more dense, and she could barely see more than five feet before the leaves and branches obscured her view.

Elsie did her best to slow her breathing so she could listen for any signs of Doug, but all she heard was the wind blowing through the treetops above her head.

As one silent minute stretched to another, everything that had happened began to penetrate. She hadn't had time to process what Doug had said, what he'd done, until that moment. He'd planned to hand her over to whomever he'd hired to kill her—to kill their *son*—without a second thought.

How in the world had a man she'd once thought she loved sunk so low?

And what did it say about *her* that she hadn't known this part of him existed?

Swallowing hard, Elsie refused to cry. She was done being Doug's victim. She wasn't that person anymore. Wasn't the meek little woman who did whatever her husband said. She'd come a hell of a long way since she'd left DC. She may not have had a lot of money, but she loved her son with all her heart. And she'd done a damn good job of raising him.

Suddenly, she heard something in the distance—and her blood ran cold. Shit, was Doug still back there? She had no idea how far she'd gone, but it seemed like miles. The police should've seen his car by the side of the road by now. They'd been listening to her and Doug's conversation.

Not only had the police been minutes behind, but Zeke and Rocky were as well. A large part of the reason she wasn't scared shitless being lost in the middle of the forest was because she knew without a shadow of a doubt that Zeke would come for her. Even if Simon ordered him to stay by the road, he'd ignore him to find her.

Praying the wire had continued to record after Doug had thrown it in the back seat, she held her breath, straining to hear whatever had made the noise.

It came again—a voice. Faint, as if whoever was yelling was quite a ways behind her...

But she distinctly heard her name in the wind.

"Elsieeeeeee!"

Zeke...

"Zeke!" she screamed back, praying it was his voice she'd heard and not her mind playing tricks on her. If she walked right into Doug's grasp, she'd never forgive herself.

Well...she wouldn't *have* to forgive herself because she'd probably be dead.

Spinning, Elsie ran back the way she came. At least she hoped so. She was useless when it came to directions in general, and even more so in the middle of the woods with no landmarks. But she found that it was fairly easy to backtrack by looking at the ground and seeing her footprints in the soft dirt, and the sticks and leaves she'd trampled in her flight.

"Elsie!" the voice came again, closer.

It *was* Zeke! She'd bet everything she owned—which wasn't a hell of a lot, but still.

One second she was batting branches out of her way as she fought to get to the man she loved, and the next, she literally bounced off his chest as she slammed into him.

But Zeke didn't let her fall. His arms went around her and held her as solidly as anything she'd felt in her life.

Elsie went limp as she clung to him.

"Thank God!" Zeke muttered as he went to his knees right

there in the middle of the forest.

Elsie saw Rocky right behind him, but all her attention was on the man who held her. She picked her head up and asked, "Doug? Did you find him?"

"Simon's got him," Rocky said after a moment, when Zeke didn't respond. "He's going down. Everything he said was caught on tape, Elsie. You did it—and you were right. His arrogance overcame his good sense."

The relief at hearing Rocky's words made Elsie weak. But she was worried that Zeke still hadn't spoken more than two words. "Zeke?" she asked. "Are you all right?"

In response, he brought a hand up to her face and lightly ran his fingertips over her swollen eye. "I've never been as scared as I was when Simon told me what was happening," he said softly. "If something happened to you, I don't know what I'd do."

"I'm okay. I'm gonna be sore, and I'm not sure taking a jog through the woods is something I'll ever want to do again...but I knew you'd find me."

"I'll always find you, Elsie. You're my life. I can't imagine not having you by my side."

Elsie took a deep breath and collapsed against him once more. "I love you," she whispered into the skin of his neck.

"I love *you*," he told her.

"And I love you both. Not in the same way, but whatever. Think we can get the hell out of here now?" Rocky quipped.

Elsie chuckled, but it didn't seem Zeke was quite ready to find anything about this situation amusing.

"Let's go home," Elsie said. "And tell Raiden, Drew, and Talon it's safe to bring Tony home too."

That got Zeke moving. He stood, keeping an arm around her waist to help her get to her feet. "Can you make it back to the road on your own?" he asked.

Elsie frowned. "How far is it?"

"I'm guessing probably about a mile and a half."

"That's it?" she asked. Rocky chuckled, but she ignored him. "I swear I ran at least ten miles!"

Zeke's lips twitched. "If that's what you want to tell people, I'll back you up. Rocky will too, or I'll pound him into the ground."

Elsie chuckled. She couldn't believe she was laughing when just minutes ago she was fleeing for her life. But she was all right. Tony was safe. And Doug was going to prison.

Not only that...but she was getting married. And she had no doubt Zeke was going to put a lot of effort into getting her pregnant.

Not an hour after her nightmarish morning began, all was right in her world.

"That's not necessary. But don't think this is going to turn me into an outdoor girl. Hiking still isn't my thing."

"Noted," Zeke said. "If you feel faint or something hurts, let me know and I'll carry you," he said as he clasped her hand in his and turned them back the way they'd come.

"Not happening," Elsie said firmly. "No *way* is that happening. First, I'm too heavy. Second, I ran in here on my own two feet, I'm leaving the same way."

"You aren't too heavy. You're perfect," Zeke said, lifting her hand and kissing her knuckles. "And I'm so damn proud of you."

"Me too," Rocky added. "Now...keep your eyes open for Bigfoot as we head back to the interstate. I've heard he likes to hang out in this area."

Elsie rolled her eyes and saw Zeke doing the same. She appreciated Rocky lightening the mood. She had a feeling Zeke really *would* carry her if he thought for one second that she was in too much pain.

Knowing she was free of Doug once and for all was enough for her to ignore the sore muscles and throbbing in her face. All she wanted to do was go home and be with her family.

Twenty minutes later, the three walked out of the woods and Elsie saw a tow truck hooking up the Mustang, along with two other vehicles. Simon and the deputy who'd been tailing her and Doug were nowhere to be seen. Neither was her ex.

The men waiting for them were the deputies who'd been stationed at the rest area. One approached and shook Zeke's hand.

"We called Ethan and Brock to see if they'd come and help find Miss Elsie, but they said you two had it under control."

"Damn straight," Rocky said.

"Germain?" Zeke asked.

"Simon's taking him to Roanoke to be booked."

"And the guy who was waiting for us at the rest area?" Elsie asked.

"He's in the wind," the other deputy said.

Elsie stiffened. Shit. If the hit man wasn't under arrest, would he continue to be a threat to her or Tony?

As if the deputy could read her mind, he said, "We've got your ex's phone. We'll trace it and figure out who he called. Without the money Doug was going to pay him, he's not going to do anything. Especially not when he hears about your ex's arrest."

"He won't try to get us?" she asked.

Zeke's hand tightened on hers.

"No," the deputy said confidently.

"How can you be sure?" she insisted.

"Because that's not how these guys operate. They want money. They aren't going to do a damn thing for free. Besides, Simon's gonna catch him, put him away. You're safe, Miss Elsie. No stranger's gonna fart in Fallport without someone reporting it. No one's getting to either of you."

Raising a brow at his choice of words, Elsie still nodded, his reassurances making her feel a lot better.

"You ready to go home?" the first deputy asked.

Home. Yeah, Elsie was more than ready to go home. She nodded.

"Rocky, will you drive?" Zeke asked.

"Of course," Rocky told him.

Zeke pulled Elsie toward his truck and climbed into the back seat with her. Rocky got in front with an officer. They headed east until they came to a turnaround, then they were once more driving toward Fallport.

"We'll get you some ice for that eye as soon as we get home," Zeke told her. "I'll call Doc Snow so he can look you over. Then you're going to get off your feet and relax while Rocky goes to tell Raiden and the others what's happened. We'll get Tony home and reassure him that he's safe. We'll also update Nissi on everything, and *then* we'll get married."

Elsie couldn't help but laugh. It was so like Zeke to be impatient about officially making her his. Not that she had any complaints.

"I love you," she blurted.

"I love you too. But today took ten years off my life. That's never happening again," he said firmly.

"Agreed." Elsie had no problem whatsoever about acquiescing on that.

"If you or Tony need to see a counselor, we'll make sure that happens," Zeke went on.

Her heart melted even more. How she'd been lucky enough to find a man who loved her as much as Zeke did, who also loved and worried about her son, she had no idea. All she knew was that she was never going to take him for granted. She'd make sure he knew every day of the rest of their lives how much she loved and appreciated him.

Closing her eyes, Elsie relaxed against him and sighed in contentment when his arm went around her shoulders, pulling her more firmly into him. The adrenaline rush she'd been on all morning was slowly receding, and the pain from where Doug had struck her and from her flight into the woods was starting to reveal itself. But a little pain was a small price to pay for her son's well-being and safety.

She felt Zeke's lips against her forehead, and she smiled. Zeke would take care of her. It was a wonderful feeling.

EPILOGUE

"I can't believe I let you talk me into this," Elsie sighed.

Zeke chuckled. Honestly, he couldn't believe it either. But when Tony had suggested the outing, his Elsie hadn't been able to say no.

They were currently hiking to the Eagle Point Lookout, but they weren't alone. Ethan and Lilly had joined them. As had Drew, Brock, and Talon. Raiden and Rocky had stayed back in Fallport, just in case the team was called out for a search.

Brock had offered to stay behind, encouraging Raid to go, but he'd declined. Zeke was a little worried about his friend. He wasn't exactly an extrovert at the best of times, but lately it seemed as if he was becoming more and more of a recluse. Zeke wasn't sure what to do about it. He decided maybe he'd have a talk with the rest of the team later.

The hike to the lookout tower was a grueling ten miles, and Zeke was well aware that Elsie wasn't exactly enjoying herself. But she'd agreed to come because Tony begged. She was doing this for her son. And him. And Zeke loved her even more because of it.

They'd taken it easy, for Elsie's sake, stopping to spend the night halfway to the tower. The team, and even Lilly, could've done the hike in a day, but no one had any problem with stopping after only five miles. Zeke carried supplies for both him and Elsie in his pack, but Tony insisted on carrying his own stuff. Elsie had a small backpack with snacks and water.

They'd made a fire, and Brock had made dinner in a Dutch oven, burying the pot in the ground to cook it. Tony had been fascinated, and Zeke wouldn't be surprised if he was asking to make dinner that way once they were home.

The last month had been full of ups and downs. Elsie and Tony had pretty much moved in with him, and Zeke was hardly complaining. It was a dream come true.

Tony was dealing remarkably well after what had happened with his dad. He'd wanted to sleep in the same room as his mom for two nights, and Zeke had pulled the mattress from Tony's room into the master bedroom. But after those two nights, he'd gone back to his own room and fallen back into a routine.

He'd come to Elsie one day and told her he wanted to give away all the things Doug had given him. He wanted no part of the bicycle, Xbox, clothes, and other toys. Elsie had agreed, and they'd made a trip to Fallport's secondhand store. Zeke had been so proud of Tony that day. He'd made other children very happy.

Elsie was also doing remarkably well. Zeke had kept a close eye on her, watching for signs she was struggling mentally. But his Else was as strong as hell. Yes, she'd cried a couple of nights, more because of what could've happened instead of what had. But she'd pulled herself together and told him she was focusing on the future instead of dwelling on the past.

Zeke hated to think about what might have happened that awful day. If Doug had been able to get his hands on Elsie, and she didn't have him and the others on their tail, he would've been able to snatch her away, kill her, then leave her body in the woods anywhere along I-480. They wouldn't have had a clue where he'd pulled over or left her. Her body would've decomposed and simply disappeared without a trace within months.

He shivered. But that hadn't happened. He'd been there, and Elsie had been smart enough to run as far and as fast as she could to get away from her ex.

The state police had been looking into finding the identity of the man Doug had hired to kill both Tony and Elsie, with no luck. But apparently Doug had picked the wrong man, or organization, for his nefarious plan. A mini-riot had broken out at mealtime in the jail where Doug was being held, and in the chaos, he'd been shivved. Word on the street said his death was retaliation for him telling the cops everything he knew in return for a plea deal. The police surmised the man he'd hired hadn't been too thrilled to learn Doug was a snitch.

Zeke had worried Elsie and Tony would be upset, but they'd both taken the news without much reaction. Tony had nodded and asked if Zeke could take him to Brock's shop so he could "work" with Brock for the day, and Elsie had looked a little sad but said that Doug had chosen his path in life, and she'd learned the hard way that nothing she said or did could have encouraged him to deviate.

So that was that.

Zeke hadn't wasted any time in getting his ring on Elsie's finger. As soon as they received a copy of the death certificate from Nissi, he'd made the appointment for them to get married. The entire Eagle Point Search and Rescue team had attended, but there were many other people in Fallport who wanted to celebrate with them.

So Zeke had opened On the Rocks for an impromptu reception, putting drinks and food on the house. Just about everyone in Fallport had stopped by. Otto, Art, and Silas. Simon and his deputies. Nissi. Most of the owners of shops on the square, including Finley, old man Grogan, and Sandra. Whitney, the woman who owned the Chestnut Street Manor B&B, also stopped by. Even Doc Snow and his partner Craig had popped in to congratulate them.

Fallport's one homeless resident, Davis Woolford, also came in, and Zeke made sure to prepare him a to-go container filled to the brim so he'd have breakfast and possibly lunch for the next day.

Tony had a blast, and had been even more excited to spend the night with Ethan and Lilly. Which meant Zeke had Elsie to himself for their wedding night. He took advantage and brought her home early in the evening, spending most of the night showing his new bride how much he loved and appreciated her.

How the idea of hiking to Eagle Point came up, Zeke couldn't remember. It was definitely Tony's idea though. He'd asked when Zeke was going to take him there, as he'd once promised. He'd planned on it being just him and Tony, but the guys heard about it and asked if they could tag along. Lilly didn't want to be left behind either. And when Tony heard almost everyone was going, he'd begged his mom to come too. She hadn't been able to say no.

So that was how they all ended up trekking out to the tower. Thankfully, an odd cold front had moved through the state this week, dropping the mid-summer temperatures to the upper 70s rather than the usual 90s, making the climb more bearable.

The group had laughed and joked as they walked, but Zeke watched Elsie closely. If she was truly miserable, he'd turn back with her and send Tony with the rest of the group. But so far she was hanging in there. Again, not loving the trek, but holding her own.

She had no idea that Zeke had a surprise planned for her once they got to the tower.

As if she could somehow feel him thinking about her, she reached for his hand and pulled him to a stop, letting the others pass them.

"You good?" Zeke asked as he closed his fingers around hers.

"Surprisingly, yeah. I'm not saying I want to do this every weekend, but it's so peaceful out here," Elsie told him begrudgingly.

"It can be, yes," Zeke said. "It's not bringing back any bad memories for you?"

Elsie chuckled. "No. This is one hundred percent different from what happened before. I'm not running, not being slapped in the face by branches, and my eye isn't swollen shut."

Zeke winced. He hated to even think about how she'd gotten hurt.

"Stop it," she scolded gently. "It's done and over with. We're here to celebrate our new life." Her hand brushed over his ring finger. "I still can't believe I'm Elsie Calhoun now."

"Believe it," Zeke said, pleasure coursing through his veins at hearing her use his last name. They'd had a discussion about it, and he told her that he was all right with her keeping Ireland as her last name if she wanted. He was well aware she hadn't changed it when she'd gotten married the first time. But she'd told him that there was no way she was *not* changing her name.

"You have the paperwork with you, right?" she asked.

Zeke nodded. "Of course. I have to admit, I'm a little nervous though."

"Nervous?" Elsie asked with a laugh. "Don't be. Tony's gonna be so excited. He already sees you as his dad, you know. And just the other day, he brought up changing his name too."

"He did?"

"Yeah."

"What'd you say?"

"Well, I couldn't exactly say we already had the ball rolling, not when we wanted to surprise him on this trip. So I kinda sidestepped the issue. He was frustrated, but because he's such a good kid, he dropped it," Elsie said. "By the time he starts school, he's gonna be Tony Calhoun."

"I love him," Zeke said. "So much." He stopped and put his hands on either side of Elsie's neck. "And I love you. I made a promise to myself that your life would get better when you started dating me, but I didn't fully realize how much *mine* would. You've changed everything, Else, for the better."

Elsie smiled up at him. "I love that," she said softly.

"Me too. Now kiss me, woman."

She giggled, grabbed his wrists, and went up on her tiptoes.

Every time Zeke kissed this woman, it felt like the first time. He hoped the excitement he felt around her would never fade.

"Come *on*, Mom!" Tony called from ahead of them. "We're never gonna get there if you stop to smooch every few hundred feet."

Zeke pulled back and burst out laughing. The joy in Elsie's giggles made him smile even wider. "We're comin'!" he yelled back. "Keep your pants on!"

"They're on!" Tony retorted. "But if it'll make you walk faster, I'll take 'em off!"

"Oh my God, where does he get these things?" Elsie muttered.

Zeke shrugged, still laughing. "No clue. But I have to admit, he's extremely entertaining."

"I'll remind you of that when he's fourteen or fifteen and driving us crazy," Elsie said.

"I can't wait. Come on, we better do as our son says and get a move on."

"Our son. I love that too," Elsie said with a tender smile aimed his way.

"So do I. But he's right. We've stalled enough, we've still got a few miles to go."

Elsie groaned. "Can we call for a chopper to come pick us up? The thought of walking back the same ten miles it took to get out here makes me long for a hot bath."

Zeke laughed. "I'll be sure to pamper you extra when we get home."

"Deal," she said. "I'd kill for a caramel macchiato right about now."

Zeke shook his head at her and put his hand on the small of her back. "Come on. I promise you're going to be awed and amazed at the view from the tower."

"Yeah, but I'm guessing I'm going to have to climb four million steps to get to the top to *see* that view," she said, with pretty accurate insight.

It wasn't quite four million, but there were over a hundred steps to get to the top of the tower. It had to be tall enough for the fire watchers of old to see over the trees as they looked for signs of smoke, indicating the start of a forest fire. The tower wasn't used for that anymore; technology had come a long way, and having people living out in the wilderness wasn't necessary.

Deciding he was better off not answering her quip about the stairs, Zeke simply encouraged her to walk.

It took another hour and a half to reach the small clearing where the Eagle Point tower was located. Every time Zeke saw it, it took his breath away. He loved this. Being in nature. Away from the pressures of the world. With good friends. With his wife and new son. Nothing could be better.

His friends had already put down their packs and were getting out the tents and other supplies. They planned on spending two nights here. Relaxing and recharging before heading back to Fallport.

Zeke put down his pack, rummaged in it for a moment and pocketed the rolled-up piece of paper he'd brought along. "How about if we head up to check out the view?" Zeke suggested.

Elsie sighed as she eyed the stairs. Then nodded. "Might as well get this over with so you can rub my feet later."

"Tony, you want to come too?" Zeke called out.

As he expected, the boy nodded and ran over. Zeke had told him about the surprise he had for his mom, and amazingly, the kid had been able to keep the secret for two whole days.

"Yes!" Tony said, then raced for the stairs and started running up.

"Oh, to have his energy once again," Elsie said wistfully.

"I seem to remember you being quite energetic the other night," Zeke told her softly.

The blush that formed on her cheeks was adorable and made him smile.

"Whatever," she said, shaking her head at him.

They stopped several times on the way to the top of the tower, but Zeke wasn't impatient in the least. He had all the time in the world, and if his Elsie needed a break, that was what she'd get.

At last they arrived at the platform that wound around the top of the tower. Tony was standing with his face to the sun as he stared out over the Appalachian Mountains. Zeke had no idea what was in the cards for the boy, but he knew whatever Tony chose to do in the future, he'd be awesome at it.

"Look, Mom!" Tony exclaimed, pointing to a spot in the distance. "Over there is Fallport. You can just barely see the top of the courthouse." He was pointing in the completely wrong direction, but Zeke didn't bother to correct him.

"Wow, it's beautiful up here," Elsie breathed after she acknowledged her son's words and looked around.

"Worth the hike and the climb?" Zeke couldn't help but ask.

Elsie turned to him and plastered herself to his chest as she hugged him tightly. "Absolutely," she said without a shred of doubt in her tone.

"Is it time, Zeke?" Tony asked, practically bouncing up and down in his excitement.

"Almost," Zeke reassured him, earning a questioning look from Elsie. "But first there's something your mom and I want to ask you."

Tony frowned. "There is?"

"Yeah. When your mom married me, she decided to take my last name. It was her choice, she didn't have to. Just like when she married the first time, she decided to keep the name she had as a little girl. The name she gave you."

"Ireland," Tony said with a nod.

"Exactly. We want to give you that choice now too. You can stay Tony Ireland. You've had that name a long time and it might feel weird to change it. But if you want...your mom and I did the paper-work to change it to Calhoun," Zeke said, pulling the paper from his back pocket. "If you agree, and want to take my last name, you'd be Tony Calhoun from now on. But no matter what you decide, we'll love you, bub. *I* love you."

Tony's eyes had widened as he looked from the paper in Zeke's hand, back to his mom and Zeke. "I'd be your son?"

"You're my son no matter what your name is," Zeke said firmly. "As I said, if you're more comfortable keeping Ireland, then that's what we'll do."

In response, Tony threw himself at Zeke. Elsie stepped back, and it was all Zeke could do to keep from crying. Apparently, Tony wasn't opposed to changing his name.

"I've always wanted a dad," Tony sniffed against Zeke. "I was happy when *he* came here, but then he was a jerk." The boy looked up at Zeke. "I want to be Tony Calhoun." He turned his head to meet his mom's gaze. "I want us all to have the same last name."

"Then when we get back, we'll go and file the paperwork," Elsie said, tears in her own eyes.

"You want to sign it to make it legal?" Zeke asked. Since Tony was a minor, he actually didn't really have a place to sign the paper-work, but when the boy's eyes got even wider and he nodded exuberantly, Zeke was glad he'd offered. He knelt on the wooden boards of the walkway around the tower with Tony and pulled a pen out of his pocket.

He flattened the paper, smiling when Tony's tongue came out as he concentrated on writing his name as neatly as he could in the bottom margin of the paper. When he was finished, he looked up at Zeke. "It's done?"

"Well, we have to file it with the courts, but yeah, basically it's done," Zeke agreed.

Tony let out a whoop and leaped to his feet. He hugged Zeke tightly again, then turned to his mom and burst into tears as he clung to her.

Elsie's face was wet too, but Zeke could tell they were happy tears.

"I'm so h-happy," Tony stuttered.

Elsie chuckled. "I see that."

"I just..." Tony tilted his head up so he could see his mom. "Zeke's awesome. He's smart, and nice, and makes you smile. He pays attention to me and teaches me stuff. He gets me books and reads with me. I love him so much."

Zeke felt himself getting a little teary at hearing Tony's words.

"He loves you too," Elsie reassured him.

Tony took a deep breath, wiped his face, and took a step away from his mom before turning to face Zeke once more. "Can I take the paper down to show everyone?" he asked.

Zeke nodded and rolled it back up. It didn't matter if this one got ruined, they could always print off a new form and resign it. "Sure," he said, holding it out to Tony.

The boy grabbed it, whooped once more, then ran for the stairs.

"Be careful!" Elsie warned.

"I will!" Tony yelled back as he raced down the stairs.

"Lord, the last thing we need is him falling and breaking every bone in his body," she muttered.

Zeke didn't respond. He had another surprise to deliver. Tony had been excited to see his mom's reaction to what Zeke had planned, but apparently showing the others the paperwork for changing his last name was preferable to sticking around.

"Come here," Zeke said. "I've got a surprise for you too."

"Please tell me it's a hot tub," Elsie joked.

"Unfortunately, it's not, but I think you might still like it." Zeke led her to the door into the small space where the former fire-watchers lived. He pushed the door open and waited.

Elsie inhaled sharply. "Holy crap. Did you do this, Zeke?"

He nodded. "Do you like it?"

"Like it? I'm totally moving in! I'm never leaving. Ever," Elsie said.

Looking around, Zeke was pleased with how the space turned out. He'd had to fib to Elsie by telling her he'd needed to map out a new trail Fallport was putting in, but her reaction was worth the small lie. He'd hiked out here and set everything up. He'd put a blow-up mattress on the floor, complete with real sheets, a blanket and two pillows. There were lanterns around the space, curtains tacked up over the three windows, and a dozen carnations he'd chosen because they were longer lasting than roses. The space looked cozy, and romantic, and he hoped it would make the hike out here worth it for Elsie.

"Well, unfortunately, there's no indoor plumbing. So if you have to pee, you're going to have to walk down the stairs and back up again," he said, wrinkling his nose. It was the only drawback to his plan to spoil her while out here.

"Don't care," Elsie told him as she snuggled against him.

Zeke sighed in contentment. His world always seemed brighter when Elsie was in his arms.

"Thank you for all this," she told him.

"If I'm being honest, I was selfish," Zeke admitted.

Elsie looked up at him in confusion.

"I knew there was no way you were gonna want to get frisky in a tent with Tony nearby. Not to mention the others. Making a love nest up here, away from everyone else, was the best way I could think of to try to convince you to make love to me under the stars."

Elsie laughed. "You're such a guy."

"I am," he agreed. "I'm *your* guy."

"And I've never been happier in my life than I am right now. I love you, Zeke."

"I love you too, Else. So much, you'll never know."

"I do know. Because I feel the same way."

Zeke kissed her then. Took his time, showing her without words how happy he was. Reluctantly, he eventually pulled away. "As much as I want to throw you on that mattress behind us and make long, slow, sweet love to you, there are a bunch of people who are dying to see what I've done up here."

"They all know?"

"Yeah."

"Well, shit."

"What?" Zeke asked. "What's wrong?"

"Everyone knows what we'll be doing tonight!" she exclaimed.

Zeke chuckled. "Yup."

Elsie smacked his arm. "It's not funny!"

"It's a *little* funny. But seriously, they don't care. Hell, they're probably jealous."

Elsie looked like she was going to hang on to her embarrassment, but then she simply shook her head. "You're too much."

"Nope. I'm madly in love with my wife. And, you should know, I think I forgot to bring any condoms."

This time, Elsie burst out laughing.

Zeke loved seeing her like this. Couldn't think about how close he'd come to losing her. And Tony.

"I'm guessing that's your way of saying you want to get me pregnant," she said dryly.

"Yup. But if you aren't ready, I bet I could probably find a box of condoms in the bottom of my bag if I looked *really* hard," he said. "I'm not going to rush you into anything you don't want."

"I want," she said immediately.

Zeke thought it was difficult before not to throw her on the mattress and make love to her, but now it took everything within him. The thought of being inside her without any kind of barrier between them had his cock throbbing in his pants.

He turned toward the door with Elsie under his arm. He needed to get out of the little love nest he'd put together while he still could. He'd have plenty of time tonight to show his wife how much he cherished her.

They stood outside on the walkway for a moment, enjoying the breeze and the view. Below them, Tony was showing off the name change paperwork to everyone and he could see tents being erected. The plan for tonight was much as it was last night. Make dinner over a fire, have s'mores, relax with friends, and enjoy simply being alive.

"Thank you for being a man I can trust," Elsie said softly. "Someone I can give my heart to and know it will be appreciated and protected."

"Thank *you* for the same thing," Zeke said. "After my first marriage, I made a promise never to give my heart to anyone again for fear they'd stomp all over it. But you made me forget the bad times and only see the blessings that were right in front of me."

"We make a good pair," she said, looking up at him with a smile.

Her hair was mussed, she had no makeup on, her face was flushed with both the exertion of climbing the stairs and his kiss, and she was the most beautiful woman Zeke had ever seen in his life. And she was his. As he was hers.

Life wasn't guaranteed. Tragedy could strike at any moment. He was going to appreciate every second of his life with Elsie.

"You ready to go down and let the others take a look up here?"

"Ready," she said, heading for the stairs.

Zeke took another look over the treetops and sighed in contentment, before turning to follow his wife.

* * *

Rocky pushed open the door to Sunny Side Up and smiled at Karen, one of the waitresses.

"Sit anywhere, hon. I'll be with you in a moment."

"No rush," he told her as he headed for the last booth on the side of the diner. He liked to have his back to the wall and be able to see people both entering the diner and walking by outside. His time as a SEAL had made him pretty paranoid. Even today, years after he'd left, he still couldn't sit with his back to a room. And clumps of dirt or trash on the side of the road made him break out into a cold sweat.

Living in a small town like Fallport had done a lot for his post-traumatic stress disorder. On the outside, he looked normal. Could even act normal most of the time, but inside, he was frequently a ball of nerves.

Taking the job with the Eagle Point Search and Rescue team had been a godsend. It allowed him to get out into the woods and decompress on a regular basis, and it satisfied the need deep within him to serve others. Finding a missing person was one of the best feelings in the world.

Even if that person wasn't alive, it was still quietly satisfying. The discovery of a loved one could save a family years of asking "what-if" and wondering what had happened. Of course, he much preferred finding someone alive, but death was a part of the job.

Sensing someone walking his way, Rocky looked up, expecting to see Karen, but instead it was Sandra Hain, the owner of the diner.

"Hey," he said, standing up to greet her properly.

"Sit, sit, sit," she said with a shake of her head. "How many times have I told you that you don't have to get up when I approach?" she asked.

"Four hundred and thirty-three," Rocky said, making the number up on the fly. "But no matter how many times you remind me, I'll still ignore you. It's just the polite thing to do."

Sandra shook her head at him in exasperation, and Rocky couldn't help but smile. "I wanted to talk to you," the older woman said as she slid into the booth across from him.

Rocky frowned. That didn't sound good. "Shoot," he said.

"Right, well, I don't *know* that anything's wrong. I'm probably just being silly. But there was a group that came in a week or so ago. Two couples. One of them didn't seem happy at all. They kind of argued the whole time they were eating. Anyway, the woman came back in the next day. And the next. By herself. She was nice. Said she loved the food. Complimented the diner and the town.

"Anyway, she opened up a little. Said she came with a friend and the other couple because they wanted to look for Bigfoot. She admitted that she thought it was silly, but came anyway for a break from her usual routine. Apologized for causing a scene and arguing with her friend the first time she came, though only their waitress and I really noticed. I guess he was pressuring her for a relationship she doesn't want. The group had been hiking every day, and she told me they were going out one more time. An overnight trip. She promised to come back to see me before she left town, but...she never did."

Rocky stared at Sandra and tried to decide what to tell her, but she kept talking before he could comment.

"I know, I know. You're going to tell me that she probably just forgot. Or got too busy or something. But...I just don't think that's it. She should've come back the day before yesterday. I was so worried about her, I drove out to the hotel by four-eighty, where she said they were staying. I didn't see the car they'd been using, so maybe they just left...but I'm scared something happened to her. To all of them."

Rocky wanted to tease the woman about being a stalker, but this clearly wasn't the time. And he wasn't really surprised she knew what kind of vehicle the group was using. This was a small town, and people tended to be much more observant than those in cities. "What do you want me to do?" he asked, getting to the point.

"She told me they were going to hike the Falling Water Trail. She actually joked that she wanted someone to know where they were just in case something happened. When I asked what she *thought* would happen, she shrugged and said just in case her friend —who wanted to be more than friends—decided he wasn't going to take no for an answer again. She was kidding, but I could read an undercurrent of...worry in her tone."

Rocky didn't like that. Not at all. He'd seen aggression and discrimination against women too much when he was overseas. He never understood why men treated women as if they were somehow less because of their gender.

He also didn't want to think about someone hurting a woman in *his* forest.

"I thought maybe you could walk the Falling Water Trail and make sure they're not still out there? Again, it's silly, but she was so sincere in telling me that she'd come back for one last meal before she left," Sandra said.

Rocky nodded. His friends had left to go out to Eagle Point with Elsie and Tony, and he'd volunteered to stay behind just for this reason. This wasn't an official case, but now his curiosity was piqued. He wouldn't be able to sleep thinking about someone possibly lost or in danger. Damn it.

"Fine. I'll go."

Sandra let out the breath she'd been holding. "Thank you so much. Her name is Bristol Wingham. She's thirty-seven and in fairly good shape. She's a tiny little thing, I'd be surprised if she was even five feet tall. She's got long, straight black hair and dark eyes. I think she's got some sort of Asian ancestry in her, but I don't know for sure as we didn't get to talk about that."

Rocky couldn't help but chuckle. "It sounds as if you talked about a lot of other stuff though."

"Well, yeah," Sandra said, sounding confused, as if it was the most normal thing in the world to get a customer's life history when they came in to eat. But he supposed for her, and most of Fallport, it kind of was.

"Anyway, she lives in Kingsport, right across the border. She's an artist. Specializes in making stained-glass windows and dabbles in jewelry and small sculptures. She told me that once upon a time, she worked eight to five in an office, but it stifled her and she quit to do what her heart called her to do."

Rocky wasn't sure what any of this had to do with her being lost in the woods, but he nodded anyway. "All right. I'll head out today and see what I can find, but I'm guessing she probably just forgot to come back and tell you goodbye," he told the worried woman in front of him.

Sandra shrugged. "And I think you're wrong. But I'd much prefer to find she *did* head out, rather than the alternative. You'll let me know what you find?"

"Of course," Rocky said.

"You're a good man," Sandra told him. "Your breakfast is on the house."

Rocky opened his mouth to protest, but Sandra was already pushing to her feet. "And you're getting the two-by-two-by-two meal. That's two pancakes, two sausage links, two slices of bacon, two pieces of toast, and two hash browns."

With that, she turned and headed for the kitchen. Rocky could only shake his head. He didn't usually eat that large of a meal first thing in the morning, but if he was going to be headed out on a hike, he'd burn the calories off easily enough.

His thoughts returned to the mysterious Bristol. He hoped Sandra was wrong and the woman was back at home in Kingsport, safe and sound, but he'd kick his own ass if she really was in danger and needed help, and he didn't at least try to find her and her friends.

He'd find out soon enough. He'd hike the trail. If the group was camping, they probably hadn't gone more than ten miles into the mountains. He'd pack enough to stay overnight himself, and tomorrow night he'd be back home in his comfortable bed.

Satisfied with the plan, Rocky took a sip of the hot black coffee Karen had delivered a moment ago and mentally prepared for the search ahead. He hoped he found nothing, which would almost certainly mean the group had made it out of the woods and gone back home.

Mentally shrugging, he figured it would be good training, if nothing else. The chances of a group of four going into the woods and only three coming out—and none of them notifying authorities of something happening to their friend—were slim to none. It was highly likely Sandra was sending him on a wild goose chase. But he was getting a free breakfast out of it, so he couldn't complain.

Smiling as a huge plate of food was placed in front of him, Rocky thanked Karen and dug in, thoughts of the maybe-missing, maybe-not-missing Bristol pushed to the back of his mind for the moment as he enjoyed the meal.

* * *

You know as well as I do that Rocky's gonna find Bristol in the forest...but what shape will she be in? And what is he going to do when he finds her? Read on to find out in *Searching for Bristol*!

Want to talk to other Susan Stoker fans? Join my reader group, Susan Stoker's Stalkers, on Facebook!

Also by Susan Stoker

Eagle Point Search & Rescue
Searching for Lilly
Searching for Elsie
Searching for Bristol (Nov 2022)
Searching for Caryn (TBA)
Searching for Finley (TBA)
Searching for Heather (TBA)
Searching for Khloe (TBA)

SEAL Team Hawaii Series
Finding Elodie
Finding Lexie
Finding Kenna (Oct 2021)
Finding Monica (May 2022)
Finding Carly (TBA)
Finding Ashlyn (TBA)
Finding Jodelle (TBA)

The Refuge Series
Deserving Alaska (Aug 2022)
Deserving Henley (Jan 2023)
Deserving Reese (TBA)
Deserving Cora (TBA)
Deserving Lara (TBA)
Deserving Maisy (TBA)
Deserving Ryleigh (TBA)

SEAL of Protection Series
Protecting Caroline
Protecting Alabama

Protecting Fiona
Marrying Caroline (novella)
Protecting Summer
Protecting Cheyenne
Protecting Jessyka
Protecting Julie (novella)
Protecting Melody
Protecting the Future
Protecting Kiera (novella)
Protecting Alabama's Kids (novella)
Protecting Dakota

SEAL of Protection: Legacy Series
Securing Caite
Securing Brenae (novella)
Securing Sidney
Securing Piper
Securing Zoey
Securing Avery
Securing Kalee
Securing Jane

Delta Force Heroes Series
Rescuing Rayne
Rescuing Aimee (novella)
Rescuing Emily
Rescuing Harley
Marrying Emily (novella)
Rescuing Kassie
Rescuing Bryn
Rescuing Casey
Rescuing Sadie (novella)
Rescuing Wendy

Rescuing Mary
Rescuing Macie (novella)
Rescuing Annie

Delta Team Two Series
Shielding Gillian
Shielding Kinley
Shielding Aspen
Shielding Jayme (novella)
Shielding Riley
Shielding Devyn
Shielding Ember
Shielding Sierra

Badge of Honor: Texas Heroes Series
Justice for Mackenzie
Justice for Mickie
Justice for Corrie
Justice for Laine (novella)
Shelter for Elizabeth
Justice for Boone
Shelter for Adeline
Shelter for Sophie
Justice for Erin
Justice for Milena
Shelter for Blythe
Justice for Hope
Shelter for Quinn
Shelter for Koren
Shelter for Penelope

Ace Security Series
Claiming Grace

ALSO BY SUSAN STOKER

Outback Hearts
Flaming Hearts
Frozen Hearts

Writing as Annie George:
Stepbrother Virgin (erotic novella)

ABOUT THE AUTHOR

New York Times, *USA Today* and *Wall Street Journal* Bestselling Author Susan Stoker has a heart as big as the state of Tennessee where she lives, but this all American girl has also spent the last fourteen years living in Missouri, California, Colorado, Indiana, and Texas. She's married to a retired Army man who now gets to follow *her* around the country.

She debuted her first series in 2014 and quickly followed that up with the SEAL of Protection Series, which solidified her love of writing and creating stories readers can get lost in.

If you enjoyed this book, or any book, please consider leaving a review. It's appreciated by authors more than you'll know.

www.stokeraces.com
www.AcesPress.com
susan@stokeraces.com

facebook.com/authorsusanstoker
twitter.com/Susan_Stoker
instagram.com/authorsusanstoker
goodreads.com/SusanStoker
bookbub.com/authors/susan-stoker
amazon.com/author/susanstoker

CPSIA information can be obtained
at www.ICGtesting.com
Printed in the USA
BVHW061425210622
640288BV00003B/272

9 781644 992524